GRAVITY

Tess Gerritsen studied medicine at the University of
California, and was awarded her MD in 1979. After
completing her internship she practised as a doctor in
Honolulu, Hawaii. While on maternity leave Gerritsen
first started writing and in 1987 her first novel, *Call After
Midnight*, was published. However, it was *Harvest*,
Gerritsen's first medical thriller, which brought her major
commercial success on its publication in 1996. It was
a *New York Times* bestseller and was translated into
twenty foreign languages. With later successes including
Bloodstream, *Gravity*, *The Surgeon* and *The Apprentice*,
Tess Gerritsen is now recognized as one of the fore-
runners in the field of gripping medical thrillers.

Tess Gerritsen lives with her husband in Maine.

By the same author

The Sinner
The Apprentice
The Surgeon
Bloodstream
Life Support
Harvest

TESS GERRITSEN

Gravity

HARPER

This novel is entirely a work of fiction.
The names, characters and incidents portrayed in it are
the work of the author's imagination. Any resemblance to
actual persons, living or dead, events or localities is
entirely coincidental.

Harper
An imprint of HarperCollins*Publishers*
77–85 Fulham Palace Road,
Hammersmith, London W6 8JB

www.harpercollins.co.uk

This paperback edition 2011
1

First published in Great Britain by
HarperCollins*Publishers* 2004

First published in the USA by Pocket Books 1999

Copyright © Tess Gerritsen 1999

Tess Gerritsen asserts the moral right to
be identified as the author of this work

A catalogue record for this book is
available from the British Library

ISBN: 978 0 00 791605 4

Set in Sabon by Palimpsest Book Production Ltd,
Falkirk, Stirlingshire

Printed and bound in Great Britain by
Clays Ltd, St Ives plc

MIX
Paper from
responsible sources
FSC® C007454

*To the men and women who
have made spaceflight a reality.*

*Mankind's greatest achievements
are launched on dreams.*

Acknowledgments

I could not have written this book without the generous assistance of people from NASA. My warmest thanks to:

Ed Campion, NASA Public Affairs, for personally guiding me on a fascinating inside tour of Johnson Space Center.

Flight Directors Mark Kirasich (ISS) and Wayne Hale (shuttle) for insights into their demanding roles.

Ned Penley, for explaining the process of payloads selection.

John Hooper, for introducing me to the new Crew Return Vehicle.

Jim Reuter (MSFC), for explaining the space station's environmental and life-support systems.

Flight Surgeons Tom Marshburn, M.D., and Smith Johnston, M.D., for the details of emergency medicine in weightlessness.

Jim Ruhnke, for answering my sometimes bizarre engineering questions.

Ted Sasseen (NASA retired) for sharing memories of his long career as an aerospace engineer.

*　　*　　*

I'm also grateful for the help of experts from a variety of other fields:

Bob Truax and Bud Meyer, the real-life rocket boys of Truax Engineering, for the inside scoop on reusable launch vehicles.

Steve Waterman, for his knowledge of decompression chambers.

Charles D. Sullivan and Jim Burkhart, for the information on amphibian viruses.

Ross Davis, M.D., for the neurosurgical details.

Bo Barber, my fountain of information about aircraft and runways. (Bo, I'll fly with you anytime!)

Finally, I must once again thank:

Emily Bestler, who let me spread my wings.

Don Cleary and Jane Berkey, of the Jane Rotrosen Agency, for knowing what makes a great story.

Meg Ruley, who makes dreams come true.

and –

My husband, Jacob. Honey, we're in this together.

The Sea

1

The Galápagos Rift
.30 Degrees South, 90.30 Degrees West
He was gliding on the edge of the abyss.

Below him yawned the watery blackness of a frigid underworld, where the sun had never penetrated, where the only light was the fleeting spark of a bioluminescent creature. Lying prone in the form-fitting body pan of *Deep Flight IV*, his head cradled in the clear acrylic nose cone, Dr Stephen D. Ahearn had the exhilarating sensation of soaring, untethered, through the vastness of space. In the beams of his wing lights he saw the gentle and continuous drizzle of organic debris falling from the light-drenched waters far above. They were the corpses of protozoans, drifting down through thousands of feet of water to their final graveyard on the ocean floor.

Gliding through that soft rain of debris, he guided *Deep Flight* along the underwater canyon's rim, keeping the abyss to his port side, the plateau floor beneath him. Though the sediment was seemingly barren, the evidence of life was everywhere. Etched in the ocean floor were the tracks and plow marks of wandering creatures, now safely concealed in

3

their cloak of sediment. He saw evidence of man as well: a rusted length of chain, sinuously draped around a fallen anchor; a soda pop bottle, half-submerged in ooze. Ghostly remnants from the alien world above.

A startling sight suddenly loomed into view. It was like coming across an underwater grove of charred tree trunks. The objects were black-smoker chimneys, twenty-foot tubes formed by dissolved minerals swirling out of cracks in the earth's crust. With the joysticks, he maneuvered *Deep Flight* gently starboard, to avoid the chimneys.

'I've reached the hydrothermal vent,' he said. 'Moving at two knots, smoker chimneys to port side.'

'How's she handling?' Helen's voice crackled through his earpiece.

'Beautifully. I want one of these babies for my own.'

She laughed. 'Be prepared to write a very big check, Steve. You spot the nodule field yet? It should be dead ahead.'

Ahearn was silent for a moment as he peered through the watery murk. A moment later he said, 'I see them.'

The manganese nodules looked like lumps of coal scattered across the ocean floor. Strangely, almost bizarrely, smooth, formed by minerals solidifying around stones or grains of sand, they were a highly prized source of titanium and other precious metals. But he ignored the nodules. He was in search of a prize far more valuable.

'I'm heading down into the canyon,' he said.

With the joysticks he steered *Deep Flight* over the plateau's edge. As his velocity increased to two and a half knots, the wings, designed to produce the opposite effect of an airplane wing, dragged the sub downward. He began his descent into the abyss.

'Eleven hundred meters,' he counted off. 'Eleven fifty . . .'

'Watch your clearance. It's a narrow rift. You monitoring water temperature?'

4

'It's starting to rise. Up to fifty-five degrees now.'

'Still a ways from the vent. You'll be in hot water in another two thousand meters.'

A shadow suddenly swooped right past Ahearn's face. He flinched, inadvertently jerking the joystick, sending the craft rolling to starboard. The hard jolt of the sub against the canyon wall sent a clanging shock wave through the hull.

'Jesus!'

'Status?' said Helen. 'Steve, what's your status?'

He was hyperventilating, his heart slamming in panic against the body pan. *The hull. Have I damaged the hull?* Through the harsh sound of his own breathing, he listened for the groan of steel giving way, for the fatal blast of water. He was thirty-six hundred feet beneath the surface, and over one hundred atmospheres of pressure were squeezing in on all sides like a fist. A breach in the hull, a burst of water, and he would be crushed.

'Steve, talk to me!'

Cold sweat soaked his body. He finally managed to speak. 'I got startled – collided with the canyon wall –'

'Is there any damage?'

He looked out the dome. 'I can't tell. I think I bumped against the cliff with the forward sonar unit.'

'Can you still maneuver?'

He tried the joysticks, nudging the craft to port. 'Yes. Yes.' He released a deep breath. 'I think I'm okay. Something swam right past my dome. Got me rattled.'

'Something?'

'It went by so fast! Just this streak – like a snake whipping by.'

'Did it look like a fish's head on an eel's body?'

'Yes. Yes, that's what I saw.'

'Then it was an eelpout. *Thermarces cerberus*.'

5

Cerberus, thought Ahearn with a shudder. The three-headed dog guarding the gates of hell.

'It's attracted to the heat and sulfur,' said Helen. 'You'll see more of them as you get closer to the vent.'

If you say so. Ahearn knew next to nothing about marine biology. The creatures now drifting past his acrylic head dome were merely objects of curiosity to him, living signposts pointing the way to his goal. With both hands steady at the controls now, he maneuvered *Deep Flight IV* deeper into the abyss.

Two thousand meters. Three thousand.

What if he had damaged the hull?

Four thousand meters, the crushing pressure of water increasing linearly as he descended. The water was blacker now, colored by plumes of sulfur from the vent below. The wing lights scarcely penetrated that thick mineral suspension. Blinded by the swirls of sediment, he maneuvered out of the sulfur-tinged water, and his visibility improved. He was descending to one side of the hydrothermal vent, out of the plume of magma-heated water, yet the external temperature continued to climb.

One hundred twenty degrees Fahrenheit.

Another streak of movement slashed across his field of vision. This time he managed to maintain his grip on the controls. He saw more eelpouts, like fat snakes hanging head down as though suspended in space. The water spewing from the vent below was rich in heated hydrogen sulfide, a chemical that was toxic and incompatible with life. But even in these black and poisonous waters, life had managed to bloom, in shapes fantastic and beautiful. Attached to the canyon wall were swaying *Riftia* worms, six feet long, topped with feathery scarlet headdresses. He saw clusters of giant clams, white-shelled, with tongues of velvety red peeking out. And he saw crabs, eerily pale and ghostlike as they scuttled among the crevices.

Even with the air-conditioning unit running, he was starting to feel the heat.

Six thousand meters. Water temperature one hundred eighty degrees. In the plume itself, heated by boiling magma, the temperatures would be over five hundred degrees. That life could exist even here, in utter darkness, in these poisonous and superheated waters, seemed miraculous.

'I'm at six thousand sixty,' he said. 'I don't see it.'

In his earphone, Helen's voice was faint and crackling. 'There's a shelf jutting out from the wall. You should see it at around six thousand eighty meters.'

'I'm looking.'

'Slow your descent. It'll come up quickly.'

'Six thousand seventy, still looking. It's like pea soup down here. Maybe I'm at the wrong position.'

'. . . sonar readings . . . collapsing above you!' Her frantic message was lost in static.

'I didn't copy that. Repeat.'

'The canyon wall is giving way! There's debris falling toward you. *Get out of there!*'

The loud *pings* of rocks hitting the hull made him jam the joysticks forward in panic. A massive shadow plummeted down through the murk just ahead and bounced off a canyon shelf, sending a fresh rain of debris into the abyss. The *pings* accelerated. Then there was a deafening clang, and the accompanying jolt was like a fist slamming into him.

His head jerked, his jaw slamming into the body pan. He felt himself tilting sideways, heard the sickening groan of metal as the starboard wing scraped over jutting rocks. The sub kept rolling, sediment swirling past the dome in a disorienting cloud.

He hit the emergency-weight-drop lever and fumbled with the joysticks, directing the sub to ascend. *Deep Flight IV* lurched forward, metal screeching against rock, and came to an unexpected halt. He was frozen in place, the sub tilted starboard. Frantically he worked at the joysticks, thrusters at full ahead.

No response.

He paused, his heart pounding as he struggled to maintain control over his rising panic. Why wasn't he moving? Why was the sub not responding? He forced himself to scan the two digital display units. Battery power intact. AC unit still functioning. Depth gauge reading, six thousand eighty-two meters.

The sediment slowly cleared, and shapes took form in the beam of his port wing light. Peering straight ahead through the dome, he saw an alien landscape of jagged black stones and bloodred *Riftia* worms. He craned his neck sideways to look at his starboard wing. What he saw sent his stomach into a sickening tumble.

The wing was tightly wedged between two rocks. He could not move forward. Nor could he move backward. *I am trapped in a tomb, nineteen thousand feet under the sea.*

'. . . copy? Steve, do you copy?'

He heard his own voice, weak with fear: 'Can't move – starboard wing wedged –'

'. . . port-side wing flaps. A little yaw might wiggle you loose.'

'I've tried it. I've tried everything. I'm not moving.'

There was dead silence over the earphones. Had he lost them? Had he been cut off? He thought of the ship far above, the deck gently rolling on the swells. He thought of sunshine. It had been a beautiful sunny day on the surface, birds gliding overhead. The sea a bottomless blue . . .

Now a man's voice came on. It was that of Palmer Gabriel, the man who had financed the expedition, speaking calmly and in control, as always. 'We're starting rescue procedures, Steve. The other sub is already being lowered. We'll get you up to the surface as soon as we can.' There was a pause, then: 'Can you see anything? What are your surroundings?'

'I – I'm resting on a shelf just above the vent.'

'How much detail can you make out?'

'What?'

'You're at six thousand eighty-two meters. Right at the depth we were interested in. What about that shelf you're on? The rocks?'

I am going to die, and he is asking about the fucking rocks.

'Steve, use the strobe. Tell us what you see.'

He forced his gaze to the instrument panel and flicked the strobe switch.

Bright bursts of light flashed in the murk. He stared at the newly revealed landscape flickering before his retinas. Earlier he had focused on the worms. Now his attention shifted to the immense field of debris scattered across the shelf floor. The rocks were coal black, like magnesium nodules, but these had jagged edges, like congealed shards of glass. Peering to his right, at the freshly fractured rocks trapping his wing, he suddenly realized what he was looking at.

'Helen's right,' he whispered.

'I didn't copy that.'

'She was right! The iridium source – I have it in clear view –'

'You're fading out. Recommend you . . .' Gabriel's voice broke up into static and went dead.

'I did not copy. Repeat, I did not copy!' said Ahearn.

There was no answer.

He heard the pounding of his heart, the roar of his own breathing. *Slow down, slow down. Using up my oxygen too fast . . .*

Beyond the acrylic dome, life drifted past in a delicate dance through poisonous water. As the minutes stretched to

9

hours, he watched the *Riftia* worms sway, scarlet plumes combing for nutrients. He saw an eyeless crab slowly scuttle across the field of stones.

The lights dimmed. The air-conditioning fans abruptly fell silent.

The battery was dying.

He turned off the strobe light. Only the faint beam of the port wing light was shining now. In a few minutes he would begin to feel the heat of that one-hundred-eighty-degree magma-charged water. It would radiate through the hull, would slowly cook him alive in his own sweat. Already he felt a drop trickle from his scalp and slide down his cheek. He kept his gaze focused on that single crab, delicately prancing its way across the stony shelf.

The wing light flickered.

And went out.

The Launch

2

Abort.

Through the thunder of the solid propellant rocket boosters and the teeth-jarring rattle of the orbiter, the command *abort* sprang so clearly into Mission Specialist Emma Watson's mind she might have heard it shouted through her comm unit. None of the crew had, in fact, said the word aloud, but in that instant she knew the choice had to be made, and quickly. She hadn't heard the verdict yet from Commander Bob Kittredge or Pilot Jill Hewitt, seated in the cockpit in front of her. She didn't need to. They had worked so long together as a team they could read each other's minds, and the amber warning lights flashing on the shuttle's flight console clearly dictated their next actions.

Seconds before, *Endeavour* had reached Max Q, the point during launch of greatest aerodynamic stress, when the orbiter, thrusting against the resistance of the atmosphere, begins to shudder violently. Kittredge had briefly throttled back to seventy percent to ease the vibrations. Now the console warning lights told them they'd lost two of their

13

three main engines. Even with one main engine and two solid rocket boosters still firing, they would never make it to orbit.

They had to abort the launch.

'Control, this is *Endeavour*,' said Kittredge, his voice crisp and steady. Not a hint of apprehension. 'Unable to throttle up. Left and center MEs* went out at Max Q. We are stuck in the bucket. Going to RTLS abort.'

'Roger, *Endeavour*. We confirm two MEs out. Proceed to RTLS abort after SRB burnout.'

Emma was already rifling through the stack of checklists, and she retrieved the card for 'Return to Launch Site Abort.' The crew knew every step of the procedure by heart, but in the frantic pace of an emergency abort, some vital action might be forgotten. The checklist was their security blanket.

Her heart racing, Emma scanned the appropriate path of action, clearly marked in blue. A two-engine-down RTLS abort was survivable – but only theoretically. A sequence of near miracles had to happen next. First they had to dump fuel and cut off the last main engine before separating from the huge external fuel tank. Then Kittredge would pitch the orbiter around to a heads-up attitude, pointing back toward the launch site. He would have one chance, and only one, to guide them to a safe touchdown at Kennedy. A single mistake would send *Endeavour* plunging into the sea.

Their lives were now in the hands of Commander Kittredge.

His voice, in constant communication with Mission Control, still sounded steady, even a little bored, as they approached the two-minute mark. The next crisis point. The CRT display flashed the Pc<50 signal. The solid rocket boosters were burning out, on schedule.

* There is a Glossary at the end of this book that contains many of these abbreviations.

Emma felt it at once, the startling deceleration as the boosters consumed the last of the fuel. Then a brilliant flash of light in the window made her squint as the SRBs exploded away from the tank.

The roar of launch fell ominously silent, the violent shudder calming to a smooth, almost tranquil ride. In the abrupt calm, she was aware of her own pulse accelerating, her heart thudding like a fist against her chest restraint.

'Control, this is *Endeavour*,' said Kittredge, still unnaturally calm. 'We have SRB sep.'

'Roger, we see it.'

'Initiating abort.' Kittredge depressed the Abort push button, the rotary switch already positioned at the RTLS option.

Over her comm unit, Emma heard Jill Hewitt call out, 'Emma, let's hear the checklist!'

'I've got it.' Emma began to read aloud, and the sound of her own voice was as startlingly calm as Kittredge's and Hewitt's. Anyone listening to their dialogue would never have guessed they faced catastrophe. They had assumed machine mode, their panic suppressed, every action guided by rote memory and training. Their onboard computers would automatically set their return course. They were continuing downrange, still climbing to four hundred thousand feet as they dissipated fuel.

Now she felt the dizzying spin as the orbiter began its pitch-around maneuver, rolling tail over nose. The horizon, which had been upside down, suddenly righted itself as they turned back toward Kennedy, almost four hundred miles away.

'*Endeavour*, this is Control. Go for main engine cutoff.'

'Roger,' responded Kittredge. 'MECO now.'

On the instrument panel, the three engine-status indicators suddenly flashed red. He had shut off the main engines, and

15

in twenty seconds, the external fuel tank would drop away into the sea.

Altitude dropping fast, thought Emma. *But we're headed for home.*

She gave a start. A warning buzzed, and new panel lights flashed on the console.

'Control, we've lost computer number three!' cried Hewitt. 'We have lost a nav-state vector! Repeat, we've lost a nav-state vector!'

'It could be an inertial-measurement malf,' said Andy Mercer, the other mission specialist seated beside Emma. 'Take it off-line.'

'No! It might be a broken data bus!' cut in Emma. 'I say we engage the backup.'

'Agreed,' snapped Kittredge.

'Going to backup,' said Hewitt. She switched to computer number five.

The vector reappeared. Everyone heaved a sigh of relief.

The burst of explosive charges signaled the separation of the empty fuel tank. They couldn't see it fall away into the sea, but they knew another crisis point had just passed. The orbiter was flying free now, a fat and awkward bird gliding homeward.

Hewitt barked, 'Shit! We've lost an APU!'

Emma's chin jerked up as a new buzzer sounded. An auxiliary power unit was out. Then another alarm screamed, and her gaze flew in panic to the consoles. A multitude of amber warning lights were flashing. On the video screens, all the data had vanished. Instead there were only ominous black and white stripes. *A catastrophic computer failure.* They were flying without navigation data. Without flap control.

'Andy and I are on the APU malf!' yelled Emma.

'Reengage backup!'

16

Hewitt flicked the switch and cursed. 'I'm getting no joy, guys. Nothing's happening –'

'Do it again!'

'Still not reengaging.'

'She's banking!' cried Emma, and felt her stomach lurch sideways.

Kittredge wrestled with the joystick, but they had already rolled too far starboard. The horizon reeled to vertical and flipped upside down. Emma's stomach lurched again as they spun right side up. The next rotation came faster, the horizon twisting in a sickening whirl of sky and sea and sky.

A death spiral.

She heard Hewitt groan, heard Kittredge say, with flat resignation, 'I've lost her.'

Then the fatal spin accelerated, plunging to an abrupt and shocking end.

There was only silence.

An amused voice said over their comm units, 'Sorry, guys. You didn't make it that time.'

Emma yanked off her headset. 'That wasn't fair, Hazel!'

Jill Hewitt chimed in with a protesting, 'Hey, you *meant* to kill us. There was no way to save it.'

Emma was the first crew member to scramble out of the shuttle flight simulator. With the others right behind her, she marched into the windowless control room, where their three instructors sat at the row of consoles.

Team Leader Hazel Barra, wearing a mischievous smile, swiveled around to face Commander Kittredge's irate crew of four. Though Hazel looked like a buxom earth mother with her gloriously frizzy brown hair, she was, in truth, a ruthless gameplayer who ran her flight crews through the most difficult of simulations and seemed to count it as a victory whenever the crew failed to survive. Hazel was well

17

aware of the fact that every launch could end in disaster, and she wanted her astronauts equipped with the skills to survive. Losing one of her teams was a nightmare she hoped never to face.

'That sim really was below the belt, Hazel,' complained Kittredge.

'Hey, you guys keep surviving. We have to knock down your cockiness a notch.'

'Come on,' said Andy. '*Two* engines down on liftoff? A broken data bus? An APU out? And then you throw in a failed number five computer? How many malfs and nits is that? It's not realistic.'

Patrick, one of the other instructors, swiveled around with a grin. 'You guys didn't even notice the other stuff we did.'

'What else was there?'

'I threw in a nit on your oxygen tank sensor. None of you saw the change in the pressure gauge, did you?'

Kittredge gave a laugh. 'When did we have time? We were juggling a dozen other malfunctions.'

Hazel raised a stout arm in a call for a truce. 'Okay, guys. Maybe we did overdo it. Frankly, we were surprised you got as far as you did with the RTLS abort. We wanted to throw in another wrench, to make it more interesting.'

'You threw in the whole damn toolbox,' snorted Hewitt.

'The truth is,' said Patrick, 'you guys are a little cocky.'

'The word is *confident*,' said Emma.

'Which is good,' Hazel admitted. 'It's good to be confident. You showed great teamwork at the integrated sim last week. Even Gordon Obie said he was impressed.'

'The Sphinx said that?' Kittredge's eyebrow lifted in surprise. Gordon Obie was the director of Flight Crew Operations, a man so bafflingly silent and aloof that no one at JSC really knew him. He would sit through entire mission management

18

meetings without uttering a single word, yet no one doubted he was mentally recording every detail. Among the astronauts, Obie was viewed with both awe and more than a little fear. With his power over final flight assignments, he could make or break your career. The fact that he had praised Kittredge's team was good news indeed.

In her next breath, though, Hazel kicked the pedestal out from under them. 'However,' she said, 'Obie is also concerned that you guys are too lighthearted about this. That it's still a game to you.'

'What does Obie expect us to do?' said Hewitt. 'Obsess over the ten thousand ways we could crash and burn?'

'Disaster is not theoretical.'

Hazel's statement, so quietly spoken, made them fall momentarily silent. Since *Challenger*, every member of the astronaut corps was fully aware that it was only a matter of time before there was another major mishap. Human beings sitting atop rockets primed to explode with five million pounds of thrust can't afford to be sanguine about the hazards of their profession. Yet they seldom spoke about dying in space; to talk about it was to admit its possibility, to acknowledge that the next *Challenger* might carry one's name on the crew roster.

Hazel realized she'd thrown a damper on their high spirits. It was not a good way to end a training session, and now she backpedaled on her earlier criticism.

'I'm only saying this because you guys are already so well integrated. I have to work hard to trip you up. You've got three months till launch, and you're already in good shape. But I want you in even *better* shape.'

'In other words, guys,' said Patrick from his console. 'Not so cocky.'

Bob Kittredge dipped his head in mock humility. 'We'll go home now and put on the hair shirts.'

'Overconfidence is dangerous,' said Hazel. She rose from the chair and stood up to face Kittredge. A veteran of three shuttle flights, Kittredge was half a head taller, and he had the confident bearing of a naval pilot, which he had once been. Hazel was not intimidated by Kittredge, or by any of her astronauts. Whether they were rocket scientists or military heroes, they inspired in her the same maternal concern: the wish that they make it back from their missions alive.

She said, 'You're so good at command, Bob, you've lulled your crew into thinking it's easy.'

'No, they make it look easy. Because *they're* good.'

'We'll see. The integrated sim's on for Tuesday, with Hawley and Higuchi aboard. We'll be pulling some new tricks out of the hat.'

Kittredge grinned. 'Okay, try to kill us. But be fair about it.'

'Fate seldom plays fair,' Hazel said solemnly. 'Don't expect me to.'

Emma and Bob Kittredge sat in a booth in the Fly By Night saloon, sipping beers as they dissected the day's simulations. It was a ritual they'd established eleven months ago, early in their team building, when the four of them had first come together as the crew for shuttle flight 162. Every Friday evening, they would meet in the Fly By Night, located just up NASA Road 1 from Johnson Space Center, and review the progress of their training. What they'd done right, what still needed improvement. Kittredge, who'd personally selected each member of his crew, had started the ritual. Though they were already working together more than sixty hours a week, he never seemed eager to go home. Emma had thought it was because the recently divorced Kittredge now lived alone and dreaded returning to his empty house. But as she'd come to know him better, she realized these meetings were simply his way of prolonging the adrenaline high of his job. Kittredge lived to fly. For sheer entertainment he read the painfully dry shuttle manuals. He spent every free moment at the controls of one of NASA's T-38s. It was almost as if he resented the force of gravity binding his feet to the earth.

He couldn't understand why the rest of his crew might want to go home at the end of the day, and tonight he seemed a little melancholy that just the two of them were sitting at their usual table in the Fly By Night. Jill Hewitt was at her nephew's piano recital, and Andy Mercer was home celebrating his tenth wedding anniversary. Only Emma and Kittredge had shown up at the appointed hour, and now that they'd finished hashing over the week's sims, there was a long silence between them. The conversation had run out of shop talk and therefore out of steam.

'I'm taking one of the T-38s up to White Sands tomorrow,' he said. 'You want to join me?'

'Can't. I have an appointment with my lawyer.'

'So you and Jack are forging ahead with it?'

She sighed. 'The momentum's established. Jack has his lawyer, and I have mine. This divorce has turned into a runaway train.'

'It sounds like you're having second thoughts.'

Firmly she set down her beer. 'I don't have any second thoughts.'

'Then why're you still wearing his ring?'

She looked down at the gold wedding band. With sudden ferocity she tried to yank it off, but found it wouldn't budge. After seven years on her finger, the ring seemed to have molded itself to her flesh, refusing to be dislodged. She cursed and gave another tug, this time pulling so hard the ring scraped off skin as it slid over her knuckle. She set the ring down on the table. 'There. A free woman.'

Kittredge laughed. 'You two have been dragging out your divorce longer than I was married. What are you two still haggling over, anyway?'

She sank back in her chair, suddenly weary. 'Everything. I admit it, I haven't been reasonable either. A few weeks ago, we tried to sit down and make a list of all our possessions. What I want, what he wants. We promised ourselves we were going to be civilized about it. Two calm and mature adults. Well, by the time we got halfway down the list, it was out-and-out war. Take no prisoners.' She sighed. In truth, that was the way she and Jack had always been. Equally obstinate, fiercely passionate. Whether in love or at war, the sparks were always flying between them. 'There was only one thing we could both agree on,' she said. 'I get to keep the cat.'

'Lucky you.'

She looked at him. 'Do you ever have any regrets?'

'You mean about my divorce? Never.' Though his answer was flatly unequivocal, his gaze had dropped, as though he was trying to hide a truth they both knew: he was still mourning the failure of his marriage. Even a man fearless enough to strap himself atop millions of pounds of explosive fuel could suffer from an ordinary case of loneliness.

'This is the problem, you see. I've finally figured it out,' he said. 'Civilians don't understand us because they can't share the dream. The only ones who'll stay married to an astronaut are the saints and the martyrs. Or the ones who just don't give a shit whether we live or die.' He gave a bitter laugh. 'Bonnie, she was no martyr. And she sure as hell didn't understand the dream.'

Emma stared down at her wedding ring, gleaming on the table. 'Jack understands it,' she said softly. 'It was his dream too. That's what ruined it for us, you know. That I'm going up and he can't. That he's the one left behind.'

22

'Then he needs to grow up and face reality. Not everyone's got the right stuff.'

'You know, I really wish you wouldn't refer to him as some sort of reject.'

'Hey, he's the one who resigned.'

'What else could he do? He knew he wasn't going to get any flight assignments. If they won't let you fly, there's no point being in the corps.'

'They grounded him for his own good.'

'It was medical guesswork. Having one kidney stone doesn't mean you'll get another.'

'Okay, Dr Watson. You're the physician. Tell me this: Would you want Jack on your shuttle crew? Knowing his medical problem?'

She paused. 'Yes. As a physician, yes, I would. Chances are, Jack would do perfectly fine in space. He has so much to offer I can't imagine why they *wouldn't* want him up there. I may be divorcing him, but I do respect him.'

Kittredge laughed and then drained his beer mug. 'You're not exactly objective about this, are you?'

She started to argue the point, then realized she had no defense. Kittredge was right. Where Jack McCallum was concerned, she had never been objective.

Outside, in the humid heat of a Houston summer night, she stopped in the Fly By Night's parking lot and glanced up at the sky. The glare of city lights washed out the stars, but she could still make out comfortingly familiar constellations. Cassiopeia and Andromeda and the Seven Sisters. Every time she looked at them, she remembered what Jack had told her as they'd lain side by side on the grass one summer night, gazing at the stars. The night she had first realized she was in love with him. *The heavens are full of women, Emma. You belong up there too.*

She said, softly, 'So do you, Jack.'

She unlocked her car and slid into the driver's seat. Reaching into her pocket, she fished out the wedding ring. Gazing at it in the gloom of her car, she thought of the seven years of marriage it represented. Almost over now.

She slipped the ring back into her pocket. Her left hand felt naked, exposed. *I'll have to get used to it*, she thought, and started the car.

3

July 10

Dr Jack McCallum heard the scream of the first ambulance siren and said, 'It's show time, folks!' Stepping outside to the ER loading dock, he felt his pulse kick into a tachycardia, felt the jolt of adrenaline priming his nervous system into crackling live wires. He had no idea what was coming to Miles Memorial Hospital, only that there was more than one patient on the way. Over the ER radio they'd been told a fifteen-car pileup on I-45 had left two fatalities at the scene and a score of injured. Although the most critical patients would be taken to Bayshore or Texas Med, all the area's smaller hospitals, including Miles Memorial, were braced for the overflow.

Jack glanced around the ambulance dock to confirm his team was ready. The other ER doctor, Anna Slezak, stood right beside him, looking grimly pugnacious. Their support staff included four nurses, a lab runner, and a scared-looking intern. Only a month out of med school, the intern was the greenest member of the ER team and hopelessly fumble-fingered. *Destined for the field of psychiatry*, thought Jack.

The siren cut off with a *whoop* as the ambulance swung

up the ramp and backed up to the dock. Jack yanked open the rear door and got his first glimpse of the patient – a young woman, head and neck immobilized in a cervical collar, her blond hair matted with blood. As they pulled her out of the ambulance and he got a closer look at her face, Jack felt the sudden chill of recognition.

'Debbie,' he said.

She looked up at him, her gaze unfocused, and did not seem to know who he was.

'It's Jack McCallum,' he said.

'Oh. Jack.' She closed her eyes and groaned. 'My head hurts.'

He gave her a comforting pat on the shoulder. 'We'll take good care of you, sweetheart. Don't worry about a thing.'

They wheeled her through the ER doors, toward the trauma room.

'You know her?' Anna asked him.

'Her husband's Bill Haning. The astronaut.'

'You mean one of the guys up on the space station?' Anna laughed. 'Now, *there's* a long distance phone call.'

'It's no problem reaching him, if we have to. JSC can put a call right through.'

'You want me to take this patient?' It was a reasonable question to ask. Doctors usually avoided treating friends and family; you cannot remain objective when the patient in cardiac arrest on the table is someone you know and like. Although he and Debbie had once attended the same social functions, Jack considered her merely an acquaintance, not a friend, and he felt comfortable acting as her physician.

'I'll take her,' he said, and followed the gurney into the trauma room. His mind was already leaping ahead to what needed to be done. Her only visible injury was the scalp laceration, but since she had clearly suffered trauma to her head, he had to rule out fractures of the skull and cervical spine.

26

As the nurses drew blood for labs and gently pulled off the rest of Debbie's clothing, the ambulance attendant gave Jack a quick history.

'She was about the fifth car in the pileup. Far as we could tell, she got rear-ended, her car spun sideways, and then she got hit again, on the driver's side. Door was caved in.'

'Was she awake when you got to her?'

'She was unconscious for a few minutes. Woke up while we were putting in the IV. We got her spine immobilized right away. BP and heart rhythm have been stable. She's one of the lucky ones.' The attendant shook his head. 'You should've seen the guy behind her.'

Jack moved to the gurney to examine the patient. Both of Debbie's pupils reacted to light, and her extraocular movements were normal. She knew her own name and where she was, but could not recall the date. Oriented only times two, he thought. It was reason enough to admit her, if only for overnight observation.

'Debbie, I'm going to send you for X rays,' he said. 'We need to make sure you haven't fractured anything.' He looked at the nurse. 'Stat CT, skull, and C-spine. And . . .' He paused, listening.

Another ambulance siren was approaching.

'Get those films done,' he ordered, and trotted back outside to the loading dock, where his staff had reassembled.

A second siren, fainter, had joined the first wail. Jack and Anna glanced at each other in alarm. Two ambulances on the way?

'It's going to be one of those days,' he muttered.

'Trauma room cleared out?' asked Anna.

'Patient's on her way to X-ray.' He stepped forward as the first ambulance backed up. The instant it rolled to a stop, he yanked open the door.

It was a man this time, middle-aged and overweight,

his skin pale and clammy. *Going into shock* was Jack's first assessment, but he saw no blood, no signs of injury.

'He was one of the fender benders,' said the EMT as they wheeled the man into the treatment room. 'Got chest pain when we pulled him out of his car. Rhythm's been stable, a little tachycardic, but no PVCs. Systolic's ninety. We gave morphine and nitro at the scene, and oxygen's going at six liters.'

Everyone was right on the ball. While Anna took the history and physical, the nurses hooked up the cardiac leads. An EKG blipped out of the machine. Jack tore off the sheet and immediately focused on the ST elevations in leads V1 and V2.

'Anterior MI,' he said to Anna.

She nodded. 'I figured he was a tPA special.'

A nurse called through the doorway, 'The other ambulance is here!'

Jack and two nurses ran outside.

A young woman was screaming and writhing on the stretcher. Jack took one look at her shortened right leg, the foot rotated almost completely sideways, and knew this patient was going straight to surgery. Jack quickly cut away her clothes, to reveal an impacted hip fracture, her thigh bone rammed into the socket by the force of her knees hitting the car's dashboard. Just looking at her grotesquely deformed leg made him queasy.

'Morphine?' the nurse asked.

He nodded. 'Give her as much as she needs. She's in a world of hurt. Type and cross six units. And get an orthopod in here as soon as –'

'Dr McCallum, stat, X-ray. Dr McCallum, stat, X-ray.'

Jack glanced up in alarm. *Debbie Haning*. He ran out of the room.

He found Debbie lying on the X-ray table, hovered over by the ER nurse and the technician.

'We'd just finished doing the spine and skull films,' said the tech, 'and we couldn't wake her up. She doesn't even respond to pain.'

'How long's she been out?'

'I don't know. She was lying on the table ten, fifteen minutes before we noticed she wasn't talking to us anymore.'

'Did you get the CT scan done?'

'Computer's down. It should be up and running in a few hours.'

Jack flashed a penlight in Debbie's eyes and felt his stomach go into a sickening free fall. Her left pupil was dilated and unreactive.

'Show me the films,' he said.

'C-spine's already up on the light box.'

Jack swiftly moved into the next room and eyed the X rays clipped to the backlit viewing box. He saw no fractures on the neck films; her cervical spine was stable. He yanked down the neck films and replaced them with the skull X rays. At first glance he saw nothing immediately obvious. Then his gaze focused on an almost imperceptible line tracing across the left temporal bone. It was so subtle it looked like a pin scratch on the film. A fracture.

Had the fracture torn the left middle meningeal artery? That would cause bleeding inside her cranium. As the blood accumulated and pressure built up, the brain would be squeezed. It explained the rapid deterioration of her mental status and the blown pupil.

The blood had to be drained at once.

'Get her back to ER!' he said.

Within seconds they had Debbie strapped to the gurney and were wheeling her at a run down the hallway. As they swung her into an empty treatment room, he yelled to the clerk, 'Page neurosurgery *stat!* Tell them we have an epidural bleed, and we're prepping for emergency burr holes.'

He knew what Debbie really needed was the operating room, but her condition was deteriorating so quickly they had no time to wait. The treatment room would have to serve as their OR. They slid her onto the table and attached a tangle of EKG leads to her chest. Her breathing had turned erratic; it was time to intubate.

He had just torn open the package containing the endotracheal tube when a nurse said, 'She's stopped breathing!'

He slipped the laryngoscope into Debbie's throat. Seconds later, the ET tube was in place and oxygen was being bagged into her lungs.

A nurse plugged in the electric shaver. Debbie's blond hair began to fall to the floor in silky clumps, exposing the scalp.

The clerk poked her head in the room. 'Neurosurgeon's stuck in traffic! He can't get here for at least another hour.'

'Then get someone else!'

'They're all at Texas Med! They've got all the head injuries.'

Jesus, we're screwed, thought Jack, looking down at Debbie. Every minute that went by, the pressure inside her skull was building. Brain cells were dying. *If this was my wife, I wouldn't wait. Not another second.*

He swallowed hard. 'Get out the Hudson brace drill. I'll do the burr holes myself.' He saw the nurses' startled looks, and added, with more bravado than he was feeling. 'It's like drilling holes in a wall. I've done it before.'

While the nurses prepped the newly shorn scalp, Jack put on a surgical gown and snapped on gloves. He positioned the sterile drapes and was amazed to find his hands were still steady, even while his heart was racing. It was true he had drilled burr holes before, but only once, and it was years ago, under the supervision of a neurosurgeon.

There's no more time. She's dying. Do it.

He reached for the scalpel and made a linear incision in

30

the scalp, over the left temporal bone. Blood oozed out. He sponged it away and cauterized the bleeders. With a retractor holding back the skin flap, he sliced deeper through the galea and reached the pericranium, which he scraped back, exposing the skull surface.

He picked up the Hudson brace drill. It was a mechanical device, powered by hand and almost antique looking, the sort of tool you might find in your grandfather's woodshop. First he used the perforator, a spade-shaped drill bit that dug just deeply enough into the bone to establish the hole. Then he changed to the rose bit, round-tipped, with multiedged burrs. He took a deep breath, positioned the bit, and began to drill deeper. Toward the brain. The first beads of sweat broke out on his forehead. He was drilling without CT confirmation, acting purely on his clinical judgment. He did not even know if he was tapping the right spot.

A sudden gush of blood spilled out of the hole and splattered the surgical drapes.

A nurse handed him a basin. He withdrew the drill and watched as a steady stream of red drained out of the skull and gathered in a glistening pool in the basin. He'd tapped the right place. With every trickle of blood, the pressure was easing from Debbie Haning's brain.

He released a deep breath, and the tension suddenly eased from his shoulders, leaving his muscles spent and aching.

'Get the bone wax ready,' he said. Then he put down the drill and reached for the suction catheter.

A white mouse hung in midair, as though suspended in a transparent sea. Dr Emma Watson drifted toward it, slender-limbed and graceful as an underwater dancer, the curlicue strands of her dark brown hair splayed out in a ghostly halo. She grasped the mouse and slowly spun around to face the camera. She held up a syringe and needle.

The footage was over two years old, filmed aboard the shuttle *Atlantis* during STS 141, but it remained Gordon Obie's favorite PR film, which is why it was now playing on all the video monitors in NASA's Teague Auditorium. Who wouldn't enjoy watching Emma Watson? She was quick and lithe, and she possessed what one could only call *sparkle*, with the fire of curiosity in her eyes. From the tiny scar over her eyebrow, to the slightly chipped front tooth (a souvenir, he'd heard, of reckless skiing) her face was a record of an exuberant life. But to Gordon, her primary appeal was her intelligence. Her competence. He had been following Emma's NASA career with an interest that had nothing to do with the fact she was an attractive woman.

As director of Flight Crew Operations, Gordon Obie wielded considerable power over crew selection, and he strove to maintain a safe – some would call it heartless – emotional distance from all his astronauts. He had been an astronaut himself, twice a shuttle commander, and even then he'd been known as the Sphinx, an aloof and mysterious man not given to small talk. He was comfortable with his own silence and relative anonymity. Although he was now sitting onstage with an array of NASA officials, most of the people in the audience did not know who Gordon Obie was. He was here merely for set decoration. Just as the footage of Emma Watson was set decoration, an attractive face to hold the audience's interest.

The video suddenly ended, replaced on the screen with the NASA logo, affectionately known as the meatball, a star-spangled blue circle embellished with an orbital ellipse and a forked slash of red. NASA administrator Leroy Cornell and JSC director Ken Blankenship stepped up to the lectern to field questions. Their mission, quite bluntly, was to beg for money, and they faced a skeptical gathering of congressmen and senators, members of the various subcommittees that determined NASA's budget. For the second straight year, NASA had suffered devastating cutbacks, and lately an air of abject gloom wafted through the halls of Johnson Space Center.

Gazing at the audience of well-dressed men and women, Gordon felt as though he were staring at an alien culture. What was wrong with these politicians? How could they be so shortsighted? It bewildered him that they did not share his most passionate belief: What sets the human race apart from the beasts is man's hunger for knowledge. Every child asks the universal question: *Why?* They are programmed from birth to be curious, to be explorers, to seek scientific truths.

Yet these elected officials had lost the curiosity that makes man unique. They'd come to Houston not to ask *why*, but *why should we?*

It was Cornell's idea to woo them with what he cynically called 'the Tom Hanks tour,' a reference to the movie *Apollo 13*, which still ranked as the best PR NASA had ever known. Cornell had already presented the latest achievements aboard the orbiting International Space Station. He'd let them shake the hands of some real live astronauts. Wasn't that what everyone wanted? To touch a golden boy, a hero? Next there'd be a tour of Johnson Space Center, starting with Building 30 and the Flight Control Room. Never mind the fact that this audience couldn't tell the difference between a flight console and a Nintendo set; all that gleaming technology would surely dazzle them and make them true believers.

But it isn't working, thought Gordon in dismay. *These politicians aren't buying it.*

NASA faced powerful opponents, starting with Senator Phil Parish, sitting in the front row. Seventy-six years old, an uncompromising hawk from South Carolina, Parish's first priority was preserving the defense budget, NASA be damned. Now he hauled his three-hundred-pound frame out of his seat and stood up to address Cornell in a gentleman's drawl.

'Your agency is billions of dollars overbudget on that space station,' he said. 'Now, I don't think the American people expected to sacrifice their defense capabilities just so you can tinker around up there with your nifty lab experiments. This is supposed to be an international effort, isn't it? Well, far as I can see, we-all are picking up most of the tab. How am I supposed to justify this white elephant to the good folks of South Carolina?'

NASA administrator Cornell responded with a camera-ready smile. He was a political animal, the glad-hander whose personal charm and charisma made him a star with the press and in Washington, where he spent most of his time cajoling Congress and the White House for more money, ever more money, to fund the space agency's perennially insufficient budget. His was the public face of NASA, while Ken Blankenship, the man in charge of day-to-day operations at JSC, was the private face known only to agency insiders. They were the yin and yang of NASA leadership, so completely different in temperament it was hard to imagine how they functioned as a team. The inside joke at NASA was that Leroy Cornell was all style and no substance, and Blankenship was all substance and no style.

Cornell smoothly responded to Senator Parish's question. 'You asked why other countries aren't contributing. Senator, the answer is, they already have. This truly is an international space station. Yes, the Russians are badly strapped for cash. Yes, we had to make up the difference. But they're committed to this station. They've got a cosmonaut up there now, and they have every reason to help us keep ISS running. As for *why* we need the station, just look at the research that's being conducted in biology and medicine. Materials science. Geophysics. We'll see the benefits of this research in our own lifetimes.'

Another member of the audience stood, and Gordon felt his

blood pressure rise. If there was anyone he despised more than Senator Parish, it was Montana congressman Joe Bellingham, whose Marlboro Man good looks couldn't disguise the fact he was a scientific moron. During his last campaign, he'd demanded that public schools teach Creationism. Throw out the biology books and open the Bible instead. *He probably thinks rockets are powered by angels.*

'What about all that sharing of technology with the Russians and Japanese?' said Bellingham. 'I'm concerned that we're giving away high-tech secrets for free. This international cooperation sounds high-minded and all, but what's to stop them from turning right around and using the knowledge against us? Why should we trust the Russians?'

Fear and paranoia. Ignorance and superstition. There was too much of it in the country, and Gordon grew depressed just listening to Bellingham. He turned away in disgust.

That's when he noticed a somber-faced Hank Millar step into the auditorium. Millar was head of the Astronaut Office. He looked straight at Gordon, who understood at once that a problem was brewing.

Quietly Gordon left the stage, and the two men stepped out into the hallway. 'What's going on?'

'There's been an accident. It's Bill Haning's wife. We hear it doesn't look good.'

'Jesus.'

'Bob Kittredge and Woody Ellis are waiting over in Public Affairs. We all need to talk.'

Gordon nodded. He glanced through the auditorium door at Congressman Bellingham, who was still blathering on about the dangers of sharing technology with the Commies. Grimly he followed Hank out the auditorium exit and across the courtyard, to the next building.

They met in a back office. Kittredge, the shuttle commander for STS 162, was flushed and agitated. Woody Ellis, flight director for the International Space Station, appeared far calmer, but then, Gordon had never seen Ellis look upset, even in the midst of crisis.

'How serious was the accident?' Gordon asked.

'Mrs Haning's car was in a giant pileup on I-45,' said Hank. 'The ambulance brought her over to Miles Memorial. Jack McCallum saw her in the ER.'

Gordon nodded. They all knew Jack well. Although he was no longer in the astronaut corps, Jack was still on NASA's active flight surgeon roster. A year ago, he had pulled back from most of his NASA duties, to work as an ER physician in the private sector.

'Jack's the one who called our office about Debbie,' said Hank.

'Did he say anything about her condition?'

'Severe head injury. She's in ICU; in a coma.'

'Prognosis?'

'He couldn't answer that question.' There was a silence as they all considered what this tragedy meant to NASA. Hank sighed. 'We're going to have to tell Bill. We can't keep this news from him. The problem is . . .' He didn't finish. He didn't need to; they all understood the problem.

Bill Haning was now in orbit aboard ISS, only a month into his scheduled four-month stay. This news would devastate him. Of all the factors that made prolonged habitation in space difficult, it was the emotional toll that NASA worried about most. A depressed astronaut could wreak havoc on a mission. Years before, on *Mir*, a similar situation had occurred when Cosmonaut Volodya Dezhurov was informed of his mother's death. For days, he'd shut himself away in one of *Mir*'s modules and refused to speak to Mission Control Moscow. His grief had disrupted the work of everyone aboard *Mir*.

'They have a very close marriage,' said Hank. 'I can tell you now, Bill's not going to handle this well.'

36

'You're recommending we replace him?' asked Gordon.

'At the next scheduled shuttle flight. He'll have a tough enough time being stuck up there for the next two weeks. We can't ask him to serve out his full four months.' Hank added quietly, 'They have two young kids, you know.'

'His backup for ISS is Emma Watson,' said Woody Ellis. 'We could send her up on STS 160. With Vance's crew.'

At the mention of Emma's name, Gordon was careful not to reveal any sign of special interest. Any emotion whatsoever. 'What do you think about Watson? Is she ready to go up three months early?'

'She's slated to relieve Bill. She's already up to speed on most of the onboard experiments. So I think that option is viable.'

'Well, I'm not happy about it,' said Bob Kittredge.

Gordon gave a tired sigh and turned to the shuttle commander. 'I didn't think you would be.'

'Watson's an integral part of *my* crew. We've crystallized as a team. I hate to break it up.'

'Your team's three months away from launch. You have time to make adjustments.'

'You're making my job hard.'

'Are you saying you can't get a new team crystallized in that time?'

Kittredge's mouth tightened. 'All I'm saying is, my crew is already a working unit. We're not going to be happy about losing Watson.'

Gordon looked at Hank. 'What about the STS 160 crew? Vance and his team?'

'No problem from their end. Watson would just be another passenger on middeck. They'd deliver her to ISS like any other payload.'

Gordon thought it over. They were still talking about options, not certainties. Perhaps Debbie Haning would wake up fine and Bill could stay on ISS as scheduled. But like everyone else at NASA, Gordon had taught himself to plan for every contingency, to carry in his head a mental flow chart of what actions to follow should a, b, or c occur.

He looked at Woody Ellis for final confirmation. Woody gave a nod.

'Okay,' said Gordon. 'Find me Emma Watson.'

She spotted him at the far end of the hospital hallway. He was talking to Hank Millar, and though his back was turned to her and he was wearing standard green surgical scrubs, Emma knew it was Jack. Seven years of marriage had left ties of familiarity that went beyond the mere recognition of his face.

This was, in fact, the same view she'd had of Jack McCallum the first time they'd met, when they'd both been ER residents in San Francisco General Hospital. He had been standing at the nurses' station, writing in a chart, his broad shoulders sloping from fatigue, his hair ruffled as though he'd just rolled out of bed. In fact, he had; it was the morning after a hectic night on call, and though he was unshaven and bleary-eyed, when he'd turned and looked at her for the first time, the attraction between them had been instantaneous.

Now Jack was ten years older, his dark hair was threaded with gray, and fatigue was once again weighing down on his shoulders. She had not seen him in three weeks, had spoken to him only briefly on the phone a few days ago, a conversation that had deteriorated into yet another noisy disagreement. These days they could not seem to be reasonable with each other, could not carry on a civilized conversation, however brief.

So it was with apprehension that she continued down the hall in his direction.

Hank Millar spotted her first, and his face instantly tensed, as though he knew a battle was imminent, and he wanted to get the hell out of there before the shooting started. Jack must have seen the change in Hank's expression as well, because he turned to see what had inspired it.

At his first glimpse of Emma, he seemed to freeze, a spontaneous smile of greeting half-formed on his face. It was almost, but not quite, a look of both surprise and gladness to see her. Then something else took control, and his smile vanished, replaced by a look that was neither friendly nor unfriendly, merely neutral. The face of a stranger, she thought, and that was somehow more painful than if he had greeted her with outright hostility. At least then there would've been *some* emotion left, some remnant, however tattered, of a marriage that had once been happy.

She found herself responding to his flat look with an expression that was every bit as neutral. When she spoke, she addressed both men at the same time, favoring neither.

'Gordon told me about Debbie,' she said. 'How is she doing?'

Hank glanced at Jack, waiting for him to answer first. Finally Hank said, 'She's still unconscious. We're sort of holding a vigil in the waiting room. If you want to join us.'

'Yes. Of course.' She started toward the visitors' waiting room.

'Emma,' Jack called out. 'Can we talk?'

'I'll see you both later,' said Hank, and he made a hasty retreat down the hall. They waited for him to disappear around the corner, then looked at each other.

'Debbie's not doing well,' said Jack.

'What happened?'

'She had an epidural bleed. Came in conscious and talking. In a matter of minutes, she went straight downhill. I was busy with another patient. I didn't realize it in time. Didn't drill the burr hole until . . .' He paused and looked away. 'She's on a ventilator.'

39

Emma reached out to touch him, then stopped herself, knowing that he would only shake her off. It had been so long since he'd accepted any words of comfort from her. No matter what she said, how sincerely she meant it, he would regard it as pity. And that he despised.

'It's a hard diagnosis to make, Jack,' was all she could say.

'I should have made it sooner.'

'You said she went downhill fast. Don't second-guess yourself.'

'That doesn't make me feel a hell of a lot better.'

'I'm not trying to make you feel better!' she said in exasperation. 'I'm just pointing out the simple fact that you did make the right diagnosis. And you acted on it. For once, can't you cut yourself some slack?'

'Look, this isn't about me, okay?' he shot back. 'It's about *you.*'

'What do you mean?'

'Debbie won't be leaving the hospital anytime soon. And that means Bill . . .'

'I know. Gordon Obie gave me the heads-up.'

Jack paused. 'It's been decided?'

She nodded. 'Bill's coming home. I'll replace him on the next flight.' Her gaze drifted toward the ICU. 'They have two kids,' she said softly. 'He can't stay up there. Not for another three months.'

'You're not ready. You haven't had time –'

'I'll *be* ready.' She turned.

'Emma.' He reached out to stop her, and the touch of his hand took her by surprise. She looked back at him. At once he released her.

'When are you leaving for Kennedy?' he asked.

'A week. Quarantine.'

He looked stunned. He said nothing, still trying to absorb the news.

'That reminds me,' she said. 'Could you take care of Humphrey while I'm gone?'

'Why not a kennel?'

'It's cruel to keep a cat penned up for three months.'

'Has the little monster been declawed yet?'

'Come on, Jack. He only shreds things when he's feeling ignored. Pay attention to him, and he'll leave your furniture alone.'

Jack glanced up as a page was announced over the address system: 'Dr McCallum to ER. Dr McCallum to ER.'

'I guess you have to go,' she said, already turning away.

'Wait. This is happening so fast. We haven't had time to talk.'

'If it's about the divorce, my lawyer can answer any questions while I'm gone.'

'No.' He startled her with his sharp note of anger. 'No, I *don't* want to talk to your lawyer!'

'Then what do you need to tell me?'

He stared at her for a moment, as though hunting for words. 'It's about this mission,' he finally said. 'It's too rushed. It doesn't feel right to me.'

'What does that mean?'

'You're a last-minute replacement. You're going up with a different crew.'

'Vance runs a tight ship. I'm perfectly comfortable with this launch.'

'What about on the station? This could stretch your stay to six months in orbit.'

'I can deal with it.'

'But it wasn't planned. It's been thrown together at the last minute.'

'What are you saying I should do, Jack? Wimp out?'

'I don't know!' He ran his hand through his hair in frustration. 'I don't know.'

They stood in silence for a moment, neither one of them quite sure what to say, yet neither one ready to end the conversation. *Seven years of marriage*, she thought, *and this is what it's come to. Two people who can't stay together, yet can't walk away from each other. And now there's no time left to work things out between us.*

A new page came over the address system: 'Dr McCallum stat to ER.'

Jack looked at her, his expression torn. 'Emma –'

'Go, Jack,' she urged him. 'They need you.'

He gave a groan of frustration and took off at a run for the ER.

And she turned and walked the other way.

4

From the observation windows of the Node 1 cupola, Dr William Haning could see clouds swirling over the Atlantic Ocean two hundred twenty miles below. He touched the glass, his fingers skimming the barrier that protected him from the vacuum of space. It was one more obstacle that separated him from home. From his wife. He watched the earth turn beneath him, saw the Atlantic Ocean slip away as North Africa and then the Indian Ocean slowly spun by, the darkness of night approaching. Though his body was weightless and floating, the burden of grief seemed to squeeze down on his chest, making it difficult for him to breathe.

At that moment, in a Houston hospital, his wife was fighting for her life, and he could do nothing to help her. For the next two weeks he would be trapped here, able to gaze down at the very city where Debbie might be dying, yet unable to reach her, touch her. The best he could do was close his eyes and try to imagine he was at her side, that their fingers were entwined.

You have to hang on. You have to fight. I'm coming home to you.

'Bill? Are you okay?'

He turned and saw Diana Estes float from the U.S. lab module into the node. He was surprised she was the one inquiring as to his well-being. Even after a month of living together in close quarters, he had not warmed up to the Englishwoman. She was too cool, too clinical. Despite her icy blond good looks, she was not a woman he'd ever feel attracted to, and she had certainly never favored him with the least hint of interest. But then, her attention was usually focused on Michael Griggs. The fact that Griggs had a wife waiting for him down on earth seemed irrelevant to them both. Up here on ISS, Diana and Griggs were like the two halves of a double star, orbiting each other, linked by some powerful gravitational pull.

This was one of the unfortunate realities of being one of six human beings from four different countries trapped in close quarters. There were always shifting alliances and schisms, a changing sense of *us* versus *them*. The stress of living so long in confinement had affected each of them in different ways. Russian Nicolai Rudenko, who had been living aboard ISS the longest, had lately turned sullen and irritable. Kenichi Hirai, from Japan's NASDA, was so frustrated by his poor command of English, he often lapsed into uneasy silence. Only Luther Ames had remained everyone's friend. When Houston broke the bad news about Debbie, Luther was the one who had known instinctively what to say to Bill, the one who had spoken from his heart, from the human part of him. Luther was the Alabama-born son of a well-loved black minister, and he had inherited his father's gift for bestowing comfort.

'There's no question about it, Bill,' Luther had said. 'You gotta go home to your wife. You tell Houston they'd better send the limo to get you, or they'll have to deal with me.'

How different from the way Diana had reacted. Ever logical, she had calmly pointed out that there was nothing Bill could do to speed his wife's recovery. Debbie was comatose; she wouldn't even know he was there. *As cold and brittle as the crystals she grows in her lab*, was what Bill thought of Diana.

That's why he was puzzled that she was now asking about him. She hung back in the node, as remote as always. Her long blond hair waved about her face like drifting sea grass.

He turned to look out the window again. 'I'm waiting for Houston to come into view,' he said.

'You've got a new batch of E-mail from Payloads.'

He said nothing. He just stared down at the twinkling lights of Tokyo, now poised at the knife edge of dawn.

'Bill, there are items that require your attention. If you don't feel up to it, we'll have to split up your duties among the rest of us.'

Duties. So that's what she had come to discuss. Not the pain he was feeling, but whether she could count on him to perform his assigned tasks in the lab. Every day aboard ISS was tightly scheduled, with little time to spare for reflection or grief. If one crew member was incapacitated, the others had to pick up the slack, or experiments went untended.

'Sometimes,' said Diana with crisp logic, 'work is the best thing to keep grief at bay.'

He touched his finger to the blur of light that was Tokyo. 'Don't pretend to have a heart, Diana. It doesn't fool anyone.'

For a moment she said nothing. He heard only the continuous background hum of the space station, a sound he'd grown so accustomed to he was scarcely aware of it now.

She said, unruffled, 'I do understand you're having a hard time. I know it's not easy to be trapped up here, with no way to get home. But there's nothing you can do about it. You just have to wait for the shuttle.'

45

He gave a bitter laugh. 'Why wait? When I could be home in four hours.'

'Come on, Bill. Get serious.'

'I am serious. I should just get in the CRV and *go*.'

'Leaving us with no lifeboat? You're not thinking straight.' She paused. 'You know, you might feel better with some medication. Just to help you get through this period.'

He turned to face her, all his pain, all his grief, giving way to rage. 'Take a pill and cure everything, is that it?'

'It could help. Bill, I just need to know you won't do something irrational.'

'Fuck you, Diana.' He pushed off from the cupola and floated past her, toward the lab hatchway.

'Bill!'

'As you so kindly pointed out, I've got work to do.'

'I told you, we can divide up your duties. If you're not feeling up to it –'

'I'll do my own goddamn work!'

He drifted into the U.S. lab. He was relieved she didn't follow him. Glancing back, he saw her float toward the habitation module, no doubt to check the status of the Crew Return Vehicle. Capable of evacuating all six astronauts, the CRV was their only lifeboat home should a catastrophe befall the station. He had spooked her with his mutterings about hijacking the CRV, and he regretted it. Now she'd be watching him for signs of emotional meltdown.

It was painful enough to be trapped in this glorified sardine can two hundred twenty miles above earth. To also be watched with suspicion made the ordeal worse. He might be desperate to go home, but he was not unstable. All those years of training, the psychological screening tests, had confirmed the fact Bill Haning was a professional – certainly not a man who'd ever endanger his colleagues.

Propelling himself with a practiced push-off from one wall,

he floated across the lab module to his workstation. There he checked the latest batch of E-mail. Diana was right about one thing: Work would distract him from thoughts of Debbie.

Most of the E-mail had come from NASA's Ames Biological Research Center in California, and the messages were routine requests for data confirmation. Many of the experiments were monitored from the ground, and scientists sometimes questioned the data they received. He scrolled down the messages, grimacing at yet another request for astronaut urine and feces samples. He kept scrolling, and paused at a new message.

This one was different. It did not come from Ames, but from a private-sector payload operations center. Private industry paid for a number of experiments aboard the station, and he often received E-mail from scientists outside NASA.

This message was from SeaScience in La Jolla, California.

To: Dr William Haning, ISS Bioscience
Sender: Helen Koenig, Principal Investigator
Re: Experiment CCU#23 (Archaeon Cell Culture)
Message: Our most recent downlinked data indicates rapid and unexpected increase in cell culture mass. Please confirm with your onboard micro mass measurement device.

Another jiggle-the-handle request, he thought wearily. Many of the orbital experiments were controlled by commands from scientists on the ground. Data was recorded within the various lab racks, using video or automatic sampling devices, and the results downlinked directly to researchers on earth. With all the sophisticated equipment aboard ISS, there were bound to be occasional glitches. That's the real reason humans were needed up here – to troubleshoot the temperamental electronics.

He called up the file for CCU#23 on the payloads computer

and reviewed the protocol. The cells in the culture were *Archaeons*, bacteria-like marine organisms collected from deep-sea thermal vents. They were harmless to humans.

He floated across the lab to the cell culture unit and slipped his stockinged feet into the holding stirrups to maintain his position. The unit was a box-shaped device with its own fluid-handling and delivery system to continuously perfuse two dozen cell cultures and tissue specimens. Most of the experiments were completely self-contained and without need of human intervention. In his four weeks aboard ISS, Bill had only once laid eyes on the tube #23.

He pulled open the cell specimen chamber tray. Inside were twenty-four culture tubes arrayed around the periphery of the unit. He identified #23 and removed it from the tray.

At once he was alarmed. The cap appeared to be bulging out, as though under pressure. Instead of a slightly turbid liquid, which was what he'd expected to see, the contents was a vivid blue-green. He tipped the tube upside down, and the culture did not shift. It was no longer liquid, but thickly viscous.

He calibrated the micro mass measurement device and slipped the tube into the specimen slot. A moment later, the data appeared on the screen.

Something is very wrong, he thought. *There has been some sort of contamination. Either the original sample of cells was not pure, or another organism has found its way into the tube and has destroyed the primary culture.*

He typed out his response to Dr Koenig:

. . . Your downlinked data confirmed. Culture appears drastically altered. It is no longer liquid, but seems to be a gelatinous mass, bright, almost neon blue-green. Must consider the possibility of contamination . . .

He paused. There was another possibility: the effect of micro-gravity. On earth, tissue cultures tended to grow in flat sheets, expanding in only two dimensions across the surface of their containers. In the weightlessness of space, freed from the effects of gravity, those same cultures behaved differently. They grew in three dimensions, taking on shapes they never could on earth.

What if #23 was not contaminated? What if this was simply how Archaeons behaved without gravity to keep them in check?

Almost immediately he discarded that notion. These changes were too drastic. Weightlessness alone could not have turned a single-celled organism into this startling green mass.

He typed:

. . . Will return a sample of culture #23 to you on next shuttle flight. Please advise if you have further instructions –

The sudden clang of a drawer startled him. He turned and saw Kenichi Hirai working at his own research rack. How long had he been there? The man had drifted so quietly into the lab Bill had not even known he'd entered. In a world where there is no up or down, where the sound of footsteps is never heard, a verbal greeting is sometimes the only way to alert others to your presence.

Noticing Bill's glance, Kenichi merely nodded in greeting and continued with his work. The man's silence irritated Bill. Kenichi was like the station's resident ghost, creeping around without a word, startling everyone. Bill knew it was because Kenichi was insecure about his English and, to avoid humili-ation, chose to converse little if at all. Still, the man could at least call out a 'hello' when he entered a module to avoid rattling the nerves of his five colleagues.

Bill turned his attention back to tube #23. What would this gelatinous mass look like under the microscope?

He slid tube #23 into the Plexiglas glove box, closed the hatch, and inserted his hands in the attached gloves. If there was any spillage, it would be confined to the box. Loose fluids floating around in microgravity could wreak havoc on the station's electrical wiring. Gently he loosened the tube seal. He knew the contents were under pressure; he could see the cap was bulging. Even so, he was shocked when the top suddenly exploded off like a champagne cork.

He jerked back as a blue-green glob splatted against the inside of the glove box. It clung there for a moment, quivering as though alive. It *was* alive; a mass of microorganisms, joined in a gelatinous matrix.

'Bill, we need to talk.'

The voice startled him. Quickly he recapped the culture tube and turned to face Michael Griggs, who had just entered the module. Floating right behind Griggs was Diana. *The beautiful people*, Bill thought. Both of them looked sleek and athletic in their navy blue NASA shirts and cobalt shorts.

'Diana tells me you're having problems,' said Griggs. 'We just spoke to Houston, and they think it might help if you considered some medication. Just to get you through the next few days.'

'You've got Houston worried now, have you?'

'They're concerned about you. We all are.'

'Look, my crack about the CRV was purely sarcastic.'

'But it makes us all nervous.'

'I don't need any Valium. Just leave me alone.' He removed the tube from the glove box and returned it to its slot in the cell culture unit. He was too angry to work on it now.

'We have to be able to trust you, Bill. We have to depend on each other up here.'

In fury, Bill turned to face him. 'Do you see a raving lunatic in front of you? Is that it?'

'Your wife is on your mind now. I understand that. And –'

'You wouldn't understand. I doubt you give *your* wife much thought these days.' He shot a knowing glance at Diana, then launched himself down the length of the module and into the connecting node. He started to enter the hab module, but stopped when he saw Luther was there, setting up the midday meal.

There's nowhere to hide. Nowhere to be alone.

Suddenly in tears, he backed out of the hatchway and retreated into the cupola.

Turning his back to the others, he stared through the windows at the earth. Already, the Pacific coast was rotating into view. Another sunrise, another sunset.

Another eternity of waiting.

Kenichi watched Griggs and Diana float out of the lab module, each propelled by a well-gauged push-off. They moved with such grace, like fair-haired gods. He often studied them when they weren't watching; in particular, he enjoyed looking at Diana Estes, a woman so blond and pale she seemed translucent.

Their departure left him alone in the lab, and he was able to relax. So much conflict on this station. It unsettled his nerves and affected his concentration. He was tranquil by nature, a man content to work in solitude. Though he could understand English well enough, it was an effort for him to speak it, and he found conversation exhausting. He was far more comfortable working alone, and in silence, with only the lab animals as company.

He peered through the viewing window at the mice in the animal habitat, and he smiled. On one side of the screened divider were twelve males; on the other were twelve females. As a boy growing up in Japan, he had raised rabbits and had enjoyed cuddling them in his lap. These mice, however, were not pets, and they were isolated from human contact, their air filtered and conditioned before being allowed to mix with the space station's environment. Any handling of the animals was done in the adjoining glove box, where all biological specimens, from bacteria to lab rats, could be manipulated without fear of contaminating the station's air.

Today was blood-sampling day. Not a task he enjoyed, because it involved pricking the skin of the mice with a needle. He murmured an apology in Japanese as he inserted his hands in the gloves and transferred the first mouse into the sealed work area. It struggled to escape his grasp. He released it, allowing it to float free as he prepared the needle. It was a pitiful sight to watch, the mouse frantically thrashing its limbs, attempting to propel itself forward. With nothing to push off against, it drifted helplessly in midair.

The needle now ready, he reached up with his gloved hand to recapture the mouse. Only then did he notice the blue-green globule floating beside the mouse. So close to it, in fact, that with one dart of a pink tongue, the mouse gave it an experimental lick. Kenichi laughed out loud. Drinking floating globules was something the astronauts did for fun, and that's what the mouse appeared to be doing now, playing with its newfound toy.

Then the thought occurred to him: Where had the blue-green substance come from? Bill had been using the glove box. Was whatever he'd spilled toxic?

Kenichi floated to the computer workstation and looked at the experimental protocol Bill had last called up. It was CCU#23, a cell culture. The protocol reassured him that the globule contained nothing dangerous. *Archaeons* were harmless single-celled marine organisms, without infectious properties.

Satisfied, he returned to the glove box and inserted his hands. He reached for the needle.

5

July 16

We have no downlink.

Jack stared up at the plume of exhaust streaking into the azure sky, and terror knifed deep into his soul. The sun was beating down on his face, but his sweat had chilled to ice. He scanned the heavens. Where was the shuttle? Only seconds before, he had watched it arc into a cloudless sky, had felt the ground shake from the thunder of liftoff. As it had climbed, he'd felt his heart soar with it, borne aloft by the roar of rockets, and had followed its path heavenward until it was just a glinting pinprick of reflected sunlight.

He could not see it. What had been a straight white plume was now a jagged trail of black smoke.

Frantically he searched the sky and caught a dizzying whirl of images. Fire in the heavens. A devil's fork of smoke. Shattered fragments tumbling toward the sea.

We have no downlink.

He woke up, gasping, his body steeped in sweat. It was daylight, and the sun shone, piercingly hot, through his bedroom window.

With a groan he sat up on the side of the bed and dropped

53

his head in his hands. He had left the air conditioner off last night, and now the room felt like an oven. He stumbled across his bedroom to flip the switch, then sank down on the bed again and breathed a sigh of relief as chill air began to spill from the vent.

The old nightmare.

He rubbed his face, trying to banish the images, but they were too deeply engraved in his memory. He had been a college freshman when *Challenger* exploded, had been walking through the dorm lounge when the first film footage of the disaster had aired on the television. That day, and in the days that followed, he'd watched the horrifying footage again and again, had incorporated it so deeply into his subconscious that it had become as real to him as if he himself had been standing in the bleachers at Cape Canaveral that morning.

And now the memory had resurfaced in his nightmares.

It's because of Emma's launch.

In the shower he stood with head bowed under a pounding stream of cool water, waiting for the last traces of his dream to wash away. He had three weeks of vacation starting next week, but he was a long way from being in a holiday mood. He had not taken out the sailboat in months. Maybe a few weeks out on the water, away from the glare of city lights, would be the best therapy. Just him, and the sea, and the stars.

It had been so long since he'd really looked at the stars. Lately it seemed he had avoided even glancing at them. As a boy, his gaze had always been drawn heavenward. His mother once told him that, as a toddler, he had stood on the lawn one night and reached up with both hands, trying to touch the moon. When he could not reach it, he had howled in frustration.

The moon, the stars, the blackness of space – it was beyond

his reach now, and he often felt like that little boy he once was, howling in frustration, his feet trapped on earth, his hands still reaching for the sky.

He shut off the shower and stood leaning with both hands pressed against the tiles, head bent, hair dripping. *Today is July sixteenth*, he thought. *Eight days till Emma's launch*. He felt the water chill on his skin.

In ten minutes he was dressed and in the car.

It was a Tuesday. Emma and her new flight team would be wrapping up their three-day integrated simulation, and she'd be tired and in no mood to see him. But tomorrow she'd be on her way to Cape Canaveral. Tomorrow she'd be out of reach.

At Johnson Space Center, he parked in the Building 30 lot, flashed his NASA badge at Security, and trotted upstairs to the shuttle Flight Control Room. Inside, he found everyone hushed and tense. The three-day integrated simulation was like the final exam for both the astronauts and the ground control crew, a crisis-packed run-through of the mission from launch to touchdown, with assorted malfunctions thrown in to keep everyone on their toes. Three shifts of controllers had rotated through this room several times in the last three days, and the two dozen men and women now sitting at the consoles looked haggard. The rubbish can was overflowing with coffee cups and diet Pepsi cans. Though a few of the controllers saw Jack and nodded hello, there was no time for a real greeting; they had a major crisis on their hands, and everyone's attention was focused on the problem. It was the first time in months Jack had visited the FCR, and once again he felt the old excitement, the electricity, that seemed to crackle in this room whenever a mission was underway.

He moved to the third row of consoles, to stand beside Flight Director Randy Carpenter, who was too busy at the moment to talk to him. Carpenter was the shuttle program's high priest of flight directors. At two hundred eighty pounds, he was an imposing presence in the FCR, his stomach bulging over his belt, his feet planted apart like a ship's captain steadying himself on a heaving bridge. In this room, Carpenter was in command. 'I'm a prime example,' he liked to say, 'of just how far a fat boy with glasses can get in life.' Unlike the legendary flight director Gene Kranz, whose quote 'Failure is not an option' made him a media hero, Carpenter was well known only within NASA. His lack of photogenic qualities made him an unlikely movie hero, in any event.

Listening in on the loop chatter, Jack quickly pieced together the nature of the crisis Carpenter was now dealing with. Jack had faced just such a problem in his own integrated sim two years ago, when he was still in the astronaut corps, preparing for STS 145. The shuttle crew had reported a precipitous drop in cabin pressure, indicating a rapid air leak. There was no time to track down the source; they had to go to emergency deorbit.

The flight dynamics officer, sitting at the front row of consoles known as the Trench, was rapidly plotting out the flight trajectories to determine the best landing site. No one considered this a game; they were too aware that if this crisis were real, the lives of seven people would be in jeopardy.

'Cabin pressure down to thirteen point nine psi,' reported Environmental Control.

'Edwards Air Force Base,' announced Flight Dynamics. 'Touchdown at approximately thirteen hundred.'

'Cabin pressure will be down to seven psi at this rate,' said Environmental. 'Recommend they don helmets now. Before initiating reentry sequence.'

Capcom relayed the advice to *Atlantis*.

'Roger that,' responded Commander Vance. 'Helmets are on. We are initiating deorbit burn.'

Against his will, Jack was caught up in the urgency of the

game. As the moments ticked by, he kept his gaze fixed on the central screen at the front of the room, where the orbiter's path was plotted on a global map. Even though he knew that every crisis was artificially introduced by a mischievous sim team, the grim seriousness of this exercise had rubbed off on him. He was scarcely aware that his muscles had tensed as he focused on the changing data flickering on the screen.

The cabin pressure dropped to seven psi.

Atlantis hit the upper atmosphere. They were in radio blackout, twelve long minutes of silence when the friction of reentry ionizes the air around the orbiter, cutting off all communications.

'*Atlantis*, do you copy?' said Capcom.

Suddenly Commander Vance's voice broke through: 'We hear you loud and clear, Houston.'

Touchdown, moments later, was perfect. Game over.

Applause broke out in the FCR.

'Okay, folks! Good job,' said Flight Director Carpenter. 'Debriefing at fifteen hundred. Let's all take a break for lunch.' Grinning, he pulled off his headset and for the first time looked at Jack. 'Hey, haven't seen you around here in ages.'

'Been playing doctor with civilians.'

'Going for the big bucks, huh?'

Jack laughed. 'Yeah, tell me what to do with all my money.' He glanced around at the flight controllers, now relaxing at their consoles with sodas and bag lunches. 'Did the sim go okay?'

'I'm happy. We made it through every glitch.'

'And the shuttle crew?'

'They're ready.' Carpenter gave him a knowing look. 'Including Emma. She's in her element, Jack, so don't rattle her. Right now she needs to focus.' This was more than just friendly advice. It was a warning: *Keep your personal issues to yourself. Don't screw around with my flight crew's morale.*

Jack was subdued, even a little contrite, as he waited outside in the sweltering heat for Emma to emerge from Building 5, where the flight simulators were housed. She walked out with the rest of her crew. Obviously they had just shared a joke, because they were all laughing. Then she saw Jack, and her smile faded.

'I didn't know you were coming,' she said.

He shrugged and said sheepishly, 'Neither did I.'

'Debriefing's in ten minutes,' said Vance.

'I'll be there,' she said. 'You all go on ahead.' She waited for her team to walk away; then she turned to face Jack again. 'I've really got to join them. Look, I know this launch complicates everything. If you're here about the divorce papers, I promise I'll sign them as soon as I get back.'

'I didn't come about that.'

'Is there something else, then?'

He paused. 'Yeah. Humphrey. What's the name of his vet? In case he swallows a hair ball or something.'

She fixed him with a perplexed look. 'The same vet he's always had. Dr Goldsmith.'

'Oh. Yeah.'

They stood in silence for a moment, the sun beating on their heads. Sweat trickled down his back. She suddenly seemed so small to him and insubstantial. Yet this was a woman who'd jumped out of an airplane. She could outrace him on horseback, spin circles around him on the dance floor. His beautiful, fearless wife.

She turned to look at Building 30, where her team was waiting for her. 'I have to go, Jack.'

'What time are you leaving for the Cape?'

'Six in the morning.'

'All your cousins flying out for the launch?'

'Of course.' She paused. 'You won't be there. Will you?'

The *Challenger* nightmare was still fresh in his mind, the angry trails of smoke etching across a blue sky. *I can't be there to watch it*, he thought. *I can't deal with the possibilities*. He shook his head.

She accepted his answer with a chilly nod and a look that said: *I can be every bit as detached as you are*. Already she was withdrawing from him, turning to leave.

'Emma.' He reached for her arm and gently tugged her around to face him. 'I'll miss you.'

She sighed. 'Sure, Jack.'

'I really will.'

'Weeks go by without a single call from you. And now you say you're going to miss me.' She laughed.

He was stung by the bitterness in her voice. And by the truth of her words. For the past few months he *had* avoided her. It had been painful to be anywhere near her because her success only magnified his own sense of failure.

There was no hope of reconciliation; he could see that now, in the coolness of her gaze. Nothing left to do but be civilized about it.

He glanced away, suddenly unable to look at her. 'I just came by to wish you a safe trip. And a great ride. Give me a wave every so often, when you pass over Houston. I'll watch for you.' A moving star was what ISS would look like, brighter than Venus, hurtling through the sky.

'You wave too, okay?'

They both managed a smile. So it would be a civilized parting after all. He held open his arms, and she leaned toward him for a hug. It was a brief and awkward one, as though they were strangers coming together for the first time. He felt her body, so warm and alive, press against him. Then she pulled away and started toward the Mission Control building.

She paused only once, to wave good-bye. The sunlight was sharp in his eyes, and squinting against its brightness, he saw her only as a dark silhouette, her hair flying in the hot wind. And he knew that he had never loved her as much as he did at that very moment, watching her walk away.

July 19
Cape Canaveral

Even from a distance, the sight took Emma's breath away. Poised on launchpad 39B, awash in brilliant floodlights, the shuttle *Atlantis*, mated to its giant orange fuel tank and the paired solid rocket boosters, was a towering beacon in the blackness of night. No matter how many times she experienced it, that first glimpse of a shuttle lit up on the pad never failed to awe her.

The rest of the crew, standing beside her on the blacktop, were equally silent. To shift their sleep cycle, they'd awakened at two that morning and had emerged from their quarters on the third floor of the Operations and Checkout building to catch a nighttime glimpse of the behemoth that would carry them into space. Emma heard the cry of a night bird and felt a cool wind blow in from the Gulf, freshening the air, sweeping away the stagnant scent of the wetlands surrounding them.

'Kind of makes you feel humble, doesn't it?' said Commander Vance in his soft Texas drawl.

The others murmured in agreement.

'Small as an ant,' said Chenoweth, the lone rookie on the crew. This would be his first trip aboard the shuttle, and he was so excited he seemed to generate his own field of electricity. 'I always forget how big she is, and then I take another look at her and I think, Jesus, all that power. And I'm the lucky son of a bitch who gets to ride her.'

They all laughed, but it was the hushed, uneasy laughter of parishioners in a church.

'I never thought a week could go by so slowly,' said Chenoweth.

'This man's tired of being a virgin,' said Vance.

'Damn right I am. I want *up* there.' Chenoweth's gaze lifted hungrily to the sky. To the stars. 'You guys all know the secret, and I can't wait to share it.'

The secret. It belonged only to the privileged few who had made the ascent. It wasn't a secret that could be imparted to another; you yourself had to live it, to see, with your own eyes, the blackness of space and the blue of earth far below. To be pressed backward into your seat by the thrust of the rockets. Astronauts returning from space often wear a knowing smile, a look that says, *I am privy to something that few human beings will ever know.*

Emma had worn such a smile when she'd emerged from *Atlantis*'s hatch over two years ago. On weak legs she had walked into the sunshine, had stared up at a sky that was startlingly blue. In the span of eight days aboard the orbiter, she had lived through one hundred thirty sunrises, had seen forest fires burning in Brazil and the eye of a hurricane whirling over Samoa, had viewed an earth that seemed heartbreakingly fragile. She had returned forever changed.

In five days, barring a catastrophe, Chenoweth would share the secret.

'Time to shine some light on these retinas,' said Chenoweth. 'My brain still thinks it's the middle of the night.'

'It *is* the middle of the night,' said Emma.

'For us it's the crack of dawn, folks,' Vance said. Of all of them, he had been the quickest to readjust his circadian rhythm to the new sleep-wake schedule. Now he strode back into the O and C building to begin a full day's work at three in the morning.

The others followed him. Only Emma lingered outside for a moment, gazing at the shuttle. The day before, they had driven over to the launchpad for a last review of crew escape procedures. Viewed up close, in the sunlight, the shuttle had seemed glaringly bright and too massive to fully comprehend. One could focus on only a single part of her at a time. The nose. The wings. The black tiles, like reptilian scales on the belly. In the light of day, the shuttle had been real and solid. Now she seemed unearthly, lit up against the black sky.

With all the frantic preparation, Emma had not allowed herself to feel any apprehension, had firmly banished all misgivings. She was ready to go up. She wanted to go up. But now she felt a sliver of fear.

She looked up at the sky, saw the stars disappear behind an advancing veil of clouds. The weather was about to change. Shivering, she turned and went into the building. Into the light.

July 23
Houston

Half a dozen tubes snaked into Debbie Haning's body. In her throat was a tracheotomy tube, through which oxygen was forced into her lungs. A nasogastric tube had been threaded up her left nostril and down her esophagus into the stomach. A catheter drained urine, and two intravenous catheters fed fluids into her veins. In her wrist was an arterial line, and a continuous blood pressure tracing danced across the oscilloscope. Jack glanced at the IV bags hanging over the bed and saw they contained powerful antibiotics. A bad sign; it meant she'd acquired an infection – not unusual when a patient has spent two weeks in a coma. Every breach in the skin, every plastic tube, is a portal for bacteria, and in Debbie's bloodstream, a battle was now being waged.

With one glance, Jack understood all of this, but he said nothing to Debbie's mother, who sat beside the bed, clasping her daughter's hand. Debbie's face was flaccid, the jaw limp, the eyelids only partially closed. She remained deeply coma-tose, unaware of anything, even pain.

Margaret looked up as Jack came into the cubicle, and gave a nod of greeting. 'She had a bad night,' said Margaret. 'A fever. They don't know where it's coming from.'

'The antibiotics will help.'

'And then what? We treat the infection, but what happens next?' Margaret took a deep breath. 'She wouldn't want it this way. All these tubes. All these needles. She'd want us to let her go.'

'This isn't the time to give up. Her EEG is still active. She's not brain dead.'

'Then why doesn't she wake up?'

'She's young. She has everything to live for.'

'This isn't *living*.' Margaret stared down at her daughter's hand. It was bruised and puffy from IVs and needle sticks. 'When her father was dying, Debbie told me she never wanted to end up like that. Tied down and force-fed. I keep thinking about that. About what she said . . .' Margaret looked up again. 'What would you do? If this was your wife?'

'I wouldn't think about giving up.'

'Even if she'd told you she didn't want to end up this way?'

He thought about it for a moment. Then said with convic-tion, 'It would be *my* decision, in the end. No matter what she or anyone else told me. I wouldn't give up on someone I loved. Ever. Not if there was the smallest chance I could save her.'

His words offered no comfort to Margaret. He didn't have the right to question her beliefs, her instincts, but she had asked his opinion, and his answer had come from his heart, not his head.

Feeling guilty now, he gave Margaret one last pat on the shoulder and left the cubicle. Nature would most likely take the decision out of their hands. A comatose patient with a systemic infection is already on death's threshold.

He left the ICU and glumly stepped into the elevator. This was a depressing way to kick off his vacation. First stop, he decided as he stepped off on the lobby level, would be the corner grocery store for a six-pack. An ice-cold beer and an afternoon loading up the sailboat was what he needed right now. It would get his mind off Debbie Haning.

'Code Blue, SICU. Code Blue, SICU.'

His head snapped up at the announcement over the hospital address system. *Debbie*, he thought, and dashed for the stairwell.

Her SICU cubicle was already crowded with personnel. He pushed his way in and shot a glance at the monitor. *Ventricular fibrillation!* Her heart was a quivering bundle of muscles, unable to pump, unable to keep her brain alive.

'One amp epinephrine going in now!' one of the nurses called out.

'Everyone stand back!' a doctor ordered, placing the defibrillator paddles on the chest.

Jack saw the body give a jolt as the paddles discharged, and saw the line shoot up on the monitor, then sink back to baseline. Still in V fib.

A nurse was performing CPR, her short blond hair flipping up with each pump on the chest. Debbie's neurologist, Dr Salomon, glanced up as Jack joined him at the bedside.

'Is the amiodarone in?' asked Jack.

'Going in now, but it's not working.'

Jack glanced at the tracing again. The V fib had gone from coarse to fine. Deteriorating toward a flat line.

'We've shocked her four times,' said Salomon. 'Can't get a rhythm.'

'Intracardiac epi?'

'We're down to Hail Marys. Go ahead!'

The code nurse prepared the syringe of epinephrine and attached a long cardiac needle. Even as Jack took it, he knew that the battle was already over. This procedure would change nothing. But he thought about Bill Haning, waiting to come home to his wife. And he thought about what he had said to Margaret only moments ago.

I wouldn't give up on someone I loved. Ever. Not if there was the smallest chance I could save her.

He looked down at Debbie, and for one disconcerting moment the image of Emma's face flashed through his mind. He swallowed hard and said, 'Hold compressions.'

The nurse lifted her hands from the sternum.

Jack gave the skin a quick swab of Betadine and positioned the tip of the needle beneath the xiphoid process. His own pulse was bounding as he pierced the skin. He advanced the needle into the chest, exerting gentle negative pressure.

A flash of blood told him he was in the heart.

With one squeeze of the plunger, he injected the entire dose of epinephrine and pulled out the needle. 'Resume compressions,' he said, and looked up at the monitor. *Come on, Debbie. Fight, damn it. Don't give up on us. Don't give up on Bill.*

The room was silent, everyone's gaze fixed on the monitor. The tracing flattened, the myocardium dying, cell by cell. No one needed to say a word; the look of defeat was on their faces.

She is so young, thought Jack. Thirty-six years old.

The same age as Emma.

It was Dr Salomon who made the decision. 'Let's end it,' he said quietly. 'Time of death is eleven-fifteen.'

The nurse administering compressions solemnly stepped away from the body. Under the bright cubicle lights, Debbie's torso looked like pale plastic. A mannequin. Not the bright and lively woman Jack had met five years ago at a NASA party held under the stars.

Margaret stepped into the cubicle. For a moment she stood in silence, as though not recognizing her own daughter. Dr Salomon placed his hand on her shoulder and said gently, 'It happened so quickly. There was nothing we could do.'

'He should have been here,' said Margaret, her voice breaking.

'We tried to keep her alive,' said Dr Salomon. 'I'm sorry.'

'It's Bill I feel sorry for,' said Margaret, and she took her daughter's hand and kissed it. 'He wanted to be here. And now he'll never forgive himself.'

Jack walked out of the cubicle and sank into a chair in the nurses' station. Margaret's words were still ringing in his head. *He should have been here. He'll never forgive himself.*

He looked at the phone. *And what am I still doing here?* he wondered.

He took the Yellow Pages from the ward clerk's desk, picked up the phone, and dialed.

'Lone Star Travel,' a woman answered.

'I need to get to Cape Canaveral.'

6

Cape Canaveral

Through the open window of his rental car, Jack inhaled the humid air of Merritt Island and smelled the jungle odors of damp soil and vegetation. The gateway to Kennedy Space Center was a surprisingly rural road slashing through orange groves, past ramshackle doughnut stands and weed-filled junkyards littered with discarded missile parts. Daylight was fading, and up ahead he saw the taillights of hundreds of cars, slowed to a crawl. Traffic was backing up, and soon his car would be trapped in the conga line of tourists searching for parking spots from which to view the morning launch.

There was no point trying to work his way through this mess. Nor did he see the point of trying to make it through the Port Canaveral gate. At this hour, the astronauts were asleep, anyway. He had arrived too late to say good-bye.

He pulled out of traffic, turned the car around, and headed back to Highway AIA. The road to Cocoa Beach.

Since the era of Alan Shepard and the original Mercury seven, Cocoa Beach had been party central for the astronauts, a slightly seedy strip of hotels and bars and T-shirt shops stretching along a spit of land trapped between the Banana

River to the west and the Atlantic Ocean to the east. Jack knew the strip well, from the Tokyo Steak House to the Moon Shot Bar. Once he had jogged the same beach where John Glenn used to run. Only two years ago, he had stood on Jetty Park and gazed across the Banana River at launchpad 39A. At *his* shuttle, the bird that was supposed to take him into space. The memories were still clouded by pain. He remembered a long run on a sweltering afternoon. The sudden, excruciating stab in his flank, an agony so terrible he was brought to his knees. And then, through a haze of narcotics, the somber face of his flight surgeon gazing down at him in the ER, telling him the bad news. A kidney stone.

He'd been scrubbed from the mission.

Even worse, his future in spaceflight was in doubt. A history of kidney stones was one of the few conditions that could permanently ground an astronaut. Microgravity caused physiologic shifts in body fluids, resulting in dehydration. It also caused bones to leach out calcium. Together, these factors raised the risk of new kidney stones while in space – a risk NASA did not want to take. Though still in the astronaut corps, Jack had effectively been grounded. He had hung on for another year, hoping for a new flight assignment, but his name never again came up. He'd been reduced to an astronaut ghost, condemned to wander the halls of JSC forever in search of a mission.

Fast-forward to the present. Here he was, back in Canaveral, no longer an astronaut but just another tourist cruising down A1A, hungry and grumpy, with nowhere to go. Every hotel within forty miles was booked solid, and he was tired of driving.

He turned into the parking lot of the Hilton Hotel and headed for the bar.

The place had been spiffed up considerably since the last time he had been here. New carpet, new barstools, ferns hanging from the ceiling. It used to be a slightly shabby hangout, a tired old Hilton on a tired old tourist strip. There were no four-star hotels on Cocoa Beach. This was as close as you came to luxury digs.

He ordered a scotch and water and focused on the TV above the bar. It was tuned to the official NASA channel, and the shuttle *Atlantis* was on the screen, aglow with floodlights, ghostly vapor rising around it. Emma's ride into space. He stared at the image, thinking of the miles of wiring inside that hull, the countless switches and data buses, the screws and joints and O-rings. Millions of things that could go wrong. It was a wonder that so little *did* go wrong, that men, imperfect as they were, could design and build a craft of such reliability that seven people are willing to strap themselves inside. *Please let this launch be one of the perfect ones*, he thought. *A launch where everyone has done their job right, and not a screw is loose. It has to be perfect because my Emma will be aboard.*

A woman sat down on the barstool beside him and said, 'I wonder what they're thinking now.'

He turned to look at her, his interest momentarily captured by a glimpse of thigh. She was a sleek and sunny blonde, with one of those blandly perfect faces whose features one forgets within an hour of parting. 'What who's thinking?' he asked.

'The astronauts. I wonder if they're thinking, "Oh, shit, what'd I get myself into?"'

He shrugged and took a sip of scotch. 'They're not thinking anything right now. They're all asleep.'

'I wouldn't be able to sleep.'

'Their circadian rhythm's completely readjusted. They probably went to bed two hours ago.'

'No, I mean, I wouldn't be able to sleep at *all*. I'd be lying awake thinking up ways to get out of it.'

69

He laughed. 'I guarantee you, if they're awake, it's because they can't wait to climb on board that baby and blast off.'

She looked at him curiously. 'You're with the program, aren't you?'

'Was. Astronaut corps.'

'Not now?'

He lifted the drink to his lips, felt the ice cubes clink sharply against his teeth. 'I retired.' Setting down his empty glass, he rose to his feet and saw disappointment flash in the woman's eyes. He allowed himself a moment's consideration of how the rest of the evening *could* go were he to stay and continue the conversation. Pleasant company. The promise of more to follow.

Instead he paid his bar tab and walked out of the Hilton.

At midnight, standing on the beach at Jetty Park, he gazed across the water toward pad 39B. *I'm here*, he thought. *Even if you don't know it, I'm with you.*

He sat down on the sand and waited for dawn.

July 24
Houston

'There's a high-pressure system over the Gulf, which is expected to keep skies clear over Cape Canaveral, so RTLS landing is a go. Edwards Air Force Base is seeing intermittent clouds, but that's expected to clear by launch. TAL site in Zaragoza, Spain, is still current and forecast go. TAL site in Morón, Spain, is also current and go. Ben Guerir, Morocco, is experiencing high winds and sandstorms, and at this time is not a viable TAL site.'

The first weather briefing of the day, broadcast simultaneously to Cape Canaveral, brought satisfactory news, and Flight Director Carpenter was happy. The launch was still a go. The poor landing conditions at Ben Guerir airport was only a minor concern, since the two alternate transatlantic-abort landing sites in Spain were clear. It was all backups within backups, anyway; the sites would be needed only in case of a major malfunction.

He glanced around at the rest of the ascent team to see if there were any new concerns. The nervous tension in the Flight Control Room was palpable and mounting, as it always was prior to a launch, and that was good. The day they *weren't* tense was the day they made mistakes. Carpenter wanted his people on edge, with all synapses snapping – a level of alertness that, at midnight, required an extra dose of adrenaline.

Carpenter's nerves were as taut as everyone else's, despite the fact that the countdown was right on schedule. The inspection team at Kennedy had finished their checks. The flight dynamics team had reconfirmed the launch time to the second. In the meantime, a far-flung cast of thousands was watching the same countdown clock.

At Cape Canaveral, where the shuttle was poised for launch, the same tension would be building in the firing room of the Launch Control Center, where a parallel team sat at their consoles, preparing for liftoff. As soon as the solid rocket boosters ignited, Houston's Mission Control would take over. Though thousands of miles apart, the two control rooms in Houston and Canaveral were so closely interconnected by communications they might as well have been located in the same building.

In Huntsville, Alabama, at Marshall Space Flight Center, research teams were waiting for their experiments to be launched.

One hundred sixty miles north-northeast of Cape Canaveral, Navy ships waited at sea to recover the solid rocket boosters, which would separate from the shuttle after burnout.

At contingency landing sites and tracking stations around the world, from NORAD in Colorado to the international

71

airfield at Banjul, Gambia, men and women watched the clock.

And at this moment, seven people are preparing to place their lives in our hands.

Carpenter could see the astronauts now on closed-circuit TV as they were helped into their orange launch-and-entry suits. The images were live from Florida, but without audio. Carpenter found himself pausing for a moment to study their faces. Though none of them revealed a trace of fear, he knew it had to be there, beneath their beaming expressions. The racing pulse, the zing of nervousness. They knew the risks, and they had to be scared. Seeing them on the screen was a sobering reminder to ground personnel that seven human beings were counting on them to do their jobs right.

Carpenter tore his gaze from the video monitor and focused his attention back on his team of flight controllers, seated at the sixteen consoles. Though he knew each member of the team by name, he addressed them by their mission-command positions, their titles reduced to the shorthand call signs that was NASA-speak. The guidance officer was nicknamed GDO. The spacecraft communicator was Capcom. The propulsion systems engineer was Prop. The trajectory officer was Traj. Flight surgeon was shortened to Surgeon. And Carpenter went by the call sign of Flight.

The countdown came out of the scheduled T-minus-three-hours hold. The mission was still a go.

Carpenter stuck his hand in his pocket and gave his shamrock key ring a jingle. It was his private good-luck ritual. Even engineers have their superstitions.

Let nothing go wrong, he thought. *Not on my watch*.

Cape Canaveral
The Astrovan ride from the O and C building to launchpad 39B took fifteen minutes. It was a strangely silent ride, none

of the crew saying much. Just a half hour before, while suiting up, they had been joking and laughing in that sharp and electric tone that comes when one's nerves are raw with excitement. The tension had been building since the moment they had been awakened at two-thirty for the traditional steak and eggs breakfast. Through the weather briefing, the suiting up, the prelaunch ritual of dealing out playing cards for the best poker hand, they had all been a little too noisy and cheerful, all engines roaring with confidence.

Now they'd fallen silent.

The van came to a stop. Chenoweth, the rookie, seated beside Emma, muttered, 'I never thought diaper rash would be one of the job hazards.'

She had to laugh. They were all wearing Depend adult diapers under their bulky flight suits; it would be a long three hours until liftoff.

With help from the launchpad technicians, Emma stepped out of the van. For a moment she paused on the pad, gazing up in wonder at the thirty-story shuttle, ablaze with spotlights. The last time she'd visited the pad, five days ago, the only sounds she'd heard were the sea wind and the birds. Now the spacecraft itself had come to life, rumbling and smoking like a waking dragon, as volatile propellants boiled inside the fuel tank.

They rode the elevator up to Level 195 and stepped onto the grated catwalk. It was still night, but the sky was washed out by the pad lights, and she could barely get a glimpse of the stars overhead. The blackness of space was waiting.

In the sterile white room, technicians in lint-free 'bunny' suits helped the crew, one by one, through the hatch and into the orbiter. The commander and pilot were seated first. Emma, assigned to mid-deck, was the last to be assisted. She settled back into her padded seat, buckles secured, helmet in place, and gave a thumbs-up.

73

The hatch swung shut, closing the crew off from the outside.

Emma could hear her own heartbeat. Even through the air-to-ground voice checks chattering over her comm unit, through the gurgles and groans of the awakening shuttle, the thud of her own heart came through in a steady drumbeat. As a middeck passenger, she had little to do in the next two hours but sit and think; the preflight checks would be conducted by the flight-deck crew. She had no view of the outside, nothing to stare at except the stowage area and food pantry.

Outside, dawn would soon light the sky, and pelicans would skim the surf at Playalinda Beach.

She took a deep breath and settled back to wait.

Jack sat on the beach and watched the sun come up.

He was not alone in Jetty Park. The sightseers had been gathering since before midnight, the arriving cars forming an endless line of headlights creeping along the Bee Line Expressway, some peeling north toward Merritt Island Wildlife Refuge, the others continuing across the Banana River to the city of Cape Canaveral. The viewing would be good from either location. The crowd around him was in a holiday mood, with beach towels and picnic baskets. He heard laughter and loud radios and the bawling of sleepy children. Surrounded by that swirl of celebrants, he was a silent presence, a man alone with his thoughts and fears.

As the sun cleared the horizon, he stared north, toward the launchpad. She would be aboard *Atlantis* now, strapped in and waiting. Excited and happy and a little afraid.

He heard a child say, 'That's a bad man, Mommy,' and he turned to look at the girl. They gazed at each other for a moment, a tiny blond princess locking eyes with an unshaven and very disheveled man. The mother snatched the girl into her arms and quickly moved to a safer spot on the beach.

Jack gave a wry shake of his head and once again turned his gaze northward. Toward Emma.

Houston
The Flight Control Room had turned deceptively quiet. It was twenty minutes till launch – time to confirm it was still a go. All the back-room controllers had completed their systems checks, and now the front room was ready to be polled.

In a calm voice, Carpenter went down the list, requesting verbal confirmation from each front-room controller.

'Fido?' asked Carpenter.

'Fido is go,' said the flight dynamics officer.

'Guido?'

'Guidance is go.'

'Surgeon?'

'Surgeon is go.'

'DPS?'

'Data Processing is go.'

When Carpenter had polled them all and received affirmatives from all, he gave a brisk nod to the room.

'Houston, are you go?' asked the launch director in Cape Canaveral.

'Mission Control is go,' affirmed Carpenter.

The launch director's traditional message to the shuttle crew was heard by everyone at Houston's Mission Control.

'*Atlantis*, you are a go. From all of us at the Cape, good luck and Godspeed.'

'Launch Control, this is *Atlantis*,' they heard Commander Vance respond. 'Thanks for gettin' this bird ready to fly.'

Cape Canaveral

Emma closed and locked her visor and turned on her oxygen supply. Two minutes till liftoff. Cocooned and isolated in her suit, she had nothing to do but count the seconds. She felt the shudder of the main engines gimballing into launch position.

T minus thirty seconds. The electrical link to ground control was now severed, and the onboard computers took control.

Her heart accelerated, the adrenaline roaring through her veins. As she listened to the countdown, she knew, second by second, what to expect, could see in her mind's eye the sequence of events that were now playing out.

At T minus eight seconds, thousands of gallons of water were dumped beneath the launchpad to suppress the roar of the engines.

At T minus five, the onboard computers opened the valves to allow liquid oxygen and hydrogen to travel into the main engines.

She felt the shuttle jerk sideways as the three main engines ignited, the spacecraft straining against the bolts that still harnessed it to the launchpad.

Four. Three. Two . . . The point of no return.

She held her breath, hands gripped tight, as the solid rocket boosters ignited. The turbulence was bone-shaking, the roar so painfully loud she could not hear communications through her headset. She had to clamp her jaw shut to stop her teeth from slamming together. Now she felt the shuttle roll into its planned arc over the Atlantic, and her body was shoved back against the seat by the acceleration to three g's. Her limbs were so heavy she could barely move them, the vibrations so violent it seemed the orbiter would surely fly apart into pieces. They were at Max Q, the peak of turbulence, and Commander Vance announced he was throttling back the main engines. In less than a minute, he would throttle up again to full thrust.

As the seconds ticked by, as the helmet rattled around her head, and the force of liftoff pressed like an unyielding hand against her chest, she felt a fresh lick of apprehension. This was the point during launch when *Challenger* had exploded.

Emma closed her eyes and remembered the simulation with Hazel two weeks ago. They were now approaching the point where everything in the sim had started to go wrong, where they'd been forced into an RTLS abort, and then Kittredge had lost control of the orbiter. This was a critical moment in the launch, and there was nothing she could do but lie back and hope that real life was more forgiving than a simulation.

Over the headset she heard Vance say, 'Control, this is *Atlantis*. Throttling up.'

'Roger, *Atlantis*. Throttle up.'

Jack stood with his gaze cast skyward, his heart in his throat, as the shuttle lifted into the sky. He heard the crackling of the solid rocket boosters as they spewed out twin fountains of fire. The trail of exhaust climbed higher, sketched by the glinting pinpoint of the shuttle. All around him, the crowd burst out in applause. A perfect launch, they all thought. But Jack knew there were too many things that could still go wrong.

Suddenly he was frantic that he'd lost track of the seconds. How much time had elapsed? Had they passed through Max Q? He shielded his eyes against the morning sunlight, straining to see *Atlantis*, but able to make out only the plume of exhaust.

Already the crowd had started to drift back to their cars.

He remained frozen, waiting in dread. He saw no terrible explosion. No black smoke. No nightmare.

77

Atlantis had safely escaped the earth and was now hurtling through space.

He felt tears trickle down his cheeks, but he didn't bother to wipe them away. He let them fall as he continued to gaze at the sky, at the dissipating trail of smoke that marked his wife's ascent into the heavens.

The Station

7

July 25
Beatty, Nevada

Sullivan Obie awakened with a groan to the sound of the ringing telephone. His head felt as if cymbals were banging on it, and his mouth tasted like an old ashtray. He reached for the phone and accidentally knocked it off the cradle. The loud thud made him wince with pain. *Aw, forget it*, he thought, and turned away, burrowing his face into a nest of tangled hair.

A woman?

Squinting against the morning light, he confirmed that there was indeed a woman lying in bed with him. A blonde. Snoring. He closed his eyes, hoping that if he just went back to sleep, she would be gone when he woke up again.

But he could not sleep now. Not with the voice yelling from the fallen receiver.

He fished around at the side of the bed and found the phone. 'What, Bridget?' he said. 'What?'

'Why aren't you here?' Bridget demanded.

''Cause I'm in bed.'

'It's ten-thirty! Hel-*lo*? Meeting with the new investors?

81

I might as well warn you, Casper is wavering between cruci-fixion and strangulation.'

The investors. Shit.

Sullivan sat up and clutched his head, waiting for the dizziness to pass.

'Look, just leave the bimbo and get over here,' said Bridget. 'Casper's already walking them over to the hangar.'

'Ten minutes,' he said. He hung up and stumbled to his feet. The bimbo didn't stir. He had no idea who she was, but he left her asleep in his bed, figuring he had nothing worth stealing, anyway.

There was no time to shower or shave. He tossed back three aspirins, chased them with a cup of nuked coffee, and roared off on his Harley.

Bridget was waiting for him outside the hangar. She *looked* like a Bridget, sturdy and redheaded, with a bad temper to match. Sometimes, unfortunately, stereotypes do ring true.

'They're about to leave,' she hissed. 'Get your butt in there.'

'Who are these guys again?'

'A Mr Lucas and a Mr Rashad. They represent a consortium of twelve investors. You blow this, Sully, and we're toast.' She paused, eyeing him in disgust. 'Ah, hell, we're already toast. Look at you. Couldn't you at least have shaved?'

'You want me to go back home? I can rent a tuxedo on the way.'

'Forget it.' She thrust a folded newspaper into his hand.

'What's this?'

'Casper wants it. Give it to him. Now get in there and convince 'em to write us a check. A big check.'

Sighing, he stepped into the hangar. After the harsh desert glare, the relative darkness was a comfort to his eyes. It took him a moment to spot the three men, standing by the black thermal barrier tiles of the orbiter *Apogee II*. The two visitors, both in business suits, looked out of place among all the aircraft tools and equipment.

'Good morning, gentlemen!' he called. 'Sorry I'm late, but I got hung up on a conference call. You know how things can drag on . . .' He glimpsed Casper Mulholland's warning look of *Don't push it, asshole* and swallowed hard. 'I'm Sullivan Obie,' he said. 'Mr Mulholland's partner.'

'Mr Obie knows every nut and bolt of this RLV,' said Casper. 'He used to work with the old master himself, Bob Truax out in California. In fact, he can explain the system better than I can. Around here, we call him our Obie-Wan.'

The two visitors merely blinked. It was not a good sign when the universal language of *Star Wars* failed to elicit a smile.

Sullivan shook hands, first with Lucas, then with Rashad, grinning broadly even as his hopes sank. Even as he felt a surge of resentment toward these two well-dressed gentlemen whose money he and Casper so desperately needed. Apogee Engineering, their baby, the dream they had nurtured for the past thirteen years, was about to go under, and only a fresh infusion of cash, from a new set of investors, could save it. He and Casper had to make the sales pitch of their lives. If it didn't work, they might as well pack up their tools and sell off the orbiter as a carnival ride.

With a flourish, Sullivan waved his arm at *Apogee II*, which looked less like a rocket plane and more like a fat fireplug with windows.

'I know she may not look like much,' he said, 'but what we've built here is the most cost-effective and practical reusable launch vehicle now in existence. She uses an assisted SSTO launch system. After vertical takeoff, upon climbing to twelve kilometers, pressure-fed rockets accelerate the vehicle to a Mach four staging point at low-dynamic

83

pressures. This orbiter is fully reusable, and weighs only eight and a half tons. It fulfills the principles we believe are the future of commercial space travel. Smaller. Faster. Cheaper.'

'What sort of lift engine do you use?' asked Rashad.

'Rybinsk RD-38 air-breathing engines imported from Russia.'

'Why Russian?'

'Because, Mr Rashad – between you, me, and the wall – the Russians know more about rocketry than anyone else on earth. They've developed dozens of liquid-fueled rocket motors, using advanced materials which can operate at higher pressures. Our country, I'm sorry to say, has developed only one new liquid-fueled rocket motor since Apollo. This is now an international industry. We believe in choosing the best components for our product – wherever those components may come from.'

'And how does this . . . *thing* land?' asked Mr Lucas, looking dubiously at the fireplug orbiter.

'Well, that's the beauty of *Apogee II*. As you'll notice, she has no wings. She doesn't need a runway. Instead she drops straight down, using parachutes to slow her descent and air bags to cushion touchdown. She can land anywhere, even in the ocean. Again, we have to tip our hats to the Russians, because we've borrowed features from their old *Soyuz* capsule. It was their reliable workhorse for decades.'

'You like that old Russki technology, huh?' said Lucas.

Sullivan stiffened. 'I like technology that works. Say what you want about the Russians, they knew what they were doing.'

'So what you have here,' said Lucas, 'is something of a hybrid. *Soyuz* mixed in with space shuttle.'

'A very *small* space shuttle. We've spent thirteen years in development and only sixty-five million dollars to get this far – that's amazingly inexpensive when you compare it to what the shuttle cost is. With multiple spacecraft, we believe you'll get an annual return on investment of thirty percent, if we launch twelve hundred times a year. Cost per flight would be eighty thousand dollars; the price per kilogram would be dirt cheap at two hundred seventy. Smaller, faster, cheaper. That's our mantra.'

'How small are we talking about, Mr Obie? What's your payload capacity?'

Sullivan hesitated. This was the point where they might lose them. 'We can launch a payload of three hundred kilograms, plus a pilot, to low earth orbit.'

There was a long silence.

Mr Rashad said, 'That's all?'

'That's almost seven hundred pounds. You can fit a lot of research experiments in –'

'I know how much three hundred kilos is. It's not much.'

'So we make up for it by more frequent launches. You can almost think of it as an airplane to space.'

'In fact – in fact, we've already got NASA's interest!' Casper interjected with a note of desperation. 'This is just the kind of system they might purchase for quick hops to the space station.'

Lucas's eyebrow shot up. 'NASA is interested?'

'Well, we have something of an inside track.'

Aw, shit, Casper, thought Sullivan. *Don't go there.*

'Show them the newspaper, Sully.'

'What?'

'*Los Angeles Times*. Second page.'

Sullivan looked down at the L.A. *Times* that Bridget had thrust in his hand. He turned to the second page and saw the article: 'NASA Launches Astronaut Replacement.' Next to it was a photograph of JSC high-muck-a-mucks at a press conference. He recognized the homely guy with the big ears and the bad haircut. It was Gordon Obie.

Casper snatched the paper and showed it to their visitors. 'See this man here, standing next to Leroy Cornell? That's the director of Flight Crew Operations. Mr Obie's brother.'

The two visitors, obviously impressed, turned and looked at Sullivan.

'Well?' said Casper. 'Would you gentlemen care to talk business?'

'We might as well tell you this up front,' said Lucas. 'Mr Rashad and I have already taken a look at what other aerospace companies have in development. We've looked over the Kelly Astroliner, the Roton, the Kistler K-1. We were impressed by all of them, especially the K-1. But we figured we should give your little company a chance to make a pitch as well.'

Your little company.

Fuck this, thought Sullivan. He hated begging for money, hated getting down on his knees before stuffed shirts. This was a hopeless campaign. His head ached, his stomach was growling, and these two-suits had wasted his time.

'Tell us why we should bet on your horse,' said Lucas. 'What makes Apogee our best choice?'

'Frankly, gentlemen, I don't think we are your best choice,' Sullivan answered bluntly. And he turned and walked away.

'Uh – excuse me,' said Casper, and he went chasing after his partner. 'Sully!' he whispered. 'What the hell are you doing?'

'These guys aren't interested in us. You heard them. They love the K-1. They want *big* rockets. To match their dicks.'

'Don't screw this up! Go back and talk to them.'

'Why? They're not writing us any checks.'

'We lose them, we lose everything.'

'We've already lost.'

'No. No, you can *sell* this to them. All you have to do is

tell the truth. Tell them what we really believe. Because you know and I know we've got the best.'

Sullivan rubbed his eyes. The aspirin was wearing off, and his head pounded. He was sick of begging. He was an engineer and a pilot, and he'd happily spend the rest of his life with his hands blackened by engine grease. But it would not happen, not without new investors. Not without new cash.

He turned and walked back to the visitors. To his surprise, both men seemed to regard him with wary respect. Perhaps because he had told the truth.

'Okay,' said Sullivan, emboldened by the fact he had nothing to lose. He might as well go down like a man. 'Here's the deal. We can back up everything we've said with one simple demonstration. Are the other companies ready to launch at the drop of a hat? No, they are not. They need *preparation* time,' he sneered. 'Months and months of it. But we can launch anytime. All we need to do is load this baby onto its booster and we can shoot her up to low earth orbit. Hell, we can send her up to hotdog the space station. So give us a date. Tell us when you want liftoff, and we'll do it.'

Casper turned as white as a – well, a ghost. And not a friendly one. Sullivan had just taken them so far out on a limb they were clawing at thin air. *Apogee II* hadn't been tested yet. She had been sitting in this hangar for over fourteen months, gathering dust while they scrounged for money. On this, her maiden voyage, Sully wanted to launch her all the way to orbit?

'In fact, I'm so confident she'll pass muster,' said Sullivan, raising the stakes even higher, 'I'll ride in the pilot's seat myself.'

Casper clutched his stomach. 'Uh . . . that's just a figure of speech, gentlemen. She can be flown perfectly well unmanned –'

'But there's no real drama in that,' said Sullivan. 'Let me take her up. It'll make it more interesting for everyone. What do you say?'

I say you're outta your fucking mind, Casper's eyes told him.

The two businessmen exchanged looks, a few whispered words. Then Lucas said, 'We'd be very interested in a demonstration. It will take us time to round up all our partners. Coordinate travel schedules. So let's say . . . a month. Can you do it?'

They were calling his bluff. Sullivan merely laughed. 'A month? No problem.' He looked at Casper, who now had his eyes closed as though in pain.

'We'll be in touch,' said Lucas, and turned toward the door.

'One last question, if I may,' said Mr Rashad. He pointed to the orbiter. 'I notice the name on your prototype is *Apogee II*. Is there an *Apogee I*?'

Casper and Sullivan looked at each other.

'Uh, yes,' said Casper. 'There was . . .'

'And what happened to her?'

Casper went mute.

What the hell, thought Sullivan. Telling the truth seemed to work with these guys; he might as well do it again.

'She crashed and burned,' he said. And walked out of the hangar.

Crashed and burned. That was the only way to describe what had happened on that cold, clear morning a year and a half ago. The morning his dreams had crashed and burned as well. Sitting at his battered desk in the company office, nursing his hangover with a cup of coffee, he couldn't help replaying every painful detail of that day. The busload of NASA officials pulling up at the launch site. His brother,

88

Gordie, grinning with pride. The air of celebration among the dozen Apogee employees and the score of investors who had assembled under the tent for prelaunch coffee and doughnuts.

The countdown. The liftoff. Everyone squinting up at the sky as *Apogee I* streaked toward the heavens and receded to a glinting pinpoint.

Then the flash of light, and it was all over.

Afterward, his brother had not said very much, barely a few words of condolence. But that's how it was with Gordon. All their lives, whenever Sullivan screwed up – and it seemed to happen all too often – Gordon would just give that sad and disappointed shake of the head. Gordon was the older brother, the sober and reliable son who had distinguished himself as a shuttle commander.

Sullivan had never even made it into the astronaut corps. Though he, too, was a pilot and an aerospace engineer, things never seemed to go Sullivan's way. If he climbed into the cockpit, that was precisely the moment a wire would short out or a line would rupture. He often thought the words *Not My Fault* should be tattooed on his forehead, because more often than not, it *wasn't* his fault when things went wrong. But Gordon didn't see it that way. Things never went wrong for *him*. Gordon thought the concept of bad luck was an excuse to cover up incompetence.

'Why don't you call him?' said Bridget.

He looked up. She was standing by his desk, her arms crossed like a disapproving schoolteacher's. 'Call who?' he asked.

'Your brother, who else? Tell him we're launching the second prototype. Invite him to watch. Maybe he'll bring the rest of NASA.'

'I don't want anyone from NASA.'

'Sully, if we impress them, we'll turn this company around.'

'Like the last time, huh?'

'A fluke. We've fixed the problem.'

'So maybe there'll be another fluke.'

'You're gonna jinx us, you know that?' She shoved the phone in front of him. 'Call Gordon. If we're gonna roll the dice, we might as well bet the whole house.'

He eyed the phone, thinking about *Apogee I*. About how a lifetime of dreams can be vaporized in an instant.

'Sully?'

'Forget it,' he said. 'My brother's got better things to do than hang out with losers.' And he tossed the newspaper into the rubbish can.

July 26
Aboard *Atlantis*

'Hey, Watson,' Commander Vance called down to the middeck. 'Come up and take a look at your new home.'

Emma floated up the access ladder and emerged on the flight deck, right behind Vance's seat. At her first glimpse through the windows, she inhaled a sharp breath of wonder. This was the closest she had ever come to the station. During her first mission, two and a half years ago, they had not docked with ISS, but had observed it only from a distance.

'Gorgeous, isn't she?' said Vance.

'She's the most beautiful thing I've ever seen,' Emma said softly.

And she was. With her vast solar arrays fanning out from the massive main truss, ISS looked like a majestic sailing ship soaring through the heavens. Built by sixteen different countries, the components had been delivered into space on forty-five separate launches. It had taken five years to assemble her, piece by piece, in orbit. Far more than merely a marvel of engineering, she was a symbol of what man can achieve when he lays down his weapons and turns his gaze skyward.

'Now, that's a nice piece of real estate,' said Vance. 'I'd call that a view apartment.'

'We're right on the R-bar,' said shuttle pilot DeWitt. 'Nice flying.'

Vance left the command seat and stationed himself at the flight deck's overhead window for visual approach as they neared the ISS docking module. This was the most delicate phase in the complicated process of rendezvous. *Atlantis* had been launched into a lower orbit than ISS, and for the last two days she had been playing a game of catch-up with the hurtling space station. They would approach her from below, using their RCS jets to fine-tune their position for docking. Emma could hear the whomp of the thrusters' firing now and felt the orbiter shudder.

'Look,' said DeWitt. 'There's that solar array that got dinged last month.' He pointed to one of the solar panels, scarred by a gaping hole. One of the inescapable perils of space is the constant rain of meteorites and manmade debris. Even a tiny fragment can be a devastating missile when it's hurtling at thousands of miles per hour.

As they drew closer and the station filled the window, Emma felt such overwhelming awe and pride that tears suddenly flashed in her eyes. *Home*, she thought. *I'm coming home*.

The air-lock hatch swung open, and a wide brown face grinned at them from the other end of the vestibule connecting *Atlantis* with ISS. 'They brought oranges!' Luther Ames called out to his station mates. 'I can smell 'em!'

'NASA home delivery service,' deadpanned Commander Vance. 'Your groceries have arrived.' Bearing a nylon sack of fresh fruit, Vance floated through *Atlantis*'s air lock into the space station.

It had been a perfect docking. With both spacecrafts

traveling at a speed of 17,500 miles per hour above the earth, Vance had approached ISS at the delicate rate of two inches per second, lining up *Atlantis*'s docking module to the ISS port for a good, tight lock.

Now the hatches were open and *Atlantis*'s crew floated one by one into the space station to be greeted with hand-shakes and hugs, and the welcoming smiles of people who have not seen new faces in over a month. The node was too small to hold thirteen people, and the crews quickly spilled into the adjoining modules.

Emma was the fifth to cross into the station. She popped out of the vestibule and inhaled a mélange of scents, the slightly sour and meaty odors of humans confined too long in a closed space. Luther Ames, an old friend from astronaut training, was the first to greet her.

'Dr Watson, I presume!' he boomed out, pulling her into a hug. 'Welcome aboard. The more ladies, the merrier.'

'Hey, you know I'm no lady.'

He winked. 'We'll keep that between us.' Luther had always been larger than life, a man whose good cheer could fill a room. Everyone liked Luther because Luther liked everyone. Emma was glad to have him aboard.

Especially when she turned to look at her other station mates. She shook hands first with Michael Griggs, the ISS commander, and found his greeting polite but almost military. Diana Estes, the Englishwoman sent up by the European Space Agency, was not much warmer. She smiled, but her eyes were a strange glacial blue. Cool and distant.

Emma turned next to the Russian, Nicolai Rudenko, who had been aboard ISS the longest – almost five months. The module lights seemed to wash all the color from his face, turning it as drab as the gray-flecked stubble of his beard. As they shook hands, his gaze barely met hers. *This man*, she thought, *needs to go home. He is depressed. Exhausted.*

Kenichi Hirai, the astronaut from NASDA, floated forward to greet her next. He, at least, had a smile on his face and a firm handshake. He stammered a greeting and quickly retreated.

By now the module had emptied out, the rest of the group dispersing to other parts of the station. She found herself alone with Bill Haning.

Debbie Haning had died three days ago. *Atlantis* would be bringing Bill home, not to his wife's bedside, but to her funeral. Emma floated across to him. 'I'm sorry,' she said softly. 'I'm so sorry.'

He merely nodded and looked away. 'It's strange,' he said. 'We always thought – if something ever happened – it would happen to me. Because I'm the big hero in the family. The one who takes all the risks. It never occurred to us that she would be the one . . .' He took a deep breath. She saw that he was fighting to maintain his composure, and she knew this was not the time for words of sympathy. Even a gentle touch might destroy his fragile control over his emotions.

'Well, Watson,' he finally said. 'I guess I should be the one to show you the ropes. Since you'll be taking on my load.'

She nodded. 'Whenever you're ready, Bill.'

'Let's do it now. There's a lot to tell you. And not much time for the changeover.'

Though Emma was familiar with the layout of the station, her first interior glimpse of the actual structure was a dizzying experience. The weightlessness of orbit meant there was no up or down, no floor or ceiling. Every surface was functional workspace, and if she turned too quickly in midair, she instantly lost all sense of direction. That, and the twinges of nausea, made her move slowly, focusing her eyes on one spot as she turned.

She knew that the core of ISS had as much inhabitable

93

airspace as two Boeing 747s, but it was distributed among a dozen bus-sized modules, plugged together like Tinkertoys into connecting points called nodes. The shuttle had docked on Node 2. Attached to that same node were the European Space Agency lab, the Japanese lab, and the U.S. lab, which served as the gateway into the rest of the station.

Bill led her out of the U.S. lab into the next connecting point, Node 1. Here they paused for a moment to look out the observation cupola. The earth slowly spun beneath them, milky clouds swirling over seas.

'This is where I spend every spare moment,' said Bill. 'Just looking out these windows. It feels almost sacred to me. I call this the Church of Mother Earth.' He tore his gaze away from the view and turned to point out the other node hatchways. 'Directly opposite is the EVA air lock,' he said. 'And the hatchway below us leads into the hab module. Your sleep station's in there. The CRV is docked at the other end of the hab, for quick evac access.'

'Three crew members sleep in this hab?'

He nodded. 'The other three sleep in the Russian service module. It's through this hatchway here. Let's head there now.'

They left Node 1, and like fish swimming through a maze of tunnels, they floated into the Russian half of the station.

This was the oldest part of ISS, the section that had been in orbit longest, and its age showed. As they passed through Zarya – the power and propulsion plant – she saw smudges on the walls, the occasional scratch and dent. What had been only a set of blueprints in her head now took on texture and sensory detail. The station was more than just a maze of gleaming labs; it was also a home for human beings, and the wear and tear of constant occupancy was evident.

They floated into the Russian service module, and Emma confronted a disorienting view of Griggs and Vance, both of them upside down. *Or am I the one who's upside down?*

thought Emma, amused by this topsy-turvy world of weight-lessness. Like the U.S. hab, the RSM contained a galley, toilet, and sleep stations for three crew members. At the far end, she spotted another hatchway.

'Does that go to the old *Soyuz?*' she asked.

Bill nodded. 'We use it for storing junk now. That's about all we can do with it.' The *Soyuz* capsule, which had once served as an emergency lifeboat, was now obsolete, and its batteries had long since drained.

Luther Ames popped his head into the RSM. 'Hey, everyone, it's show time! Group hug in the media conferencing center. NASA wants the taxpayers to see our international love fest up here.'

Bill gave a weary sigh. 'We're like animals in a zoo. Every day it's *smile* for the damn cameras.'

Emma was the last to join the exodus to the hab module. By the time she reached it, a dozen people were already crowded inside. It looked like a tangle of arms and legs in there, everyone bobbing, trying not to collide with each other.

While Griggs struggled to get things organized, Emma hung back in Node 1. Drifting in midair, she found herself slowly turning toward the cupola. The view beyond those windows took her breath away.

The earth stretched below in all its magnificence, a rim of stars crowning the gentle curve of the horizon. They were passing into night now, and below, she saw familiar land-marks slipping into darkness. Houston. It was their first passover of the night.

She leaned close to the window, pressing her hand to the glass. *Oh, Jack*, she thought. *I wish you were here. I wish you could see this.*

Then she waved. And she knew, without the slightest doubt, that somewhere in the darkness below, Jack was waving back.

8

July 28
Personal E-mail to: Dr Emma Watson (ISS)
From: Jack McCallum

Like a diamond in the sky. That's what you look like
from down here. Last night I stayed up to watch you
pass over. Gave you a big wave.

This morning on CNN, you were being touted as
Ms Right Stuff. 'Girl astronaut blasts off, doesn't chip
a nail,' or something equally hokey. They interviewed
Woody Ellis and Leroy Cornell, and both of them
were beaming like proud daddies. Congratulations.
You're America's sweetheart.

Vance and crew made a picture-perfect landing.
Bloodsucking reporters were all over poor Bill when
he arrived in Houston. I caught a glimpse of him on
TV – he looks like he's aged twenty years. Services
for Debbie are this afternoon. I'll be there.

Tomorrow, I'll be sailing on the Gulf.

Em, I got the divorce papers today, and I'll be
honest with you. It doesn't feel good. But then, I guess
it's not supposed to, is it?

Anyway, they're ready for us to sign. Maybe now that it's finally over, we can get back to being friends again. The way we used to be.

Jack

P.S.: Humphrey's a little shit. You owe me a new couch.

Personal E-mail to: Jack McCallum
From: Emma Watson

America's sweetheart? Puh-leeze. This has turned into a high-wire act, with everyone on earth watching and waiting for me to screw up. And when I do, I'll be the shoulda-sent-a-man Exhibit #1. I hate that.

On the other hand, I do love it up here. How I wish you could see this view! When I look down at the earth and see how incredibly beautiful she is, I want to shake some sense into everyone living down there. If only they could see how small and fragile and very alone the earth is, surrounded by all this cold black space. They'd take much better care of her.

(Uh, oh, here she goes again, getting teary-eyed about the home planet. Shoulda sent a man.)

I'm happy to report the nausea's gone. I can zip around from mod to mod with scarcely a twinge. I still get a little woozy when I catch an unexpected glimpse of earth through a window. It screws up my sense of up and down, and it takes me a few seconds to reorient. I'm trying to keep up the exercise, but two hours every day is a big chunk of time, especially when I've got so much to do. Dozens of experiments to monitor, a zillion E-mails from Payload Operations, every scientist demanding top priority for their pet projects. Eventually, I'll get up to speed. But this morning I was so tired, I slept right through Houston's

97

wakeup music. (And Luther says they blasted us with Wagner's Valkyrie!)

As for the divorce being final, it doesn't feel good for me, either. But, Jack, at least we had seven good years. That's more than a lot of couples can say. I know you must be anxious to finish this business. I promise I'll sign the papers as soon as I get home.

Don't stop waving.

Em

P.S.: Humphrey never attacked my furniture. What did you do to upset him?

Emma turned off her laptop computer and folded it shut. Answering personal E-mail was the last task of the day. She had looked forward to hearing from home, but Jack's mention of the divorce had stung her. *So he's ready to move on*, she thought. *He's ready to 'be friends' again.*

As she zipped herself into her sleep restraint bag, she was angry at him, at how easily he'd accepted the end of their marriage. Early in their divorce, when their arguments were still raging, she'd felt strangely reassured by every noisy disagreement. But now the conflicts had ended, and Jack had reached the stage of calm acceptance. No pain, no regrets. *And here I am, still missing you. And I hate myself for it.*

Kenichi hesitated to wake her. He lingered outside her sleep station privacy curtain, wondering if he should call out again. It was such a small matter, and he hated to disturb her. She had looked so tired at supper, had actually dozed off still clutching her fork. Without the constant pull of gravity, the body does not crumple when you fall unconscious, and there is no warning jerk of the head to startle you awake. Tired astronauts had been known to fall asleep in the midst of repairs, while still holding a tool in their hand.

98

He decided not to wake her and returned, alone, to the U.S. lab.

Kenichi had never needed more than five hours of rest a night, and while the others slept, he would often wander the labyrinth of the space station, checking on his various experiments. Inspecting, exploring. It seemed that only when the human crew slept did the station assert its own gleaming personality. It became an autonomous being that hummed and clicked, its computers directing a thousand different functions, electronic commands zinging through its nervous system of wires and circuits. As Kenichi drifted through the maze of tunnels, he thought of all the human hands that had worked to fashion just a single square inch of this structure. The electronics and metal workers, the molders of plastic. The glassmakers. Because of their labor, a farmer's son who had grown up in a mountain village of Japan now floated two hundred twenty miles above the earth.

Kenichi had been aboard the station for a month, and the wonder of it all had not left him.

He knew his stay here was limited. He knew the toll now being exacted on his body: the steady seepage of calcium from his bones, the wasting of his muscles, the declining vigor of arteries and heart, now freed from the challenge of pumping against gravity. Every moment aboard ISS was precious, and he did not want to waste a minute of it. So, during the hours scheduled for sleep, he roamed the station, lingering at windows, visited the animals in the lab.

That was how he had discovered the dead mouse.

It had been floating with legs frozen and extended, pink mouth gaping open. Another one of the males. It was the fourth mouse to die in sixteen days.

He confirmed that the habitat was functioning properly, that the temperature set points had not been violated and the airflow rate was maintained at the standard twelve

99

changes per hour. Why were they dying? Could it be contamination of the water or food? Several months ago, the station had lost a dozen rats when toxic chemicals had seeped into the animal habitat's water supply.

The mouse floated in a corner of the enclosure. The other males were bunched at the far end, as though repulsed by the corpse of their cage mate. They seemed frantic to get away from it, paws clinging to the cage screen. On the other side of the wire divider, the females, too, were bunched together. All except one. She was twitching, spiraling slowly in midair, her claws thrashing in seizure-like movements.

Another one is sick.

Even as he watched, the female gave what looked like a last tortured gasp and suddenly went limp.

The other females bunched even tighter, a panicked mass of writhing white fur. He had to remove the corpses, before the contagion – if it was a contagion – spread to the other mice.

He interfaced the habitat to the life-sciences glove box, snapped on latex gloves, and inserted his hands through the rubber dams. Reaching first into the male side of the enclosure, he removed the corpse and bagged it in plastic. Then he opened the females' enclosure and reached in for the second dead mouse. As he removed it, a flash of white fur shot out past his hand.

One of the mice had escaped into the glove box.

He snatched her in midair. And almost immediately released her when he felt the sharp nip of pain. She had bitten right through the glove.

At once he pulled his hands out of the box, quickly peeled off the gloves, and stared at his finger. A drop of blood welled up, the sight of it so unexpected, he felt nauseated. He closed his eyes, berating himself. This was nothing – barely a prick. The mouse's rightful vengeance for all those needles he had stuck in them. He opened his eyes again, but the nausea was still there.

I need to rest, he thought.

He recaptured the struggling mouse and thrust it into the cage. Then he removed the two bagged corpses and placed them in the refrigerator. Tomorrow, he'd deal with the problem. Tomorrow, when he felt better.

July 30

'I found this one dead today,' said Kenichi. 'It is number six.'

Emma frowned at the mice in the animal habitat. They were housed in a divided cage, the males separated from the females only by a wire barrier. They shared the same air, the same food and water supply. On the male side, a dead mouse floated motionless, limbs extended and rigid. The other males were clustered at the opposite end of the enclosure, scrabbling at the screen as though frantic to escape.

'You've lost six mice in seventeen days?' said Emma.

'Five males. One female.'

Emma studied the remaining live animals for signs of illness. They all appeared alert, their eyes bright, with no mucus discharge from their nostrils.

'First, let's get this dead one out,' she said. 'Then we'll take a close look at the others.'

Using the glove box, she reached into the cage and removed the corpse. It was already in rigor mortis, the legs stiff, the spine inflexible. The mouth was partly open, and the tip of the tongue protruded in a soft flap of pink. It was not unusual for lab animals to die in space. On one shuttle flight in 1998, there had been almost a hundred percent mortality among newborn rats. Microgravity was an alien environment, and not all species adapted well.

Prior to launch, these mice would have been screened for

a number of bacteria, fungi, and viruses. If this was an infection, then they had picked it up while aboard ISS.

She put the dead mouse in a plastic pouch, changed gloves, and reached into the enclosure for one of the live mice. It squirmed with great vigor, showing no signs of illness. The only unusual feature was a tattered ear that had been chewed by its cage mates. She flipped it over to look at its belly and gave an exclamation of surprise.

'This is a female,' she said.

'What?'

'You had a female in the male enclosure.'

Kenichi leaned close to peer through the glove box window at the mouse's genitals. The evidence was plain to see. His face flushed deep red with embarrassment.

'Last night,' he explained. 'She bit me. I put her back in a hurry.'

Emma gave him a sympathetic smile. 'Well, the worst that can happen is an unexpected baby boom.'

Kenichi slipped on gloves and inserted his hands in the second pair of glove box armholes. 'I make the mistake,' he said. 'I fix it.'

Together they examined the rest of the mice in the enclosure, but found no other misplaced specimens. All appeared healthy.

'This is very strange,' said Emma. 'If we're dealing with a contagious disease, there ought to be some evidence of infection . . .'

'Watson?' a voice called over the module intercom.

'In the lab, Griggs,' she answered.

'You've got priority E-mail from Payloads.'

'I'll get it now.' She sealed off the animal enclosure and said to Kenichi, 'Let me check my message. Why don't you take out the dead mice you put in cold storage. We'll look at them.'

He nodded and floated across to the refrigerator.

At the workstation computer, she called up her priority E-mail.

To: Dr Emma Watson
From: Helen Koenig, Principal Investigator
Re: Experiment CCU#23 (Archaeon Cell Culture)
Message: Immediately abort this experiment. Latest specimens returned by Atlantis show fungal contamination. All Archaeon cultures, along with the containers holding them, should be incinerated in onboard crucible and the ashes jettisoned.

Emma read and reread the message on the screen. Never before had she received such a strange request. Fungal contamination was not dangerous. To incinerate the cultures seemed a drastic overreaction. She was so preoccupied by this puzzling request she paid no attention to Kenichi, who was taking the dead mice out of the refrigerator. Only when she heard him gasp did she turn to look at him.

At first all she saw was his shocked face, splattered with a foul slurry of entrails. Then she looked at the plastic bag that had just burst open. In his horror, he had released it, and it floated free, hanging in the air between them.

'What is *that*?' she said.

He said, in disbelief, 'The mouse.'

But it was not a dead mouse she saw in the bag. It was a mass of disintegrated tissue, a putrefied gumbo of flesh and fur that even now was leaking out foul-smelling globules.

Biohazard!

She shot the length of the module to the caution-and-warning panel and hit the button to shut off airflow between modules. Kenichi had already opened the emergency rack and pulled out two filter masks. He tossed one to her, and she clapped it over her nose and mouth. They didn't need to exchange a word; they both knew what had to be done.

Quickly they closed the hatches on either end of the module, effectively isolating the lab from the rest of the station. Then Emma took out a biocontainment bag and carefully moved toward the drifting bag of liquefied flesh. Surface tension had bound the liquids together in one globule; if she was careful not to stir the air, she could trap it in the bag, without scattering droplets. Gently she lowered the containment bag over the free-floating specimen and quickly sealed it off. She heard Kenichi give a sigh of relief. Hazard contained.

'Did it leak into the refrigerator?' she asked.

'No. Only when I took it out.' He wiped his face with an alcohol swab and sealed the swab for safe disposal. 'The bag, it was . . . you know, blown up big. Like a balloon.'

The contents had been under pressure, the process of decomposition releasing gases. Through the plastic containment bag, she could see the date of death on the label. *This is impossible*, she thought. In just five days, the corpse had deteriorated to a black puree of rotted flesh. The bag was cold to the touch, so the refrigerator was functioning. Despite cold storage, something had accelerated the body's decomposition. Flesh-eating *streptococcus?* she wondered. Or another bacteria, equally destructive?

She looked at Kenichi and thought, *It splashed him in the eye*.

'We need to talk to your principal investigator,' she said. 'The one who sent up these mice.'

It was only five A.M., Pacific Daylight Time, but the voice of Dr Michael Loomis, principal investigator for the experiment 'Conception and gestation in mice during spaceflight,' was fully alert and obviously concerned. He was speaking

104

to Emma from Ames Research Center in California. Though she couldn't see him, she could picture the man who belonged to this reedy voice: tall, energetic. A man for whom five in the morning is a normal part of the workday.

'We've been monitoring these animals for over a month,' said Loomis. 'It's a relatively low-stress experiment for the animals. We'd planned to mingle the males and females next week, in hopes they'd successfully mate and conceive. This research has important applications for long-term spaceflight. Planetary colonization. As you can imagine, these deaths are pretty upsetting.'

'We've already got cultures incubating,' said Emma. 'All the dead mice appear to be decomposing more quickly than they should. Based on the condition of the corpses, I'm concerned about *clostridia* or *streptococcus* infections.'

'Dangerous bugs like that on the station? That would be a serious problem.'

'Exactly. Especially in a closed environment like ours. We'd all be vulnerable.'

'What about autopsying the dead mice?'

Emma hesitated. 'We're only set up to deal with Level Two contamination up here. Nothing more dangerous. If this is a serious pathogen, I can't afford to risk infecting other animals. Or people.'

There was a silence. Then Loomis said, 'I understand. And I guess I have to agree with you. So you'll be safely disposing of all the corpses?'

'Immediately,' said Emma.

July 31

For the first time since he'd arrived on ISS, Kenichi could not sleep. He had zipped himself into his restraint bag hours ago, yet he was still awake, still mulling over the puzzle of the dead mice. Though no one had uttered a word of reproach, somehow he felt responsible for the failed experiment. He tried to think of what he might have done wrong. Had he used a contaminated needle, perhaps, when he'd sampled their blood, or a bad setting in the animal rack's environmental controls? Thoughts of all the possible mistakes he might have made kept sleep at bay.

Also, his head was throbbing.

He had first noticed the discomfort this morning, when it had started as a vague tingling around his eye. As the day wore on, the tingling had become an ache, and now the left half of his head hurt. Not an excruciating pain, just a nagging annoyance.

He unzipped his bag. He was getting no rest in any event; he might as well check on the mice again.

He floated past Nicolai's curtained sleep station and headed through the series of connecting modules that led to the U.S. half of the station. Only when he'd entered the lab did he realize someone else was awake.

Voices murmured in the adjoining NASDA lab. Silently he floated into Node 2 and peered through the open hatch. He saw Diana Estes and Michael Griggs, limbs tangled together, mouths locked in hungry exploration. At once he backed out unnoticed, his face burning with embarrassment at what he'd just witnessed.

Now what? Should he grant them their privacy and return to his sleep station? *This is not right*, he thought with sudden resentment. *I am here to work, to fulfill my duties*.

He floated to the animal habitat. Deliberately he made a great deal of noise as he opened and closed the rack drawers. A moment later, as he'd expected, Diana and Griggs suddenly appeared, both of them looking flushed. *And well they should be*, he thought, *considering what they've been up to*.

'We had a problem with the centrifuge,' lied Diana. 'I think it's fixed now.'

Kenichi merely nodded, betraying no sign that he knew the truth. Diana was cool as ice about it, and that both appalled and angered him. Griggs, at least, had the decency to look a little guilty.

Kenichi watched as they floated out of the lab and disappeared through the hatch. Then he turned his attention back to the animal habitat. He peered into the cage.

Another mouse was dead. A female.

August 1

Diana Estes calmly held out her arm for the tourniquet and squeezed her hand open and shut several times to plump up her antecubital vein. She did not flinch or look away as the needle pierced her skin; indeed, Diana was so detached, she might have been watching someone else's blood being drawn. Every astronaut was poked and prodded many times during the course of his or her career. At selection screening, they endured multiple blood draws and physical exams and the most probing of questions. Their serum chemistries and EKGs and cell counts were on permanent record, to be pored over by aerospace physiologists. They panted and sweated on treadmills with electrodes attached to their chests; their body fluids were cultured, their bowels probed; every inch of skin was examined. Astronauts were not just highly trained personnel; they were also experimental subjects. They were the equivalent of lab rats, and while in orbit, they resigned themselves to a sometimes painful battery of tests.

Today was specimen collection day. As the physician on board, Emma was the one wielding the needles and syringes. No wonder most of her crewmates groaned when they saw her coming.

Diana, though, had simply held out her arm and submitted to the needle. As Emma waited for the syringe to fill with blood, she sensed the other woman's gaze appraising her skill

107

and technique. If Princess Diana had been England's rose, went the joke at JSC, then Diana Estes was England's ice cube, an astronaut whose poise never cracked, even in the heat of real calamity.

Four years ago, Diana had been aboard *Atlantis* when a main engine failed. On tapes of the crew transmissions, the voices of the shuttle commander and pilot had risen in alarm as they scrambled to guide the shuttle in a transatlantic abort. But not Diana's voice. She could be heard coolly reading the checklist as *Atlantis* hurtled to an uncertain landing in North Africa. What had sealed her icy reputation were the bio-telemetry readings. On that particular launch, the entire crew had been wired to record their blood pressure and pulse. While the heart rates of everyone else had skyrocketed, Diana's had barely accelerated to a leisurely ninety-six beats per minute. 'That's because she's not human,' Jack had joked. 'She's really an android. The first in NASA's newest line of astronauts.'

Emma had to admit there was something not quite human about the woman.

Diana glanced at the puncture site on her arm, saw that the bleeding had stopped, and matter-of-factly turned back to her protein crystal growth experiments. She was indeed almost android perfect, long-limbed and slender, her flawless skin paled to milky white from a month in space. All that plus a genius IQ, according to Jack, who had trained with Diana for the shuttle mission he had never completed.

Diana had a doctorate in materials science and had published over a dozen research papers on zeolites – crystal-line materials used in petroleum refinement – prior to being accepted into the astronaut program. Now she was the scientist in charge of both organic and inorganic crystals research. On earth, crystal formation was distorted by gravity. In space, crystals grew larger and more elaborate, allowing thorough analysis of their structure. Hundreds of human proteins, from angiotensin to chorionic gonadotropin, were being grown as crystals aboard ISS – vital pharmaceutical research that could lead to the development of new drugs.

Finished with Diana, Emma left the ESA lab and floated into the hab, to find Mike Griggs. 'You're next,' she said.

He groaned and reluctantly held out his arm. 'All in the name of science.'

'It's just one tube this time,' said Emma, tying on the tourniquet.

'We've gotten so many needle sticks we look like junkies.'

She gave his skin a few gentle slaps to bring out the antecubital vein. It plumped up, blue and cordlike on his muscular arm. Griggs had been compulsive about staying in condition – not a simple thing while in orbit. Life in space took its toll on the human body. Astronauts' faces were bloated, swollen by shifts in fluids. Their thigh and calf muscles shrank until they had 'chicken legs,' poking out pale and scrawny from their bloomerlike shorts. Duties were exhausting, the irritations too numerous to count. And then there was the emotional toll of being confined for months with crewmates who were under stress, scarcely bathed, and wearing dirty clothes.

Emma swabbed the skin with alcohol and pierced the vein. Blood shot back into the syringe. She glanced at him and saw his gaze was averted. 'Okay?'

'Yeah. I do appreciate a skillful vampire.'

She released the tourniquet and heard his sigh of relief when she withdrew the needle. 'You can eat breakfast now. I've drawn everyone's blood but Kenichi's.' She glanced around the hab. 'Where is he?'

'I haven't seen him this morning.'

'I hope he hasn't eaten. That'll screw up his glucose level.'

Nicolai, who'd been floating off in a corner, quietly finishing his breakfast, said, 'He is still asleep.'

109

'Strange,' said Griggs. 'He's always up before everyone else.'

'His sleep is not so good,' said Nicolai. 'Last night, I hear him vomit. I ask if he needs help, and he tells me no.'

'I'll check on him,' said Emma.

She left the hab and headed up the long tunnel to the RSM, where Kenichi's sleep station was. She found his privacy curtain was closed.

'Kenichi?' she called out. There was no response. 'Kenichi?' She hesitated a moment, then opened the curtain and saw his face.

His eyes were a brilliant bloodred.

'Oh, my God,' she said.

The Sickness

9

The flight surgeon manning the console for ISS Mission Control was Dr Todd Cutler, a physician who was so fresh-faced and youthful the astronauts had dubbed him 'Doogie Howser' after the TV show about a teenage doctor. Cutler was, in reality, a ripe old thirty-two and known for his cool competence. He acted as Emma's personal physician while she was in orbit, and once a week, during their private medical conference, she spoke to him on a closed communications loop, reporting the most intimate details about her health. She trusted Todd's medical skills and was relieved that he was the surgeon on duty at that hour in the ISS control room at Johnson.

'He's got scleral hemorrhages in both eyes,' she said. 'It scared the hell out of me when I first saw it. I think he got them from vomiting so hard last night – the sudden changes in pressure popped a few vessels in his eyes.'

'That's a relatively minor concern right now. The hemorrhages will clear up,' said Todd. 'What about the rest of the exam?'

'He's got a fever of thirty-eight point six. Pulse one twenty, blood pressure one hundred over sixty. The heart and lungs sound fine. He does complain of a headache, but I can't find any neurologic changes. What really worries me is the fact he has no bowel sounds, and his abdomen is diffusely tender. He's vomited several times in just the last hour – so far, it's negative for blood.' She paused. 'Todd, he looks *sick*. And here's the bad news. I just ran his amylase level. It's six hundred.'

'Oh, shit. You think he's got pancreatitis?'

'With a rising amylase, it's certainly possible.' Amylase was an enzyme produced by the pancreas, and its levels usually skyrocketed when the organ became inflamed. But a high amylase level could also indicate other acute abdominal processes. A bowel perforation or a duodenal ulcer.

'His white blood cell count is also high,' said Emma. 'I've drawn blood cultures, just in case.'

'What's the history? Anything worth noting?'

'Two things. First, he's been under some emotional stress. One of his experiments is crashing on him, and he feels responsible.'

'And the second thing?'

'He was splashed in the eye two days ago, with body fluids from a dead lab mouse.'

'Tell me more.' Todd's voice had gone very quiet.

'The mice in his experiment have been dying, for reasons unknown. The corpses have decomposed at an amazing rate. I was concerned about pathogenic bacteria, so I took samples of the body fluids for culture. Unfortunately, all those cultures are ruined.'

'How?'

'I think it's fungal contamination. The plates have all turned green. No known pathogens can be identified. I had to discard the plates. The same thing happened to another experiment, a cell culture of marine organisms. We had to abort that project because fungi got into the culture tube.'

114

Fungal overgrowth, unfortunately, was not an uncommon problem in closed environments like ISS, despite the continually recirculating air. Aboard the old *Mir* station, the windows were sometimes coated with a fuzzy layer of fungi. Once the air of a spacecraft has been contaminated by these organisms, it is next to impossible to eliminate them. Luckily, they were by and large harmless to people and lab animals.

'So we don't know if he's been exposed to any pathogens,' said Todd.

'No. Right now, it looks more like a case of pancreatitis, not a bacterial infection. I've got an IV started, and I think it's time for a nasogastric tube.' She paused, then added reluctantly, 'We need to think about emergency evacuation.'

There was a long silence. This was the scenario everyone dreaded, the decision no one wanted to make. The Crew Return Vehicle, which remained docked to ISS whenever personnel were aboard, was large enough to evacuate all six astronauts. Since the *Soyuz* capsules were no longer functioning, the CRV was the only escape vehicle on the station. If it left, they would all have to be aboard it. For the sake of one sick crew member, they would be forced to abandon ISS, ending hundreds of in-flight experiments. It would be a crippling setback to the station.

But there was an alternative. They could wait for the next shuttle flight to evacuate Kenichi. Now it came down to a medical decision. *Could* he wait? Emma knew NASA was relying on her clinical judgment, and the responsibility weighed heavily on her shoulders.

'What about a shuttle evac?' she asked.

Todd Cutler understood the dilemma. 'We have *Discovery* on the pad for STS 161, launch minus fifteen days. But her mission is classified military. Satellite retrieval and repair. One sixty-one's crew hasn't been prepping for ISS docking and rendezvous.'

'What about replacing them with Kittredge's team? My old crew from 162? They're scheduled to dock here in seven weeks. They're fully prepared.'

Emma glanced at Mike Griggs, who was hovering nearby, listening to the conversation. As ISS commander, his primary goal was to keep the station up and running, and he was firmly opposed to abandoning her. He joined the conversation.

'Cutler, this is Griggs. If my crew evacuates, we lose experiments. That's months of work down the drain. A shuttle rescue makes the most sense. If Kenichi needs to get home, then you folks come pick him up. Let the rest of us stay here and do our jobs.'

'Can a rescue wait that long?' asked Todd.

'How soon can you get that bird up here?' said Griggs.

'We have to talk logistics. Launch windows –'

'Just tell us how long.'

Cutler paused. 'Flight Director Ellis is standing by. Go ahead, Flight.'

What had started as a closed and confidential loop between two physicians was now open to the flight director. They heard Woody Ellis say, 'Thirty-six hours. That's the earliest possible launch.'

A lot could change in thirty-six hours, Emma thought. An ulcer could perforate or hemorrhage. Pancreatitis could lead to shock and circulatory collapse.

Or Kenichi could recover completely, the victim of nothing worse than a severe intestinal infection.

'Dr Watson's the one examining the patient,' Ellis said. 'We're relying on her judgment here. What's the clinical call?'

Emma thought about it. 'He doesn't have an acute surgical abdomen – not at the moment. But things could go bad fast.'

'So you're not sure.'

'No, I'm not.'

116

'The instant you give us the word, we'll still need twenty-four hours for fueling.'

A whole day's lag between a call for rescue, and the actual launch, plus additional time for rendezvous. If Kenichi suddenly took a turn for the worse, could she keep him alive that long? The situation had turned nerve-racking. She was a physician, not a fortune-teller. She had no X rays at her disposal, no operating room. The physical exam and blood tests were abnormal but non-specific. If she chose to delay rescue, Kenichi might die. If she called for help too soon, millions of dollars would be wasted on an unnecessary launch.

A wrong decision either way would end her career with NASA.

This was the tightrope Jack had warned her about. *I screw up, and the whole world knows. They're waiting to see if I've got the right stuff.*

She looked down at the printout of Kenichi's blood tests. Nothing she saw there justified hitting the panic button. Not yet.

She said, 'Flight, I'm going to keep him on IVs and start NG suction. Right now his vital signs are looking stable. I just wish I knew what was going on in his belly.'

'So in your opinion, emergency shuttle launch is not yet indicated?'

She released a deep breath. 'No. Not yet.'

'We will nevertheless be poised and ready to light *Discovery*'s candle, should it be necessary.'

'I appreciate that. I'll get back to you later with a medical update.' She signed off and looked at Griggs. 'I hope I'm making the right call.'

'Just cure him, okay?'

She went to check on Kenichi. Because he would need attention throughout the night, she'd moved him out of the hab module and into the U.S. lab, so the rest of the crew would not have their sleep disturbed. He was zipped into a restraint bag. An infusion pump fed a steady flow of saline solution into his intravenous line. He was awake and obviously in discomfort.

Luther and Diana, who'd been watching the patient, both looked relieved to see Emma. 'He vomited again,' said Diana.

Emma anchored her feet to hold her position and slipped the stethoscope on her ears. Gently she placed the diaphragm on Kenichi's abdomen. Still no bowel sounds. His digestive tract had shut down, and fluid would begin to accumulate in his stomach. That fluid needed to be drained.

'Kenichi,' she said, 'I'm going to insert a tube into your stomach. It will help the pain, and maybe stop the vomiting.'

'What – what tube?'

'A nasogastric tube.' She opened the ALSP medical kit. Inside was a broad array of supplies and drugs, a collection as complete as a modern ambulance's. In the drawer marked 'Airway' were various tubes, suction devices, collection bags, and a laryngoscope. She tore open the packet containing the long nasogastric tube. It was thin and coiled, made of flexible plastic, with a perforated tip.

Kenichi's bloodred eyes widened.

'I'll be as gentle as I can,' she said. 'You can help it go faster by taking a sip of water when I ask you to. I'm going to insert this end into your nostril. The tube will go down the back of your throat, and when you swallow the water, the tube will pass into your stomach. The only uncomfortable part will be right at the beginning, when I first slip it in. After it's in place, it should hardly bother you at all.'

'How long does it stay inside?'

'A day, at least. Until your intestines start working again.' She added, gently, 'It really is necessary, Kenichi.'

He sighed and nodded.

Emma glanced at Luther, who was looking more and more

118

horrified by the idea of this tube. 'He'll need water to sip. Could you get some?' Then she looked at Diana, who was floating nearby. As usual, Diana looked unperturbed, coolly detached from the crisis. 'I need NG suction set up.'

Diana automatically reached into the ALSP kit for the suction device and collection bag.

Emma uncoiled the NG tube. First she dipped the tip in lubricant gel, to ease its passage through the nasopharynx. Then she handed Kenichi the pouch of water, which Luther had filled.

She gave Kenichi's arm a reassuring squeeze. Though dread was plain to see in his eyes, he returned a nod of consent.

The perforated end of the tube glistened with lubricant. She inserted the tip into his right nostril and gently advanced it deeper, into his nasopharynx. He gagged, eyes watering, and began to cough in protest as the tube slid down the back of his throat. She threaded it deeper. He was twitching now, fighting the overwhelming instinct to thrust her away, to yank the tube out of his nose.

'Swallow some water,' she urged.

He wheezed and with a trembling hand brought the straw to his lips.

'Swallow, Kenichi,' she said.

When a bolus of water is passed from the throat into the esophagus, the epiglottis reflexively closes over the opening to the trachea, preventing any leakage into the lungs. It would also direct an NG tube down the correct passageway. The instant she saw him begin to swallow, she swiftly advanced the tube, threading it past the throat and down the esophagus, until it slid in far enough for the tip to be in the stomach.

'All done,' she said, taping the tube to his nose. 'You did fine.'

'Suction's ready,' said Diana.

Emma connected the NG tube to the suction device.

They heard a few gurgles, then fluid suddenly appeared in the tube, flowing out of Kenichi's stomach, into the drainage bag. It was a bilious green; no blood, Emma noted with relief. Perhaps this was all the treatment he needed – bowel rest, NG suction, and intravenous fluids. If he did indeed have pancreatitis, this therapy alone would carry him through the next few days, until the shuttle arrived.

'My head – it hurts,' said Kenichi, closing his eyes.

'I'll give you something for the pain,' said Emma.

'So what do you think? Crisis averted?' It was Griggs speaking. He had watched the procedure from the hatchway, and even though the tube was now inserted, Griggs hung back, as though repulsed by the mere sight of illness. He did not even look at the patient, but kept his gaze focused on Emma.

'We'll have to see,' she said.

'What do I tell Houston?'

'I just got the tube in. It's too early.'

'They need to know soon.'

'Well, I *don't* know!' she snapped. Then, swallowing her temper, she said more calmly, 'Can we discuss this in the hab?' She left Luther to stay with the patient and headed through the hatchway.

In the hab module, she and Griggs were joined by Nicolai. They gathered around the galley table as though sharing a meal. What they were sharing, instead, were their frustrations over an uncertain situation.

'You're the M.D.,' said Griggs. 'Can't you make a decision?'

'I'm still trying to stabilize him,' said Emma. 'Right now I don't know what I'm dealing with. It could resolve in another day or two. Or it could suddenly get worse.'

'And you can't tell us which is going to happen.'

'Without an X ray, without an OR, I can't see what's going

on inside him. I can't predict what his condition will be tomorrow.'

'Great.'

'I do think he should go home. I'd like the launch moved up as soon as possible.'

'What about a CRV evac?' asked Nicolai.

'A controlled shuttle ride is always better for transporting a sick patient,' said Emma. A CRV return was a rough ride, and depending on weather conditions on earth, they might not be able to touch down in the best possible location for medical transport.

'Forget CRV evac,' said Griggs flatly. 'We're not abandoning this station.'

Nicolai said, 'If he becomes critical –'

'Emma will just have to keep him alive long enough for *Discovery* to get here. Hell, this station's like an orbiting ambulance! She *should* be able to keep him stable.'

'What if she cannot?' pressed Nicolai. 'A man's life is worth more than these experiments.'

'It's the option of last resort,' said Griggs. 'We all jump on the CRV, we're abandoning months of work.'

'Look, Griggs,' said Emma. 'I don't want to leave the station any more than you do. I fought like hell to make it up here, and I'm not about to cut my stay short. But if my patient needs instant evac, then it's *my* call.'

'Excuse me, Emma,' said Diana, floating in the hatchway. 'I just finished running Kenichi's last blood tests. I think you should see this.' She handed Emma a computer printout.

Emma stared at the results: *Creatine kinase: 20.6 (normal 0–3.08).*

This illness was more than pancreatitis, more than just a gastrointestinal disturbance. A high CK meant there had been damage to either his muscles or his heart.

Vomiting is sometimes a symptom of a heart attack.

She looked at Griggs. 'I've just made the decision,' she said. 'Tell Houston to fire up the shuttle. Kenichi has to get home.'

August 2
Jack tightened the jib sheet, his sunburned arms gleaming with sweat as he strained against the crank. With a satisfying *whomp* the sail went taut, and *Sanneke* heeled leeward, her bow suddenly slicing faster through the muddy waters of Galveston Bay. He had left the Gulf of Mexico behind him, had sailed around Point Bolivar earlier that afternoon, dodging the ferry from Galveston Island, and was now tacking past the string of refineries on the shores of Texas City as he sailed north toward Clear Lake. Toward home.

Four days at sea on the Gulf had turned him brown and shaggy. He had informed no one of his plans, had simply stocked up on food and set sail toward open water, beyond sight of land, into nights so black his eyes had been dazzled by the stars. Lying on his back on deck, the Gulf waters gently rocking the hull beneath him, he'd gazed for hours at the night sky. With that field of stars stretching in every direction, as far as he could see, he could almost imagine he was hurtling through space, that each rise of the swells was thrusting him deeper into the coil of another galaxy. He had emptied his mind of everything but the stars and the sea. Then a meteor had streaked by in a brilliant slash of light, and suddenly he'd thought of Emma. He could not put up barricades high enough to keep her out. She was always there, hovering at the edges, waiting to slip into his thoughts when he least expected it. Least wanted it. He had gone rigid, his eyes fixed on that dying streak of the meteor's trail, and even though nothing else had changed, not the direction of the wind nor the rise and fall of the swells, he had felt suddenly, deeply, alone.

It was still dark when he'd raised the sails and turned back for home.

Now, as he motored up the channel into Clear Lake, past rooflines silhouetted against the glare of sunset, he regretted his decision to return home so soon. On the Gulf there had been a constant breeze, but here, the heat hung unstirred and the humidity was stifling.

He tied up at his slip and stepped onto the dock, his legs unsteady from days at sea. First order of business, he thought, was a cold shower. He'd save the boat cleanup for tonight, when it was cooler. And as for Humphrey, well – another day in the kennel wouldn't hurt the little hair ball. Lugging his duffel bag, he headed up the dock and was walking past the marina's small grocery store when his gaze fell on the newsstand. His duffel bag slipped from his grasp and hit the ground. He stared at the banner headline across that morning's *Houston Chronicle*:

'Emergency Shuttle Countdown Begins – Liftoff Tomorrow.'
What has happened? he thought. *What has gone wrong?*

With shaking hands he pulled quarters from his pockets, fed the coins into the slot, and grabbed a copy from the stand. Two photos accompanied the news article. One was of Kenichi Hirai, the NASDA astronaut from Japan. The other was of Emma.

He snatched up the duffel bag and ran for a phone.

There were three flight surgeons at the meeting – an indication to Jack that the crisis they faced was medical. As he walked into the room, heads turned in surprise. He read the unspoken question in space station flight director Woody Ellis's eyes: *What's Jack McCallum doing back in the fold?*

Dr Todd Cutler gave the answer. 'Jack helped develop our emergency medical procedures protocol for the station's first crew. I thought he should join us.'

Ellis said, uneasily, 'The personal angle makes this complicated.' *Emma* was what he meant.

'Every member of that crew is like family to us,' said Todd. 'So in a way, it's *all* personal.'

Jack took a seat beside Todd. Sitting at the table were the NSTS deputy director, the ISS mission operations director, flight surgeons, and several program managers. Also present was NASA's public affairs officer, Gretchen Liu. With the exception of launch days, the news media largely ignored NASA operations. Today, though, journalists from every news agency were crammed into the tiny pressroom in NASA's Public Information building, awaiting Gretchen's appearance. What a difference a day made, thought Jack. Public attention was fickle. It demanded explosions, tragedy. Crisis. The miracle of a flawless operation drew no one's attention.

Todd passed a sheaf of papers to him, with a note scrawled on top: *'Hirai's labs and clinical findings last 24 hours. Welcome back.'*

Jack flipped through the medical reports while he listened to the meeting. He had a day's worth of developments to catch up on, and it took him a while to absorb the essentials. Astronaut Kenichi Hirai was seriously ill, his lab findings puzzling to everyone. The shuttle *Discovery* was poised for a six A.M. EDT launch manned by Kittredge's crew, along with an astronaut-physician. Countdown was on schedule.

'Any change in your recommendations?' the NSTS deputy director asked the flight surgeons. 'Do you still think Hirai can wait for a shuttle evac?'

Todd Cutler answered. 'We still believe a shuttle evac is the safest option. We aren't changing our recommendations in that regard. ISS is a fairly well-equipped medical facility, with all the drugs and equipment needed for cardiopulmonary resuscitation.'

'So you still believe he's had a heart attack?'

Todd looked at his fellow flight surgeons. 'Frankly,' he admitted, 'we're not entirely certain. There are things that do point to a myocardial infarction – a heart attack, in layman's terms. Mainly, the rising levels of cardiac enzymes in his blood.'

'Then why are you still unsure?'

'The EKG shows only nonspecific changes – a few T wave inversions. It's not a classic pattern for an MI. Also, Hirai was thoroughly screened for cardiovascular disease prior to his acceptance in the program. He had no risk factors. Frankly, we're not sure what's going on. But we do have to assume he has had a heart attack. Which makes a shuttle evac the best option. It's a gentler reentry and a controlled landing. Far less stress on the patient than coming home in the CRV. In the meantime, ISS can deal with any arrhythmias he may have.'

Jack looked up from the lab reports he'd been scanning. 'Without the necessary lab equipment, the station can't fractionate these CK levels. So how can we be sure this enzyme is really from the heart?'

Everyone's attention turned to him.

'What do you mean by "fractionate"?' asked Woody Ellis.

'Creatine kinase is an enzyme that helps muscle cells utilize stored energy. It's found in both striated and cardiac muscle. When there's damage to heart cells, say, in a heart attack, the CK levels rise in the blood. That's why we're assuming he had a heart attack. But what if it's not the heart?'

'What else could it be?'

'Some other type of muscle damage. Trauma, for instance, or convulsions. Inflammation. In fact, just a simple intramuscular injection can cause the CK to rise. You need to fractionate the CK in order to tell if it's from heart muscle. The station can't do that test.'

'So he may not have had a heart attack at all.'

'Correct. And here's another puzzling detail. After acute muscle damage, his CK levels should drop back to normal. But look at the pattern.' Jack flipped through the lab sheets and read off the numbers. 'In the last twenty-four hours, his levels have been steadily *rising*. Which indicates continued damage.'

'It's just part of the bigger puzzle,' said Todd. 'We've got abnormal results all over the board, without any recognizable pattern. Liver enzymes, renal abnormalities, sedimentation rate, white blood cell counts. Some labs go up while others are dropping. It's as though different organ systems are taking turns being attacked.'

Jack looked at him. 'Attacked?'

'Just a figure of speech, Jack. I don't know *what* process we're dealing with. I know it's not lab error. We've run controls on the other crew members, and they're perfectly normal.'

'But is he sick enough to warrant *any* evac?' The question was asked by the mission operations director for the shuttle. He was not happy about any of this. *Discovery*'s original mission was to retrieve and repair the classified *Capricorn* spy satellite. Now her mission had been usurped by this crisis. 'Washington is not happy about postponing the satellite repair. You've commandeered their flight so *Discovery* can play flying ambulance. Is it really necessary? Can't Hirai recover on the station?'

'We can't predict it. We don't know what's wrong with him,' said Todd.

'You have a physician up there, for God's sake. Can't *she* figure it out?'

Jack tensed. This was an attack on Emma. 'She doesn't have X-ray vision,' he said.

'She's got just about everything else at her disposal. What'd you call the station, Dr Cutler? "A well-equipped medical facility"?'

'Astronaut Hirai needs to get home, as expeditiously as possible,' said Todd. 'That remains our position. If you want to second-guess your flight surgeons, that's your choice. All I can say is, I'd never presume to second-guess an engineer on propulsion systems.'

That effectively ended the argument.

The NSTS deputy director said, 'Are there any other concerns?'

'Weather,' said the NASA forecaster. 'I just thought I'd mention there's a storm system developing west of Guadeloupe and moving very slowly westward. It won't affect the launch. But depending on its path, it could be a problem for Kennedy in the next week or so.'

'Thanks for the heads up.' The deputy director glanced around the room and saw no further questions. 'Then launch is still a go for five A.M. CDT. See you all there.'

10

Punta Arena, Mexico

The Sea of Cortez shimmered like beaten silver in the fading light. From her table on the outdoor deck of the Las Tres Virgenes café, Helen Koenig could see fishing boats heading back to Punta Colorado. This was the time of day she loved best, the evening breeze cool against her sun-flushed skin, her muscles pleasantly weary from an afternoon's swim. A waiter brought the margarita she'd ordered and set the drink before her.

'*Gracias, señor,*' she murmured.

For an instant he met her gaze. She saw a quiet and dignified man with tired eyes and silver-streaked hair, and she felt a prick of discomfort. Yankee guilt, she thought as she watched him walk back to the bar. A feeling she experienced every time she drove down to Baja. She sipped her drink and gazed at the sea, listening to the whining trumpets of a mariachi band playing somewhere up the beach.

It had been a good day, and she'd spent almost all of it in the sea. A two-tank dive in the morning followed by a shallower dive in the afternoon. And then, just before dinner, a swim in the sunset-gilded waters. The sea was her comfort, her sanctuary. It had always been so. Unlike the love of a man, the sea was constant and it never disappointed her. It was always ready to embrace her, soothe her, and in moments of crisis she found herself fleeing into its waiting arms.

This was why she had come to Baja. To swim in warm waters and to be alone, where no one could reach her. Not even Palmer Gabriel.

Her lips puckered from the tang of the margarita. She drank it down and ordered a second. Already the alcohol made her feel as if she were floating. No matter; she was now a free woman. The project was finished, aborted. The cultures destroyed. Even though Palmer was furious with her, she knew she had done the right thing. The safe thing. Tomorrow she would sleep in, order hot chocolate and huevos rancheros for breakfast. Then she'd slip beneath the waters for another dive, another return to her sea-green lover.

A woman's laughter drew her attention. Helen looked at the bar, where a couple was flirting, the woman slim and tanned, the man with muscles like steel cord. A vacation fling in the making. They would probably have dinner together, walk along the beach, hold hands. Then there would be a kiss, an embrace, all the hormone-charged rituals of mating. Helen watched them with both a scientist's interest and a woman's envy. She knew such rituals did not apply to her. She was forty-nine years old and she looked it. Her waist was thick, her hair more than half gray, and her face was unremarkable save for the intelligence of her eyes. She was not the sort of woman who attracted looks from sun-bronzed Adonises.

She finished the second margarita. By now the floating sensation had spread to her whole body, and she knew it was time to get some food in her stomach. She opened the menu. '*Restaurante de Las Tres Virgenes*' it said at the top.

129

The Three Virgins. An appropriate place for her to eat. She might as well be a virgin.

The waiter came to take her order. She looked up at him and had just requested the grilled dorado when her eyes focused on the TV over the bar, on the image of the space shuttle poised on the launchpad.

'What's happening?' she said, pointing to the TV.

The waiter shrugged.

'Turn up the sound,' she called out to the bartender. 'Please, I need to hear it!'

He reached for the volume knob, and the broadcast spilled out in English. An American channel. Helen crossed to the bar counter and stared at the television.

'. . . medical evacuation of astronaut Kenichi Hirai. NASA has not released any further information, but reports indicate their flight surgeons remain baffled by his illness. Based on today's blood tests, they felt it was prudent to launch a shuttle rescue. *Discovery* is expected to lift off tomorrow at six A.M. Eastern Daylight Time.'

'*Señora?*' said the waiter.

Helen turned and saw he was still holding his order pad. 'Do you wish another drink?'

'No. No, I have to leave.'

'But your food –'

'Cancel my order. Please.' She opened her purse, handed him fifteen dollars, and hurried out of the restaurant.

Back in her hotel room she tried to call Palmer Gabriel in San Diego. It took half a dozen tries to connect with the international operator, and when the call finally went through, she got only Palmer's voice mail.

'They have a sick astronaut on ISS,' she said. 'Palmer, this is what I was afraid of. What I warned all of you about. If it's confirmed, we have to move fast. Before . . .' She paused, glancing at the clock. *To hell with this*, she thought, and

130

hung up. *I have to get home to San Diego. I'm the only one who knows how to deal with this. They'll need me.*

She threw her clothes into the suitcase, checked out of the hotel, and climbed into a taxi for the fifteen-mile ride to the tiny airstrip in Buena Vista. A small plane would be waiting for her there to fly her to La Paz, where she could catch a commercial flight to San Diego.

It was a rough taxi ride, the road bumpy and winding, the dust flying in the open windows. But the part of the trip she truly dreaded was the flight coming up. Small planes terrified her. If not for her rush to get home, she would have made the long drive up the Baja Peninsula in her own car, which was now safely parked at the resort. She clung to the armrest with sweaty palms, imagining what sort of aviation disaster awaited her.

Then she glimpsed the night sky, clear and velvety black, and she thought of the people aboard the space station. Thought of the risks other, braver human beings took. It was all a matter of perspective. A ride in a small plane is nothing compared to the dangers an astronaut faces.

This was not the time to be a coward. Lives might hang in the balance. And she was the only one who knew what to do about it.

The spine-rattling ride suddenly smoothed out. They were now on a paved road, thank God, and Buena Vista was just a few miles away.

Sensing the urgency of this journey, her driver accelerated, and the wind whipped through the open windows, stinging her face with dust. She reached down to crank up the glass. Suddenly she felt the taxi swerve left to pass a slow-moving car. She glanced up and saw to her horror they were on a curve.

'*Señor! Más despacio!*' she said. *Slow down.*

They were neck and neck with the other car now, the taxi

just pulling ahead, the driver unwilling to surrender his gain. The road ahead wound to the left, dipping out of sight.

'Don't pass!' she said. 'Please, don't—' Her gaze shot forward and froze on the blinding lights of another car.

She raised her arms to cover her face, blotting out the brilliance of those lights. But she could not shut out the scream of the tires or the shriek of her own voice as the headlights leaped toward them.

August 3

From his seat behind the glass partition of the crowded visitors' gallery, Jack had a clear view down into the Flight Control Room, where every console was manned, every controller neatly attired for the TV cameras. Though the men and women working below might be intently focused on their duties, they never entirely forgot they were being observed, that the public eye was trained on them, and every gesture, every nervous shake of the head, could be seen through the wall of glass behind them. Only a year ago, Jack had manned the flight surgeon's console during a shuttle launch, and he had felt the gaze of strangers, like a vague but uncomfortable heat trained on the back of his neck. He knew the people below were feeling it now.

The atmosphere in the FCR appeared icy calm, as were the voices on the comm loop. It was the image NASA strove to maintain, of professionals doing their job and doing it well. What the public seldom saw were the crises in the back controller rooms, the near-disasters, the Chinese fire drills when things went wrong and confusion reigned.

Not today, he thought. *Carpenter's at the helm. Things will go right.*

Flight Director Randy Carpenter was leading the ascent team. He was old enough and experienced enough to have witnessed a multitude of crises during his career. It was his belief that space-flight tragedies were not usually the result of one major malfunction, but rather a series of small problems that piled up until they resulted in disaster. He was therefore a stickler for details, a man for whom every problem was a potential crisis. His team looked up to him – quite literally, because Carpenter was a giant of a man, six foot four and nearly three hundred pounds.

Gretchen Liu, the public affairs officer, was sitting at the far left, last-row console. Jack saw her turn and give the viewing gallery an A-OK smile. She was dressed in her TV best today, a navy blue suit and gray silk scarf. This mission had caught the world's attention, and although most of the press was gathered at the launch site in Cape Canaveral, there were enough reporters here in JSC's Mission Control to pack the observation gallery.

The ten-minute countdown hold ended. On audio, they heard final weather clearance, and then the countdown proceeded. Jack leaned forward, his muscles tensing as events cascaded toward liftoff. That old launch fever was back. A year ago, when he'd walked away from the space program, he thought he'd left all this behind. But here he was, caught up once again in the excitement. The dream. He imagined the crew strapped into their seats, the vehicle trembling beneath them as the chambers of liquid oxygen and hydrogen built up pressure. He thought of their claustrophobia as they closed their visors. The hiss of oxygen. The quickening of their pulses.

'We have SRB ignition,' said the public affairs officer in KSC's Launch Control. 'And liftoff! We have liftoff! Control has now shifted to Houston's JSC . . .'

Tracing across the central screen, the shuttle's course arced eastward along its planned flight path. Jack was still tense, his heart racing. On the TV screens mounted above the gallery, images of the shuttle were being transmitted from

Kennedy. Communications between Capcom and shuttle commander Kittredge played on the speakers. *Discovery* had gone into its roll and was climbing into the upper reaches of the atmosphere, where blue sky would soon darken to the blackness of space.

'We're looking good,' said Gretchen over the media loop. In her voice they heard the triumph of a perfect launch. And so far it *was* perfect. Right through Max Q, through SRB sep, through main engine cutoff.

In the FCR, Flight Director Carpenter stood immobile, his gaze fixed on the front screen.

'*Discovery*, you are go for ET sep,' said Capcom.

'Roger, Houston,' said Kittredge. 'We have ET sep.'

It was the sudden jerking up of Carpenter's massive head that told Jack something had just changed. In the FCR, a flutter of activity seemed to animate all the flight controllers at once. Several of them glanced sideways at Carpenter, whose normally slouching shoulders had snapped up to attention. Gretchen had her hand pressed to her earpiece as she listened intently to the loop.

Something has gone wrong, thought Jack.

The air-to-ground loop continued to play on the gallery audio.

'*Discovery*,' said Capcom, 'MMACS reports umbilical doors have failed to close. Please confirm.'

'Roger that, and we confirm. The doors are not closing.'

'Suggest you go to manual command.'

There was an ominous silence. Then they heard Kittredge say, 'Houston, we're A-OK now. The doors have just closed.'

Only then, when Jack released a sharp breath, did he realize he'd been holding it. So far this was the only glitch. Everything else, he thought, is perfect. Yet the effects of that sudden surge of adrenaline still lingered, and his hands were sweating. They'd just been reminded of how many things can go wrong, and he could not shake off this new sense of uneasiness.

He stared down at the FCR and wondered if Randy Carpenter, the best of the best, felt the same sense of foreboding.

August 4

It was as though the clock in his brain had automatically reset itself, shifting his sleep and wake cycles so that his mind snapped to alertness at one A.M. Jack lay in bed, eyes wide open, the luminous glow of his nightstand clock staring back at him. Like the shuttle *Discovery*, he thought, I am racing to catch up with ISS. With Emma. Already his body was synchronizing itself to hers. In an hour, she would be waking up, and her workday would begin. And here was Jack, awake already, their rhythms in near parallel.

He did not try to go back to sleep, but rose and got dressed.

At one-thirty A.M., Mission Control was quietly humming with activity. He glanced first in the FCR, where the shuttle controllers sat. So far, no crises had occurred aboard *Discovery*.

He went down the hall to Special Vehicle Operations, the separate control room for ISS. It was much smaller than the shuttle's FCR, with its own array of consoles and personnel. Jack headed straight to the flight surgeon's console and sank into the chair next to Roy Bloomfeld, the physician on duty. Bloomfeld glanced at him with surprise.

'Hey, Jack. I guess you're really back in the program.'

'Couldn't stay away.'

'Well, it can't be the money. So it must be the thrill of the job.' He leaned back, yawning. 'Not many thrills tonight.'

'Patient's stable?'

'Has been for the last twelve hours.' Bloomfeld nodded

to the biotelemetry readings on his console. Kenichi Hirai's EKG and blood pressure readings blipped across the screen. 'Rhythm's steady as a rock.'

'No new developments?'

'Last status report was four hours ago. His headache's worse, and he still has that fever. Antibiotics don't seem to be doing much of anything. We're all scratching our heads over this one.'

'Does Emma have any ideas?'

'At this point, she's probably too exhausted to think. I told her to get some sleep, since we're watching the monitor anyway. So far, it's been pretty boring.' Bloomfeld yawned again. 'Listen, I gotta take a leak. Can you watch the console for a few minutes?'

'No problem.'

Bloomfeld left the room, and Jack slipped on the headset. It felt familiar and good to be sitting in front of a console again. To hear the muted conversation from the other controllers, to watch the front screen, where the station's orbital path traced a sine wave across the map. This might not be a seat on the shuttle, but it was as close as he could get to one. *I won't ever touch the stars, but I can be here to see that others do.* It was a startling revelation to him, that he had accepted that bitter twist in his life. That he could stand on the periphery of his old dream and still admire the view from afar.

His gaze suddenly focused on Kenichi Hirai's EKG, and he leaned forward. The heart tracing had shuddered up and down in a few rapid oscillations. Now it sketched a completely straight line across the top of the screen.

Jack relaxed. This was nothing to worry about; he recognized it as an electrical anomaly – probably a loose EKG lead. The blood pressure tracing continued across the screen, unchanged. Perhaps the patient had moved, accidentally

136

pulling off a lead. Or Emma had disconnected the monitor, to allow him to use the toilet in private. Now the blood pressure tracing abruptly cut off – another indication that Kenichi was off the monitors. He watched the screen for a moment longer, expecting the readings to reappear.

When they did not, he got on the loop.

'Capcom, this is Surgeon. I'm seeing a loose lead pattern on the patient's EKG.'

'Loose lead?'

'Looks like he's been disconnected from his monitor. There's no heart tracing coming across. Could you check with Emma to confirm?'

'Roger, Surgeon. I'll give her a jingle.'

A soft whine pulled Emma from a dreamless sleep, and she awakened to the cold kiss of moisture on her face. She had not intended to doze. Though Mission Control was continually monitoring Kenichi's EKG on biotelemetry and would alert her to any changes in his status, she had planned to stay awake throughout the crew's designated sleep period. But in the last two days, she had caught only brief snatches of rest, and those were often interrupted by her crewmates, waking her with questions about her patient's status. Exhaustion, and the utter relaxation of weightlessness, had finally caught up with her. Her last waking memory was of watching Kenichi's heart rhythm blip across the screen in a hypnotic squiggle, the line fading to a blur of green. To black.

Aware of the cold splash of water clinging to her cheek, she opened her eyes and saw a globule float toward her, twirling with a rainbow of reflections. It took her a few dazed seconds to understand what she was looking at, another few seconds to register the dozens of other globules dancing like silvery Christmas ornaments all around her.

Static, then a voice, crackled over her comm unit. 'Uh,

137

Watson, this is Capcom. We hate to wake you, but we need to confirm status of the patient's EKG leads.'

Hoarse with exhaustion, Emma replied, 'I'm awake, Capcom. I think.'

'Biotelemetry shows an anomaly on your patient's EKG. Surgeon thinks you've got a loose lead up there.'

She had been drifting, turning in midair while asleep, and now she reoriented herself in the module and turned to where her patient should be.

His sleep restraint bag was empty. The disconnected IV tube floated free, the catheter end releasing drops of glistening saline into the air. Loose electrode wires drifted in a tangle.

At once she shut off the infusion pump and quickly glanced around. 'Capcom, he's not here. He's left the module! Stand by.' She pushed off the wall, shot into Node 2, leading to the NASDA and ESA labs. A glance through the hatchways told her he was not there.

'Have you located him?' Capcom asked.

'Negative. I'm still looking.'

Had he become disoriented, wandered away in confusion? Backtracking through the U.S. lab, she shot through the node hatchway. A droplet splattered her face. She swiped at the pinpoint of moisture and was startled to see her finger was smeared with blood.

'Capcom, he's passed through Node One. Bleeding from his IV puncture site.'

'Recommend you shut off airflow between modules.'

'Roger that.' She glided through the hatchway of the hab module. The lights had been dimmed, and in the gloom, she saw Griggs and Luther, both sound asleep and zipped into their restraint bags. No Kenichi.

Don't panic, she thought as she shut off the intermodule airflow. *Think. Where would he go?*

Back to his own sleep station, at the Russian end of ISS.

Without waking Griggs or Luther, she left the hab and moved quickly into the tunnel of connecting nodes and modules, her gaze darting left and right in search of her fugitive patient. 'Capcom, I still haven't located him. I'm through Zarya and heading for the RSM.'

She slipped into the Russian service module, where Kenichi normally slept. In the gloom she saw Diana and Nicolai both asleep, floating as though drowned, their arms drifting free of their restraint bags. Kenichi's station was empty.

Her anxiety turned to real fear.

She gave Nicolai a shake. He was slow to awaken, and even after he opened his eyes, it took him a moment to understand what she was telling him.

'I can't find Kenichi,' she repeated. 'We need to search every module.'

'Watson,' said Capcom over her headset. 'Engineering reports intermittent anomaly in Node One air lock. Please check status.'

'What anomaly?'

'Off and on readings indicate the hatch between the equipment and crew locks may not be fully secure.'

Kenichi. He's in the air lock.

With Nicolai right behind her, she shot like a flying bird through the station and dove into Node 1. At her first frantic glance through the open hatch, into the equipment lock, Emma caught a startling glimpse of what looked like three bodies. Two were only the pair of EVA suits, the hard-shelled torsos mounted on the air lock walls for easy donning.

Hanging in midair, his body arched backward in a convulsive spasm, was Kenichi.

'Help me get him out of here!' said Emma. She maneuvered behind him and, bracing her feet against the outer hatch, shoved him toward Nicolai, who pulled him out of the air lock. Together, they propelled him toward the lab module, where the medical equipment had been set up.

'Capcom, we've located the patient,' said Emma. 'He appears to be seizing – grand mal. I need Surgeon on the loop!'

'Stand by, Watson. Go ahead, Surgeon.'

Emma heard a startlingly familiar voice over her headset. 'Hey, Em. Hear you've got yourself a problem up there.'

'*Jack?* What are you doing –'

'How's your patient?'

Still in a state of shock, she focused her attention on Kenichi. Even as she restarted the IV, attached EKG wires, she was wondering what Jack was doing in Mission Control. He had not sat at a flight surgeon's console in a year; now here he was on the comm loop, his voice calm, even casual, as he asked about Kenichi's status.

'Is he still seizing?'

'No. No, he's making purposeful movements now – fighting us –'

'Vital signs?'

'Pulse is rapid – one twenty, one thirty. He's moving air.'

'Good. So he's breathing.'

'We're just getting the EKG hooked up now.' She glanced at the monitor, at the cardiac rhythm racing across the screen. 'Sinus tach, rate of one twenty-four. Occasional PVCs.'

'I see it on biotelemetry.'

'Taking BP now . . .' She whiffed up the cuff, listened to the brachial pulse as the pressure was slowly released. 'Ninety-five over sixty. Not significantly –'

The blow caught her by surprise. She gave a sharp cry of pain as Kenichi's hand flailed out, striking her across the mouth. The impact spun her away, and she flew across the module, colliding with the opposite wall.

'Emma?' said Jack. '*Emma?*'

Dazed, she reached up to touch her throbbing lip.

'You're bleeding!' said Nicolai.

Over her headset, Jack's frantic voice demanded, 'What the hell is going on up there?'

'I'm okay,' she murmured. And repeated, irritably, 'I'm okay, Jack. Don't have a cow.'

But her head was still buzzing from the blow. As Nicolai strapped Kenichi to the patient restraint board, she hung back, waiting for her dizziness to pass. At first she did not register what Nicolai was saying.

Then she saw the look of disbelief in his eyes. 'Look at his stomach,' Nicolai whispered. '*Look!*'

Emma moved closer. 'What the hell is that?' she whispered.

'Talk to me, Emma,' said Jack. 'Tell me what's going on.'

She stared at Kenichi's abdomen, where the skin seemed to ripple and boil. 'There's something moving – under his skin –'

'What do you mean, moving?'

'It looks like muscle fasciculations. But it's migrating across the belly . . .'

'Not peristalsis?'

'No. No, it's moving *upwards*. It's not following the intestinal tract.' She paused. The squirming had suddenly stopped, and she was staring at the smooth, unworried surface of Kenichi's abdomen.

Fasciculations, she thought. The uncoordinated twitching of muscle fibers. It was the most likely explanation, except for one detail: Fasciculations do not migrate in waves.

Suddenly Kenichi's eyes shot open, and he stared at Emma.

The cardiac alarm squealed. Emma turned to see the EKG whipsawing up and down on the screen.

'V tach!' said Jack.

'I see it, I see it!' She flipped on the defibrillator charge button, then felt for a carotid pulse.

141

There it was. Faint, barely palpable.

His eyes had rolled up, and only the bloodred sclerae were visible. He was still breathing.

She slapped on defibrillator pads, positioned the paddles on the chest, and pressed the discharge buttons. An electric charge of one hundred joules shot through Kenichi's body.

His muscles contracted in a violent and simultaneous spasm. His legs thrashed against the board. Only the restraints kept him from flying across the module.

'Still in V tach!' said Emma.

Diana came flying into the module. 'What can I do?' she asked.

'Get the lidocaine ready!' snapped Emma. 'CDK drawer, right side!'

'Found it.'

'He's not breathing!' said Nicolai.

Emma grabbed the ambu-bag and said, 'Nicolai, brace me!'

He maneuvered into position, planting his feet on the opposite wall, his back pressed against Emma's to hold her in place as she applied the oxygen mask. On earth, performing cardiopulmonary resuscitation is demanding enough; in microgravity, it is a nightmare of complex acrobatics, with drifting equipment, tubes twisting and tangling in midair, syringes filled with precious drugs floating away. The simple act of pressing your hands against a patient's chest can send you tumbling across the room. Although the crew had practiced this scenario, no rehearsal could reproduce the genuine chaos of bodies frantically maneuvering in a closed space, racing against the clock of a dying heart.

With the mask over Kenichi's mouth and nose, she squeezed the ambu-bag, forcing oxygen into his lungs. The EKG line continued to thrash across the screen.

'One amp lidocaine IV push now,' said Diana.

'Nicolai, shock him again!' said Emma.

After the briefest hesitation, he reached for the paddles, placed them on the chest, and pressed the discharge buttons. This time two hundred joules arced through Kenichi's heart.

Emma glanced at the monitor. 'He's gone into V fib! Nicolai, start cardiac compressions. I'm going to intubate!'

Nicolai released the defib paddles, and they floated off, dangling at the ends of the wires. Bracing his feet against the opposite wall of the module, he was about to place his palms on Kenichi's sternum when he suddenly jerked his hands away.

Emma looked at him. 'What is it?'

'His chest. Look at his chest!'

They stared.

The skin on Kenichi's chest was boiling, squirming. At the contact points where the defib paddles had delivered their electric jolts, two raised circles had formed and were now spreading, like ripples cast by a stone in water.

'Asystole!' came Jack's voice over her headset.

Nicolai was still frozen, staring at Kenichi's chest.

It was Emma who swung into position, bracing her back against Nicolai's.

Asystole. The heart has stopped. He will die without cardiac compressions.

She felt nothing moving, nothing unusual. Just skin stretched over the bony landmarks of his breastbone. *Muscle fasciculations*, she thought. *It had to be. There's no other explanation.* With her body braced in position, she began chest compressions, her hands performing the work for Kenichi's heart, pumping blood to his vital organs.

'Diana, one amp IV epinephrine!' she ordered.

Diana injected the drug into the IV line.

They all looked at the monitor, hoping for, praying for, a blip on the screen.

11

'There has to be an autopsy,' said Todd Cutler.

Gordon Obie, director of Flight Crew Operations, flashed him an irritated look. Some of the others in the conference room gave Cutler dismissive nods as well, because he had merely stated the obvious. Of course there would be an autopsy.

Over a dozen people had gathered together for this crisis meeting. An autopsy was the least of their concerns. Right now, Obie was dealing with more urgent issues. Normally a man of few words, he'd suddenly found himself in the uncomfortable position of having reporters' microphones thrust at his face whenever he appeared in public. The excruciating process of assigning blame had begun.

Obie had to accept a portion of responsibility for this tragedy, because he had approved the choice of every member of the flight crew. If the crew screwed up, in essence, *he* had screwed up. And his choice of Emma Watson was starting to look like a major error.

That, at least, was the message he was hearing in this room. As the only physician aboard ISS Emma Watson should have realized Hirai was dying. An immediate CRV evac might

144

have saved him. Now a shuttle had been launched, and a multimillion-dollar rescue mission had turned into nothing more than a morgue run. Washington was hungry for scapegoats, and the foreign press was asking a politically incendiary question: Would an *American* astronaut have been allowed to die?

The PR fallout was, in fact, this meeting's major topic of discussion.

Gretchen Liu said, 'Senator Parish has gone on the record with a statement.'

JSC director Ken Blankenship groaned. 'I'm afraid to ask.'

'CNN-Atlanta faxed it over. And I quote: "Millions of tax dollars went into the development of the emergency Crew Return Vehicle. Yet NASA chose not to use it. They had a critically ill man up there whose life might have been saved. Now that courageous astronaut is dead, and it's apparent to everyone that a terrible mistake was made. One death in space is one death too many. A congressional inquiry is in order."' Gretchen looked up with a grim expression. 'Our favorite senator speaks.'

'I wonder how many people remember that he tried to kill our Crew Return Vehicle program?' said Blankenship. 'I'd love to rub that in his face right now.'

'You can't,' said Leroy Cornell. As NASA administrator, it was second nature for Cornell to weigh all the political ramifications. He was their link to Congress and the White House, and he never lost sight of how things would play out in Washington. 'You launch a direct attack on the senator, and things will really hit the fan.'

'He's attacking *us*.'

'That's nothing new, and everyone knows it.'

'The public doesn't,' said Gretchen. 'He's making headlines with these attacks.'

'That's the whole point – the senator wants headlines,'

145

said Cornell. 'We fire back, it'll feed the media beast. Look, Parish has never been our friend. He's fought every budget increase we've ever asked for. He wants to buy gunships, not spaceships, and we'll never change his mind.' Cornell took a deep breath and looked around the room. 'So we might as well take a good hard look at his criticism. And ask ourselves if it isn't justified.'

The room went momentarily silent.

'Obviously, mistakes were made,' said Blankenship. 'Errors in medical judgment. Why didn't we know how sick the man was?'

Obie saw an uneasy glance fly between the two flight surgeons. Everyone was now focused on the performance of the medical team. And on Emma Watson.

She wasn't here to defend herself; Obie would have to speak up for her.

Todd Cutler beat him to it. 'Watson's at a disadvantage up there. Any doctor would be,' he said. 'No X ray, no OR. The truth is, none of us know why Hirai died. That's why we need the autopsy. We have to know what went wrong. And whether microgravity was a contributing factor.'

'There's no question about an autopsy,' said Blankenship. 'Everyone's agreed on that point.'

'No, the reason I mention it is because of the . . .' Cutler dropped his voice, 'preservation problem.'

There was a pause. Obie saw gazes drop in uneasy contemplation of what that meant.

'The lack of refrigeration on the station is what he's talking about,' said Obie. 'Not for something as large as a human body. Not in a pressurized environment.'

ISS flight director Woody Ellis said, 'Shuttle rendezvous is in seventeen hours. How badly can the body deteriorate in that time?'

'There's no refrigeration aboard the shuttle either,' pointed

146

out Cutler. 'Death occurred seven hours ago. Add to that the time for rendezvous, the transfer of the corpse, as well as other cargo, and the undocking. We're talking at least three days with the body at room temperature. And that's if everything goes like clockwork. Which, as we all know, is not a given.'

Three days. Obie thought of what could happen to a dead body in two days. Of how badly raw chicken parts stank if he left them in his garbage can for just one night . . .

'You're saying *Discovery* can't delay her return home, even for an extra day?' said Ellis. 'We were hoping there'd be time for other tasks. There are numerous experiments on ISS ready to come home. Scientists on the ground are waiting for them.'

'An autopsy won't be of much help if the body's deteriorated,' said Cutler.

'Isn't there some way to preserve it? Embalm it?'

'Not without affecting its chemistry. We need an unembalmed body. And we need it home soon.'

Ellis sighed. 'There has to be a compromise. A way to get *something* else accomplished while they're docked.'

Gretchen said, 'From a PR point of view, it looks bad, going about your usual business while a corpse is stored in the middeck. Besides, isn't there some, well, health hazard? And then there's . . . the odor.'

'The body is sealed in a plastic shroud,' said Cutler. 'They can curtain it off out of view in a sleep station.'

The subject had turned so grim that most faces in the room were looking pale. They could talk about the political fallout and the media crisis. They could talk about hostile senators and mechanical anomalies. But dead bodies and bad smells and deteriorating flesh were not things they wanted to concentrate on.

Leroy Cornell finally broke the silence. 'I understand your sense of urgency about getting the body back for autopsy, Dr Cutler. And I understand the PR angle as well. The

147

seeming . . . lack of sensitivity if we go about our business. But there *are* things we have to do, even in light of our losses.' He looked around the table. 'That is our prime objective, isn't it? One of our strengths as an organization? No matter what goes wrong, no matter what we suffer, we always strive to get the job done?'

That's the moment Obie sensed the sudden shift of mood in the room. Up till then, they had been laboring under the pall of tragedy, the pressure of media attention. He had seen gloom and defeat in these faces, and defensiveness. Now the pall was lifting. He met Cornell's gaze and felt some of his old disdain toward the man fall away. Obie had never trusted smooth talkers like Cornell. He thought of NASA administrators as a necessary evil and tolerated them only as long as they kept their noses out of operational decisions.

At times, Cornell had strayed over that line. Today, though, he had done them a service by making them step back and view the big picture. Everyone had come to this meeting with his or her private concerns. Cutler wanted a fresh corpse to autopsy. Gretchen Liu wanted the right media spin. The shuttle management team wanted *Discovery*'s mission expanded.

Cornell had just reminded them that they had to look beyond this death, beyond their individual concerns, and focus on what was best for the space program.

Obie gave a small nod of agreement, which was noted by others at the table. The Sphinx had finally made his opinion known.

'Every successful launch is a gift from heaven,' he said. 'Let's not waste this one.'

August 5
Dead.

Emma's running shoes pounded rhythmically on the TVIS treadmill, and every slap of her soles against the moving belt,

148

every impact jolting her bones and joints and muscles, was another self-administered blow of punishment.

Dead.

I lost him. I fucked up and I lost him.

I should have realized how sick he was. I should have pushed for a CRV evac. But I delayed, because I thought I could handle it. I thought I could keep him alive.

Muscles aching, sweat beading on her forehead, she continued to punish herself, enraged by her own failure. She had not used the TVIS in three days because she'd been too busy tending to Kenichi. Now she was making up for it, had snapped on the side restraints, turned the treadmill to active mode, and started her run.

On earth she enjoyed running. She was not particularly fast, but she'd developed endurance and had learned to slip into that hypnotic trance that comes to long-distance runners as the miles melt away beneath their feet, as the burn of working muscles gives way to euphoria. Day after day she had worked to build up that endurance, had forced herself, through sheer stubbornness, to go longer, farther, always in competition with her last run, never cutting herself a break. It was the way she'd been since she was a girl, smaller than the others, but fiercer. All her life she had been fierce, but never more so than with herself.

I made mistakes. And now my patient's dead.

Sweat soaked through her shirt, a big wet blotch spreading between her breasts. Her calves and thighs were beyond the burn stage. The muscles were twitching, on the verge of collapse from the constant tension of the restraints.

A hand reached over and flicked off the TVIS power switch. The running belt abruptly shuddered to a halt. She glanced up and met Luther's gaze.

'I think that's more than enough, Watson,' he said quietly.

'Not yet.'

149

'You've been at it for more than three hours.'

'I'm just getting started,' she muttered grimly. She switched on the power, and once again her shoes pounded on the moving belt.

Luther watched her for a moment, his body floating at her eye level, his gaze unavoidable. She hated being studied, even hated *him* at that instant, because she thought he could see right through to her pain, her self-disgust.

'Wouldn't it be quicker just to smash your head against a wall?' he said.

'Quicker. But not painful enough.'

'I get it. To be punishment, it's gotta hurt, huh?'

'Right.'

'Would it make a difference if I told you this is bullshit? Because it is. It's a waste of energy. Kenichi died because he was sick.'

'That's where I'm supposed to come in.'

'And you couldn't save him. So now you're the corps fuckup, huh?'

'That's right.'

'Well, you're wrong. Because *I* claimed that title before you.'

'Is this some sort of contest?'

Again, he shut off the TVIS power. Again the treadmill belt ground to a halt. He was staring her right in the eye, his gaze angry. As fierce as hers.

'Remember *my* fuckup? On *Columbia*?'

She said nothing; she didn't have to. Everyone at NASA remembered it. It had happened four years ago, during a mission to repair an orbiting comm satellite. Luther had been the mission specialist responsible for redeploying the satellite after repairs were completed. The crew had ejected it from its cradle in the payload bay and watched it drift away. The rockets had ignited right on schedule, sending the satellite into its correct altitude.

Where it failed to respond to any commands. It was dead in orbit, a multimillion-dollar piece of junk uselessly circling the earth. Who was responsible for this calamity?

Almost immediately, the blame fell on the shoulders of Luther Ames. In his haste to deploy, he had forgotten to key in vital software codes – or so the private contractor claimed. Luther insisted he *had* keyed in the codes, that he was the scapegoat for mistakes made by the satellite's manufacturer. Though the public heard very little about the controversy, within NASA, the story was known by all. Luther's flight assignments dried up. He was condemned to the status of astronaut ghost, still in the corps, but invisible to those who chose shuttle crews.

Complicating the mess was the fact Luther was black.

For three years, he suffered in obscurity, his resentment mounting. Only the support of close friends among the other astronauts – Emma most of all – had kept him in the corps. He knew he'd made no mistakes, but few at NASA believed him. He knew people talked behind his back. Luther was the man the bigots pointed to as evidence minorities didn't have the 'right stuff.' He'd struggled to maintain his dignity, even as he'd felt despair closing in.

Then the truth came out. The satellite had been flawed. Luther Ames was officially absolved of blame. Within a week, Gordon Obie offered him a flight assignment: a four-month mission aboard ISS.

But even now, Luther felt the lingering stain on his reputation. He knew, only too painfully, what Emma was now going through.

He stuck his face right in front of hers, forcing her to look at him. 'You're not perfect, okay? We're all human.' He paused, and added dryly, 'With the possible exception of Diana Estes.'

Against her will, she laughed.

151

'Punishment over. Time to move on, Watson.'

Her respirations had returned to normal, even though her heart continued pounding, because she was still angry at herself. But Luther was right; she had to move on. It was time to deal with the aftermath of her mistakes. A final report still needed to be transmitted to Houston. Medical summary, clinical course. Diagnosis. Cause of death.

Doctor fuckup.

'*Discovery* docks in two hours,' said Luther. 'You've got work to do.'

After a moment, she nodded and unclipped the TVIS restraints. Time to get on with the job; the hearse was on its way.

August 7

The tethered corpse, sealed in its shroud, slowly spun in the gloom. Surrounded by the clutter of excess equipment and spare lithium canisters, Kenichi's body was like one more unneeded station part stowed away in the old *Soyuz* capsule. *Soyuz* had not been operational in over a year, and the station crew used its service compartment as excess storage space. It seemed a terrible indignity to keep Kenichi in here, but the crew had been shaken badly by his death. To be confronted repeatedly with his corpse, floating in one of the modules where they worked or slept, would have been too upsetting.

Emma turned to Commander Kittredge and Medical Officer O'Leary of the shuttle *Discovery*. 'I sealed the remains immediately after death,' she said. 'It hasn't been touched since.' She paused, her gaze returning to the corpse. The shroud was black, and small pouches of plastic billowed out, obscuring the human form within.

'The tubes are still in?' asked O'Leary.

'Yes. Two IVs, the endotracheal, and the NG.' She had

152

disturbed nothing; she knew the pathologists performing the autopsy would want everything left in place. 'You have all the blood cultures, all the specimens we collected from him. Everything.'

Kittredge gave a grim nod of the head. 'Let's do it.'

Emma unhooked the tether and reached for the corpse. It felt stiff, bloated, as though its tissues were already undergoing anaerobic decomposition. She refused to think about what Kenichi must look like beneath the layer of dark plastic.

It was a silent procession, as grim as a funeral cortege, the mourners floating like wraiths as they escorted the corpse through the long tunnel of modules. Kittredge and O'Leary led the way, gently guiding the body through hatchways. They were followed by Jill Hewitt and Andy Mercer, no one saying a word. When the orbiter had docked a day and a half ago, Kittredge and his crew had brought smiles and hugs, fresh apples and lemons, and a long-awaited copy of the Sunday *New York Times*. This was Emma's old team, the people she had trained with for a year, and seeing them again had been like having a bittersweet family reunion. Now the reunion was over, and the last item to be moved aboard *Discovery* was making its ghostly passage toward the docking module.

Kittredge and O'Leary floated the corpse through the hatchway and into *Discovery*'s middeck. Here, where the shuttle crew slept and ate, was where the body would be stowed until landing. O'Leary maneuvered it into one of the horizontal sleep pallets. Prior to launch, the pallet had been reconfigured to serve as a medical station for the ailing patient. Now it would be used as a temporary coffin for the returning corpse.

'It's not going in,' said O'Leary. 'I think the body's too distended. Was it exposed to heat?' He looked at Emma.

'No. *Soyuz* temperature was maintained.'

'Here's your problem,' said Jill. 'The shroud's snagged on the vent.' She reached in and freed the plastic. 'Try it now.'

This time the corpse fit. O'Leary slid the panel shut so no one would have to look at the pallet's occupant.

There followed a solemn ceremony of farewell between the two crews. Kittredge pulled Emma into a hug and whispered, 'Next mission, Watson, you're my first choice.' When they separated, she was crying.

It ended with the traditional handshake between the two commanders, Kittredge and Griggs. Emma caught one last glimpse of the orbiter crew – *her* crew – waving good-bye, and then the hatches swung shut. Though *Discovery* would remain attached to ISS for another twenty-four hours while its crew rested and prepared for the undocking, the closing of those airtight hatches effectively ended all human contact between them. They were once again separate vehicles, temporarily attached, like two dragonflies hurtling together in a mating dance through space.

Pilot Jill Hewitt was having trouble getting to sleep.

Insomnia was new to her. Even on the night before a launch, she could manage to drop off cleanly into a deep sleep, trusting in a lifetime of good luck to carry her through the next day. It was a point of pride for her that she'd never needed a sleeping pill. Pills were for nervous Nellies who fretted about a thousand awful possibilities. For the neurotics and obsessives. As a naval pilot, Jill had known more than her share of mortal danger. She'd flown missions over Iraq, had landed a crippled jet on a heaving carrier, had ejected into a stormy sea. She figured she'd cheated Death so many times that surely he'd given up on her and gone home in defeat. And so she usually slept just fine at night.

But tonight, sleep was not coming. It was because of the corpse.

No one wanted to be near it. Though the privacy panel was shut, concealing the body, they all felt its presence. Death shared their living space, cast its shadow over their evening meal, stifled their usual jokes. It was the unwanted fifth member of their crew.

As though to escape it, Kittredge, O'Leary, and Mercer had abandoned their usual sleep stations and had moved up to the flight deck. Only Jill remained on the middeck, as though to prove to the men that she was less squeamish than they were, that she, a woman, wasn't bothered by a corpse.

But now, with the cabin lights dimmed, she found that sleep was eluding her. She kept thinking about what lay beyond that closed-off panel. About Kenichi Hirai, when he was alive.

She remembered him quite vividly as pale and soft-spoken, with black hair stiff as wire. Once, in weightlessness training, she had brushed against his hair and had been surprised by its boarlike bristliness. She wondered what he looked like now. She felt a sudden, sickening curiosity about what had become of his face, what changes Death had wrought. It was the same curiosity that used to compel her, as a child, to poke twigs into the corpses of the dead animals she sometimes encountered in the woods.

She decided to move further away from the body.

She brought her sleep restraint bag to the port side and anchored it behind the flight-deck access ladder. It was as far away as she could get, yet still be on the same deck. Once again she zipped herself into the bag. Tomorrow she would need every reflex, every brain cell, to be operating at peak performance for reentry and landing. Through sheer strength of will, she forced herself into a deepening trance.

She was asleep when the swirl of iridescent liquid began to seep through Kenichi Hirai's shroud.

* * *

155

It had begun with a few glistening droplets oozing through a tiny rent in the plastic, torn open when the shroud had snagged. For hours the pressure had been building, the plastic slowly inflating as the contents swelled. Now the breach widened, and a shimmering ribbon streamed out. Escaping through the pallet ventilation holes, the ribbon broke apart into blue-green droplets that briefly danced in weightless abandon before recongealing into large globules that undulated in the dimly lit cabin. The opalescent fluid continued to spill forth. The globules spread, riding the gentle currents of circulating air. Drifting across the cabin, they found their way to the limp form of Jill Hewitt, who slept unaware of the shimmering cloud enveloping her, unaware of the mist she inhaled with every soft breath or of the droplets that settled like condensation on her face. Only briefly did she stir, to brush the tickle on her cheek as the opalescent drops slid toward her eye.

Rising with the air currents, the dancing droplets passed through the opening of the interdeck access and began to spread through the gloom of the flight deck, where three men drifted in the utter relaxation of weightless sleep.

12

August 8

The ominous swirl had begun to take shape over the eastern Caribbean days before. It had started as a short wave trough aloft, a gentle undulation of clouds formed from the evaporated waters of the sun-baked equatorial sea. Butting up against a bank of cooler air from the north, the clouds had begun to rotate, spinning around a calm eye of dry air. Now it was a definite spiral that seemed to grow with every new image transmitted by the geostationary GOES weather satellite. The NOAA National Weather Service had been tracking it since its birth, had watched as it meandered, directionless, off the eastern end of Cuba. Now the newest buoy data was coming in, with measurements of temperature, wind speed and direction. This data reinforced what the meteorologists were now seeing on their computer screens.

It was a tropical storm. And it was moving northwest, toward the tip of Florida.

This was the sort of news shuttle flight director Randy Carpenter dreaded. They could tinker with engineering problems. They could troubleshoot multiple systems failures. But against the forces of Mother Nature, they were helpless. The primary concern of this morning's mission management team meeting was a go-no-go decision on deorbit, and they had planned for shuttle undocking and deorbit burn in six hours' time. The weather briefing changed everything.

'NOAA Spaceflight Meteorology Group reports the tropical storm is moving north-northwest, bearing toward the Florida Keys,' said the forecaster. 'Radar from Patrick Air Force Base and NexRad Doppler from the National Weather Service in Melbourne show radial wind velocities of up to sixty-five knots, with intensifying rain. Rawinsonde balloon and Jimsphere balloon both confirm. Also, both the Field Mill network around Canaveral as well as LDAR show increasing lightning activity. These conditions will probably continue for the next forty-eight hours. Possibly longer.'

'In other words,' said Carpenter, 'we're not landing at Kennedy.'

'Kennedy is definitely out. At least for the next three to four days.'

Carpenter sighed. 'Okay, we sorta guessed that was coming. Let's hear about Edwards.'

Edwards Air Force Base, tucked into a valley east of the Sierra Nevada in California, was not their first choice. A landing at Edwards delayed shuttle processing and turnaround for the next mission because the shuttle would have to be transported back to Kennedy, piggybacked to a 747.

'Unfortunately,' said the forecaster, 'there's a problem with Edwards as well.'

A knot had formed in Carpenter's stomach. A premonition that this was the beginning of a bad chain of events. As lead shuttle flight director, he had made it his personal mission to review every mishap on record and analyze what had gone wrong. With the advantage of hindsight, he could usually trace the problem backward, through a succession of bad but seemingly innocuous decisions. Sometimes it started back at the factory with a distracted technician, a miswired panel. Hell, even something as big and expensive as the Hubble Telescope lens had started off screwed up from the very beginning.

Now he could not shake off the feeling that he would later think back to this very meeting and ask himself, *What should I have done differently? What could I have done to prevent a catastrophe?*

He asked, 'What are the conditions at Edwards?'

'Currently they're looking at a cloud ceiling at seven thousand feet.'

'That's an automatic no-go.'

'Right. So much for sunny California. But there's the possibility of partial clearing within the next twenty-four to thirty-six hours. We might have reasonable landing conditions if we just wait it out. Otherwise, it's off to New Mexico we go. I just checked the MIDDS, and White Sands looks good. Clear skies, head winds at five to ten knots. No adverse weather forecast.'

'So it's down to a choice,' said Carpenter. 'Wait till Edwards clears up. Or go for White Sands.' He looked around the room at the rest of the team, seeking opinions.

One of the program managers said, 'They're fine up there right now. We could leave them docked to ISS as long as we need to, until the weather cooperates. I don't see the necessity of rushing them home to a less than optimal site.'

Less than optimal was an understatement. White Sands was little more than an isolated landing strip equipped with heading alignment cylinders.

'There's the matter of getting the corpse back as soon as possible,' said Todd Cutler. 'While an autopsy's still useful.'

'We're all aware of that,' said the program manager. 'But weigh it against the negatives. White Sands is limited. Civilian medical backup just isn't there, if we have any problems on landing. In fact, all things considered, I'd suggest we wait it out even longer, till Kennedy's clear. Logistically, it's the best thing for the program. Quicker orbiter turnaround, get her right back on the pad for the next mission. In the meantime, the flight crew can use ISS as a hotel for the next few days.'

Several other program managers nodded. They were all taking the most conservative approach. The crew was safe where they were; the urgency of bringing home Hirai's corpse paled in light of all the problems of a White Sands landing. Carpenter thought of all the ways he could be second-guessed should there, God forbid, be a catastrophic landing at White Sands. He thought of the questions *he* would ask, were he reviewing the decisions of another flight director. *Why didn't you wait out the weather? Why did you hurry them home?*

The right decision was the one that minimized risk, yet met mission goals.

He decided to choose the middle ground.

'Three days is stretching it out too long,' he said. 'So Kennedy's out. Let's go for Edwards. Maybe we'll get clear skies tomorrow.' He looked at the forecaster. 'Make those clouds go away.'

'Sure. I'll just do a reverse rain dance.'

Carpenter glanced at the wall clock. 'Okay, crew's wake-up call is in four hours. We'll give 'em the news then. They can't come home quite yet.'

August 9

Jill Hewitt woke up gasping. Her first conscious thought was that she was drowning, that with every breath, she was inhaling water.

She opened her eyes, and with her first panicked glance saw what looked like a swarm of jellyfish drifting around her. She coughed, at last managed to draw in a deep breath,

160

and coughed again. The sharply expelled air sent all the jellyfish tumbling away.

She scrambled out of her restraint bag and turned up the cabin lights. In amazement she stared at the shimmering air.

'Bob!' she yelled. 'We've got a spill!'

She heard O'Leary say, up on flight deck, 'Jesus, what the hell is *this*?'

'Get out the masks!' ordered Kittredge. 'Until we know this isn't toxic.'

Jill opened the emergency locker, pulled out the contaminant-protection kit, and tossed masks and goggles to Kittredge, O'Leary, and Mercer as they came diving down the access opening into middeck. There'd been no time to get dressed; everyone was still in their underwear, still shaking off sleep.

Now, with their masks on, they stared at the blue-green globules drifting around them.

Mercer reached out and captured one in his hand. 'Weird,' he said, rubbing it between his fingers. 'It feels thick. Slimy. Like some sort of mucus.'

Now O'Leary, the medical officer, caught one and held it up to his goggles for a closer look. 'It's not even liquid.'

'Looks to me like a liquid,' said Jill. 'It behaves like one.'

'But it's more gelatinous. Almost like –'

They all gave a start as loud music abruptly blared out. It was Elvis Presley's velvet voice singing 'Blue Suede Shoes.' Their morning wake-up call from Mission Control.

'And a good mornin' to you, *Discovery*,' came Capcom's cheery voice. 'Time to rise and shine, folks!'

Kittredge responded, 'Capcom, we're already awake. We've, uh, got ourselves a strange situation up here.'

'Situation?'

'We have some sort of spill in the cabin. We're trying to identify it. It's a viscous substance. Sort of a milky blue-green.

161

Almost looks like little opals floating around. It's already spread to both decks.'

'You guys wearing your masks?'

'Affirmative.'

'You know where it's coming from?'

'Not a clue.'

'Okay, we're consulting ECLSS right now. They may have an idea what it is.'

'Whatever it is, it doesn't seem to be toxic. We've all been asleep with this stuff hanging in the air. None of us seems to be sick.' Kittredge glanced around at his masked crew, and they all shook their heads.

'Is there any odor to the spill?' asked Capcom. 'ECLSS wants to know if it could be from the waste collection system.'

Suddenly Jill felt queasy. Was this stuff they'd been breathing in, swimming in, leaked toilet waste?

'Uh – I guess one of us has to take a sniff,' said Kittredge. He looked around at his crew, who merely stared back. 'Gee, guys, don't all volunteer at once,' he muttered, and finally lifted his mask. He smeared a globule between his fingers and took a whiff. 'I don't think this is sewage. It doesn't smell chemical, either. At least, not petroleum-based.'

'What does it smell like?' asked Capcom.

'Sort of . . . fishy. Like the slime off a trout. Something from the galley, maybe?'

'Or it could be leakage from one of the life-science payloads. You're carrying a few experiments back from ISS. Aren't there aquarium enclosures onboard?'

'This stuff does sort of remind me of frog eggs. We'll inspect the enclosures,' said Kittredge. He looked around the cabin, at the glistening clumps adhering to the walls. 'It's landing on everything now. We're gonna be cleaning up the splatters for a while. It'll set back our reentry.'

'Uh, *Discovery*, I hate to break the news,' said Capcom.

'But reentry's going to be delayed in any event. You'll have to sit tight.'

'What's the problem?'

'We've got some weather down here. Kennedy's looking at crosswinds of up to forty knots, with thunderstorm anvils in the vicinity. Tropical storm's moving in from the southeast. She's already made a mess of the Dominican Republic, and she's headed for the Keys.'

'What about Edwards?'

'They're currently reporting a seven-thousand-foot cloud ceiling. It should clear up in the next two days. So unless you guys are anxious to land at White Sands, we're looking at a delay of at least thirty-six hours. We may have you reopen the hatches and join the crew on ISS again.'

Kittredge eyed the globules drifting by. 'Negative on that, Capcom. We'd contaminate the station with this spill. We've gotta get things cleaned up.'

'Roger that. Surgeon is standing by here, wants to confirm that your crew is experiencing no adverse effects. Is that correct?'

'The spill appears harmless. No one's showing any signs of illness.' He batted away a clump of globules, and they went spinning off like scattered pearls. 'They're really kind of pretty. But I hate to think of them gunking up our electronics, so we'd better get cracking on cleanup detail.'

'We'll update you on the weather as it changes, *Discovery*. Now get out those mops and buckets.'

'Yeah,' laughed Kittredge. 'Just call us the sky-high cleaning service. We even do windows.' He pulled off his mask. 'I guess it's safe to take 'em off.'

Jill took off her mask and goggles and glided across to the emergency locker. She had just stowed the equipment when she found Mercer staring at her.

'What?' she said.

'Your eye – what happened to it?'

'What's wrong with my eye?'

'You'd better take a look.'

She floated across to the hygiene station. Her first glimpse in the mirror was shocking. The sclera of one of her eyes was blood red. Not merely streaked, but a solid crimson.

'Jesus,' she murmured, horrified by her own reflection. *I'm a pilot. I need my eyes. And one of them looks like a bag of blood.*

O'Leary turned her around by the shoulders and examined her eye. 'It's nothing to worry about, okay?' he said. 'It's just a scleral hemorrhage.'

'Just?'

'A small bleed into the white of your eye. It looks more serious than it is. It'll clear up without any effect on your vision.'

'How did I get it?'

'Sudden changes in intracranial pressure can do it. Sometimes a violent cough or heavy vomiting is all it takes to pop a tiny vessel.'

She gave a relieved sigh. 'That must be it. I woke up coughing on one of those floating goombahs.'

'See? Nothing to worry about.' He gave her a pat. 'That'll be fifty bucks. Next patient!'

Reassured, Jill turned back to the mirror. *It's merely a small bleed*, she thought. *Nothing to worry about.* But the image staring back horrified her. One normal eye, one eye an evil and brilliant red. Something alien. Satanic.

August 10

'They're the houseguests from hell,' said Luther. 'We shut the door on 'em and they still refuse to leave.'

Everyone in the galley laughed, even Emma. In the last few days there had not been much in the way of humor

164

aboard ISS, and it was a relief to hear people joking again. Since they'd transferred Kenichi's corpse to *Discovery*, everyone's mood seemed brighter. His shrouded body had been a grim and constant reminder of death, and Emma was relieved she no longer had to confront the evidence of her own failure. She could focus, once again, on her work.

She could even laugh at Luther's crack, although the subject of his humor – the orbiter's failure to depart – was not, in fact, very funny. It complicated their day. They had expected *Discovery* to undock early yesterday morning. Now it was a day later, and she was still mated and could not leave for at least the next twelve hours. Her uncertain departure time threw the station's work schedule into uncertainty as well. Undocking was more than just a simple matter of the orbiter detaching itself and flying away. It was a delicate dance between two massive objects hurtling at 17,500 miles per hour, and it required the cooperation of both the orbiter and ISS crews. During undocking, the space station's control software had to be temporarily reconfigured for proximity operations, and its crew suspended many of its research activities. Everyone had to be focused on the orbiter's departure.

On avoiding calamity.

Now a cloudy day over an air force base in California had delayed everything, wreaking havoc on the space station's work schedule. But this was the nature of spaceflight; the only thing predictable about it was the unpredictable.

An alarming blob of grape juice came floating by Emma's head. And here was more unpredictability, she thought, laughing, as a sheepish Luther went chasing after it with a straw. You let your attention wander for just an instant, and there goes a vital tool or a sip's worth of juice drifting away. Without gravity, an unrestrained object could end up anywhere.

This was something the crew of *Discovery* was now

confronting. 'We had glops of this stuff land all over our aft DAP controls,' she heard Kittredge say over the radio. *Discovery*'s commander was conversing with Griggs on the space-to-space subsystem. 'We're still trying to clean off the toggle switches, but it's like thick mucus when it dries. I just hope it hasn't plugged up any data ports.'

'You find out where it's coming from?' asked Griggs.

'We found a small crack in the toadfish enclosure. But it doesn't look like much leaked out – not enough to account for what's flying around the cabin.'

'Where else could it be coming from?'

'We're checking the galley and commode now. We've been so busy cleaning up, we haven't had a chance to identify the source. I just can't figure out what this stuff is. It sort of reminds me of frog eggs. Round clumps, in this sticky green mass. You should see my crew – it's like they've been slimed on *Ghostbusters*. And then Hewitt's got this evil red eye. Man, we're scary looking.'

Evil red eye? Emma turned to Griggs. 'What's wrong with Hewitt's eye?' she said. 'I didn't hear about it.'

Griggs relayed the question to *Discovery*.

'It's just a scleral bleed,' answered Kittredge. 'Nothing serious, according to O'Leary.'

'Let me talk to Kittredge,' said Emma.

'Go ahead.'

'Bob, this is Emma,' she said. 'How did Jill get that scleral bleed?'

'She woke up coughing yesterday. We think that's what did it.'

'Is she having any abdominal pains? Headaches?'

'She did complain of a headache a little while ago. And we've all got muscle aches. But we've been working like dogs here.'

'Nausea? Vomiting?'

'Mercer's got an upset stomach. Why?'

'Kenichi had a scleral bleed too.'

'But that's not a serious condition,' said Kittredge. 'That's what O'Leary says.'

'No, it's the *cluster* of symptoms that concerns me,' said Emma. 'Kenichi's illness started with vomiting and a scleral hemorrhage. Abdominal pains. A headache.'

'Are you saying this is some sort of contagion? Then why aren't *you* sick? You took care of him.'

A good question. She couldn't answer that.

'What disease are we talking about?' asked Kittredge.

'I don't know. I do know Kenichi was incapacitated within a day of his first symptoms. You guys need to undock and go home now. Before anyone on *Discovery* gets sick.'

'No can do. Edwards is still under clouds.'

'Then White Sands.'

'Not a good option right now. They've got a problem with one of their TACANs. Hey, we're doing fine. We'll just wait out the weather. It shouldn't be more than another twenty-four hours.'

Emma looked at Griggs. 'I want to talk to Houston.'

'They're not going to head for White Sands just because Hewitt's got a red eye.'

'It could be more than just a scleral hemorrhage.'

'How would they catch Kenichi's illness? They weren't exposed to him.'

The corpse, she thought. *His corpse is on the orbiter.*

'Bob,' she said. 'This is Emma again. I want you to check the shroud.'

'What?'

'Check Kenichi's shroud for a breach.'

'You saw for yourself it's sealed tight.'

'Are you sure it still is?'

167

'Okay,' he sighed. 'I have to admit, we haven't checked the body since it came aboard. I guess we were all a little creeped-out about it. We've kept the pallet panel closed so we wouldn't have to look at him.'

'How does the shroud look?'

'I'm trying to get the panel open now. It seems to be sticking a little, but . . .' There was a silence. Then a murmured 'Jesus.'

'Bob?'

'The spill's coming from the shroud!'

'What is it? Blood, serum?'

'There's a tear in the plastic. I can see it leaking out!'

What was leaking out?

She heard other voices in the background. Loud groans of disgust, and the sound of someone retching.

'Seal it off. *Seal it off!*' said Emma. But they didn't answer.

Jill Hewitt said, 'His body feels like mush. As if he's . . . *dissolving*. We should find out what's happening to it.'

'*No!*' cried Emma. '*Discovery*, do *not* open the shroud!'

To her relief, Kittredge finally responded, 'Roger that, Watson. O'Leary, seal it up. We're not going to let any more of . . . that stuff . . . leak out.'

'Maybe we should jettison the body,' said Jill.

'No,' Kittredge answered. 'They want it for autopsy.'

'What sort of fluid is it?' asked Emma. 'Bob, answer me!'

There was a silence. Then he said, 'I don't know. But whatever it is, I hope it's not infectious. Because we've all been exposed.'

Twenty-eight pounds of flab and fur. That was Humphrey, sprawled like a fat pasha on Jack's chest. *This cat is trying to murder me*, thought Jack, staring up into Humphrey's malevolent green eyes. He'd fallen asleep on the couch, and the next thing he knew, a ton of kitty lard was crushing his ribs, squeezing the air out of his lungs.

Purring, Humphrey sank a claw into Jack's chest.

With a yelp, Jack shoved him away, and Humphrey landed on all fours with a ponderous thump.

'Go catch a mouse,' Jack muttered, and turned on his side to resume his nap, but it was hopeless. Humphrey was yowling to be fed. Again. Yawning, Jack dragged himself off the couch and stumbled into the kitchen. As soon as he opened the cupboard where the cat food was stored, Humphrey began to yowl louder. Jack filled the cat bowl with Little Friskies and stood watching in disgust as his nemesis chowed down. It was only three in the afternoon, and Jack had not yet caught up on his sleep. He'd been awake all night, manning the surgeon's console in the space station control room, and then had come home and settled on the couch to review the ECLSS subsystems for the space station. He was back in the game, and it felt good. It even felt good to wade through a bone-dry MOD training manual. But fatigue had finally caught up with him, and he'd dropped off to sleep around noon, surrounded by stacks of flight manuals.

Humphrey's bowl was already half empty. Unbelievable.

As Jack turned to leave the kitchen, the phone rang.

It was Todd Cutler. 'We're rounding up medical personnel to meet *Discovery* at White Sands,' he said. 'The plane's leaving Ellington in thirty minutes.'

'Why White Sands? I thought *Discovery* was going to wait for Edwards to clear up.'

'We've got a medical situation on board, and we can't wait for the weather to clear. They're going to deorbit in an hour. Plan on infectious precautions.'

'What's the infection?'

'Not yet identified. We're just playing it safe. Are you with us?'

'Yeah, I'm with you,' said Jack, without an instant's hesitation.

'Then you'd better get moving or you'll miss the plane.'

'Wait. Who's the patient? Which one's sick?'

'They all are,' said Cutler. 'The entire crew.'

13

Infectious precautions. Emergency deorbit. What are we dealing with?

The wind was blowing, kicking up dust as Jack trotted across the tarmac toward the waiting jet. Squinting against flying grit, he climbed the steps and ducked into the aircraft. It was a Gulfstream IV seating fifteen passengers, one of a fleet of sturdy and reliable workhorses that NASA used to shuttle personnel between its many far-flung centers of operation. There were already a dozen people aboard, including a number of nurses and doctors from the Flight Medicine Clinic. Several of them gave Jack waves of greeting.

'We've got to get going, sir,' said the copilot. 'So if you could buckle right in.'

Jack took a window seat near the front of the plane.

Roy Bloomfeld was the last to step aboard, his bright red hair stiff from the wind. As soon as Bloomfeld took his seat, the copilot closed the hatch.

'Todd isn't coming?' asked Jack.

'He's manning the console for landing. Looks like we're gonna be the shock troops.'

171

The plane began to taxi out onto the runway. They could waste no time; it was an hour-and-a-half flight to White Sands.

'You know what's going on?' Jack asked. 'Cause I'm in the dark.'

'I got a brief rundown. You know that spill they had on *Discovery* yesterday? The one they've been trying to identify? Turns out it was fluids leaking from Kenichi Hirai's body bag.'

'That bag was sealed tight. How did it leak?'

'Tear in the plastic. The crew says the contents seem to be under pressure. Some sort of advanced decomposition going on.'

'Kittredge described the fluid as green and only mildly fishy smelling. That hardly sounds like fluid from a decomposing corpse.'

'We're all puzzled. The bag's been resealed. We'll have to wait till they land to find out what's going on inside. It's the first time we've dealt with human remains in microgravity. Maybe there's something different about the process of decomposition. Maybe the anaerobic bacteria die off, and that's why it's not giving off foul odors.'

'How sick is the crew?'

'Both Hewitt and Kittredge are complaining of severe headaches. Mercer's throwing up like a dog now, and O'Leary's got abdominal pain. We're not sure how much of it is psychological. There's gotta be an emotional reaction when you've been gulping in a decomposing colleague.'

Psychological factors certainly complicated the picture. Whenever there is an outbreak of food poisoning, a significant percentage of victims are, in fact, uninfected. The power of suggestion is so strong it can produce vomiting as severe as any real illness.

'They had to put off the undocking. White Sands has been

172

having problems too – one of their TACANs was transmitting erroneous signals. They needed a few hours to get it up and functioning again.'

The TACAN, or tactical air navigation locating system, was a series of ground transmitters that provided the orbiter with updates on its navigation-state vector. A bad TACAN signal could cause the shuttle to miss the runway entirely.

'Now they've decided they can't wait,' said Bloomfeld. 'In just the last hour, the crew's gotten sicker. Kittredge and Hewitt *both* have scleral hemorrhages. That's how it started with Hirai.'

Their plane began its takeoff roll. The roar of the engines filled their ears, and the ground dropped away.

Jack yelled over the noise, 'What about ISS? Is anyone sick on the station?'

'No. They kept the hatches closed between vehicles to contain the spill.'

'So it's confined to *Discovery?*'

'So far as we know.'

Then Emma's okay, he thought, releasing a deep breath. *Emma's safe.* But if a contagion had been brought aboard *Discovery* inside Hirai's corpse, why wasn't the space station crew infected as well?

'What's the shuttle's ETA?' he asked.

'They're undocking now. Burn target's in forty-five minutes, and touchdown should be around seventeen hundred.'

Which didn't give the ground crew much time to prepare. He stared out the window as they broke through the clouds into a golden bath of sunlight. *Everything is working against us*, he thought. *An emergency landing. A broken TACAN shack. A sick crew.*

And it will all come together on a runway in the middle of nowhere.

* * *

Jill Hewitt's head hurt, and her eyeballs were aching so badly she could barely focus on the undocking checklist. In just the last hour pain had crept into every muscle of her body, and now it felt as if jagged bolts were ripping through her back, her thighs. Both her sclerae had turned red; so had Kittredge's. His eyeballs looked like twin bags of blood. Glowing. Red. He was in pain too; she could see it in the way he moved, the slow and guarded turning of his head. They were both in agony, yet neither of them dared accept an injection of narcotics. Undocking and landing required peak alertness, and they could not risk losing even the slightest edge of performance.

Get us home. Get us home. That was the mantra that kept running through Jill's head as she struggled to stay on task, as sweat drenched her shirt and the pain ate into her concentration.

They were racing through the departure checklist. She had plugged the IBM ThinkPad's computer cable into the aft console data port, booted up, and opened the Rendezvous and Proximity Operations program.

'There's no data flow,' she said.

'What?'

'The port must be gunked up by the spill. I'll try the middeck PCMMU.' She unplugged the cable. Every bone in her face screamed with pain as she made her way through the interdeck access, carrying the ThinkPad. Her eyes were throbbing so badly they felt as if they were about to pop out of their sockets. Down on middeck, she saw Mercer was already dressed in his launch-and-entry suit and strapped in for reentry. He was unconscious – probably from the dose of narcotics. O'Leary, also strapped in, was still awake but looking dazed. Jill floated across to the middeck data port and plugged in the ThinkPad.

Still no data stream.

'Shit. *Shit.*'

Now struggling to focus, she made her way back to the flight deck.

'No luck?' said Kittredge.

'I'll change out the source cable and try this port again.' Her head was pounding so badly now it brought tears to her eyes. Teeth gritted, she pulled out the cable, replaced it with a new one. Rebooted. From Windows, she opened RPOP.

The *Rendezvous and Proximity Operations* logo appeared on the screen.

Sweat broke out on her upper lip as she began to type in the mission elapsed time. Days, hours, minutes, seconds. Her fingers weren't obeying as they should. They were sluggish, clumsy. She had to back up to correct the numbers. At last she selected 'Prox Ops' and clicked on 'OK.'

'RPOP initialized,' she said with relief. 'Ready to process data.'

Kittredge said, 'Capcom, are we go for sep?'

'Stand by, *Discovery.*'

The wait was excruciating. Jill looked down at her hand and saw that her fingers had started to twitch, that the muscles of her forearm were contracting like a dozen writhing worms beneath the skin. As if something alive were tunneling through her flesh. She fought to keep her hand steady, but her fingers kept twitching in electric spasms. *Get us home now. While we can still fly this bird.*

'*Discovery,*' said Capcom. 'You are a go for undocking.'

'Roger that. Digital autopilot on low Z. Go for undocking.' Kittredge shot Jill a look of profound relief. 'Now let's get the hell home,' he muttered, and grasped the hand controls.

Flight Director Randy Carpenter stood like the statue of Colossus, his gaze fixed on the front screen, his engineer's brain coolly monitoring simultaneous streams of visual data and loop conversations. As always, Carpenter was thinking several steps ahead. The docking base was now depressurized. The latches connecting the orbiter to ISS would unhook, and preloaded springs in the docking system would gently push the two vehicles apart, causing them to free drift away from each other. Only when they were two feet apart would *Discovery*'s RCS jets be turned on to steer the orbiter away. At any point in this delicate sequence of events, things could go wrong, but for every possible failure, Carpenter had a contingency plan. If the docking latches failed to unhook, they'd fire pyrotechnic charges and shear off the latch retention bolts. If that failed, two crew members from ISS could perform an EVA and manually remove the bolts. They had backup plans for backup plans, a contingency for every failure.

At least, every failure they could predict. What Carpenter dreaded was the glitch that no one had thought about. And now he asked himself the same question he always did at the beginning of a new mission phase: *What have we failed to anticipate?*

'ODS has successfully disengaged,' he heard Kittredge announce. 'Latches have released. We're now in free drift.'

The flight controller beside Carpenter gave a little punch of triumph in the air.

Carpenter thought ahead, to the landing. The weather at White Sands was holding steady, head winds at fifteen knots. The TACAN would be up and operational in time for the shuttle's arrival. Ground crews were at this moment converging on the runway. There were no new glitches in sight, yet he knew one had to be waiting just around the corner.

All this was going through his mind, but not a flicker of expression crossed his face. Not a hint to any of the flight controllers in the room that he was feeling dread, as sour as bile, in his throat.

Aboard ISS, Emma and her crewmates also watched and waited. All research activities were at a temporary standstill. They had gathered at the Node 1 cupola to look at the massive shuttle as it undocked. Griggs was also monitoring the operation on an IBM ThinkPad, which showed the same RPOP wireframe display that Houston's Mission Control was now looking at.

Through the cupola windows, Emma saw *Discovery* begin to inch away, and she gave a sigh of relief. The orbiter was now in free drift, and on its way home.

Medical Officer O'Leary floated in a narcotic daze. He'd injected fifty milligrams of Demerol into his own arm, just enough to take the edge off his pain, to allow him to strap in Mercer, to prepare the cabin for reentry. Even that small dose of narcotic was clouding his mental processes.

He sat strapped in his middeck seat, ready for deorbit. The cabin seemed to drift in and out of focus, as though he were seeing it underwater. The light hurt his eyes, and he closed them. Moments ago, he thought he'd seen Jill Hewitt float past with the ThinkPad; now she was gone, but he could hear her strained voice over his headset, along with Kittredge's and Capcom's. They had undocked.

Even in his mental fog, he felt a sense of impotence, of shame, that he was strapped into his seat like an invalid while his crewmates up on flight deck were laboring to get them home. Pride made him fight his way back from the comfortable oblivion of sleep, and he surfaced into the hard glare of the middeck lights. He felt for his harness release, and as the straps came free, he floated out of his seat. The middeck began to shift around him, and he had to close his eyes to stem the sudden tide of nausea. *Fight it*, he thought. *Mind over matter. I'm the one who always had the iron stomach*. But he could not bring himself to open his eyes, to confront that disorienting drift of the room.

Until he heard the sound. It was a creaking, so close by that he thought it must be Mercer, stirring in his sleep. O'Leary turned toward the sound – and found that he was not facing Mercer. He was staring at Kenichi Hirai's body bag.

It was bulging. Expanding.

My eyes, he thought. *They're playing tricks on me*.

He blinked and refocused. The shroud was still swollen, the plastic ballooning out over the corpse's abdomen. Hours ago, they had patched the leak; now the pressure inside must be building up again.

Moving through a dreamlike haze, he floated across to the sleeping pallet. He placed his hand on the bulging body bag.

And jerked away in horror. For in that brief moment of contact, he had felt it swell, retract, and swell again.

The corpse was pulsating.

Sweat beading her upper lip, Jill Hewitt watched through the overhead window as *Discovery* unlatched from ISS. Slowly the gap widened between them, and she glanced at the data streaming across her computer screen. One foot separation. Two feet. *Going home*. Pain suddenly arced through her head, its stab so unbearable she felt herself beginning to black out. She fought back, holding on to consciousness with the stubbornness of a bulldog.

'ODS is clear,' she said through clenched teeth.

Kittredge responded with, 'Switching to RCS OP, low Z.'

Using the reaction-control-system thrusters, Kittredge would now gently steer away from ISS, moving to a point three thousand feet below the station, where their differing orbits would automatically begin to pull them farther apart.

Jill heard the *whomp* of the thrusters firing and felt the orbiter shudder as Kittredge, at the aft controls, slowly backed them down the R-bar. His hand shook, and his face went tight with the effort to retain control of his grip. He, not the computer, was flying the orbiter, and a wayward jerk of the control stick could send them careening off course.

Five feet apart. Ten. They were past the crucial separation phase now, moving further and further away from the station.

Jill began to relax.

And then she heard the shriek on middeck. A cry of horror and disbelief. *O'Leary*.

She turned, just as a gruesome fountain of human debris burst onto the flight deck and exploded toward her.

Kittredge, nearest the interdeck access, caught the brunt of the force and went flying against the rotational hand controller. Jill tumbled backward, her headset flying off, her body pummelled by foul-smelling fragments of intestine and skin and clumps of black hair, still attached to scalp. *Kenichi's hair*. She heard the *whomps* of firing thrusters, and the orbiter seemed to lurch around her. The cloud of disintegrated human parts had spread throughout the flight deck, and a nightmarish galaxy swirled, floating bits of plastic shroud and shattered organs and those strange greenish clumps. A grape-like mass of them floated by and splattered against a nearby wall.

When droplets collide with, and adhere to, flat surfaces in microgravity, they tremble briefly from the impact, then fall still. This splatter had not stopped moving.

In disbelief, she watched as the quivering intensified, as a ripple disturbed the surface. Only then did she see, embedded deep within the gelatinous mass, a core of something black, something moving. It writhed like the larva of a mosquito.

179

Suddenly a new image caught her eye, even more startling. She stared up through the window above the flight deck and saw the space station rapidly zooming toward them, so close now she could almost make out the rivets on the solar array truss.

In a burst of panic, she shoved against the wall and dove through that gruesome cloud of exploded flesh, her arms outstretched in desperation toward the orbiter control stick.

'Collision course!' yelled Griggs over space-to-space radio. '*Discovery*, you are on a collision course!'

There was no response.

'*Discovery! Reverse course!*'

Emma watched in horror as disaster hurtled toward them. Through the space station's cupola window, she saw the orbiter simultaneously pitch up and roll to starboard. She saw *Discovery*'s delta wing slicing toward them with enough momentum to ram it through the station's aluminum hull. She saw, in the imminent collision, the approach of her own death.

The plumes of firing rockets suddenly spewed out from the forward RCS thruster in the orbiter's nose. *Discovery* began to pitch downward, reversing momentum. Simultaneously the starboard delta wing rolled upward, but not quickly enough to clear the space station's main solar truss. She felt her heartbeat freeze.

Heard Luther whisper, 'Lord Jesus.'

'CRV!' Griggs shouted in panic. 'Everyone to the evac vehicle!'

Arms and legs churned in midair, feet flying in every direction as the crew scrambled to evacuate the node. Nicolai and Luther were first through the hatch, into the hab. Emma had just grabbed the hatch handhold when her ears filled with the squeal of rending metal, the groan of aluminum being twisted and deformed by the collision of two massive objects.

The space station shuddered, and in the ensuing quake, she caught a disorienting glimpse of the node walls tilting away, of Griggs's ThinkPad spinning in midair and Diana's terrified face, slick with sweat.

The lights flickered and went out. In the darkness, a red warning light flashed on and off, on and off.

A siren shrieked.

14

Shuttle flight director Randy Carpenter was watching death on the front screen.

At the instant of the orbiter's impact, he felt the blow as surely as if a fist had been rammed into his own sternum, and he actually lifted his hand and pressed it to his chest.

For a few seconds, the Flight Control Room went absolutely silent. Stunned faces stared at the front wall. On the center screen was the world map with the shuttle trajectory trace. To the right was the frozen RPOP display, *Discovery* and ISS represented by wireframe diagrams. The orbiter was now melded like a crumpled toy to the silhouette of ISS. Carpenter felt his lungs suddenly expand, realized that, in his horror, he had forgotten to breathe.

The FCR erupted in chaos.

'Flight, we have no voice downlink,' he heard Capcom say. '*Discovery* is not responding.'

'Flight, we're still getting data stream from TCS –'

'Flight, no drop in orbiter cabin pressure. No indication of oxygen leak –'

'What about ISS?' Carpenter snapped. 'Do we have downlink from them?'

'SVO's trying to hail them. The station pressure is dropping –'

'How low?'

'It's down to seven hundred ten . . . six hundred ninety. Shit, they're decompressing fast!'

Breach in the station's hull! thought Carpenter. But that wasn't his problem to fix; it belonged to Special Vehicle Operations, down the hall.

The propulsion systems engineer suddenly broke into the comm loop. 'Flight, I'm reading RCS ignition, F2U, F3U, and F1U. *Someone's* working the orbiter controls.'

Carpenter's head snapped to attention. The RPOP display was still locked and frozen, with no new images appearing. But Propulsion's report told him that *Discovery's* steering rockets had just fired. It had to be more than just a random discharge; the crew was trying to move the orbiter away from ISS. But until they had radio downlink, they could not confirm the orbiter crew's status. They could not confirm they were alive.

It was the most terrible scenario of all, the one he feared most. A dead crew on an orbiting shuttle. Though Houston could control most of the orbiter's maneuvers by ground command, they could not bring it home without crew help. A functioning human being was necessary to flip the arming switches for the OMS deorbit burn. It took a human hand to deploy the air-data probes and to lower the landing gear for touchdown. Without someone at the controls to perform these functions, *Discovery* would remain in orbit, a ghost ship circling silently around the earth until its orbit decayed months from now, and it fell to earth in a streak of fire. It was this nightmare that passed through Carpenter's head as the seconds ticked by, as panic slowly gathered force around him in the FCR. He could not afford to think about the space station, whose crew even now might be in the agonal throes of a decompressive death. His focus had to remain on *Discovery*. On *his* crew, whose survival seemed less and less likely with every second of silence that passed.

Then, suddenly, they heard the voice. Faint, halting.

'Control, this is *Discovery*. Houston. Houston . . .'

'It's Hewitt!' said Capcom. 'Go ahead, *Discovery!*'

'. . . major anomaly . . . could not avoid collision. Structural damage to orbiter appears minimal . . .'

'*Discovery*, we need visual on ISS.'

'Can't deploy Ku antenna – closed circuit gone –'

'Do you know the extent of their damage?'

'Impact tore off their solar truss. I think we punched a hole in their hull . . .'

Carpenter felt sick. They still had heard no word from the ISS crew. No confirmation they had survived.

'What is your crew's status?' asked Capcom.

'Kittredge is barely responding. Hit his head on the aft control panel. And the crew on middeck – I don't know about them –'

'What's your status, Hewitt?'

'Trying to . . . oh, God, my head . . .' There was a soft sob. Then she said, 'It's alive.'

'Did not copy.'

'The stuff floating around – the spill from the body bag. It's moving all around me. It's *inside* me. I can see it moving under my skin, and it's *alive*.'

A chill crawled all the way up Carpenter's spine. Hallucinations. A head injury. They were losing her, losing their only chance of getting the orbiter down intact.

'Flight, we're approaching burn target,' warned FDO. 'We can't afford to miss it.'

'Tell her to go for deorbit,' Carpenter ordered.

'*Discovery*,' said Capcom. 'Go to APU prestart.'

184

There was no response.

'*Discovery?*' repeated Capcom. 'You're going to miss your burn target!'

As the seconds stretched to minutes, Carpenter's muscles tensed, and his nerves felt like live wires. He gave a sigh of relief when Hewitt finally responded.

'Middeck crew's in landing position. They're both unconscious. I've strapped them in. But I can't get Kittredge into his LES –'

'Screw his reentry suit!' said Carpenter. 'Let's not miss that target. Just get the bird down!'

'*Discovery*, we advise you proceed directly to APU prestart. Just strap him into the starboard seat, and you get on with deorbit.'

They heard a ragged sigh of pain. Then Hewitt said, 'My head – having trouble focusing . . .'

'We roger that, Hewitt.' Capcom's voice became gentler. Almost soothing. 'Look, Jill. We know you're the one in the commander's seat now. We know you're hurting. But we can guide you in on autoland, all the way to wheel stop. If you just *stay with us*.'

She let out a tortured sob. 'APU prestart complete,' she whispered. 'Loading OPS 3-0-2. Tell me when, Houston.'

'Go for deorbit burn,' said Carpenter.

Capcom relayed the decision. 'Go for deorbit burn, *Discovery*.' And he added softly, 'Now, let's get you home.'

In the hellish darkness, Emma braced herself for the shock of decompression. She knew exactly what to expect. How she would die. There would be the roar of air rushing out of the hull. The sudden popping of her eardrums. The rapid crescendo of pain as her lungs expanded and her alveoli exploded. As the air pressure drops toward vacuum, the boiling temperature of liquid also drops, until it becomes

185

the same as the freezing temperature. One instant, the blood is boiling. In the next, it freezes solid in the veins.

The red warning lights, the siren, confirmed her worst fears. It was a Class 1 emergency. They had a breached hull, and their air was leaking into space.

She felt her ears pop. *Evacuate now!*

She and Diana dove into the hab, flying through gloom lit only by the bright red flashes of the warning panels. The siren was so loud everyone had to yell to hear each other. In her panic, Emma bounced into Luther, who grabbed her before she could ricochet off in a new direction.

'Nicolai's already in the CRV. You and Diana next!' he shouted.

'Wait. Where's Griggs?' said Diana.

'Just *get in!*'

Emma turned. In the psychedelic flash of red warning lights, she saw no one else in the hab. Griggs had not followed them. A strange, fine mist seemed to hang in the gloom, but there was no hurricane whoosh of air sucking them toward the breach.

And no pain, she suddenly realized. She'd felt her ears pop, but there was no chest pain, no symptoms of explosive decompression.

We can save this station. We have time to isolate the leak.

She did a quick swimmer's turn, kicked off the wall, and went flying back toward the node.

'Hey! What the fuck, Watson?' yelled Luther.

'Don't give up the ship!'

She was moving so fast she slammed against the edge of the hatchway, bashing her elbow. *Here* was the pain now, not from decompression but from her own stupid clumsiness. Her arm was throbbing as she kicked off again, into the node.

Griggs wasn't there, but she saw his ThinkPad, drifting at

186

the end of its data cord. The screen flashed a bright red 'Decompression' warning. The air pressure was down to six hundred fifty and dropping. They had only minutes to work, minutes before their brains would not function.

He must have gone in search of the leak, she thought. *He's going to close off the damaged module.*

She dove into the U.S. lab, through that thickening white mist. *Was* it mist or was it her vision fogging over from hypoxia? A warning that unconsciousness was closing in? She shot through the darkness and felt disoriented by the warning lights continuing to flash like a strobe. She banged into the far hatchway. Her coordination was off, and her clumsiness getting worse. She slipped through the hatch opening, into Node 2.

Griggs was there. He was struggling to disconnect a tangle of cables strung between the NASDA and European modules.

'The leak's in NASDA!' he yelled over the screaming sirens. 'If we can clear the cables from this hatchway and close it off, we can isolate the module.'

She dove forward to help him yank the cables apart. Then she found one that could not be disconnected. 'What the hell's this?' she said. All cables leading through hatchways were supposed to be easy to pull apart in case of an emergency. This one was continuous – a violation of safety rules. 'It doesn't have a quick release!' she yelled.

'Get me a knife and I'll cut it!'

She spun around, dove back into the U.S. lab. *A knife. Where the hell is a knife?* Through the red flashes of light, she saw the medical locker. *A scalpel.* She yanked open the drawer, reached into the instrument tray, and went flying back into Node 2.

Griggs took the scalpel and began to sever the cable.

'What can we do to help?' came Luther's shout.

Emma turned and saw him, along with Nicolai and Diana, hovering anxiously in the hatchway.

'The breach is in NASDA!' she said. 'We're gonna close off the module!'

Sparks suddenly shot out like fireworks. Griggs yelped and jerked away from the cable. 'Shit! It's a live wire!'

'We've got to cut it!' said Emma.

'And get fried to a crisp? I don't think so.'

'Then how do we seal the hatch?'

Luther said, 'Pull back! Pull back into the lab! We'll close off the whole node. Isolate this end of the station.'

Griggs looked at the sparking wire. He didn't want to close off Node 2, because it meant sacrificing both the NASDA and European modules, which would be completely depressurized and unreachable. And it meant sacrificing the shuttle docking port, which also led off Node 2.

'Pressure's dropping, folks!' called Diana, reading a hand-held pressure gauge. 'We're down to six hundred twenty-five millimeters! Just pull the fuck back, and let's close off the node!'

Emma could already feel herself breathing faster, trying to catch her breath. Hypoxia. They were all going to black out if they didn't do something soon.

She tugged Griggs's arm. 'Pull back! It's the only way to save the station!'

He gave a stunned nod and retreated with Emma into the U.S. lab.

Luther tried to tug the hatch shut, but he couldn't get it to budge. Now that they were outside Node 2, they had to pull, not push the hatch shut. And they were working against the rush of escaping air, in a rapidly depressurizing atmosphere.

'We'll have to abandon this module too!' yelled Luther. 'Retreat to Node 1 and close off the next hatch!'

'Hell no!' Griggs said. 'I'm not giving up this module as well!'

188

'Griggs, we've got no choice. I can't pull this hatch shut!'

'Then let me do it!' Griggs grabbed the handle and strained to pull it shut, but the hatch moved only a few inches before he had to let go in exhaustion.

'You're gonna kill us all just to save this fucking module!' shouted Luther.

It was Nicolai who suddenly yelled out the solution. '*Mir!* Feed the leak! Feed the leak!' He shot out of the lab, headed toward the Russian end of the station.

Mir. Everyone immediately knew what he was talking about. 1997. The *Progress* collision with *Mir*'s Spektr module. There had been a breach in the hull, and *Mir* had begun to leak its precious air into space. The Russians, with years more experience in manned space stations, were ready with their emergency response: feeding the leak. Pour extra oxygen into the module to raise the pressure. Not only would it buy them time to work, it might narrow the pressure gradient enough so they could pull the hatch shut.

Nicolai came flying back into the lab with two oxygen tanks. Frantically he opened the valves all the way. Even over the screaming sirens, they could hear the screech of air escaping from the tanks. Nicolai tossed both tanks into Node 2. *Feeding the leak.* They were building air pressure on the other side of the hatch.

They were also pouring oxygen into a module with a live wire, thought Emma, remembering the sparks. It could trigger an explosion.

'Now!' Nicolai shouted. 'Try to close the hatch!'

Luther and Griggs both grabbed the handle and pulled. They would never know if it was due to their combined desperation or if the oxygen tanks had succeeded in dropping the pressure gradient across that hatchway, but the hatch slowly began to swing shut.

Griggs locked it in place.

For a moment he and Luther simply hung limp in midair, both of them too exhausted to say a word. Then Griggs turned, his face bright with sweat in the flashing lights.

'Now let's shut off that fucking racket,' he said.

The ThinkPad was still floating where he'd left it in Node 1. Peering at the glowing screen, he rapidly tapped in a series of commands. To everyone's relief, the sirens stopped screaming. The flashing red lights also stopped, leaving only a constant yellow glow on the caution-and-warning panels. At last they could communicate without shouting.

'Air pressure is back up to six hundred ninety and rising,' he said, and gave a laugh of relief. 'Looks like we're home free.'

'Why are we still at Class 3 caution?' asked Emma, pointing to the yellow light on the screen. A Class 3 caution meant one of three possibilities: Their backup guidance computer was down, one of their control motion gyros was inoperative, or they'd lost their S-band radio link to Mission Control.

Griggs tapped a few more keys. 'It's the S-band. We've lost it. *Discovery* must have hit our P-1 truss and taken out the radio. Looks like they also hit our port solar arrays. We've lost a photovoltaic module. That's why we're still in power down.'

'Houston must be going bonkers, wondering what's happening,' said Emma. 'And now they can't reach us. What about *Discovery*? What's happened to them?'

Diana, already working the space-to-space radio, said, '*Discovery* isn't responding. They may be out of UHF range.'

Or they were all dead and couldn't respond.

'Can we get these lights back?' said Luther. 'Cross-strap primary power?'

Griggs began to tap on the keyboard again. Part of the beauty of ISS's design lay in its redundancy. Each of its power channels were configured to supply electricity for specific loads, but those channels could be rerouted – 'cross-strapped' – as needed. Though they'd lost one photovoltaic module, they had three others to tap into.

Griggs said, 'I know this is a cliché, but "let there be light."' He hit a computer key, and the module lights barely brightened. But it was enough to navigate through hatchways. 'I've rerouted power. Nonessential payload functions are now off the grid.' He released a deep breath and looked at Nicolai. 'We need to contact Houston. It's your show, Nicolai.'

The Russian understood at once what he had to do. Moscow's Mission Control maintained its own separate communications link with the station. The collision should not have affected the Russian end of ISS.

Nicolai gave a terse nod. 'Let us hope Moscow has paid its electric bill.'

ITEM 3–7-EXEC
ITEM 3–8-EXEC
OPS 3–0–4 PRO

Jill Hewitt was gasping in pain, short little whimpers that punctuated every push of a new button on the control panel. Her head felt like a melon ripe to explode. Her field of vision had contracted so that it seemed as if she were peering down a long black tunnel and the controls had receded almost beyond her reach. It took every ounce of concentration for her to focus on each switch she had to flip, on each button wavering beyond her finger. Now she struggled to make out the attitude-direction indicator, her vision blurring as the eight-ball display seemed to spin wildly in its casing. *I can't see it. I can't read pitch or yaw . . .*

'*Discovery*, you are at entry interface,' said Capcom. 'Body flap on auto.'

Jill squinted at the panel and reached for the switch, but it seemed so far away . . .

'Discovery?'

Her trembling finger made contact. She switched to 'auto.' 'Confirm,' she whispered, and let her shoulders go slack. The computers were now in control, flying the ship. She did not trust herself on the stick. She did not even know how long she could stay conscious. Already the black tunnels were closing over her vision, swallowing the light. For the first time she could hear the sound of rushing air across the hull, could feel her body being shoved back against her seat.

Capcom had gone silent. She was in communications blackout, the spacecraft hurtling against the atmosphere with such force it stripped the electrons from air molecules. That electromagnetic storm interrupted all radio waves, cut off all communication. For the next twelve minutes it was only her, and the ship, and the roaring air.

She had never felt so alone.

She felt the autopilot begin to steer into the first high bank, rolling the spacecraft on its side, slowing it down. She imagined the glow of heat on the cockpit windows, could feel its warmth, like the sun radiating on her face.

She opened her eyes. And saw only darkness.

Where are the lights? she thought. *Where is the glow on the window?*

She blinked, again and again. Rubbed her eyes, as though to force them to see, to force her retinas to draw in light. She reached out toward the control panel. Unless she flipped the right switches, unless she deployed the air-data probes and lowered the landing gear, Houston could not land the ship. They could not get her home alive. Her fingers brushed against a mind-numbing array of dials and buttons, and she gave a howl of despair.

She was blind.

15

At 4,093 feet above sea level, the air at White Sands Missile Proving Grounds was dry and thin. The landing strip traced across an ancient dried-out seabed located in a desert valley formed between the Sacramento and Guadalupe mountain ranges to the east, and the San Andres Mountains to the west. The closest town was Alamogordo, New Mexico. The terrain was stark and arid, and only the hardiest of desert vegetation could survive.

The area had long served as a training base for fighter pilots. It had also seen other uses through the decades. During World War II, it was the site of a German prisoner of war camp. It was also the location of the Trinity site, where the U.S. exploded its first atomic bomb, assembled not far away in Los Alamos, New Mexico. Barbed wire and unmarked government buildings had sprouted up in this desert valley, their functions a mystery even to the residents of nearby Alamogordo.

Through binoculars, Jack could see the landing strip shimmering with heat in the distance. Runway 16/34 was oriented just slightly off due north-south. It was fifteen thousand feet long and three hundred feet wide – large enough to accept the heaviest of jets, even in that rarefied air, which forces long landing and takeoff rolls.

Just west of the touchdown point, Jack and the medical team waited, along with a small convoy of NASA and United Space Alliance vehicles, for *Discovery*'s arrival. They had stretchers, oxygen, defibrillators, and ACLS kits – everything one could find in a modern ambulance, and more. For landings at Kennedy, there would be over one hundred fifty ground team members prepared to meet the orbiter. Here, on this desert strip, they had barely three dozen, and eight of them were medical personnel. Some of the ground crew were wearing self-contained atmospheric protective suits, to insulate them from any propellant leaks. They would be the first to meet the orbiter and, with atmospheric sensors, would quickly assess the potential for explosions before allowing doctors and nurses to approach.

A distant rumble made Jack lower his binoculars and glance due east. Choppers were approaching, so many of them they looked like an ominous swarm of black wasps.

'What's this?' said Bloomfeld, also noticing the choppers. Now the rest of the ground crew was staring at the sky, many of them murmuring in bewilderment.

'Could be backup,' said Jack.

The convoy leader, listening on his comm unit, shook his head. 'Mission Control says they're not ours.'

'This airspace should be clear,' said Bloomfeld.

'We're trying to hail the choppers, but they're not responding.'

The rumble had crescendoed, and Jack could feel it in his bones now, a deep and constant thrum in his sternum. They were going to invade the orbiter's airspace. In fifteen minutes, *Discovery* would drop out of the sky and find those choppers in her flight path. He could hear the convoy leader talking urgently into his headset, could feel panic begin to ripple through the ground crew.

'They're holding position,' said Bloomfeld.

Jack raised his binoculars. He counted almost a dozen choppers. They had indeed halted their approach and were now landing like a flock of vultures, due east of the orbiter's touchdown point.

'What do you suppose that's all about?' said Bloomfeld.

Two minutes left of communications blackout. Fifteen minutes till touchdown.

Randy Carpenter was feeling the first flush of optimism. He knew they could bring *Discovery* down safely. Barring a catastrophic computer failure, they could fly that bird from the ground. The key was Hewitt. She had to stay conscious, had to be able to flip two switches at the right times. Minimal tasks, but crucial. At their last radio contact, ten minutes before, Hewitt had sounded alert, but in pain. She was a good pilot, a woman with a steel backbone tempered by the refiner's fire of the U.S. Navy. All she had to do was stay conscious.

'Flight, we have good news from NASCOM,' said Ground Control. 'Mission Control Moscow has made radio contact with ISS on Regul S-Band.'

Regul was the Russian S-band radio system aboard ISS. It was completely separate and independent of the U.S. system, and it operated via Russian ground stations and their LUCH satellite.

'Contact was brief. They were on the tail end of LUCH satellite comm pass,' said Ground Control. 'But the crew is all alive and well.'

Carpenter's optimism flared even brighter, and he tightened his plump fingers in a triumphant fist. 'Damage report?'

'They had a breach of the NASDA module and had to close off Node Two and everything forward of that. They've

195

also lost at least two solar arrays and several truss segments. But no one's hurt.'

'Flight, we should be coming out of comm blackout,' said Capcom.

At once Carpenter's attention snapped back to *Discovery*. He was happy about the news from ISS, but his first responsibility was to the shuttle.

'*Discovery*, do you copy?' said Capcom. '*Discovery?*'

The minutes went by. Too many. Suddenly Carpenter was back dancing on the brink of panic.

Guidance said, 'Second S-turn completed. All systems look good.'

Then why wasn't Hewitt responding?

'*Discovery*,' repeated Capcom, his voice now urgent. 'Do you copy?'

'Going into third S-turn,' said Guidance.

We've lost her, thought Carpenter.

Then they heard her voice. Soft and unsteady. 'This is *Discovery*.'

Capcom's sigh of relief huffed loudly over the loop. '*Discovery*, welcome back! It's good to hear your voice! Now you need to deploy your air-data probes.'

'I – I'm trying to find the switches.'

'Your air-data probes,' Capcom repeated.

'I know, I know! *I can't see the panel!*'

Carpenter felt as if his blood had just frozen in his veins. *Dear God, she's blind. And she's seated in the commander's seat. Not in her own.*

'*Discovery*, you need to deploy now!' said Capcom. 'Panel C-three –'

'I *know* which panel!' she cried. There was silence. Then the sound of her breath rushing out in a whoosh of pain.

'Probes have been deployed,' said MMACS. 'She did it. She found the switch!'

Carpenter allowed himself to breathe again. To hope again.

'Fourth S-turn,' said Guidance. 'Now at TAEM interface.'

'*Discovery*, how ya doing?' said Capcom.

One minute, thirty seconds to touchdown. *Discovery* was now traveling at six hundred miles per hour, at an altitude of eight thousand feet and dropping rapidly. The pilots called it the 'flying brick' – heavy, with no engines, gliding in on delta-wing slivers. There'd be no second chances, no abort and fly around for another try. It was going to land, one way or the other.

'*Discovery?*' said Capcom.

Jack could see it glinting in the sky, puffs of smoke trailing from its yaw jets. It looked like a bright chip of silver as it swept around on its final turn to line up with the runway.

'Come on, baby. You're lookin' good!' whooped Bloomfeld.

His enthusiasm was shared by all three dozen members of the ground crew. Every shuttle landing is a celebratory event, a victory so moving it brings tears to the eyes of those who watch from the ground. Every eye was now turned to the sky, every heart pounding as they watched that chip of silver, *their* baby, gliding toward the runway.

'Gorgeous. God, she's beautiful!'

'Yee-haw!'

'Linin' up just fine! Yes *sir!*'

The convoy leader, listening on his earpiece to Houston, suddenly snapped straight, his spine rigid in alarm. 'Oh, shit,' he said. 'Landing gear isn't down!'

Jack turned to him. '*What?*'

'Crew hasn't deployed the landing gear!'

Jack's head whipped around to stare at the approaching shuttle. It was barely one hundred feet above the ground, moving at over three hundred miles an hour. He could not see the wheels.

The crowd suddenly went dead silent. Their celebration had just turned into disbelief. Horror.

Get them down. Get those wheels down! Jack wanted to scream.

The shuttle was seventy-five feet above the runway, lined up perfectly. Ten seconds till touchdown.

Only the flight crew could lower the landing gear. No computer could flip the switch, could perform the task meant for a human hand. No computer could save them.

Fifty feet and still traveling over two hundred miles an hour.

Jack did not want to see the final event, but he could not help himself. He could not turn away. He saw *Discovery*'s tail slam down first, spewing up a shower of sparks and shattered heat tiles. He heard the screams and sobs of the crowd as *Discovery*'s nose slammed down next. The shuttle began to slide sideways, trailing a maelstrom of debris. A delta wing broke off, went flying like a black scythe through the air. The shuttle kept scraping sideways in a deafening screech.

The other wing broke off, tumbling, shattering.

Discovery slid off the tarmac, onto the desert sand. A tornado of dust flew up, obscuring Jack's view of the final seconds. His ears rang with the crowd's screams, but he could not utter a sound. Nor could he move; shock had numbed him so profoundly he felt as if he had left his own body and were hovering, ghostlike, in some nightmare dimension.

Then the cloud of dust began to clear, and he saw the shuttle, lying like a broken bird, in a terrible landscape of scattered debris.

Suddenly the ground convoy was moving. As engines roared to life, Jack and Bloomfeld jumped in back of the medical vehicle and began the bouncing ride across the desert floor to the crash site. Even over the roar of the convoy engines, Jack heard another sound, throbbing and ominous.

The choppers were moving in too.

Their vehicle suddenly braked to a halt. Jack and Bloomfeld, both clutching emergency medical kits, jumped to the ground in a cloud of dust. *Discovery* was still a hundred yards ahead. The choppers had already landed, forming a ring around the shuttle. Barring the convoy.

Jack began to run toward *Discovery*, ready to duck his head beneath the whirring rotor blades. He was stopped before he reached the ring of choppers.

'What the hell is going on?' yelled Bloomfeld as uniformed soldiers suddenly poured out of the choppers and formed an armed wall against the NASA ground crew.

'Back off! Back off!' one of the soldiers yelled.

The convoy leader pushed to the front. 'My crew needs to get to the orbiter!'

'You people will stay back!'

'You have no authority here! This is a NASA operation!'

'Everyone get the fuck back *now!*'

Rifles suddenly came up, barrels pointed at the unarmed ground crew. NASA personnel began to back away, all eyes focused on the guns, on the implied threat of mass slaughter.

Looking past the soldiers, Jack saw that a white plastic tent was rapidly being erected over *Discovery*'s hatch, closing it off from the outside air. A dozen hooded figures, completely clad in bright orange suits, emerged from two of the choppers and approached the orbiter.

'Those are Racal biological space suits,' said Bloomfeld.

The orbiter hatch was now completely hidden by the plastic tent. They could not see the hatch being opened. They could not see those space-suited men enter the middeck.

That's our *flight crew in there, thought Jack. Our people who might be dying in that orbiter. And we can't reach them. We've got doctors and nurses standing here, with a truck full of medical equipment, and they won't let us do our jobs.*

He pushed toward the line of soldiers, stepping directly in front of the Army officer who appeared to be in charge. 'My medical crew is coming in,' he said.

The officer gave a smirk. 'I don't think so, sir.'

'We're employees of NASA. We're doctors, charged with the health and well-being of that flight crew. You can shoot us if you'd like. But then you'd have to kill everyone else here too, because they'd be witnesses. And I don't think you're going to do that.'

The rifle came up, the barrel pointed directly at Jack's chest. His throat was dry, and his heart was slamming against his ribs, but he stepped around the soldier, ducked under the chopper blades, and kept walking. He didn't even glance back as the soldier ordered,

'Halt, or I'll shoot!'

He walked on, his gaze fixed on the billowing tent ahead of him. He saw the men in their Racal space suits turn and stare at him in surprise. He saw the wind kick up a puff of dust and send it swirling across his path. He was almost at the tent when he heard Bloomfeld yell.

'Jack, look out!'

The blow caught him right at the base of the skull. He went down on his knees, pain exploding in bright bursts in his head. Another blow slammed into his flank, and he sprawled forward, tasting sand, hot as ash in his face. He rolled over, onto his back, and saw the soldier looming over him, rifle butt raised to deliver yet another blow.

'That's enough,' said an oddly muffled voice. 'Leave him alone.'

The soldier backed away. Now another face loomed into view, staring down at Jack through a clear Racal hood.

'Who are you?' the man said.

'Dr Jack McCallum.' The words came out in barely a whisper. He sat up, and his vision suddenly blurred, danced on the edge of darkness. He clutched his head, willing himself to stay conscious, fighting the blackness threatening to drag him down. 'Those are *my* patients in that orbiter,' Jack said. 'I demand to see them.'

'That's not possible.'

'They need medical attention –'

'They're dead, Dr McCallum. All of them.'

Jack froze. Slowly he raised his head and met the man's gaze through the clear face shield. He could read no expression there, could see nothing that reflected the tragedy of four lost lives.

'I'm sorry about your astronauts,' the man said, and turned to walk away.

Jack struggled to stand up. Though swaying and dizzy, he managed to stay on his feet. 'And who the fuck are *you?*' he demanded.

The man paused and turned back. 'I'm Dr Isaac Roman, USAMRIID,' he said. 'That orbiter is now a hot zone. The Army is assuming control.'

USAMRIID. Dr Roman had pronounced it as one word, but Jack knew what the letters stood for. The U.S. Army Medical Research Institute of Infectious Diseases. Why was the Army here? Since when had this turned into a military operation?

Jack squinted in the flying dust, his skull still ringing from the blow, and struggled to absorb this bewildering information. An eternity seemed to pass, a surreal progression of images in slow motion. Men in Racal suits striding toward the orbiter. The soldier staring at him with expressionless eyes. The isolation tent billowing in the wind like a living, breathing organism. He looked at the ring of soldiers, still holding the ground crew at bay. He looked at the orbiter and saw the men in space suits carry the first stretcher out of the tent. The body was sealed in a bag. The plastic had

201

been stamped repeatedly with the bright red biohazard symbol, like blossoms strewn across a corpse.

The sight of that stretcher made Jack's mind snap back into focus. He said, 'Where are you taking the bodies?'

Dr Roman did not even turn to look at him, but directed the stretcher to a waiting chopper. Jack started to walk toward the orbiter, and once again found a soldier standing in front of him, rifle butt raised to deliver another blow.

'Hey!' came a shout from the ground crew. 'You dare to hit him again and we've got thirty witnesses!'

The soldier turned and stared at the angry NASA and United Space Alliance employees, who were now surging forward, voices raised in outrage.

'You think this is Nazi Germany?'

'– think you can beat up civilians now?'

'Who the hell *are* you guys?'

The nervous soldiers tightened ranks as the ground crew continued to push forward, shouting, feet churning up dust.

A rifle shot exploded into the air. The crowd went dead still.

There is something terribly wrong here, thought Jack. *Something we don't understand*. These soldiers were fully prepared to shoot. To kill.

The convoy leader understood this as well, because he blurted out in panic, 'I'm in comm link with Houston! At this moment, a hundred men and women in Mission Control are listening!'

Slowly the soldiers lowered their rifles and glanced toward their officer. A long silence passed, broken only by the wind and the scatter shot of sand pinging the choppers.

Dr Roman appeared at Jack's side. 'You people don't understand the situation,' he said.

'Explain it to us.'

'We are dealing with a serious biohazard. The White House

Security Council has activated the Army's Biological Rapid Response Team – a team created by an act of Congress, Dr McCallum. We're here on orders from the White House.'

'What biohazard?'

Roman hesitated. He glanced toward the NASA ground crew, who stood in a tense huddle beyond the line of soldiers.

'What is the organism?' Jack said.

At last Roman met his gaze through the plastic face shield. 'That information is classified.'

'We're the medical team, charged with the health of that flight crew. Why weren't we told about this?'

'NASA doesn't realize what it's dealing with.'

'And how is it that you do?' The question, heavy with significance, went unanswered.

Another stretcher emerged from the tent. And whose body was that? Jack wondered. The faces of the four crew members flashed through his mind. All dead now. He could not grasp that fact. He could not imagine those vibrant, healthy people reduced to shattered bones and ruptured organs.

'Where are you taking the bodies?' he asked.

'A Level Four facility for autopsy.'

'Who's doing the autopsy?'

'I am.'

'As the crew's flight surgeon, I should be present.'

'Why? Are you a pathologist?'

'No.'

'Then I don't see how you could contribute anything useful.'

'How many dead pilots have you examined?' Jack shot back. 'How many aircraft accidents have you investigated? Aerospace trauma is *my* training. My field of expertise. You might need me.'

'I don't think so,' said Roman. And he walked away.

Stiff with rage, Jack crossed back to the NASA ground

crew and said to Bloomfeld. 'The Army's in control of this site. They're taking the bodies.'

'By what authority?'

'He says it comes straight from the White House. They've activated something called a Biological Rapid Response Team.'

'That's an anti-terrorist team,' said Bloomfeld. 'I've heard about them. They were created to deal with bioterrorism.'

They watched a chopper lift off, carrying two of the bodies. *What the hell is really going on?* Jack wondered. *What are they hiding from us?*

He turned to the convoy leader. 'Can you patch me through to JSC?'

'Anyone in particular?'

Jack thought of whom he could trust, and who was high enough in the NASA bureaucracy to carry the battle to the very top.

'Get me Gordon Obie,' he said. 'Flight Crew Operations.'

The Autopsy

16

Gordon Obie walked into the video conference room prepared for bloody battle, but none of the officials sitting around the table suspected the depth of his rage. And no wonder; Obie was wearing his usual poker face, and he didn't say a word as he took his place at the table, next to a tearful and puffy-eyed Public Affairs Officer Gretchen Liu. Everyone looked shell-shocked. They didn't even notice Gordon's entrance.

Also at the table was NASA administrator Leroy Cornell, JSC director Ken Blankenship, and a half dozen senior NASA officials, all of them grimly staring at the two video display screens. On the first screen was a Colonel Lawrence Harrison from USAMRIID, speaking from the Army base in Fort Detrick, Maryland. On the second monitor was a solemn, dark-haired man in civilian clothes, identified as 'Jared Profitt, White House Security Council.' He did not look like a bureaucrat. With his mournful eyes and his gaunt, almost ascetic features, he looked like a medieval monk, unwillingly transported into a modern age of suits and ties.

Blankenship was talking, his comments directed at Colonel Harrison. 'Not only did your soldiers prevent my people from doing their jobs, they threatened them at gunpoint. One of our flight surgeons was assaulted – knocked to the ground with a rifle butt. We have three dozen witnesses –'

'Dr McCallum broke through our security cordon. He refused to halt as ordered,' Colonel Harrison responded. 'We had a hot zone to protect.'

'So now the U.S. Army is prepared to attack, even shoot, civilians?'

'Ken, let's try to look at it from USAMRIID's point of view,' said Cornell, placing a calming hand on Blankenship's arm. The diplomat's touch, thought Gordon with distaste. Cornell might be NASA's spokesman at the White House and their best asset when it came to cajoling Congress for money, but many at NASA had never really trusted him. They could never trust any man who thought more like a politician than an engineer. 'Protecting a hot zone is a valid reason to apply force,' said Cornell. 'Dr McCallum did breach the security line.'

'And the results could have been disastrous,' said Harrison over the audio feed. 'Our intelligence reports that Marburg virus may have been purposefully introduced to the space station. Marburg is a cousin of Ebola virus.'

'How would it get aboard?' said Blankenship. 'Every experimental protocol is reviewed for safety. Every lab animal is certified healthy. We don't send up biohazards.'

'That's your agency line, of course. But you receive your experimental payloads from scientists all around the country. You may screen their protocols, but you can't examine every bacteria or tissue culture as it arrives for launch. To keep biological materials alive, the payloads are loaded right onto the shuttle. What if one of those experiments was contaminated? Consider how easy it is to replace a harmless culture with a dangerous organism like Marburg.'

'Are you saying this was a deliberate sabotage attempt on the station?' said Blankenship. 'An act of bioterrorism?'

'That's precisely what I'm saying. Let me describe what happens to you if you are infected with this particular virus. First your muscles begin to ache and you have a fever. The ache is so severe, so agonizing, you can scarcely bear to be touched. An intramuscular injection makes you shriek in pain. Then your eyes turn red. Your belly begins to hurt, and you vomit, again and again. You begin to throw up blood. It comes up black at first, because of digestive processes. Then it comes faster and turns bright red, as rapid as a gushing pump. Your liver swells, cracks. Your kidneys fail. Your internal organs are being destroyed, turning to foul, black mush. And suddenly, disastrously, your blood pressure crashes. And you're dead.' Harrison paused. 'That's what we may be dealing with, gentlemen.'

'This is *bullshit!*' blurted Gordon Obie.

Everyone at the table stared at him in astonishment. The Sphinx had spoken. On the rare occasions Obie did say anything at a meeting, it was usually in a monotone, his words used to convey data and information, not emotion. This outburst had shocked them all.

'May I ask who just spoke?' asked Colonel Harrison.

'I'm Gordon Obie, director of Flight Crew Operations.'

'Oh. The astronauts' top dog.'

'You could call me that.'

'And why is this bullshit?'

'I don't believe this is Marburg virus. I don't know what it is, but I do know you're not telling us the truth.'

Colonel Harrison's face froze into a rigid mask. He said nothing.

It was Jared Profitt who spoke. His voice sounded exactly as Gordon had expected, thin and reedy. He was not a bully like Harrison, but a man who preferred to appeal to one's intellect and reason. 'I understand your frustration, Mr Obie,' Profitt said. 'There's so much we're unable to tell you because

209

of security concerns. But Marburg is not something we can be careless about.'

'If you already know it's Marburg, then why are you excluding our flight surgeons from the autopsy? Are you afraid we'll learn the truth?'

'Gordon,' Cornell said quietly, 'why don't we discuss this in private?'

Gordon ignored him and said to the screen, 'What disease are we really talking about? An infection? A toxin? Something loaded on board the shuttle in a military payload, perhaps?'

There was a silence. Then Harrison blustered, 'There's that NASA paranoia! Your agency likes to blame the military for everything that goes wrong.'

'Why do you refuse to allow my flight surgeon into the autopsy?'

'Are we speaking of Dr McCallum?' asked Profitt.

'Yes. McCallum has training in aviation trauma and pathology. He is a flight surgeon as well as a former member of the astronaut corps. The fact you refuse to let him or *any* of our doctors view the autopsies makes me wonder what you don't want NASA to see.'

Colonel Harrison glanced sideways, as though to look at someone else in the room. When he gazed back at the camera, his face was flushed and angry. 'This is absurd. You people just crashed the shuttle! You screw up the landing, kill your own crew, and then you point an accusing finger at the U.S. *Army*?'

'The entire astronaut corps is up in arms about this,' said Gordon. 'We want to know what really happened to our colleagues. We insist you allow one of *our* doctors to view the bodies.'

Leroy Cornell again tried to intercede. 'Gordon, you can't make unreasonable demands like this,' he said quietly. 'They know what they're doing.'

'So do I.'

'I'm going to ask you to back down *now*.'

Gordon looked Cornell in the eye. Cornell was NASA's representative to the White House, NASA's voice in Congress. Opposing him was career suicide.

He did it anyway. 'I speak for the astronauts,' he said. '*My* people.' He turned to the video screen, his gaze fixed on the stony face of Colonel Harrison. 'And we're not above taking our concerns to the press. We don't consider this move lightly – exposing confidential NASA matters. The astronaut corps has always been discreet. But if we're forced to, we will demand a public inquiry.'

Gretchen Liu's jaw dropped. 'Gordon,' she whispered, 'what the hell are you doing?'

'What I have to do.'

The silence at the table stretched to a full minute.

Then, to everyone's astonishment, Ken Blankenship said, 'I side with our astronauts.'

'So do I,' said another voice.

'Me too –'

'–and me.'

Gordon looked around the table at his colleagues. Most of these people were engineers and operational managers whose names seldom turned up in the press. More often than not, they were in conflict with the astronauts, whom they considered flyboys with big egos. The astronauts got all the glory, but these men and women, who performed the unseen and unglamorous jobs that made spaceflight a reality, were the heart and soul of NASA. And they were now united behind Gordon.

Leroy Cornell looked stricken, the leader abandoned by his own troops. He was a proud man, and this was a humiliatingly public blow. He cleared his throat and slowly squared his shoulders. Then he faced the video image of Colonel

211

Harrison. 'I have no choice but to support my astronauts as well,' he said. 'I insist that one of our flight surgeons be allowed to view the autopsies.'

Colonel Harrison said nothing. It was Jared Profitt who made the final decision – Jared Profitt who was obviously the real man in charge. He turned to confer with someone standing offscreen. Then he looked at the camera and nodded.

Both screens went blank. The video conference had ended.

'Well, you certainly thumbed your nose at the U.S. Army,' said Gretchen. 'Did you see how pissed-off Harrison looked?'

No, thought Gordon, remembering Colonel Harrison's expression just before the image went blank. *That wasn't anger I saw on his face. It was fear.*

The bodies had not been taken to USAMRIID headquarters in Fort Detrick, Maryland, as Jack had expected. They'd been transported barely sixty miles away from the White Sands landing strip to a windowless concrete-block building, much like the dozens of other anonymous government buildings that had sprung up in that dry desert valley. But this one had a distinguishing feature: a series of ventilation pipes jutting up from the roofline. Barbed wire bristled atop the perimeter fence. As they drove through the military checkpoint, Jack heard the hum of high-voltage wires.

Flanked by his armed escort, Jack approached the front entrance – the only entrance, he realized. On the door was a chillingly familiar symbol: the bright red biohazard blossom. *What is this facility doing in the middle of nowhere?* he wondered. Then he scanned the featureless horizon, and his question was answered. The building was here precisely because it *was* in the middle of nowhere.

He was escorted through the door and into a series of stark corridors heading deeper into the heart of the building. He saw men and women in Army uniforms, others in lab coats. All lighting was artificial, and the faces appeared bluish and sickly.

The guards stopped outside a door labeled 'Men's Lockers.'

'Go in,' he was told. 'Follow the written instructions to the letter. Then go through the next door. They're waiting for you.'

Jack entered the room. Inside were lockers, a laundry cart containing various sizes of green surgical scrub suits, a shelf with paper caps, a sink, and a mirror. A list of instructions was posted on the wall, starting with 'Remove ALL street clothes, including underwear.'

He took off his clothes, left them in an unsecured locker, and dressed in a scrub suit. Then he pushed through the next door, again labeled with the universal biohazard symbol, into an ultraviolet-lit room. There he paused, wondering what to do next.

A voice over the intercom said, 'There's a shelf of socks beside you. Put on a pair and walk through the door.'

He did.

A woman in a scrub suit was waiting for him in the next room. She was brusque, unsmiling, as she told him to don sterile gloves. Then she angrily ripped off strips of tape and sealed his sleeves and pant cuffs. The Army may have resigned themselves to Jack's visit, but they weren't going to make it a friendly one. She slipped an audio headset over his head, then gave him a 'Snoopy' hat, like a swimming cap, to hold the equipment in place.

'Now suit up,' she barked.

Time for the space suit. This one was blue, with the gloves already attached. As his hostile assistant lowered the hood over his head, Jack felt a dart of anxiety about the woman. In her anger, she could sabotage the process, see to it that he wasn't completely sealed off from contamination.

She closed the seal on his chest, hooked him up to a wall

hose, and he felt the whoosh of air blow into his suit. It was too late now to worry about what could go wrong. He was ready to cross into the hot area.

The woman unplugged his hose and pointed to the next door.

He stepped through, into the air lock. The door slammed shut behind him. A man in a space suit was waiting for him. He did not speak, but gestured to Jack to follow him through the far door.

They stepped through and walked down a hallway to the autopsy room.

Inside was a stainless steel table with a body on it, still sealed in its bag. Two men in space suits were already standing on either side of the body. One of the men was Dr Roman. He turned and saw Jack.

'Don't touch anything. Don't interfere. You're only here to observe, Dr McCallum, so stay the hell out of our way.'

Nice welcome.

The space-suited escort plugged a wall hose into Jack's suit, and once again air hissed into his helmet. If not for the audio headset, he'd be unable to hear anything the other three men said.

Dr Roman and his two associates opened the body bag.

Jack felt his breath catch, his throat constrict. The corpse was Jill Hewitt's. Her helmet had been removed, but she was still wearing the orange launch-and-entry suit, embroidered with her name. Even without that identification, he would have known it was Jill, because of her hair. It was a silky chestnut, cut in a bob and streaked with the first hints of gray. Her face was strangely intact. Her eyes were half open. Both sclerae were a bright and shocking red.

Roman and his colleagues unzipped the LES and stripped the corpse. The fabric was fire-retardant, too tough to cut through. They had to peel it off. They worked efficiently,

214

their comments matter-of-fact and without even a hint of emotion. When they had removed her clothing, she looked like a broken doll. Both her hands were deformed by fractures, reduced to masses of crushed bone. Her legs, too, were broken and akilter, the shins bent at impossible angles. The tips of two broken ribs penetrated her chest wall, and black bruises marked the strap lines of her seat restraint.

Jack felt his breaths coming too fast, and he had to quell his rising horror. He had witnessed many autopsies, on bodies in much worse shape. He had seen aviators burned into little more than charred twigs, skulls exploded from the pressure of cooking brains. He had seen a corpse whose face had been sliced off from walking into a chopper's tail rotor. He had seen a Navy pilot's spine broken in half and folded backward from ejecting through a closed canopy.

This was far, far worse because he knew the deceased. He remembered her as a living, breathing woman. His horror was mingled with rage, because these three men viewed Jill's exposed body with such cold dispassion. She was a slab of meat on the table, nothing more. They ignored her injuries, her grotesquely fractured limbs. The cause of death was only of secondary concern to them. They were more interested in the microbiological hitchhiker harbored within her corpse.

Roman began his Y incision. In one hand he gripped a scalpel; the other hand was safely encased in a steel-mesh glove. One slash ran from the right shoulder, diagonally through the breast, to the xiphoid process. Another diagonal slash ran from the left shoulder and met the first slash at the xiphoid. The incision continued straight down the abdomen, with a small jag around the umbilicus, ending near the pubic bone. He cut through the ribs, freeing the sternum. The bony shield was lifted to reveal the chest cavity.

The cause of death was immediately apparent.

When a plane crashes, or an automobile slams into a wall,

215

or a despondent lover makes a suicide leap from a ten-story building, the same forces of deceleration apply. A human body traveling at great speed is abruptly brought to a halt. The impact itself can shatter ribs and send missiles of bone shards into vital organs. It can fracture vertebrae, rupture spinal cords, crush skulls against dashboards or instrument panels. But even when pilots are fully strapped in and helmeted, even when no part of their body makes contact with the aircraft, the force of deceleration alone can be fatal, because although the torso may be restrained, the internal organs are not. The heart and lungs and great vessels are suspended inside the chest by only tissue attachments. When the torso comes to an abrupt halt, the heart continues to swing forward like a pendulum, moving with such force it shears tissues and rips open the aorta. Blood explodes into the mediastinum and pleural cavity.

Jill Hewitt's chest was a lake of blood.

Roman suctioned it out, then frowned at the heart and lungs. 'I can't see where she bled out,' he said.

'Why don't we remove the entire block?' said his assistant. 'We'd have better visibility.'

'The tear is most likely in the ascending aorta,' said Jack. 'Sixty-five percent of the time, it's located just above the aortic valve.'

Roman glanced at him in annoyance. Up till then, he'd managed to ignore Jack; now he resented this intrusive comment. Without a word, he positioned his scalpel to sever the great vessels.

'I advise examining the heart in situ first,' said Jack. 'Before you cut.'

'How and where she bled out is not my primary concern,' Roman retorted.

They don't really care what killed her, thought Jack. *All they want to know is what organism might be growing, multiplying, inside her.*

216

Roman sliced through the trachea, esophagus, and great vessels, then removed the heart and lungs in one block. The lungs were covered with hemorrhages. Traumatic or infectious? Jack didn't know. Next Roman examined the abdominal organs. The small bowel, like the lungs, was splotchy with mucosal hemorrhages. He removed it and set the glistening coils of intestines in a bowl. He resected the stomach, pancreas, and liver. All would be sectioned and examined microscopically. All tissue would be cultured for bacteria and viruses.

The body was now missing almost all its internal organs. Jill Hewitt, Navy pilot, triathlete, lover of J&B Scotch and high-stakes poker and Jim Carrey movies, was now nothing but a hollow shell.

Roman straightened, looking vaguely relieved. So far, the autopsy had revealed nothing unexpected. If there was gross evidence of Marburg virus, Jack did not see it.

Roman circled behind the corpse, to the head.

This was the part Jack dreaded. He had to force himself to watch as Roman sliced the scalp, his incision running across the top of the crown, from ear to ear. He peeled the scalp forward and folded the flap over the face, a fringe of chestnut hair flopping down over her chin. With a rongeur, they cracked the skull. No saws, no flying bone dust, could be allowed in a Level 4 autopsy. They pried off the cap of bone.

A fist-sized mass of clotted blood plopped out, splattering the stainless steel table.

'Big subdural hematoma,' said one of Roman's associates. 'From the trauma?'

'I don't think so,' said Roman. 'You saw the aorta – death would have been nearly instantaneous on impact. I'm not sure her heart was pumping long enough to produce this much intracranial bleeding.' Gently he slid his gloved fingers into the cranial cavity, probing the surface of gray matter.

A gelatinous mass slithered out and splashed onto the table.

Roman jerked back, startled.

'What the hell is *that?*' his assistant said.

Roman didn't answer. He just stared at the clump of tissue. It was covered with a blue-green membrane. Through the glistening veil, the mass appeared irregular, a knot of formless flesh. He was about to slit the membrane open, then he stopped himself and shot a glance toward Jack. 'It's a tumor of some kind,' he said. 'Or a cyst. That would explain the headache she reported.'

'No it wouldn't,' Jack spoke up. 'Her headache came on suddenly – within hours. A tumor takes months to grow.'

'How do you know she hasn't been hiding her symptoms these past months?' countered Roman. 'Keeping it a secret so she wouldn't get scrubbed from the launch?'

Jack had to concede that was a possibility. Astronauts were so eager for flight assignments they might well conceal any symptoms that would pull them from a mission.

Roman looked at his associate standing across the table from him. The other man nodded, slid the mass into a specimen container, and carried it out of the room.

'Aren't you going to section it?' said Jack.

'It needs to be fixed and stained first. If I start slicing now, I could deform the cellular architecture.'

'You don't know if it *is* a tumor.'

'What else would it be?'

Jack had no answer. He had never seen anything like it.

Roman continued his examination of Jill Hewitt's cranial cavity. Clearly the mass, whatever it was, had increased pressure on her brain, deforming its structures. How long had it been there? Months, years? How was it possible that Jill had been able to function normally, much less pilot a complicated vehicle like the shuttle? All this raced through Jack's head as he watched Roman remove the brain and slide it into a steel basin.

'She was close to herniating through the tentorium,' said Roman.

No wonder Jill had gone blind. No wonder she hadn't lowered the landing gear. She had already been unconscious, her brain about to be squeezed like toothpaste out the base of her skull.

Jill's corpse – what remained of it – was sealed into a new body bag and wheeled out of the room, along with the biohazard containers holding her organs.

A second body was brought in. It was Andy Mercer.

With fresh gloves pulled over his space suit gloves, and a clean scalpel, Roman set to work on the Y incision. He was moving more quickly, as though Jill had just been the warm-up and he was only now hitting his stride.

Mercer had complained of abdominal pain and vomiting, Jack remembered as he watched Roman's scalpel slice through skin and subcutaneous fat. Mercer hadn't complained of a headache, as Jill had, but he'd had a fever and had coughed up a little blood. Would his lungs show the effects of Marburg virus?

Again, Roman's diagonal cuts met below the xiphoid, and he sliced a shallow line down the abdomen to the pubis. Again he cut through the ribs, freeing up the triangular shield that covered the heart. He lifted the sternum.

Gasping, he stumbled backward, dropping his scalpel. It clanged onto the table. His assistants stood frozen in disbelief.

In Mercer's chest cavity was a cluster of blue-green cysts, identical to the cyst in Jill Hewitt's brain. They were massed around his heart, like tiny translucent eggs.

Roman stood paralyzed, his gaze fixed on the gaping torso. Then his gaze shifted to the glistening peritoneal membrane.

It was distended, full of blood and bulging out through the abdominal incision.

Roman stepped toward the body, staring at the outpouching of peritoneal membrane. When he'd made his incision through the abdominal wall, his scalpel had nicked the surface of that membrane. A trickle of blood-tinged fluid leaked out. At first it was barely a few drops. Then, even as they watched, the trickle turned into a stream. The slit suddenly burst open into a gaping rent as blood gushed out, carrying with it a slippery flood of blue-green cysts.

Roman gave a cry of horror as the cysts plopped onto the floor in splatters of blood and mucus.

One of them skittered across the concrete and bumped against Jack's rubber boot. He bent down, to touch it with his gloved hand. Abruptly he was yanked backward as Roman's associates pulled him away from the table.

'Get him out of here!' Roman ordered. 'Get him out of the room!'

The two men pushed Jack toward the door. He resisted, shoving away the gloved hand now grasping his shoulder. The man stumbled backward, tipped over a tray of surgical instruments, and sprawled to the floor, slippery with cysts and blood.

The second man wrenched Jack's air hose from its connection and held up the kinked end. 'I advise you to walk out with us, Dr McCallum,' he said. 'While you've still got breathable air.'

'My suit! Jesus, I've got a breach!' It was the man who'd stumbled into the instrument tray. He was now staring in horror at a two-inch-long tear in his space suit sleeve – a sleeve that was coated with Mercer's body fluids.

'It's wet. I can feel it. My inner sleeve is wet –'

'*Go!*' barked Roman. 'Decon *now!*'

The man unplugged his suit and went running in panic

out of the room. Jack followed him to the air lock door, and they both stepped through, into the decon shower. Water shot out of the overhead jets, pounding down like hard rain on their shoulders. Then the shower of disinfectant began, a torrent of green liquid that splattered noisily against their plastic helmets.

When it finally stopped, they stepped through the next door and pulled off their suits. The man immediately peeled off his already-wet scrub suit and thrust his arm under a faucet of running water, to rinse away any body fluids that had leaked through the sleeve.

'You have any breaks in your skin?' asked Jack. 'Cuts, hangnails?'

'My daughter's cat scratched me last night.'

Jack looked down at the man's arm and saw the claw marks, three scabbed lines raking up the inner arm. The same arm as the torn space suit. He looked at the man's eyes and saw fear.

'What happens now?' said Jack.

'Quarantine. I go to lockup. Shit . . .'

'I already know it's not Marburg,' said Jack.

The man released a deep breath. 'No. It's not.'

'Then what is it? Tell me what we're dealing with,' said Jack.

The man clutched the sink with both hands and stared down at the water gurgling into the drain. He said softly, 'We don't know.'

17

Sullivan Obie was riding his Harley on Mars.

At midnight, with the full moon shining down and the pock-marked desert stretched out before him, he could imagine it was the Martian wind whipping his hair and red Martian dust churning beneath his tires. This was an old fantasy from boyhood, from the days when those precocious Obie brothers shot off homemade rockets and built cardboard moon landers and donned space suits of crinkled foil. The days when he and Gordie knew, just knew, that their futures lay in the heavens.

And this is where those big dreams end up, he thought. *Drunk on tequila, popping wheelies in the desert.* No way was he ever getting to Mars, or to the moon either. Chances were he wouldn't even get off the goddamn launchpad, but would be instantly atomized. A quick, spectacular death. What the hell; it beat dying at seventy-five with cancer.

He skidded to a stop, his bike spitting up dirt, and stared across the moonlit ripples of sand at *Apogee II*, gleaming like a streak of silver, her nose cone pointed at the stars. They had moved her to the launchpad yesterday. It was a slow and celebratory procession, the dozen Apogee employees honking horns and beating on their car roofs as they followed the flatbed truck across the desert. When she had finally been hoisted into position and everyone squinted up against the blazing sun to look at her, they had suddenly fallen silent. They all knew this was the last roll of the dice. In three weeks, when *Apogee II* lifted off, she would be carrying all their hopes and dreams.

And my sorry carcass as well, thought Sullivan.

A chill shot through him as he realized he might be staring at his own coffin.

He goosed the Harley and roared back toward the road, bouncing across dunes, leaping over dips. He rode with abandon, his recklessness fueled by tequila and by the sudden and unshakable certainty that he was already a dead man. That in three weeks he would be riding that rocket to oblivion. Until then, nothing could touch him, nothing could hurt him.

The promise of death had made him invincible.

He accelerated, flying across the bleak moonscape of his boyhood fantasies. *And here I am in the lunar rover, speeding across the Sea of Tranquility. Roaring up a lunar hill. Launching off to a soft landing . . .*

He felt the ground drop away. Felt himself soaring through the night, the Harley growling between his knees, the moon shining in his eyes. Still soaring. How far? How high?

The ground hit with such force he lost control and tumbled sideways, the Harley falling on top of him. For a moment he lay stunned, pinned between his bike and a flat rock. *Well, this is one fucking stupid position to be in*, he thought.

Then the pain hit him. Deep and grinding, as though his hips were crushed to splinters.

He gave a cry and fell back, his face turned to the sky. The moon shone down, mocking him.

*   *   *

'His pelvis is fractured in three places,' said Bridget. 'The doctors pinned it last night. They tell me he's gonna be confined to bed for at least six weeks.'

Casper Mulholland could almost hear the sound of his dreams popping, like the loud burst of a balloon. 'Six . . . *weeks?*'

'And then he'll be in rehab for another three or four months.'

'Four *months?*'

'For God's sake, Casper. Say something original.'

'We're screwed.' He slapped his palm against his forehead, as though to punish himself for daring to dream they could ever succeed. It was that old Apogee curse again, cutting them off at the ankles just as they reached the finish line. Blowing up their rockets. Burning down their first office. And now, taking their only pilot out of commission. He paced the waiting room, thinking, *Nothing has ever gone right for us.* They'd invested all their combined savings, their reputations, and the last thirteen years of their lives. This was God's way of telling them to give up. To cut their losses before something *really* bad happened.

'He was drunk,' said Bridget.

Casper halted and turned to look at her. She stood with her arms grimly crossed, her red hair like the flaming halo of an avenging angel.

'The doctors told me,' she said. 'Blood alcohol level of point one nine. As pickled as a herring. This isn't just our usual bad luck. This is our own dear Sully fucking up again. My only consolation is that for the next six weeks, he's gonna have a big tube stuck up his dick.'

Without a word, Casper walked out of the visitors' waiting room, headed up the hall, and pushed into Sullivan's hospital room. 'You moron,' he said.

Sully looked up at him with morphine-glazed eyes. 'Thanks for the sympathy.'

'You don't deserve any. Three weeks before launch and you pull some goddamn Chuck Yeager stunt in the desert? Why didn't you just finish the job? Splatter your brains while you were at it? Hell, we wouldn't have known the difference!'

Sully closed his eyes. 'I'm sorry.'

'You always are.'

'I screwed up. I know . . .'

'You promised them a manned flight. It wasn't my idea, it was *yours*. Now they're expecting it. They're excited about it. When was the last time any investor was excited about us? This could have made the difference. If you'd just kept the bottle corked –'

'I was scared.'

Sully had spoken so softly Casper wasn't sure he'd heard him right. 'What?' he said.

'About the launch. Had a . . . bad feeling.'

A bad feeling. Slowly Casper sank into the bedside chair, all his anger instantly dissolving. Fear is not something a man readily admits to. The fact that Sully, who regularly courted destruction, would confess to being afraid left Casper feeling shaken.

And, at last, sympathetic.

'You don't need me for the launch,' said Sully.

'They expect to see a pilot climb into that cockpit.'

'You could put a goddamn monkey in my seat and they'd never know the difference. She doesn't need a pilot, Cap. You can uplink all the commands from the ground.'

Casper sighed. They had no choice now; it would have to be an unmanned flight. Clearly they had a valid excuse not to launch Sully, but would the investors accept it? Or would they believe, instead, that Apogee had lost its nerve? That it lacked the confidence to risk a human life?

'I guess I just lost my nerve,' said Sully softly. 'Got to drinking last night. Couldn't stop . . .'

Casper understood his partner's fear – the way he understood how one defeat can lead inexorably to another and then another until the only certainty in a man's life is failure. No wonder Sully was scared; he had lost faith in their dream. In Apogee.

Maybe they all had.

Casper said, 'We can still make this launch work. Even without a monkey in the cockpit.'

'Yeah. You could send up Bridget instead.'

'Then who'd answer the phones?'

'The monkey.'

Both men laughed. They were like two old soldiers, mustering up a shred of cheer on the eve of certain defeat.

'So we're gonna do it?' said Sully. 'We're gonna launch?'

'That was the whole idea of building a rocket.'

'Well, then.' Sully took a deep breath, and a ghost of the old bravado returned to his face. 'Let's do it right. Press release to all the wire services. One mother of a tent party with champagne. Hell, invite my sainted brother and his NASA pals. If she blows up on the pad, at least we'll go outta business in style.'

'Yeah. We always had an excess of style.'

They grinned.

Casper rose to leave. 'Get better, Sully,' he said. 'We'll need you for *Apogee III*.'

He found Bridget still sitting in the visitors' waiting room. 'So what happens now?' she said.

'We launch on schedule.'

'Unmanned?'

He nodded. 'We fly her from the control room.'

To his surprise, she huffed out a sigh of relief. 'Hallelujah!'

'What're you so happy about? Our man's laid up in a hospital bed.'

'Exactly.' She slung her purse over her shoulder and

turned to leave. 'It means he won't be up there to fuck things up.'

August 11

Nicolai Rudenko floated in the air lock, watching as Luther wriggled his hips into the lower torso assembly of the EVA suit. To the diminutive Nicolai, Luther was an exotic giant, with those broad shoulders and legs like pistons. And his skin! While Nicolai had turned pasty during his months aboard ISS, Luther was still a deep and polished brown, a startling contrast to the pale faces that inhabited their otherwise colorless world. Nicolai had already suited up, and now he hovered beside Luther, ready to assist his partner into the EVA suit's upper torso assembly. They said little to each other; neither man was in the mood for idle chatter.

The two of them had spent a mostly conversationless night sleeping in the air lock, allowing their bodies to adjust to a lower atmospheric pressure of 10.2 pounds per square inch – two thirds that of the space station. The pressure in their suits would be even less, at 4.3. The suits could not be inflated any higher, or the limbs would be too stiff and bulky, the joints impossible to flex. Moving directly from a fully pressurized spacecraft into the lower air pressure of an EVA suit was like surfacing too fast from the depths of the ocean. An astronaut could suffer the bends. Nitrogen bubbles formed in the blood, clogging capillaries, cutting off precious oxygen to the brain and spinal cord. The consequences could be devastating: paralysis and stroke. Like deep-sea divers, astronauts had to give their bodies time to adjust to the changing pressures. The night before a space walk, the EVA crew washed out their lungs with a hundred percent oxygen and shut themselves into the air lock for 'the camp-out.' For hours they were trapped together in a small chamber already crammed full of equipment. It was not a place for claustrophobics.

With his arms extended over his head, Luther squirmed into the suit's hard-shelled upper torso, which was mounted on the air lock wall. It was an exhausting dance, like wriggling into an impossibly small tunnel. At last his head popped out through the neck hole, and Nicolai helped him close the waist ring, sealing the two halves of the suit.

They put on their helmets. As Nicolai looked down to fit his helmet to the torso assembly, he noticed something glistening on the rim of the suit's neck ring. Just spittle, he thought, and locked on the helmet. They donned their gloves. Sealed into their suits, they opened the equipment lock hatch, floated into the adjoining crew lock, and shut the hatch behind them. They were now in an even smaller compartment, barely large enough to contain both the men and their bulky life-support backpacks.

Thirty minutes of 'prebreathe' came next. While they inhaled pure oxygen, purging their blood of any last nitrogen, Nicolai floated with his eyes closed, mentally preparing for the space walk ahead. If they could not get the beta gimbal assembly to unlock, if they could not reorient the solar panels toward the sun, they would be starved for power. Crippled. What Nicolai and Luther accomplished in the next six hours could well determine the fate of the space station.

Though this responsibility weighed heavily on his tired shoulders, Nicolai was anxious to open the hatch and float out of the air lock. To go EVA was like being reborn, the fetus emerging from that small, tight opening, the umbilical restraint dangling as one swims out into the vastness of space. Were the situation not so grave, he would be looking forward to it, would be giddily anticipating the freedom of floating in a universe without walls, the dazzling blue earth spinning beneath him.

But the images that came to mind, as he waited with his eyes closed for the thirty minutes to pass, were not of space-walking. What he saw instead were the faces of the dead. He imagined *Discovery* as she plunged from the sky. He saw the crew, strapped into their seats, bodies shaken like dolls, spines snapping, hearts exploding. Though Mission Control had not told them the details of the catastrophe, the nightmarish visions filled his head, made his heart pound, his mouth turn dry.

'Your thirty minutes are up, guys,' came Emma's voice over the intercom. 'Time for depress.'

Hands clammy with sweat, Nicolai opened his eyes and saw Luther start the depressurization pump. The air was being sucked out, the pressure in the crew lock slowly dropping. If there was a leak in their suits, they would now detect it.

'A-OK?' asked Luther, checking the latches on their umbilical tethers.

'I am ready.'

Luther vented the crew lock atmosphere to space. Then he released the handle and pulled open the hatch.

The last air hissed out.

They paused for a moment, clutching the side of the hatch, staring out in awe. Then Nicolai swam out, into the blackness of space.

'They're coming out now,' said Emma, watching on closed-circuit TV as the two men emerged from the crew lock, umbilical tethers trailing after them. They removed tools from the storage box outside the airlock. Then, pulling themselves from handhold to handhold, they made their way toward the main truss. As they passed by the camera mounted just under the truss, Luther gave a wave.

'You watching the show?' came his voice over the UHF audio system.

'We see you fine on external camera,' said Griggs. 'But your EMU cameras aren't feeding in.'

'Nicolai's too?'

'Neither one. We'll try to track down the problem.'

'Okay, well, we're heading up onto the truss to check out the damage.'

The two men moved out of the first camera's range. For a moment they disappeared from view. Then Griggs said, 'There they are,' and pointed to a new screen, where the space-suited men were moving toward the second camera, propelling themselves hand over hand along the top of the truss. Again they passed out of range. They were now in the blind zone of the damaged camera and could no longer be seen.

'Getting close, guys?' asked Emma.

'Almost – almost there,' said Luther, sounding short of breath. *Slow down*, she thought. *Pace yourselves.*

For what seemed like an endless wait, there was only silence from the EVA crew. Emma felt her pulse quicken, her anxiety rising. The station was already crippled and starved for power. Nothing must go wrong with these repairs. *If only Jack was here*, she thought. Jack was a talented tinkerer who could rebuild any boat engine or cobble together a shortwave radio from junkyard scraps. In orbit, the most valuable tools are a clever pair of hands.

'Luther?' said Griggs.

There was no answer.

'Nicolai? Luther? Please respond.'

'Shit,' said Luther's voice.

'What is it? What do you see?' said Griggs.

'I'm looking at the problem right now, and man, it's a mess. The whole P-6 end of the main truss is twisted around. *Discovery* must've clipped the 2-B array and bent that end right up. Then she swung over and snapped off the S-band antennas.'

'What do you think? Can you fix anything?'

'The S-band's no problem. We got an ORU for the antennas, and we'll just replace 'em. But the port-side solar arrays – forget it. We need a whole new truss on that end.'

'Okay.' Wearily Griggs rubbed his face. 'Okay, so we're definitely down one PVM. I guess we can deal with that. But we need the P-4 arrays reoriented, or we're screwed.'

There was a pause as Luther and Nicolai headed back along the main truss. Suddenly they were in camera range; Emma saw them moving slowly past in their bulky suits and enormous backpacks, like deep-sea divers moving through water. They stopped at the P-4 arrays. One of the men floated down the side of the truss and peered at the mechanism joining the enormous solar wings to the truss backbone.

'The gimbal assembly is bent,' said Nicolai. 'It cannot turn.'

'Can you free it up?' asked Griggs.

They heard a rapid exchange of dialogue between Luther and Nicolai. Then Luther said, 'How elegant do you want this repair to be?'

'Whatever it takes. We need the juice soon, or we're in trouble, guys.'

'I guess we can try the body shop approach.'

Emma looked at Griggs. 'Does that mean what I think it means?'

It was Luther who answered the question. 'We're gonna get out a hammer and bang this sucker back into shape.'

He was still alive.

Dr Isaac Roman gazed through the viewing window at his unfortunate colleague, who was sitting in a hospital bed watching TV. Cartoons, believe it or not. The Nickelodeon channel, which the patient stared at with almost desperate concentration. He didn't even glance at the space-suited nurse who'd come into the room to remove the untouched lunch tray.

Roman pressed the intercom button. 'How are you feeling today, Nathan?'

Dr Nathan Helsinger turned his startled gaze to the viewing window, and for the first time noticed that Roman was standing on the other side of the glass. 'I'm fine. I'm perfectly healthy.'

'You have no symptoms whatsoever?'

'I told you, I'm *fine*.'

Roman studied him for a moment. The man looked healthy enough, but his face was pale and tense. Scared.

'When can I come out of isolation?' said Helsinger.

'It's been scarcely thirty hours.'

'The astronauts had symptoms by eighteen hours.'

'That was in microgravity. We don't know what to expect here, and we can't take chances. You know that.'

Abruptly Helsinger turned to stare at the TV again, but not before Roman saw the flash of tears in his eyes. 'It's my daughter's birthday today.'

'We sent a gift in your name. Your wife was informed you couldn't make it. That you're on a plane to Kenya.'

Helsinger gave a bitter laugh. 'You do tie up those loose ends well, don't you? And what if I die? What will you tell her?'

'That it happened in Kenya.'

'As good a place as any, I suppose.' He sighed. 'So what did you get her?'

'Your daughter? I believe it was a Dr Barbie.'

'That's exactly what she wanted. How did you know?'

Roman's cell phone rang. 'I'll check back on you later,' he said, then turned from the window to answer the phone.

'Dr Roman, this is Carlos. We've got some of the DNA results. You'd better come up and see this.'

'I'm on my way.'

He found Dr Carlos Mixtal sitting in front of the lab computer. Data was scrolling down the monitor in a continuous stream:

```
GTGATTAAAGTGGTTAAAGTTGCTC
ATGTTCAATTATGCAGTTGTTGCG
GTTGCTTAGTGTCTTTAGCAGACA
CATATGAAAAGCTTTTAGATGTTTT
GAATTCAATTGAGTTGGTTTATTGT
CAAACTTTAGCAGATGCAAGAGAAA
TTCCTGAATGCGATATTGCTTTAGT
TGAAGGCTCTGT . . .
```

The data was made up of only four letters, G, T, A, and C. It was a nucleotide sequence, and each of the letters represented the building blocks that make up DNA, the genetic blueprint for all living organisms.

Carlos turned at the sound of Roman's footsteps, and the expression on his face was unmistakable. Carlos looked scared. *Just like Helsinger*, Roman thought. *Everyone is scared.*

Roman sat down beside him. 'Is that it?' he asked, pointing to the screen.

'This is from the organism infecting Kenichi Hirai. We took it from the remains that we were able to . . . scrape from the walls of *Discovery*.'

Remains was the appropriate word for what was left of Hirai's body. Ragged clumps of tissue, splattered throughout the walls of the orbiter. 'Most of the DNA remains unidentifiable. We have no idea what it codes for. But this particular sequence, here on the screen, we can identify. It's the gene for coenzyme F420.'

'Which is?'

'An enzyme specific to the Archaeon domain.'

Roman sat back, feeling faintly nauseated. 'So it's confirmed,' he murmured.

'Yes. The organism definitely has Archaeon DNA.' Carlos paused. 'I'm afraid there's bad news.'

'What do you mean, "bad news"? Isn't this bad enough?'

Carlos tapped on the keyboard and the nucleotide sequence scrolled to a different segment. 'This is another gene cluster we found. I thought at first it had to be a mistake, but I've since confirmed it. It's a match with *Rana pipiens*. The northern leopard frog.'

'What?'

'That's right. Lord knows how it picked up frog genes. Now here's where it gets really scary.' Carlos scrolled to yet another segment of the genome. 'Another identifiable cluster,' he said.

Roman felt a chill creeping up his spine. 'And what are these genes?'

'This DNA is specific to *Mus musculis*. The common mouse.'

Roman stared at him. 'That's impossible.'

'I've confirmed it. This life-form has somehow incorporated mammalian DNA into its genome. It's added new enzymatic capabilities. It's changing. Evolving.'

Into what? Roman wondered.

'There's more.' Again Carlos tapped on the keyboard, and a new sequence of nucleotide bases scrolled onto the monitor. 'This cluster is not of Archaeon origin, either.'

'What is this? More mouse DNA?'

'No. This part is human.'

The chill shot all the way up Roman's spine. The hairs on the back of his neck were bristling. Numbly he reached for the telephone.

'Connect me to the White House,' he said. 'I need to speak to Jared Profitt.'

234

His call was answered on the second ring. 'This is Profitt.'
'We've analyzed the DNA,' said Roman.
'And?'
'The situation is worse than we thought.'

18

Nicolai paused to rest, his arms trembling from fatigue. After months of living in space, his body had grown weak and unaccustomed to physical labor. In microgravity there is no heavy lifting and little need to exert one's muscles. In the last five hours, he and Luther had worked nonstop, had repaired the S-band antennas, had dismantled and reassembled the gimbal. Now he was exhausted. Just the extra effort of bending his arms in the turgid EVA suit made simple tasks difficult.

Working in the suit was an ordeal in itself. To insulate the human body from extreme temperatures ranging from -250 to 250 degrees Fahrenheit and to maintain pressure against the vacuum of space, the suit was constructed of multiple layers of aluminized Mylar insulation, nylon ripstop, an Ortho-fabric cover, and a pressure-garment bladder. Beneath the suit, an astronaut wore an undergarment laced with water-cooling tubes. He also had to wear a life-support backpack containing water, oxygen, self-rescue jet pack, and radio equipment. In essence, the EVA suit was a personal spacecraft, bulky and difficult to maneuver in, and just the act of tightening a screw required strength and concentration.

The work had exhausted Nicolai. His hands were cramping in the clumsy space suit gloves, and he was sweating.

He was also hungry.

He took a sip of water from the mouthpiece mounted inside his suit and released a heavy sigh. Though the water tasted strange, almost fishy, he thought nothing of it. Everything tasted strange in microgravity. He took another sip and felt wetness splash onto his jaw. He could not reach into his helmet to brush it away, so he ignored it and gazed down at the earth. That sudden glimpse of it, spread out in breathtaking glory beneath him, made him feel a little dizzy, a little nauseated. He closed his eyes, waiting for the feeling to pass. It was motion sickness, nothing more; it often happened when you unexpectedly caught sight of earth. As his stomach settled, he became aware of a new sensation: The spilled water was now trickling up his cheek. He twitched his face, trying to shake off the droplet, but it continued to slide across his skin.

But I am in microgravity, where there is no up or down. Water should not be trickling at all.

He began to shake his head, tapped his gloved hand on his helmet.

Still he felt the droplet moving up his face, tracing a wet line up his jaw. Toward his ear. It had reached the edge of his comm-assembly cap now. Surely the fabric would soak up the moisture, would prevent it from trickling further . . .

All at once his body went rigid. The wetness had slid beneath the edge of the cap. It was now squirming toward his ear. Not a droplet of water, not a stray trickle, but something that moved with purpose. *Something alive.*

He thrashed left, then right, trying to dislodge it. He banged hard on his helmet. And still he felt it moving, sliding under his comm assembly.

He caught dizzying glimpses of earth, then black space,

then earth again, as he flailed and twisted around in a frantic dance.

The wetness slithered into his ear.

'Nicolai? Nicolai, please respond!' said Emma, watching him on the TV monitor. He was turning around and around, gloved hands battering frantically at his helmet. 'Luther, he looks like he's having a seizure!'

Luther appeared on camera, moving quickly to assist his EVA partner. Nicolai kept thrashing, shaking his head back and forth. Emma could hear them on UHF, Luther asking frantically, 'What is it, what is it?'

'My ear – It is in my ear –'

'Pain? Does your ear hurt? *Look* at me!'

Nicolai slapped his helmet again. 'It's going *deeper!*' he screamed. 'Get it out! Get it out!'

'What's wrong with him?' cried Emma.

'I don't know! Jesus, he's panicking –'

'He's getting too close to the tool stanchion. Get him away before he damages his suit!'

On the TV monitor, Luther grabbed his partner by the arm. 'Come on, Nicolai! We're going back in the air lock.'

Suddenly Nicolai clutched at his helmet, as though to rip it off.

'No! *Don't!*' screamed Luther, clutching at both of his partner's arms in a desperate attempt to restrain him. The men thrashed together, umbilical tethers winding, tangling around them.

Griggs and Diana had joined Emma at the TV monitor, and the three of them watched in horror as the drama unfolded outside the station.

'Luther, the tool stanchion!' said Griggs. 'Watch your suits!'

Even as he said it, Nicolai suddenly and violently twisted in Luther's grasp. His helmet slammed into the tool stanchion.

238

A fine stream of what looked like white mist suddenly spurted out of his faceplate.

'Luther!' cried Emma. 'Check his helmet! Check his helmet!'

Luther stared at Nicolai's faceplate. 'Shit, he's got a crack!' he yelled. 'I can see air leaking out! He's decompressing!'

'Tap his emergency O2 and get him in *now!*'

Luther reached over and flipped the emergency oxygen supply switch on Nicolai's suit. The extra airflow might keep the suit inflated long enough for Nicolai to make it back alive. Still struggling to keep his partner under control, Luther began to haul him toward the air lock.

'Hurry,' murmured Griggs. 'Jesus, *hurry.*'

It took precious minutes for Luther to drag his partner into the crew lock, for the hatch to be closed and the atmosphere repressurized. They didn't wait for the usual air-lock integrity check, but pumped the pressure straight up to one atmosphere.

The hatch swung open, and Emma dove through into the equipment lock.

Luther had already removed Nicolai's helmet and was frantically trying to pull him out of the upper torso shell. Working together, they wriggled a struggling Nicolai out of the rest of his EVA suit. Emma and Griggs dragged him through the station and into the RSM, where there was full power and light. He was screaming all the way, clawing at the left side of his comm-assembly cap. Both eyes were swollen shut, the lids ballooned out. She touched his cheeks and felt crepitus – air trapped in the subcutaneous tissues from the decompression. A line of spittle glistened on his jaw.

'Nicolai, calm down!' said Emma. 'You're all right, do you hear me? You'll be all right!'

He shrieked and yanked off the comm cap. It went flying away.

'Help me get him onto the board!' said Emma.

It took all hands to set up the medical restraint board, strip off Nicolai's ventilation long johns, and strap him down. They had him fully restrained now. Even as Emma checked his heart and lungs and examined his abdomen, he continued to whimper and rock his head from side to side.

'It's his ear,' said Luther. He had shed his bulky EVA suit and was staring wide-eyed at the tormented Nicolai. 'He said there was something in his ear.'

Emma looked closer at Nicolai's face. At the line of spittle that traced from his chin, up the curve of his left jaw. To his ear. A drop of moisture was smeared on the pinna.

She turned on the battery-powered otoscope and inserted the earpiece into Nicolai's canal.

The first thing she saw was blood. A bright drop of it, glistening in the otoscope's light. Then she focused on the eardrum.

It was perforated. Instead of the gleam of the tympanic membrane, she saw a black and gaping hole. *Barotrauma* was her first thought. Had the sudden decompression blown out his eardrum? She checked the other eardrum, but it was intact.

Puzzled, she turned off the otoscope and looked at Luther. 'What happened out there?'

'I don't know. We were both taking a breather. Resting up before we brought the tools back in. One minute he's fine, the next minute he's panicking.'

'I need to look at his helmet.'

She left the RSM and headed back to the equipment lock. She swung open the hatch and gazed in, at the two EVA suits, which Luther had remounted on the wall.

'What are you doing, Watson?' said Griggs, who'd followed her.

'I want to see how big the crack was. How fast he was decompressing.'

She went to the smaller EVA suit, labeled 'Rudenko,' and removed the helmet. Peering inside, she saw a dab of moisture adhering to the cracked faceplate. She took out a cotton swab from one of her patch pockets and touched the tip to the fluid. It was thick and gelatinous. Blue-green.

A chill slithered up her spine.

Kenichi was in here, she suddenly remembered. *The night he died, we found him in this air lock. He has somehow contaminated it.*

At once she was backing out in panic, colliding with Griggs in the hatchway. 'Out!' she cried. 'Get out now!'

'What is it?'

'I think we've got a biohazard! Close the hatch! Close it!'

They both scrambled out of the air lock, into the node. Together they slammed the hatch shut and sealed it tight. They exchanged tense glances.

'You think anything leaked out?' Griggs said.

Emma scanned the node, searching for any droplets spinning through the air. At first glance she saw nothing. Then a flash of movement, a telltale sparkle, seemed to dance at the furthest periphery of her vision.

She turned to stare at it. And it was gone.

Jack sat at the surgeon's console in Special Vehicle Operations, his tension growing with every passing minute as he watched the clock on the front screen. The voices coming over his headset were speaking with new urgency, the chatter fast and staccato, as status reports flew back and forth between the controllers and ISS flight director Woody Ellis. Similar in layout to the shuttle Flight Control Room and housed in the same building, the SVO room was a smaller, more specialized version, manned by a team dedicated only to space station operations. Over the last thirty-six hours, ever since *Discovery* had collided with ISS, this room had been the scene of relentlessly mounting anxiety, laced with intermittent panic. With so many people in the room, so many hours of unrelieved stress, the air itself smelled of crisis, the mingled odors of sweat and stale coffee.

Nicolai Rudenko was suffering from decompression injuries and clearly needed to be evacuated. Because there was only one lifeboat – the Crew Return Vehicle – the entire crew was coming home. This would be a controlled evacuation. No shortcuts, no mistakes. No panic. NASA had run through this simulation many times before, but a CRV evac had never actually been done, not with five living, breathing human beings aboard.

Not with someone I love aboard.

Jack was sweating, almost sick with dread.

He kept glancing at the clock, cross-checking it with his watch. They had waited for ISS's orbital path to reach the right position before vehicle separation could proceed. The goal was to bring the CRV down in the most direct approach possible to a landing site immediately accessible to medical personnel. The entire crew would need assistance. After weeks of living in space, they would be weak as kittens, their muscles unable to support them.

The time for separation was approaching. It would take them twenty-five minutes to coast away from ISS and acquire GPS guidance, fifteen minutes for the deorbit burn setup. An hour to land.

In less than two hours, Emma would be back on earth. *One way or another.* The thought came before he could suppress it. Before he could stop himself from remembering the terrible sight of Jill Hewitt's flayed body on the autopsy table.

He clenched his hands into fists, forcing himself to concentrate on Nicolai Rudenko's biotelemetry readings. The heart rate was fast but regular; blood pressure holding steady. *Come on, come on. Let's bring them home now.*

He heard Griggs, on board ISS, report, 'Capcom, my crew is all aboard the CRV and the hatch is closed. It's a little cozy in here, but we're ready when you are.'

'Stand by to power up,' said Capcom.

'Standing by.'

'How is the patient doing?'

Jack's heart gave a leap as he heard Emma's voice join the loop. 'His vitals remain stable, but he's disoriented times three. The crepitus has migrated to his neck and upper torso, and it's causing him some discomfort. I've given him another dose of morphine.'

The sudden decompression had caused air bubbles to form in his soft tissues. The condition was harmless, but painful. What Jack worried about were air bubbles in the nervous system. Could that be the reason Nicolai was confused?

Woody Ellis said, 'Go for power up. Remove ECCLES seals.'

'ISS,' said Capcom, 'you are now go for –'

'Belay that!' a voice cut in.

Jack looked at Flight Director Ellis in confusion. Ellis looked just as confused. He turned to face JSC director Ken Blankenship, who'd just walked into the room, accompanied by a dark-haired man in a suit and a half dozen Air Force officers.

'I'm sorry, Woody,' said Blankenship. 'Believe me, this is not my decision.'

'What decision?' said Ellis.

'The evacuation is off.'

'We have a sick man up there! The CRV's ready to go –'

'He can't come home.'

'Whose decision is that?'

The dark-haired man stepped forward. He said, with what was almost a quiet note of apology, 'The decision is mine. I'm Jared Profitt, White House Security Council. Please tell your crew to reopen the hatches and exit the CRV.'

'My crew is in trouble,' said Ellis. 'I'm bringing them home.'

Trajectory cut in, 'Flight, we have to go to sep now if we want them landing on target.'

Ellis nodded to Capcom. 'Proceed to CRV power up. Let's go to sep.'

Before Capcom could utter another word, his headset was yanked off and he was hauled from his chair and pushed aside. An Air Force officer took Capcom's place at the console.

'Hey!' yelled Ellis. '*Hey!*'

All the flight controllers froze as the other Air Force officers immediately fanned out across the room. Not a weapon was drawn, but the threat was apparent.

'ISS, do not power up,' said the new Capcom. 'The evacuation has been canceled. Reopen the hatches and exit the CRV.'

A baffled Griggs responded, 'I don't think I copied that, Houston.'

'The evacuation is off. Exit the CRV. We are experiencing difficulties with both TOPO and GNC computers. Flight has decided it's best to hold off the evac.'

'How long?'

'Indefinitely.'

Jack shot to his feet, ready to wrestle away Capcom's headset.

Jared Profitt suddenly stepped in front of him, barring his way. 'You don't understand the situation, sir.'

'My wife is on that station. We're bringing her home.'

'They can't come home. They may all be infected.'

'With what?'

Profitt didn't answer.

In fury, Jack lunged toward him, but was hauled back by two Air Force officers.

'Infected with *what?*' Jack yelled.

'A new organism,' said Profitt. 'A chimera.'

Jack looked at Blankenship's stricken face. He looked at the Air Force officers who now stood poised to assume control of the consoles. Then he noticed another familiar face: that of Leroy Cornell, who'd just come into the room. Cornell looked pale and shaken. That's when Jack understood that this decision had been made at the very top. That nothing he, or Blankenship, or Woody Ellis said would make a difference.

NASA was no longer in control.

The Chimera

The Chimera

19

August 13

They gathered at Jack's house, where all the shades were drawn. They didn't dare meet at JSC, where they would most certainly be noticed. They were all so stunned by the sudden takeover of NASA operations they had no idea how to proceed. This was one crisis for which they had no operations manual, no contingency plans. Jack had invited only a handful of people, all of them from inside NASA operations: Todd Cutler, Gordon Obie, Flight Directors Woody Ellis and Randy Carpenter, and Liz Gianni from the Payload Directorate.

The doorbell rang, and everyone tensed.

'He's here,' said Jack, and he opened the door.

Dr Eli Petrovitch from NASA's Life Sciences Directorate stepped in, clutching a laptop carrying case. He was a thin and fragile man who, for the past two years, had been battling lymphoma. Clearly he was losing the war. Most of his hair had fallen out, and only a few brittle white strands remained. His skin looked like yellowed parchment, stretched over the jutting bones of his face. But there was the glow of excitement in his eyes, lit by a scientist's unflagging curiosity.

'Did we get it?' asked Jack.

249

Petrovitch nodded and patted his briefcase. On that skeletal face, his smile looked ghoulish. 'USAMRIID has agreed to share some of its data.'

'Some?'

'Not all. Much of the genome remains classified. We were given only parts of the sequence, with large gaps. They're showing us just enough to prove that the situation is grave.' He carried the laptop to the dining room table and flipped it open. As everyone crowded around to watch, Petrovitch booted up the computer, then slipped in a floppy disk.

Data began to scroll down, line after line of seemingly random letters marching at a dizzying pace down the screen. It was not text; these letters did not spell out words at all, but a code. The same four letters reappeared again and again, in a changing sequence: A, T, G, and C. They represented the nucleotides adenine, thymine, guanine, and cytosine. The building blocks that made up DNA. This string of letters was a genome, the chemical blueprint for a living organism.

'This,' said Petrovitch, 'is their chimera. The organism that killed Kenichi Hirai.'

'What *is* this "*ky-mir-ra*" thing I keep hearing about?' asked Randy Carpenter. 'For the sake of us ignorant engineers, maybe you could explain it?'

'Certainly,' said Petrovitch. 'And there's no reason to feel ignorant. It's not a term used much outside of molecular biology. The word comes from the ancient Greeks. Chimera was a mythological beast, said to be unconquerable. A fire-breathing creature with a lion's head, a goat's body, and a serpent's tail. She was eventually slain by a hero named Bellerophon. It wasn't exactly a fair fight, because he cheated. He hitched a ride on Pegasus, the winged horse, and shot arrows down at Chimera from above.'

'This mythology is interesting,' cut in Carpenter impatiently, 'but what's the relevance?'

'The Greek Chimera was a bizarre creature made up of three different animals. Lion, goat, and serpent, all combined into one. And that's exactly what we're seeing here, in this chromosome. A creature as bizarre as the beast killed by Bellerophon. This is a *biological* chimera whose DNA comes from at least three unrelated species.'

'Can you identify those species?' asked Carpenter.

Petrovitch nodded. 'Over the years, scientists around the world have amassed a library of gene sequences from a variety of species, from viruses to elephants. But collecting this data is slow and tedious. It's taken decades just to analyze the human genome. So as you can imagine, there are a number of species that haven't been sequenced. Large areas of this chimera's genome can't be identified; they're nowhere in the library. But here's what we have been able to identify so far.' He clicked on the icon for 'species matches.'

On the screen appeared:

Mus musculis (common mouse)
Rana pipiens (northern leopard frog)
Homo sapiens

'This organism is part mouse, part amphibian. And part human.' He paused. 'In a sense,' he said, 'the enemy is *us*.'

The room fell silent.

'Which of our genes is on that chromosome?' Jack asked softly. 'What part of Chimera is human?'

'An interesting question,' said Petrovitch, nodding in approval. 'It deserves an interesting answer. You and Dr Cutler will appreciate the significance of this list.' He typed on the keyboard.

On the screen appeared:

Amylase
Lipase
Phospholipase A
Trypsin
Chymotrypsin
Elastase
Enterokinase

'My God,' murmured Todd Cutler. 'These are all digestive enzymes.'

The organism is primed to devour its host, thought Jack. *It uses these enzymes to digest us from the inside, reducing our muscles and organs and connective tissue to little more than a foul soup.*

'Jill Hewitt – she told us Hirai's body had disintegrated,' said Randy Carpenter. 'I thought she was hallucinating.'

Jack said suddenly, 'This has got to be a bioengineered organism! Someone cooked this thing up in a lab. Took a bacteria or virus and grafted on genes from other species, to make it a more effective killing machine.'

'But *which* bacteria? *Which* virus?' said Petrovitch. 'That's the mystery here. Without more of the genome to examine, we can't identify which species they started off with. USAMRIID refuses to show us the most important part of this organism's chromosome. The part that identifies this killer.' He looked at Jack. 'You're the only one here who's actually seen the pathology at autopsy.'

'It was only a glimpse. They pushed me out of the room so fast I barely got a look. What I saw appeared to be some sort of cysts. The size of pearls, embedded in a blue-green matrix. They were in Mercer's thorax and abdomen. In Hewitt's cranium. I've never seen anything like it before.'

'Could they have been hydatid cysts?' asked Petrovitch.

'What's that?' asked Woody.

'It's an infection by the larval stage of a parasitic tapeworm called *echinococcus*. It causes cysts in the liver and lungs. For that matter, in any organ.'

'You think this could be a parasite?'

Jack shook his head. 'Hydatid cysts take a long time to grow. Years, not days. I don't think this was a parasite.'

'Maybe they weren't cysts at all,' said Todd. 'Maybe they were spores. Fungus balls. *Aspergillus* or *cryptococcus*.'

Liz Gianni from Payloads cut in, 'The crew reported a problem with fungal contamination. One of the experiments had to be destroyed because of overgrowth.'

'Which experiment?' asked Todd.

'I'd have to look it up. I remember it was one of the cell cultures.'

'But simple fungal contamination wouldn't account for these deaths,' said Petrovitch. 'Remember, there were fungi floating around *Mir* all the time, and no one died of it.' He looked at the computer screen. 'This genome tells us we're dealing with an entirely new life-form. I agree with Jack. It must have been engineered.'

'So it's bioterrorism,' said Woody Ellis. 'Someone's sabotaged our station. They must have sent it up in one of the payloads.'

Liz Gianni vigorously shook her head. Aggressive and intense, she was a forceful presence at any meeting, and she spoke up now with absolute assurance. 'Every payload goes through safety review. There are hazard reports, three-phase analyses of all containment devices. Believe me, we would have nixed anything this dangerous.'

'Assuming you knew it was dangerous,' said Ellis.

'Of course we'd know!'

'What if there was a breach in security?' said Jack. 'Many of the experimental payloads arrive directly from the principal investigators – the scientists themselves. We don't know what *their* security is like. We don't know if they have a terrorist working in their lab. If they switched a bacterial culture at the last minute, would we necessarily know?'

For the first time Liz looked uncertain. 'It . . . it's unlikely.'

'But it could happen.'

Though she wouldn't admit the possibility, dismay registered in her eyes. 'We'll grill every principal investigator,' she said. 'Every scientist who sent up an experiment. If they had a lapse in security, I'm fucking well gonna find out about it.'

She probably will, thought Jack. Like the other men in the room, he was a little afraid of Liz Gianni.

'There's one question we haven't asked yet,' said Gordon Obie, speaking up for the first time. As always, he'd been the Sphinx, listening without comment, silently processing information. 'The question is *Why?* Why would anyone sabotage the station? Is this someone with a grudge against us? A fanatic opposed to technology?'

'The biological equivalent of the Unabomber,' said Todd Cutler.

'Then why not just release the organism at JSC and kill off our infrastructure? That would be easier, and far more logical.'

'You can't apply logic to a fanatic,' Cutler pointed out.

'You can apply logic to everyone, including fanatics,' Gordon responded. 'As long as you know the framework in which they operate. And that's why this bothers me. That's why I wonder if we're really dealing with sabotage.'

'What else would it be,' said Jack, 'if *not* sabotage?'

'There is another possibility. It could be something just as frightening,' said Gordon, his troubled gaze lifting to Jack's. 'A mistake.'

Dr Isaac Roman ran down the hall, his pager alarm squealing on his belt, dreading what he was about to face. He silenced the pager and opened the door leading into the Level 4 isolation suite. He did not enter the patient's room, but stood safely outside and stared at the horror unfolding beyond the observation window.

There was blood splattered on the walls and pooling on the floor where Dr Nathan Helsinger lay seizing. Two nurses and a physician in space suits were trying to stop him from injuring himself, but his spasms were so violent and so powerful they could not restrain him. His leg shot out and a nurse went sprawling, sliding across the blood-slicked concrete floor.

Roman hit the intercom button. 'Your suit! Is there a breach?'

As she slowly rose to her feet, he could see her expression of terror. She looked down at her gloves, her sleeves, then at the juncture where the hose fed air into her suit. 'No,' she said, and it was almost a sob of relief. 'No breach.'

Blood splattered the window. Roman jerked back as bright droplets trickled down the glass. Helsinger was banging his head against the floor now, his spine relaxing, then hyper-extending. Opisthotonos. Roman had seen this bizarre posture only once before, in a victim of strychnine poisoning, the body curved backward like a bow strung under tension. Helsinger spasmed again, and his skull slammed backward against the concrete. Blood sprayed the faceplates of the two nurses.

'Back off!' Roman commanded through the intercom.

'He's hurting himself!' said the physician.

'I don't want anyone else exposed.'

'If we could get these seizures under control –'

'There's nothing you can do to save him. I want you all to move away *now*. Before you get hurt.'

Reluctantly the two nurses backed away. After a pause, so did the physician. They stood in silent tableau as the scene of horror played out at their feet.

New convulsions sent Helsinger's head whipping backward. The scalp split open, like cloth ripping along a seam. The pool of blood widened into a lake.

'Oh, God, look at his eyes!' one of the nurses cried.

The eyes were popping out, like two giant marbles straining to burst out of the sockets. *Traumatic proptosis*, thought Roman. The eyeballs thrust forward by catastrophic intracranial pressure, the lids shoved apart, wide and staring.

The seizures continued, unrelenting, the head battering the floor. Splinters of bone flew up and ticked against the window. It was as though he were trying to crack open his own skull, to release whatever was trapped inside.

Another crack. Another spattering of blood and bone.

He should have been dead. Why was he still seizing?

But even decapitated chickens continue to twitch and thrash, and Helsinger's death throes were not yet over. His head lifted off the floor, his spine curling forward like a spring winding up to unbearable tension just before it snaps. His neck lashed backward. There was a *crack*, and the skull split open like an egg. Shards of bone flew. A lump of gray matter splashed the window.

Roman gasped and stumbled backward, nausea rising in his throat. He dropped his head, fighting to stay in control. Fighting the darkness that threatened to envelop his vision.

Sweating, shaking, he managed to lift his head. To look, once again, through the window.

Nathan Helsinger at last lay still. What was left of his head rested in a lake of blood. There was so much blood that for a moment Roman could not focus on anything else but that spreading pool of scarlet. Then his gaze settled on the dead man's face. On the blue-green mass that clung, quivering, to his forehead. Cysts.

Chimera.

256

August 14

'Nicolai? Nicolai, please respond!'

'My ear – It is in my ear –'

'Pain? Does your ear hurt? Look at me!'

'It's going deeper! Get it out! Get it . . .'

White House Security Council science adviser Jared Profitt pressed the OFF button on the cassette recorder and looked at the men and women seated around the table. All of them wore expressions of horror. 'What happened to Nicolai Rudenko was more than just a decompressive accident,' he said. 'That's why we took the action we did. That's why I urge you all to stay the course. There's too much at stake. Until we learn more about this organism – how it reproduces, how it infects – we can't let those astronauts come home.'

The response was stunned silence. Even NASA administrator Leroy Cornell, who had led off the meeting with an outraged protest about the takeover of his agency, sat utterly speechless.

It was the president who asked the first question. 'What *do* we know about this organism?'

'Dr Isaac Roman from USAMRIID can answer that better than I can,' said Profitt, and he nodded to Roman, who was not seated at the table, but on the periphery, where he'd been largely unnoticed by everyone in the room. Now he stood so that he could be seen, a tall and graying man with the look of exhaustion in his eyes.

'I'm afraid the news is not good,' he said. 'We've injected Chimera into a number of different mammalian species including dogs and spider monkeys. Within ninety-six hours, all were dead. A mortality rate of one hundred percent.'

'And there's no treatment? Nothing has worked?' asked the secretary of defense.

'Nothing. Which is frightening enough. But there's worse news.'

The room went very still as fear rippled across faces. How could this get any worse?

'We have repeated the DNA analysis of the most recent generation of eggs, collected from the dead monkeys. Chimera has acquired yet a new cluster of genes, specific to *Ateles geoffroyi*. The spider monkey.'

The president blanched. He looked at Profitt. 'Does this mean what I think it means?'

'It's devastating,' said Profitt. 'Every time this life-form cycles through a new host, every time it produces a new generation, it seems to acquire new DNA. It has the ability to stay several steps ahead of us by picking up new genes, new capabilities it's never had before.'

'How the hell can it do this?' asked General Moray of the Joint Chiefs of Staff. 'An organism that picks up new genes? That keeps remaking itself? It sounds impossible.'

Roman said, 'It's not impossible, sir. In fact, a similar process occurs in nature. Bacteria often share genes with each other, trading them back and forth by using viruses as couriers. That's how they develop antibiotic resistance so quickly. They spread around the genes for resistance, adding new DNA to their chromosomes. Like everything else in nature, they'll use every weapon they have to survive. To perpetuate their species. That's what this organism is doing.' He moved to the head of the table, where a blowup of an electron micrograph was displayed. 'You can see here, in this photograph of the cell, what looks like tiny granules. They're clumps of helper virus. Couriers that travel into the host cell, raid its DNA, and bring back bits and pieces of genetic material to Chimera. Adding new genes, new weapons to its arsenal.' Roman looked at the president. 'This organism came equipped to survive any environmental conditions. All it needs to do is raid the local fauna's DNA.'

The president looked ill. 'So it's still changing. Still evolving.'

258

There were murmurs of dismay around the table. Frightened glances, creaking chairs.

'What about that doctor who got infected?' asked a woman from the Pentagon. 'The one USAMRIID had in Level Four isolation? Is he still alive?'

Roman paused, a look of pain in his eyes. 'Dr Helsinger died late last night. I witnessed the terminal event and it was . . . a horrible death. He began to convulse so violently we didn't dare control him for fear someone's space suit would be torn and someone else exposed. These were seizures unlike any I've ever seen. It was as though every single neuron in his brain fired at once in a massive electrical storm. He broke the bed rail. Snapped it cleanly off the frame. Rolled off the mattress and began to – to batter his head on the floor. So hard, we could . . .' He swallowed. 'We could hear the skull crack. By then there was blood flying everywhere. He kept smashing his head against the floor, almost as if he was trying to break it open. To release the pressure building up inside. The trauma only made it worse, because he began to bleed into his brain. At the end, the intracranial pressure was so great, it bulged his eyes out of their sockets. Like a cartoon character. Like an animal you see squashed on the road.' He took a deep breath. 'That,' he said quietly, 'was the terminal event.'

'Now you understand the possible epidemic we face,' said Profitt. 'This is why we can't afford to be weak or careless. Or sentimental.'

There was another long silence. Everyone looked at the president. They were all waiting for – hoping for – an unequivocal decision.

Instead, he swiveled his chair toward the window and stared outside. 'I wanted to be an astronaut, once,' he said sadly.

Didn't we all? thought Profitt. *Which child in this country has not dreamed of riding a rocket into space?*

259

'I was there when they launched John Glenn on the shuttle,' the president said. 'And I cried. Just like everyone else. Goddamn it, but I cried like a baby. Because I was proud of him. And proud of this country. And proud of just being part of the human race . . .' He paused. Took a deep breath and wiped his hand across his eyes. 'How the hell do I condemn those people to death?'

Profitt and Roman exchanged unhappy glances.

'We have no choice, sir,' said Profitt. 'It's five lives versus the lives of God knows how many people here on earth.'

'They're *heroes*. Honest-to-God heroes. And we're going to leave them up there to die.'

'The chances are, Mr President, we wouldn't be able to save them anyway,' said Roman. 'All of them are probably infected. Or they soon will be.'

'Then some of them may *not* be infected?'

'We don't know. We do know Rudenko definitely is. We believe he was exposed while in his EVA suit. If you'll recall, Astronaut Hirai was found seizing in the EVA equipment lock ten days ago. That would explain how the suit got contaminated.'

'Why aren't the others sick yet? Why only Rudenko?'

'Our studies indicate this organism needs incubation time before it reaches the infectious stage. We think it's most contagious around the time the host dies, or afterwards, when it's released from the corpse. But we're not certain. We can't afford to be wrong. We have to assume they're all carriers.'

'Then keep them in Level Four isolation until you know. But at least get them *home*.'

'Sir, that's where the risk comes in,' said Profitt. 'In just bringing them home. The CRV's not like the shuttle, which you actually guide down to a specific landing strip. They'd be coming home in a far less controllable vehicle – essentially a pod with parachutes. What if something goes wrong? What if the CRV breaks up in the atmosphere, or crashes on landing? This organism would be released into the air. The wind could carry it anywhere! By then, it will have so much human DNA in its genome, we won't be able to fight it. It will be too much like *us*. Any drug we use against it would kill humans as well.' Profitt paused, letting the impact of his words sink in. 'We can't let emotions affect our decision. Not with so much at stake.'

'Mr President,' cut in Leroy Cornell, 'with all due respect, may I point out that this would be a politically disastrous move. The public will not allow five heroes to die in space.'

'Politics should be our last concern right now!' said Profitt. 'Our first priority is public health!'

'Then why the secrecy? Why have you cut NASA out of the loop? You've shown us only parts of the organism's genome. Our life-sciences people are ready and willing to contribute their expertise. We want to find a cure every bit as much as – even more than – you do. If USAMRIID would just share all its data with us, we could work together.'

'Our concern is security,' said General Moray. 'A hostile country could turn this into a devastating bioweapon. Giving out Chimera's genetic code is like handing out a blueprint for that weapon.'

'Meaning you don't trust NASA with that information?'

General Moray met Cornell's gaze head-on. 'I'm afraid NASA's new philosophy of sharing technology with every two-bit country under the sun does not make your agency a good security risk.'

Cornell flushed with anger but said nothing.

Profitt looked at the president. 'Sir, it *is* a tragedy that five astronauts must be left up there to die. But we have to look beyond that, to the possibility of a far greater tragedy. A worldwide epidemic, caused by an organism we're just beginning to understand. USAMRIID is working around the clock to learn what makes it tick. Until then, I urge you to stay the course. NASA is not equipped to deal with a biological disaster. They have one planetary-protection officer. *One*. The Army's Biological Rapid Response Team is prepared for just this sort of crisis. As for NASA operations, leave that under the control of U.S. Space Command, backed up by the Fourteenth Air Force. NASA has too many personal and emotional ties to the astronauts. We need a firm grip on the helm. We need absolute discipline.' Profitt slowly looked around at the men and women seated at the long table. Only a few of these people did he truly respect. Some were interested only in prestige and power. Others had earned a seat here because of political connections. Still others were easily swayed by public sentiment. Few had motives as uncomplicated as his.

Few had suffered his nightmares, had awakened soaked with sweat in the darkness, shaken by the terrible vision of what they might face.

'Then you're saying the astronauts can never come home,' said Cornell.

Profitt looked at the NASA administrator's ashen face and felt genuine sympathy. 'When we find a way to cure it, when we know we can kill this organism, then we can talk about bringing your people home.'

'If they're still alive,' murmured the president.

Profitt and Roman glanced at each other, but neither responded. They already understood the obvious. They would not find a cure in time. The astronauts would not be coming home alive.

Jared Profitt wore his jacket and tie as he walked through that sweltering day, but he scarcely noticed the heat. Others might complain of the miseries of a D.C. summer. He did not mind the soaring temperatures. It was winter he dreaded, because he was so sensitive to cold, and on frosty days his lips would turn blue and he'd shiver under layers of scarves and sweaters. Even in summer he kept a sweater in his office to combat the effects of the air conditioner. Today the temperature was in the nineties, and perspiration gleamed on all the faces he passed on the street, but he did not remove his jacket or loosen his tie.

The meeting had left him deeply chilled, both in body and soul.

He was carrying his lunch in a brown paper bag, the identical lunch he packed every morning before he left for work. The route he walked was the one he always took, west toward the Potomac, the Reflecting Pool on his left. He took comfort in the routine, the familiar. There were so few things in his life that offered much reassurance these days, and as he grew older, he found himself adhering to certain rituals, much as a monk in a religious order adheres to the daily rhythm of work and prayer and meditation. In many ways, he was like those ancient ascetics, a man who ate only to fuel his body and dressed in suits only because it was required of him. A man for whom wealth meant nothing.

The name *Profitt* could not be further from the reality of the man.

He slowed his pace as he walked along the grassy slope past the Vietnam War Memorial, and gazed down at the solemn line of visitors shuffling past the wall etched with names of the dead. He knew what they were all thinking as they confronted those panels of black granite, as they considered the horrors of war: *So many names. So many dead.*

And he thought, *You have no idea.*

He found an empty bench in the shade and sat down to eat. From his brown bag he removed an apple, a wedge of cheddar, and a bottle of water. Not Evian or Perrier, but straight from the tap. He ate slowly, watching the tourists as they made the circuit from memorial to memorial. *And so we honor our war heroes*, he thought. Society erected statues, engraved marble plaques, raised flags. It shuddered at the number of lives lost on both sides in the slaughterhouse of war. Two million soldiers and civilians dead in Vietnam. Fifty million dead in World War II. Twenty-one million dead in World War I. The numbers were appalling. People might ask: Could man have a more lethal enemy than himself?

The answer was yes.

Though humans could not see it, the enemy was all around them. Inside them. In the air they breathed, the food they drank. Throughout the history of mankind, it has been their nemesis, and it would survive them long after they have vanished from the face of the earth. The enemy was the microbial world, and over the centuries, it has killed more people than all of man's wars combined.

From A.D. 542 to 767, forty million dead of the plague in the Justinian pandemic.

In the 1300s, twenty-five million dead when the Black Death returned.

In 1918 and 1919, thirty million dead of influenza.

And in 1997, Amy Sorensen Profitt, age forty-three, dead of pneumococcal pneumonia.

He finished his apple, placed the core in the brown bag, and carefully rolled his rubbish into a tight bundle. Though the lunch had been meager, he felt satisfied, and he remained on the bench for a while, sipping the last of the water.

A tourist walked by, a woman with light brown hair. When she turned just so and the light slanted across her face, she looked like Amy. She felt him staring, and she glanced his way. They regarded each other for a moment, she with wariness, he with silent apology. Then she walked away, and he decided she did not look like his dead wife after all. No one did. No one could.

He rose to his feet, discarded his trash in a receptacle, and began to walk back the way he'd come. Past the wall. Past the uniformed veterans, gray and shaggy now, keeping vigil. Honoring the memory of the dead.

But even the memories fade, he thought. The image of her smile across the kitchen table, the echo of her laughter – all those were receding as time went by. Only the painful memories hung on. A San Francisco hotel room. A late-night phone call. Frantic images of airports and taxis and phone booths as he raced across the country to reach Bethesda Hospital in time.

But necrotizing streptococcus has its own agenda, its own timetable for killing. *Just like Chimera.*

He drew in a breath of air and wondered how many viruses, how many bacteria, how many fungi, had just swirled into his lungs. And which of those might kill him.

20

August 15

'I say fuck'em,' said Luther. The air-to-ground comm was off, their conversation unmonitored by Mission Control. 'Let's get back on the CRV, flip the switches, and *go*. They can't make us turn around and come back.'

Once they left the station, they *couldn't* turn around. The CRV was essentially a glider with drag chutes. After separation from ISS, it could travel a maximum of four revolutions around the earth before it was forced to deorbit and land.

'We've been advised to sit tight,' said Griggs. 'That's exactly what we're going to do.'

'Follow stupid shit orders? Nicolai's going to *die* on us if we don't get him home!'

Griggs looked at Emma. 'Opinion, Watson?'

For the last twenty-four hours, Emma had been hovering by her patient, monitoring Nicolai's condition. They could all see for themselves that he was in critical condition. Tied down to the medical restraint board, he twitched and trembled, his limbs sometimes flailing out with such violence Emma was afraid he'd snap his bones. He looked like a boxer who had been pummeled mercilessly in the ring.

266

Subcutaneous emphysema had bloated the soft tissues of his face, swelling his eyelids shut. Through the narrow slits, his sclerae were a brilliant, demonic red.

She didn't know how much Nicolai could hear and understand, so she didn't dare say aloud what she was thinking. She motioned her crewmates out of the Russian service module.

They met in the hab, where Nicolai could not hear them, and where they could safely remove their goggles and masks.

'Houston needs to clear our evac now,' she said, 'or we're going to lose him.'

'They're aware of the situation,' said Griggs. 'They can't authorize an evac until the White House clears it.'

'So we're just gonna hang around up here and watch each other get sick?' said Luther. 'What if we just got in the CRV and left? What're they gonna do, shoot us down?'

Diana said quietly, 'They could.'

The truth of what she'd just said made them all fall silent. Every astronaut who had ever climbed aboard the shuttle and sweated through a countdown knew that sitting in a bunker at KSC was a team of Air Force officers whose only job was to blow up the shuttle, incinerating the crew. Should the steering system go awry during launch, should the shuttle veer disastrously toward a populated area, it was the duty of these range-safety officers to press the destruct buttons. They had met every member of the shuttle's flight crew. They had probably seen photographs of the astronauts' families. They knew exactly who they would be killing. It was a terrible responsibility, yet no one doubted those Air Force officers would carry it out.

Just as they would almost certainly destroy the CRV if so ordered. When faced with the specter of a new and lethal epidemic, the lives of five astronauts would seem trivial.

Luther said, 'I'm willing to bet they'll let us land safely. Why wouldn't they? Four of us are still healthy. We haven't caught anything.'

'But we've already been exposed,' said Diana. 'We've breathed the same air, shared the same quarters. Luther, you and Nicolai slept together in that air lock.'

'I feel perfectly fine.'

'So do I. So do Griggs and Watson. But if this is an infection, we may already be in the incubation stages.'

'That's why we have to follow orders,' said Griggs. 'We stay right where we are.'

Luther turned to Emma. 'Do you go along with this martyr shit?'

'No,' she said. 'I don't.'

Griggs looked at her in surprise. 'Watson?'

'I'm not thinking about myself,' said Emma. 'I'm thinking about my patient. Nicolai can't talk, so I have to do it for him. I want him in a hospital, Griggs.'

'You heard what Houston said.'

'What I heard was a lot of confusion. Evac Orders being given, then belayed. First they tell us it's Marburg virus. Then they say it's not a virus at all, but some new organism cooked up by bioterrorists. I don't know what the hell's going on down there. All I know is, my patient is . . .' She abruptly lowered her voice. 'He's dying,' she said softly. 'My primary responsibility is to keep him alive.'

'And my responsibility is to act as commander of this station,' said Griggs. 'I have to believe that Houston is calling the shots the best they can. They wouldn't put us in this danger unless the situation was truly grave.'

Emma could not disagree. Mission Control was manned by people she knew, people she trusted. *And Jack is there*, she thought. There was no human being she trusted more than him.

'Looks like we have data being uplinked,' said Diana, glancing at the computer. 'It's for Watson.'

Emma glided across the module to read the message glowing on the screen. It was from NASA Life Sciences.

Dr Watson,
  We think you should know exactly what you're dealing with – what we're all dealing with. This is the DNA analysis of the organism infecting Kenichi Hirai.

Emma called up the attached file.

It took her a moment to mentally process the nucleotide sequence that flowed across the screen. A few minutes more to actually *believe* the conclusions.

Genes from three *different* species were on one chromosome. Leopard frog. Mouse. And human.

'What is this organism?' asked Diana.

Emma said softly, 'A new life-form.'

It was a Frankenstein's monster. An abomination of nature. She suddenly focused on the word 'mouse,' and she thought, *The mice. They were the first to get sick.* Over the past week and a half they had continued to die. The last time she had checked the cage, only one mouse, a female, was still alive.

She left the hab and headed deeper into the powered-down half of the station.

The U.S. lab was deep in gloom. She floated across the semi-darkness to the animal holding rack. Had the mice been the original carriers for this organism, the vessels in which the chimera had been brought aboard ISS? Or were they just the accidental victims, infected through exposure to something else aboard the station?

And was the last mouse alive?

She opened the rack drawer and peered into the cage at the lone resident.

Her heart sank. The mouse was dead.

She had come to think of this female with the chewed-up ear as a fighter, the scrappy survivor who, through sheer orneriness, had outlasted its cage mates. Now Emma felt an unexpected pang of grief as she gazed at the lifeless body floating at the far end of the cage. Its abdomen already looked bloated. The corpse would have to be removed immediately and discarded with the contaminated trash.

She interfaced the cage to the glove box, inserted her hands into the gloves, and reached in to grab the mouse. The instant her fingers closed over it, the corpse suddenly scrabbled to life. Emma gave a scream of surprise and released it.

The mouse flipped over and glared at her, whiskers twitching in irritation.

Emma gave a startled laugh. 'So you're not dead after all,' she murmured.

'*Watson!*'

She turned toward the intercom, which had just spat out her name. 'I'm in the lab.'

'Get in here! The RSM. Nicolai's seizing!'

She flew out of the lab, caroming off walls in the gloom as she shot toward the Russian end. The first thing she saw as she popped into the RSM were the faces of her crewmates, their horror evident even through their goggles. Then they moved aside and she saw Nicolai.

His left arm was jerking spasmodically and with such power the whole restraint board shuddered. The seizures marched down the left side of his body, and his leg began to thrash as well. Now his hips were lurching, thrusting off the board as the seizures continued their inexorable march across his body. The jerking intensified, the wrist restraints scraping his skin bloody. Emma heard a sickening *crack* as the bones of his left forearm snapped. The right wrist restraint flew apart, and his arm thrashed unchecked, the back of his hand pummeling the edge of the table, smashing bones and flesh.

'Hold him still! I'm going to pump him full of Valium!' yelled Emma, frantically rummaging inside the medical kit.

Griggs and Luther each grabbed an arm, but even Luther was not powerful enough to control the unrestrained limb. Nicolai's right arm flew up like a whip, flinging Luther aside. Luther went tumbling, and his foot clipped Diana on the cheek, knocking her goggles askew.

Nicolai's head suddenly slammed backward against the table. He gasped in a gurgling breath, and his chest bloated up with air. A cough exploded from his throat.

Phlegm sprayed out, catching Diana in the face. She gave a yelp of disgust and released her grip, drifting backward as she wiped her exposed eye.

A globule of blue-green mucus floated past Emma. Encased in that gelatinous mass was a pearllike kernel. Only as it drifted past the luminaire assembly of the lighting system did Emma realize what she was looking at. When a hen's egg is held in front of a candle flame, the contents can be seen through the shell. Now the luminaire assembly was acting as the candle, its glow penetrating the kernel's opaque membrane.

Inside, something was moving. Something was alive.

The cardiac monitor squealed. Emma spun around to look at Nicolai, and she saw that he had stopped breathing. A flat line traced across the monitor.

August 16

Jack slipped the comm unit on his head. He was alone in a back room of Mission Control, and this conversation was supposed to be confidential, but he knew that what he and Emma said today would not, in fact, be private. He suspected that all communications with ISS were now being monitored by the Air Force and U.S. Space Command.

He said, 'Capcom, this is Surgeon. I'm ready for private family conference.'

'Roger, Surgeon,' said Capcom. 'Ground Control, secure air to ground loop.' There was a pause, then: 'Surgeon, proceed to PFC.'

Jack's heart was pounding. He took a deep breath and said, 'Emma, it's me.'

'He might have lived if we'd gotten him home,' she said. 'He might have had a chance.'

'We weren't the ones who stopped the evac! Again and again, NASA's been overruled. We're fighting to get you home, as soon as possible. If you'll just hang in –'

'It won't be soon enough, Jack.' She said it quietly. Matter-of-factly. Her words chilled him to the marrow. 'Diana is infected,' she said.

'Are you sure?'

'I just ran her amylase level. It's rising. We're watching her now. Waiting for the first symptoms. The stuff flew all over the module. We've cleaned it up, but we're not sure who else was exposed.' She paused, and he heard her take a shaky breath. 'You know those things you saw inside Andy and Jill? The things you thought were cysts? I sectioned one under the microscope. I've just downlinked the images to Life Sciences. They're not cysts, Jack. And they're not spores.'

'What are they?'

'They're eggs. Something is inside them. Something is growing.'

'Growing? Are you saying they're multicellular?'

'Yes. That's exactly what I'm saying.'

He was stunned. He had assumed they were dealing with a microbe, nothing larger than a single-celled bacteria. Mankind's deadliest enemies have always been microbial – bacteria and viruses and protozoa, too small to be seen by the human eye. If Chimera was multicellular, then it was far more advanced than a simple bacteria.

'The one I saw was still unformed,' she said. 'It was more like a – a *cluster* of cells than anything else. But with vascular channels. And contractile movements. As though the whole thing was pulsating, like a culture of myocardial cells.'

'Maybe it *was* a culture. A group of single cells clumped together.'

'No. No, I think it was all one organism. And it was still young, still developing.'

'Into what?'

'USAMRIID knows,' she said. 'These things were growing inside Kenichi Hirai's corpse. Digesting his organs. When his body disintegrated, they must have been splashed all over that orbiter.'

Which the military immediately placed under quarantine, thought Jack, remembering the choppers. The space-suited men.

'They're growing in Nicolai's corpse as well.'

He said, 'Jettison his body, Emma! Don't waste any time.'

'We're doing it now. Luther's preparing to release the body from the air lock. We have to hope the vacuum of space will kill this thing. It's a historic event, Jack. The first human burial in space.' She gave a strange laugh, but it quickly choked off into silence.

'Listen to me,' he said. 'I'm going to bring you home. If I have to ride a goddamn rocket myself and come pick you up.'

'They won't let us come home. I know that now.'

He had never heard such defeat in her voice, and it made him angry. Desperate. 'Don't wimp out on me, Emma!'

'I'm only being realistic. I've seen the enemy, Jack. Chimera is a complex multicellular life-form. It moves. It reproduces. It uses *our* DNA, *our* genes, against us. If this is a bioengineered organism, some terrorist has just created the perfect weapon.'

273

'Then he must have designed a defense as well. No one unleashes a new weapon without knowing how to protect himself against it.'

'A fanatic might. A terrorist whose only interest is in killing people – lots of people. And this thing could do that. Not only does it kill, it reproduces. It *spreads*.' She paused. And the sound of exhaustion seeped into her voice. 'Given those facts, it's clear we won't be coming home.'

Jack pulled off the comm unit and dropped his head in his hands. For a long time he sat alone in the room, the sound of Emma's voice still vivid in his mind. *I don't know how to save you*, he thought. *I don't even know where to begin.*

He did not hear the door open. Only when Liz Gianni from Payload Operations said his name did he finally look up.

'We have a name,' she said.

He shook his head in bewilderment. 'What?'

'I told you, I was going to look up which experiment had to be destroyed because of fungal overgrowth. It turns out it was a cell culture. The principal investigator is a Dr Helen Koenig, a marine biologist out in California.'

'What about her?'

'She's disappeared. She resigned two weeks ago from the lab at SeaScience where she works. Hasn't been heard from since. And Jack, here's the kicker. I just spoke to someone at SeaScience. She told me that federal investigators raided Koenig's lab on August ninth. They removed all her files.'

Jack sat up straight. 'What was Koenig's experiment? What kind of cell culture did she send up?'

'A single-celled marine organism. They're called Archaeons.'

21

'It was supposed to be a three-month protocol,' said Liz. 'A study of how Archaeons multiply in microgravity. The culture began to show some bizarre results. Rapid growth, clump formation. It was multiplying at amazing rates.'

They were walking along one of the pathways that wound through the JSC campus, past a pond where a fountain sprayed water into the listless air. The day was uncomfortably hot and muggy, but they felt safer talking outside; here, at least, they could speak in private.

'Cells behave differently in space,' said Jack. That, in fact, was the reason cultures were grown in orbit. On earth, tissue grows flat like a sheet, covering the surface of the culture plate. In space, the absence of gravity allows tissues to grow in three dimensions, assuming shapes it can never achieve on earth.

'Considering how exciting these developments were,' said Liz, 'it's surprising the experiment was abruptly terminated at six and a half weeks.'

'Who terminated the experiment?' asked Jack.

'The order came directly from Helen Koenig. Apparently, she analyzed the Archaeon samples which had been returned to earth aboard *Atlantis* and found them contaminated by fungi. She ordered the culture on ISS destroyed.'

'And was it?'

'Yes. But the weird part was *how* it was destroyed. The crew wasn't allowed to just bag and dispose of it in the contaminated wet trash, which is what they'd normally do with a nonhazardous organism. No, Koenig told them to put the cultures in the crucible and *incinerate* them. And then to jettison the ash.'

Jack stopped on the path and stared at her. 'If Dr Koenig is a bioterrorist, why would she destroy her own weapon?'

'Your guess is as good as mine.'

He thought about it for a moment, trying to make sense of it, but not coming up with an answer.

'Tell me more about her experiment,' he said. 'What, exactly, *is* an Archaeon?'

'Petrovitch and I reviewed the scientific literature. *Archaeons* are a bizarre domain of single-celled organisms called *extremophiles* – "lovers of extreme conditions." They were discovered only twenty years ago, living – and thriving – near boiling volcanic vents on the sea floor. They've also been found buried in polar ice caps and in rocks deep in the earth's crust. Places we thought life couldn't exist.'

'So they're sort of like hardy bacteria?'

'No, they're a completely separate branch of life. Literally, their name means "the ancient ones." They're so ancient, their origins date back to the universal ancestor of *all* life. A time before even bacteria existed. Archaeons were some of the first inhabitants of our planet, and they'll probably be the last to survive. No matter what happens – nuclear war, asteroid impact – they'll be here, long after we're extinct.' She paused. 'In a sense, they're earth's ultimate conquerors.'

'Are they infectious?'

'No. They're harmless to humans.'

'Then this isn't our killer organism.'

'But what if something *else* was in that culture instead? What if she slipped in a different organism just before she shipped us the payload? I find it interesting that Helen Koenig vanished just as this crisis was heating up.'

Jack said nothing for a moment, his thoughts focused on why Helen Koenig would abruptly order her own experiment incinerated. He remembered what Gordon Obie had said at their meeting. Perhaps this was not an act of sabotage at all, but something just as frightening. A mistake.

'There's more,' said Liz. 'Something else about this experiment that raises the red flag for me.'

'What?'

'How it got funded. Experiments that come from outside NASA have to compete for room aboard the station. The scientist fills out the OLMSA application, explaining the possible commercial uses for the experiment. It gets reviewed by us and goes through various committees before we prioritize which ones get launched. The process takes a long time – at least a year or more.'

'How long did the Archaeon application take?'

'Six months.'

He frowned. 'It was rushed through that quickly?'

Liz nodded. 'Fast track. It didn't have to compete for NASA funding, like most experiments do. It was a commercial reimbursable. Someone *paid* to send up that experiment.'

That was, in fact, one of the ways NASA kept ISS financially viable – by selling payload space aboard the station to commercial users.

'So why would a company spend big bucks – and I do mean big bucks – to grow a test tube of essentially worthless organisms? Scientific curiosity?' She gave a skeptical snort. 'I don't *think* so.'

'Which company paid for it?'

'The firm Dr Koenig worked for. SeaScience in La Jolla, California. They develop commercial products from the sea.'

The despair Jack had felt earlier was finally lifting. Now he had information to work with. A plan of action. At last he could *do* something.

He said, 'I need the address and phone number of SeaScience. And the name of that employee you spoke to.'

Liz gave a brisk nod. 'You got it, Jack.'

August 17

Diana awakened from a restless sleep, her head aching, the dreams still clouding her mind. Dreams of England, of her childhood home in Cornwall. Of the neat brick pathway leading to the front door, overhung by climbing roses. In her dream, she had pushed open the little gate and heard it squeal as it always did, the hinges in need of oil. She had started up the walkway to the stone cottage. Only half a dozen paces and she would be on the front stoop, opening the door. Calling out that she was home, at last home. She wanted her mother's hugs, her mother's forgiveness. But the half dozen paces became a dozen. Two dozen. And still the cottage was out of reach, the pathway stretching longer and longer until the house had receded to the size of a doll's.

Diana awakened with both arms reaching out, a cry of despair bursting from her throat.

She opened her eyes and saw Michael Griggs staring at her. Though his face was partly obscured by a protective filter mask and goggles, she could see his expression of horror.

She unzipped her sleep restraint and floated across the Russian service module. Even before she looked in the mirror at her own reflection, she knew what she would see.

A flame of brilliant red was splashed across the white of her left eye.

*　　*　　*

Emma and Luther spoke in hushed voices as they floated together in the dimly lit hab. Most of the station was still in power down; only the Russian segment, which had its own self-contained electrical supply, was operating at full power. The U.S. end of the station was reduced to an eerie maze of shadowy tunnels, and in the gloom of the hab, the brightest source of light was the computer screen, on which the Environmental Control and Life Support System diagrams were currently displayed. Emma and Luther were already familiar with the ECLS system, had memorized its components and subsystems during their training on earth. Now they had an urgent reason to review the system. They had a contagion on board, and they could not be certain if the entire station was contaminated. When Nicolai had coughed, spraying eggs throughout the Russian service module, the hatch had been open. Within seconds, the station's circulation system, designed to keep pockets of dead air from building up, had swirled the airborne droplets into other parts of the station. Had the environmental-control system filtered out and trapped the airborne particles, as it was designed to do? Or was the contagion everywhere now, in every module?

On the computer screen were diagrams of airflow into and out of the station's atmosphere. Oxygen was supplied by several independent sources. The primary source was the Russian Elektron generator, which electrolyzed water into hydrogen and oxygen. A solid-fuel generator using chemical cartridges was one of the backup sources, as were the oxygen storage tanks, which were recharged by the shuttle. A plumbed system distributed the oxygen, mixed with nitrogen, throughout the station, and fans kept the air circulating between modules. Fans also drew in air through various scrubbers and filters, removing carbon dioxide, water, and airborne particles.

'These HEPA filters should've trapped every egg or larva

within fifteen minutes,' said Luther, pointing to the high-efficiency particulate air filters in the diagram. 'The system's ninety-nine point nine percent efficient. Everything bigger than a third of a micron should've been filtered out.'

'Assuming the eggs stayed airborne,' said Emma. 'The problem is, they adhere to surfaces. And I've seen them move. They could crawl into crevices, hide behind panels where we can't see them.'

'It'd take months for us to rip out every panel and look for them. Even then, we'd probably miss a few.'

'Forget ripping out the panels. That's hopeless. I'll change out the rest of the HEPA filters. Recheck the microbial air samplers tomorrow. We have to assume that'll do it. But if those larvae have crawled into the electrical conduits, we'll never find them.' She sighed, her fatigue so heavy she had to struggle to think. 'Whatever we do, it may not make a difference. It may be too late.'

'It's definitely too late for Diana,' Luther said softly.

Today, the scleral hemorrhages had appeared in Diana's eyes. She was now confined to the Russian service module. A plastic sheet had been draped over the hatchway, and no one was allowed in without a respiratory mask and goggles. A *useless exercise*, thought Emma. They had all breathed the same air; they had all touched Nicolai. Perhaps they were all infected.

'We have to assume the Russian service module is now hopelessly contaminated,' said Emma.

'That's the only livable module with full power. We can't close it off entirely.'

'Then I guess you know what we have to do.'

Luther gave a weary sigh. 'Another EVA.'

'We need to restore full power to this end,' she said. 'You've got to finish those repairs on the beta gimbal assembly, or we'll be on the edge of catastrophe. If anything

280

else goes wrong with our remaining power supply, we could lose Environmental Control next. Or the Guidance and Nav computers.' It was what the Russians used to call *the coffin scenario*. Without the power to orient itself, the station would begin to spin out of control.

'Even if we do restore power,' said Luther, 'it doesn't address our real problem. The biocontamination.'

'If we can contain it to the Russian end –'

'But she's incubating larvae right now! She's like a bomb, waiting to go off.'

'We jettison her body as soon as she dies,' said Emma. 'Before she sheds any eggs or larvae.'

'That may not be soon enough. Nicolai coughed up those eggs when he was still alive. If we wait till Diana dies . . .'

'What are you suggesting, Luther?' Griggs's voice startled them both, and they turned to look at him. He was staring at them from the hatchway, his face gleaming in the shadows. 'Are you saying we shove her out while she's still alive?'

Luther drifted deeper into the gloom, as though retreating from attack. 'Jesus, that's not what I was saying.'

'Then what *were* you saying?'

'Just that the larvae – we know they're inside her. We know it's a matter of time.'

'Maybe they're inside all of us. Maybe they're inside *you*. Growing, developing right now. Should we jettison your body?'

'If that's what it takes to stop it from spreading. Look, we all know she's going to die. There's nothing we can do about it. We've got to think ahead –'

'Shut up!' Griggs shot across the hab and grabbed Luther by his shirt. Both men slammed into the far wall and bounced off again. They twisted around and around in midair, Luther trying to pry off Griggs's hands, Griggs refusing to release him.

281

'Stop it!' yelled Emma. 'Griggs, let him *go!*'

Griggs released his hold. The two men drifted apart, still breathing hard. Emma positioned herself like a referee between them.

'Luther's right,' she said to Griggs. 'We have to think ahead. We may not want to do it, but we have no choice.'

'And if it was you, Watson?' Griggs shot back. 'How would you like us discussing what to do with your body? How quickly we can bag you up, dispose of you?'

'I'd *expect* you to be making those plans! There are three other lives at stake, and Diana knows it. I'm trying my best to keep her alive, but right now, I don't have a clue what will work. All I can do is pump her full of antibiotics and wait for Houston to give us some answers. As far as I'm concerned, we're on our own up here. We have to plan for the worst!'

Griggs shook his head. His eyes were red-rimmed, his face haggard with grief. He said softly, 'How can it get any worse?'

She didn't answer. She looked at Luther and read her own thoughts in his eyes. *The worst is yet to come.*

'ISS, we have Surgeon standing by,' said Capcom. 'Go ahead, ISS.'

'Jack?' said Emma.

She was disappointed to hear Todd Cutler's voice instead. 'It's me, Emma. I'm afraid Jack's left JSC for the day. He and Gordon took off for California.'

Damn you, Jack, she thought. *I need you.*

'We're all in agreement down here about the EVA,' said Todd. 'It needs to be done, and soon. My first question to you is, how is Luther Ames? Both physically and mentally? Is he up to it?'

'He's tired. We're all tired. We've hardly slept in the last twenty-four hours. The cleanup is keeping us busy.'

'If we give him a day to rest, could he manage the EVA?'

'Right now, a day of rest seems like an impossible dream.'

'But would it be enough time?'

She considered it for a moment. 'I think so. He just needs to catch up on his sleep.'

'Okay. Then here's my second question. Are *you* up to an EVA?'

Emma paused in surprise. 'You want *me* to be his partner?'

'We don't think Griggs is up to it. He's withdrawn from all communication with the ground. Our psychologist feels he's too unstable at this point.'

'He's grieving, Todd. And very bitter that you won't let us come home. You may not be aware of this, but he and Diana are . . .' She paused.

'We know. And these emotions seriously undercut his effectiveness. It makes an EVA dangerous. That's why you need to be Luther's partner.'

'What about a suit? The other EMU is too big for me.'

'There's an Orlan-M suit stored in the old *Soyuz*. It was tailored for Elena Savitskaya and was left on board several missions ago. Elena was about your height and weight. It should fit.'

'It's my first EVA.'

'You've gone through WET-F training. You can handle it. Luther just needs you out there to assist.'

'What about my patient? If I'm outside doing the EVA, who's going to attend to her?'

'Griggs can change her IVs, see to her needs.'

'And if there's a medical crisis? What if she starts to convulse?'

Todd said quietly, 'She's dying, Emma. We don't think there's anything you can do to change that fact.'

'That's because you haven't given me any useful information to work with! You're more interested in keeping this

283

station alive! It seems you care more about the goddamn solar arrays than the crew. We need a cure, Todd, or we're all going to die up here.'

'We don't have a cure. Not yet –'

'Then get us the fuck home!'

'You think we *want* to leave you stranded up there? You think we have a choice? It's like the Nazi high command down here! They've got Air Force assholes posted all over Mission Control, and –'

There was sudden silence.

'Surgeon?' said Emma. 'Todd?'

Still no answer.

'Capcom, I've lost Surgeon,' she said. 'I need comm link restored.'

A pause. Then, 'Stand by, ISS.'

She waited for what seemed like an eternity. When Todd's voice finally came back on, it was subdued. *Cowed*, thought Emma.

'They're listening, aren't they?' she said.

'That's affirmative.'

'This is supposed to be a PMC! A private loop!'

'Nothing's private anymore. Remember that.'

She swallowed hard, suppressing her anger. 'Okay. Okay, I'll dispense with the ranting. Just tell me what you've got on this organism. Tell me what I can use against it.'

'I'm afraid there's not much to tell you. I just spoke to USAMRIID. To a Dr Isaac Roman, who's in charge of the Chimera project. His news isn't good. All their antibiotic and antihelminth trials have failed. He says Chimera has so much foreign DNA it's now closer to a mammalian genome than anything else. Which means any drug we use against it kills *our* tissues as well.'

'Have they tried cancer drugs? This thing multiplies so fast, it's behaving like a tumor. Could we attack it that way?'

284

'USAMRIID tried antimitotics, hoping they could kill it during the cell-division phase. Unfortunately, the doses they needed were so high they ended up killing the hosts as well. The entire gastrointestinal mucosa sloughed off. The host animals bled out.'

The worst death imaginable, thought Emma. Massive hemorrhage into the bowels and stomach. Blood pouring from both mouth and rectum. She had witnessed such a death on earth. In space, it would be even more horrifying, giant globules of blood filling the cabin like bright red balloons, splashing onto every surface, every crew member.

'Then nothing has worked,' she said.

Todd said nothing.

'Isn't there something? Some cure that won't kill the host?'

'There was only one thing they mentioned. But Roman believes it's only a temporary effect. Not a cure.'

'What's the treatment?'

'A hyperbaric chamber. It requires a minimum of ten atmospheres of pressure. The equivalent of diving to a depth of over three hundred feet. Infected animals kept at those high pressures are still alive, six days after exposure.'

'It has to be a *minimum* of ten atmospheres?'

'Anything less, and the infection runs its course. The host dies.'

She let out a cry of frustration. 'Even if we *could* pump our air pressure that high, ten atmospheres is more than this station can tolerate.'

'Even two would stress the hull,' said Todd. 'Plus, you'd need a heli-ox atmosphere. You can't reproduce that on the station. That's why I didn't want to mention it. In your situation, it's useless information. We've already looked into the possibility of flying a hyperbaric chamber up to ISS, but equipment that bulky – something capable of producing pressures that high – needs to go into *Endeavour*'s cargo bay.

The problem is, she's already out of horizontal processing. It would take a minimum of two weeks to get a chamber loaded up and launched. And it means docking the orbiter to ISS. Exposing *Endeavour* and its crew to your contamination.' He paused. 'USAMRIID says that's not an option.'

She was silent, her frustration boiling into rage. Their only hope, a hyperbaric chamber, required their return to earth. That was not an option either.

'There has to be something we can do with this information,' she said. 'Explain to me. Why would hyperbaric therapy work? Why did USAMRIID even think of testing it?'

'I asked Dr Roman that same question.'

'What did he say?'

'That this was a new and bizarre organism. That it requires us to consider unconventional therapy.'

'He didn't answer your question.'

'It's all he would tell me.'

Ten atmospheres of pressure was near the upper limit of human tolerance. Emma was an avid scuba diver, but she had never dared go deeper than a hundred twenty feet. A depth of three hundred feet was only for the foolhardy. Why had USAMRIID tested such extreme pressures?

They must have had a reason, she thought. *Something they know about this organism made them think it would work.*

Something they're not telling us.

22

The reason why Gordon Obie was known as the Sphinx had never been more apparent than on their flight to San Diego. They had signed out one of the T-38 jets from Ellington Field, with Obie at the controls and Jack squeezed into the single passenger seat. That they hardly said a word to each other while in the air was not surprising. A T-38 is not conducive to conversation, since passenger and pilot sit one behind the other like two peas crammed in a pod. But even during the refueling stop in El Paso, when they had both climbed out to stretch their legs after an hour and a half in cramped quarters, Obie could not be drawn into conversation. Only once, as they stood on the edge of the tarmac drinking Dr Peppers from the hangar vending machine, did he offer a spontaneous comment. He squinted up at the sun, already past its noon height, and said, 'If she was my wife, I'd be scared shitless too.'

Then he tossed his empty soda can into the trash bin and walked back to the jet.

After landing at Lindbergh Field, Jack took the wheel of their rental car, and they headed north on Interstate 5 to La Jolla. Gordon said almost nothing, but simply stared out the window. Jack had always thought Gordon was more machine than man, and he imagined that computerlike brain registering the passing scenery like bits of data: HILL. OVERPASS. HOUSING DEVELOPMENT. Though Gordon had once been an astronaut, no one in the corps really knew him. He would dutifully show up at all their social events, but would stand off by himself, a quiet and solitary figure sipping nothing stronger than his favorite Dr Pepper. He seemed perfectly at ease with his own silence, accepted it as part of his personality, just as he'd accepted his comically protruding ears and his bad haircuts. If no one really knew Gordon Obie, it was because he saw no reason to reveal himself.

That was why his comment in El Paso had surprised Jack. *If she was my wife, I'd be scared shitless too.*

Jack could not imagine the Sphinx ever being scared, nor could he imagine him being married. As far as he knew, Gordon had always been a bachelor.

Afternoon fog was already rolling in from the sea by the time they wound their way up the La Jolla coastline. They almost missed the entrance to SeaScience; the turnoff was marked by one small sign, and the road beyond it seemed to lead into a grove of eucalyptus trees. Only when they'd driven a half mile down the turnoff did they spot the building, a surreal, almost fortresslike complex of white concrete overlooking the sea.

A woman in a white lab coat met them at the security desk. 'Rebecca Gould,' she said, shaking their hands. 'I work down the hall from Helen. I spoke to you this morning.' With her shorn hair and stout build, Rebecca might have passed for either sex. Even her deep voice was ambiguous.

They took the elevator down to the basement level. 'I don't really know why you insisted on coming out here,' said Rebecca. 'As I told you on the phone, USAMRIID's already picked Helen's lab clean.' She pointed to a doorway. 'You can see for yourself how little they left behind.'

Jack and Gordon stepped into the lab and looked around in dismay. Empty filing cabinet drawers hung open. Shelves and countertops had been swept clean of all equipment, and not even a test tube rack was in sight. Only the wall decorations had been left behind, mostly framed travel posters, seductive photographs of tropical beaches and palm trees and brown women glistening in the sun.

'I was in my lab down the hall the day they showed up. Heard a lot of upset voices and breaking glass. I looked out my door and saw men carting out files and computers. They took everything. The incubators with her cultures. Racks of seawater samples. Even the frogs she kept in that terrarium over there. My assistants tried to stop the raid, and they got hauled out for questioning. Naturally, I called upstairs to Dr Gabriel's office.'

'Gabriel?'

'Palmer Gabriel. Our company president. He came down himself, along with a SeaScience attorney. They couldn't stop the raid, either. The Army just came in with their carton boxes and hauled everything away. They even took the employees' lunches!' She opened the refrigerator and pointed to the empty shelves. 'I don't know what the hell they thought they'd find.' She turned to face them. 'I don't know why you're here, either.'

'I think we're all looking for Helen Koenig.'

'I told you. She resigned.'

'Do you know why?'

Rebecca shrugged. 'That's what USAMRIID kept asking. Whether she was angry at SeaScience. Whether she was mentally unstable. I certainly didn't see that. I think she was just tired. Burned out from working here seven days a week, for God knows how long.'

'And now no one can find her.'

Rebecca's chin jutted up in anger. 'It's not a crime to leave town. It doesn't mean she's a bioterrorist. But USAMRIID treated this lab like a crime scene. As if she was growing Ebola virus or something. Helen was studying Archaeons. Harmless sea microbes.'

'Are you certain that was the only project going on in this lab?'

'Are you asking whether I kept tabs on Helen? Of course not. I'm too busy doing my own work. But what else would Helen be doing? She's devoted years to Archaeon research. That particular strain she sent up to ISS was her discovery. She considered it her personal triumph.'

'Is there a commercial application for Archaeons?'

Rebecca hesitated. 'Not that I'm aware of.'

'Then why study them in space?'

'Haven't you heard of pure science, Dr McCallum? Knowledge for its own sake? These are weird, fascinating creatures. Helen found her species in the Galápagos Rift, near a volcanic vent, at a depth of nineteen thousand feet. Six hundred atmospheres of pressure, at boiling temperatures, this organism was *thriving*. It shows us how adaptable life can be. It's only natural to wonder what would happen if you took that life-form out of its extreme conditions and brought it up to a friendlier environment. Without thousands of pounds of pressure crushing it. Without even gravity to distort its growth.'

'Excuse me,' interrupted Gordon, and they both turned to look at him. He had been wandering around the lab, poking in empty drawers and looking into trash cans. Now he was standing beside one of the travel posters hanging on the wall. He pointed to a snapshot that had been taped to a corner of the picture frame. It showed a large aircraft parked on a tarmac. Posed under the wing were the two pilots. 'Where did this photo come from?'

Rebecca shrugged. 'How would I know? This is Helen's lab.'

'It's a KC-135,' said Gordon.

Now Jack understood why Gordon had focused on the photo. The KC-135 was the same aircraft NASA used to introduce astronauts to microgravity. When flown in giant parabolic curves, it was like an airborne roller coaster, producing up to thirty seconds of weightlessness per dive.

'Did Dr Koenig use a KC-135 in any of her research?' asked Jack.

'I know she spent four weeks out at some airfield in New Mexico. I have no idea what kind of plane they were using.'

Jack and Gordon exchanged thoughtful looks. Four weeks of KC-135 research would cost a fortune.

'Who would authorize an expense like that?' asked Jack.

'It would have to be approved by Dr Gabriel himself.'

'Could we speak to him?'

Rebecca shook her head. 'You don't just drop in on Palmer Gabriel. Even the scientists who work here hardly ever see him. He has research facilities all over the country, so he may not even be in town right now.'

'Another question,' Gordon interrupted. He had wandered over to the empty terrarium and was peering down at the moss and pebbles lining the bottom. 'What's this enclosure for?'

'The frogs. I told you about them, remember? They were Helen's pets. USAMRIID carted them off along with everything else.'

Gordon suddenly straightened and looked at her. 'What kind of frogs?'

She gave a startled laugh. 'Do you NASA guys always ask such weird questions?'

'I'm just curious what variety one would keep as a pet.'

'I think they were some sort of leopard frog. Me, I'd

291

recommend a poodle instead. They're a lot less slimy.' She glanced at her watch. 'So, gentlemen. Any other questions?'

'I think I'm through here, thank you,' said Gordon. And without another word he walked out of the lab.

They sat in the rental car, the sea mist now swirling past their windows, moisture filming the glass. *Rana pipiens*, thought Jack. The northern leopard frog. One of the three species on Chimera's genome.

'This is where it came from,' he said. 'This lab.'

Gordon nodded.

'USAMRIID knew about this place a week ago,' said Jack. 'How did they find out? How did they know Chimera came from SeaScience? There has to be some way to force them to share their information with us.'

'Not if it's a matter of national security.'

'NASA is *not* the enemy.'

'Maybe they think we are. Maybe they believe the threat comes from *inside* NASA,' said Gordon.

Jack looked at him. 'One of ours?'

'It's one of two reasons why Defense would keep us out of the loop.'

'And the other reason?'

'Because they're assholes.'

Jack gave a laugh and slumped back against his seat. Neither one of them spoke for a moment. The day had already wearied them both, and they still had the flight back to Houston.

'I feel like I'm punching at thin air,' said Jack, pressing his hand to his eyes. 'I don't know who or what I'm fighting. But I can't afford to *stop* fighting.'

'She's not a woman I'd give up on, either,' said Gordon.

Neither one of them had said her name, but they both knew they were talking about Emma.

'I remember her first day at Johnson,' said Gordon. In the dim light of the misted windows, Gordon's homely face was sketched in shades of gray on gray. He sat very still, his gaze focused straight ahead, a somber and colorless man. 'I addressed her incoming astronaut class. I looked around the room at all those new faces. And there she was, front and center. Not afraid to be picked on. Not afraid of humiliation. Not afraid of anything.' He paused and gave a small shake of his head. 'I didn't like sending her up. Every time she was chosen for a crew assignment, I wanted to scratch her name off the list. Not because she wasn't good. Hell, no. I just didn't like watching her ride off to that launchpad, knowing what I know about everything that can go wrong.' He suddenly stopped talking. It was more than Jack had ever heard him say in one stretch, more than Gordon had ever revealed of his feelings. Yet none of what he'd said came as a surprise to Jack. He thought of the countless ways he loved Emma. *And what man would not love her?* he wondered. *Even Gordon Obie is not immune.*

He started the car, and the windshield cleared as the wipers scraped away the veil of mist. It was already five o'clock; they would be flying back to Houston in darkness. He pulled out of the parking space and drove toward the exit.

Halfway across the lot, Gordon said, 'What the hell is this?'

Jack slammed on the brakes as a black sedan barreled toward them through the mist. Now a second car screeched into the parking lot and skidded to a stop, its front bumper just kissing theirs. Four men emerged.

Jack froze as his door was yanked open and a voice commanded, 'Gentlemen, please step out of the car. Both of you.'

'Why?'

'You will step out of the car *now.*'

Gordon said softly, 'I get the feeling this is not negotiable.'

Reluctantly they both climbed out and were swiftly patted down and relieved of their wallets.

'He wants to talk to you two. Get in the backseat.' The man pointed to one of the black cars.

Jack glanced around at the four men watching them. *Resistance is futile* just about summed up their situation. He and Gordon walked to the black car and slid into the rear seat.

There was a man sitting in front. All they saw was the back of his head and shoulders. He had thick silvery hair, swept back, and wore a gray suit. His window whisked down, and the two confiscated wallets were handed to him. He slid the window shut again, a darkly tinted barrier against prying eyes. For a few minutes he studied the contents of the wallets. Then he turned to face his backseat visitors. He had dark, almost obsidian eyes, and they seemed strangely devoid of reflected images. Two black holes trapping light. He tossed the wallets into Jack's lap.

'You're a long way from Houston, gentlemen.'

'Must have been that wrong turn in El Paso,' said Jack.

'What does NASA want here?'

'We want to know what was really in that cell culture you sent up.'

'USAMRIID's already been here. They swept the place clean. They have everything. Dr Koenig's research files, her computers. If you have any questions, I suggest you ask *them*.'

'USAMRIID'S not talking to us.'

'That's your problem, not mine.'

'Helen Koenig was working for *you*, Dr Gabriel. Don't you know what goes on in your own labs?'

Jack saw, by the man's expression, that he had guessed

294

correctly. This was the founder of SeaScience. *Palmer Gabriel*. An angelic last name for a man whose eyes gave off no light.

'I have hundreds of scientists working for me,' said Gabriel. 'I have facilities in Massachusetts and Florida. I can't possibly know everything that goes on in those labs. Nor can I be held responsible for any crimes my employees commit.'

'This is not just any crime. This is a bioengineered chimera – an organism that's killed an entire shuttle crew. And it came from your lab.'

'My researchers direct their own projects. I don't interfere. I'm a scientist myself, Dr McCallum, and I know that scientists work best when allowed complete independence. The freedom to indulge their curiosity. Whatever Helen did was her business.'

'Why study Archaeons? What was she hoping to find?'

He turned to face forward, and they saw only the back of his head, with its silvery sweep of hair. 'Knowledge is always useful. At first we may not recognize its value. For instance, what possible benefit is there to knowing the reproductive habits of the sea slug? Then we learn about all the valuable hormones we can extract from that lowly sea slug. And suddenly, its reproduction is of utmost importance.'

'And what's the importance of Archaeons?'

'That's the question, isn't it? That's what we do here. Study an organism until we learn its usefulness.' He pointed toward his research facility, now shrouded in mist. 'You'll notice it's by the sea. All my buildings are by the sea. It's my oil field. That's where I look for the next new cancer drug, the next miracle cure. It makes perfect sense to look there, because that's where *we* come from. Our birthplace. All life comes from the sea.'

'You haven't answered my question. Is there a commercial value for *Archaeons?*'

'That remains to be seen.'

'And why send them into space? Was there something she discovered on those KC-135 flights? Something to do with weightlessness?'

Gabriel rolled down his window and signaled to the men. The back doors swung open. 'Please step out now.'

'Wait,' said Jack. 'Where is Helen Koenig?'

'I haven't heard from her since she resigned.'

'Why did she order her own cell cultures incinerated?'

Jack and Gordon were hauled out of the backseat and shoved toward their rental car.

'What was she afraid of?' Jack yelled.

Gabriel did not answer. His car window rolled shut, and his face disappeared behind the shield of tinted glass.

23

August 18

Luther vented the last air in the crew lock to space and opened the EVA hatch. 'I'll go first,' he said. 'You take it slow. It's always scary the first time out.'

That first glimpse of the emptiness beyond made Emma grasp the edge of the hatchway in panic. She knew the sensation was common, and that it would pass. That brief paralysis of fear gripped almost everyone on their first spacewalk. The mind had trouble accepting the vastness of space, the absence of up or down. Millions of years of evolution had imprinted in the human brain the terror of falling, and this was what Emma now struggled to overcome. Every instinct told her that if she released her grip, if she ventured out the hatchway, she would plummet, shrieking, in an endless fall. On a rational level, she knew this would not happen. She was connected to the crew lock by her tether. If that tether broke, she could use her SAFER jet pack to propel herself back to the station. It would take an unlikely series of independent mishaps to cause a catastrophe.

Yet that is exactly what has happened to this station, she thought. Mishap after mishap. Their own *Titanic* in space. She could not shake the premonition of yet another disaster.

Already they had been forced to violate protocol. Instead of the usual overnight camp-out at reduced air pressures, they had spent only four hours in the air lock. Theoretically, it should be long enough to prevent the bends, but any change in normal procedures added an element of risk.

She took a few deep breaths and felt the paralysis begin to melt away.

'How ya doing?' she heard Luther ask over her comm unit.

'I'm just . . . taking a minute to enjoy the view,' she said.

'No problems?'

'No. I'm A-OK.' She released her grip and floated out of the hatch.

Diana is dying.

Griggs stared with mounting bitterness at the closed-circuit TV monitors showing Luther and Emma at work outside the station. Drones, he thought. Obedient robots, leaping at Houston's command. For so many years, he, too, had been a drone. Only now did he understand his position in the greater scheme of things. He, and everyone else, were disposable. On-orbit replacement units whose real function was to maintain NASA's glorious hardware. *We may all be dying up here, but yes, sir, we'll keep the place in fucking shipshape order.*

They could count him out. NASA had betrayed him, had betrayed all of them. Let Watson and Ames play the good little soldiers; he would have no more of it.

Diana was all he cared about.

He left the hab and headed toward the Russian end of the station. Slipping under the plastic sheeting draped over the hatchway, he entered the RSM. He didn't bother to put on his mask or goggles; what difference did it make? They were all going to die.

Diana was strapped to the treatment board. Her eyes were swollen, the lids puffy. Her abdomen, once so flat and firm, was now bloated. *Filled with eggs*, he thought. He pictured them growing inside her, expanding beneath that pale tent of skin.

Gently he touched her cheek. She opened her blood-streaked eyes and struggled to focus on his face.

'It's me,' he whispered. He saw that she was trying to free her hand from the wrist restraint. He clasped her hand in his. 'You need to keep your arm still, Diana. For the IV.'

'I can't see you.' She gave a sob. 'I can't see anything.'

'I'm here. I'm right with you.'

'I don't want to die this way.'

He blinked away tears and started to say something, false reassurance that she would not die, that he would not let her. But the words wouldn't come. They had always been truthful with each other; he would not lie to her now. So he said nothing.

She said, 'I never thought . . .'

'What?' he prompted gently.

'That this is . . . how it would happen. No chance to play the hero. Just sick and useless.' She gave a laugh, then grimaced in pain. 'Not my idea of going out . . . in a blaze of glory.'

A blaze of glory. That was how every astronaut imagined it would be to die in space. A brief moment of terror, and then the quick demise. Sudden decompression or fire. Never had they imagined a death like this, a slow and painful ebbing away as one's body is consumed and digested by another life-form. Abandoned by the ground. Quietly sacrificed to the greater good of mankind.

Expendable. He could accept it for himself, but he could

not accept Diana's expendability. He could not accept the fact he was about to lose her.

It was hard to believe that on the first day they'd met, during training at JSC, he had thought her cold and forbidding, an icy blonde with too much confidence. Her British accent had put him off as well, because it made her sound so superior. It was crisp and cultured compared to his Texas drawl. By the first week, they disliked each other so much they were scarcely speaking to each other.

By the third week, at Gordon Obie's insistence, they'd reluctantly declared a truce.

By the eighth week, Griggs was showing up at her house. Just for a drink at first, two professionals reviewing their upcoming mission. Then the mission talk had given way to conversations of a more personal nature. Griggs's unhappy marriage. The thousand and one interests he and Diana had in common. It all led, of course, to the inevitable.

They had concealed the affair from everyone at JSC. Only here, on the station, had their relationship become apparent to their colleagues. Had there been even a whiff of suspicion before this, Blankenship would have scrubbed them from the mission. Even in this modern day and age, an astronaut's divorce was a black mark against him. And if that divorce had resulted from a liaison with another member of the corps – well, so much for any future flight assignments. Griggs would have been reduced to an invisible member of the corps, neither seen nor heard.

For the last two years he had loved her. For two years, whenever he had lain beside his sleeping wife, he had yearned for Diana and plotted out the ways they might be together. Someday, they *would* be together, even if they had to resign from NASA. That was the dream that had sustained him through all those unhappy nights. Even after these two months with her in close quarters, even after their occasional flares of temper, he had not stopped loving her. He had not surrendered the dream. Until now.

'What day is this?' she murmured.

'It's Friday.' He began to stroke her hair again. 'In Houston, it's five-thirty in the afternoon. Happy hour.'

She smiled. 'TGIF.'

'They're sitting at the bar now. Chips and margaritas. God, I could do with a stiff drink. A nice sunset. You and me, on the lake . . .'

The tears glistening on her lashes almost broke his heart. He no longer gave a damn about biocontamination, about the dangers of infecting himself. With his bare hand he wiped away the tears.

'Are you in pain?' he said. 'Do you need more morphine?'

'No. Save it.' *Someone else will need it soon,* was what she didn't say.

'Tell me what you want. What I can do for you.'

'Thirsty,' she said. 'All that talk of margaritas.'

He gave a laugh. 'I'll mix one up for you. The nonalcoholic version.'

'Please.'

He floated across to the galley and opened the food locker. It was stocked with Russian supplies, not the same items as in the U.S. hab. He saw vacuum-packed pickled fish. Sausages. An array of unappetizing Russian staples. And vodka – a small bottle of it, sent by the Russians, ostensibly for medicinal purposes.

This may be the last drink we'll ever have together.

He shook some vodka into two drink bags and restowed the bottle. Then he added water to the bags, diluting hers so that it was barely alcoholic. Just a taste, he thought, to bring back happy memories. To remind her of the evenings they had spent together, watching sunsets from her patio.

He gave the bags a few good shakes to mix the water and vodka. Then he turned to look at her.

A bright red balloon of blood was oozing from her mouth.

She was convulsing. Her eyes were rolled back, her teeth clamped down on her tongue. One raw and ragged slice of it was still hanging on by a thread of tissue.

'Diana!' he screamed.

The balloon of blood broke off and the satiny globule drifted away. At once another began to form, fed by the blood pouring out of the torn flesh.

He grabbed a plastic bite block, already taped to the restraint board, and tried to force it between her teeth, to protect her soft tissues from any more trauma. He could not pry the teeth apart. The human jaw has one of the strongest muscles in the body, and hers was clamped tight. He grabbed the syringe of Valium, premeasured and ready to inject, and shoved the tip into the IV stopcock. Even as he pressed the plunger, her seizure was starting to fade. He gave her the whole dose.

Her face relaxed. Her jaw fell limp.

'Diana?' he said. She didn't respond.

The new bubble of blood was growing, spilling from her mouth. He had to apply pressure, to stop it.

He opened the medical kit, found the sterile gauze, and ripped open the package, sending a few squares flying away. He positioned himself behind her head and gently opened her mouth to expose the torn tongue.

She coughed and tried to turn her face away. She was choking on her own blood. Aspirating it into her lungs.

'Don't move, Diana.' With his right wrist pressing down on her lower teeth, to keep her jaw open, he wadded up a bundle of gauze in his left hand and began to dab away the blood. Her neck suddenly jerked taut in a new convulsion, and her jaw snapped shut.

He screamed, the meaty part of his hand caught between

her teeth, the pain at once so terrible his vision began to blacken. He felt warm blood splash against his face, saw a bright globule fountaining up. His blood, mingled with hers. He tried to pull free, but her teeth had sunk in too deeply. The blood was pouring out, the globule inflating to the size of a basketball. *Severed artery!* He could not pry her jaw open; the seizure had caused her muscle to contract with superhuman strength.

Blackness was closing in on his vision.

In desperation, he rammed his free fist against her teeth. The jaw did not relax.

He hit her again. The basketball of blood flew apart in a dozen smaller globules, splashing his face, his eyes. Still he could not open her jaw. There was so much blood now it was as though he were swimming in a lake of it, unable to draw in a breath of clean air.

Blindly he swung his fist against her face and felt bones crack, yet he could not pull free. The pain was crushing, unbearable. Panic seized him, blinding him to anything but making the agony stop. He was scarcely aware of what he was doing as he hit her again. And again.

With a scream he finally yanked his hand free and went flying backward, clutching his wrist, releasing swirls of blood in bright ribbons all around him. It took him a moment to stop caroming off walls, to shake his vision clear. He focused on Diana's broken face, on the bloodied stumps of her teeth. The damage done by his own fist.

His howl of despair echoed off the walls, filling his ears with the sound of his own anguish. *What have I done? What have I done?*

He floated to her side, held her shattered face in his hands. He no longer felt the pain of his own wound; it receded to nothing, overshadowed by the greater horror of his own actions.

He gave another howl, this time of rage. He battered his fist against the module wall. Ripped the plastic sheeting that covered the hatchway. *We're all dying anyway!* Then he focused on the medical kit.

He reached in and grabbed a scalpel.

Flight Surgeon Todd Cutler stared at his console and felt a stab of panic. On his screen were the biotelemetry readings for Diana Estes. Her EKG tracing had just burst into a sawtooth pattern of rapid spikes. To his relief, it was not sustained. Just as abruptly, the tracing reverted back to a rapid sinus rhythm.

'Flight,' he said, 'I'm seeing a problem with my patient's heart rhythm. Her EKG just showed a five-second run of ventricular tachycardia.'

'Significance?' Woody Ellis responded briskly.

'It's a potentially fatal rhythm if it's prolonged. Right now she's back in sinus, around one thirty. That's faster than she's been running. Not dangerous, but it worries me.'

'Your advice, Surgeon?'

'I'd give her antiarrhythmics. She needs IV lidocaine or amiodarone. They've got both drugs in their ALS pack.'

'Ames and Watson are still out on EVA. Griggs'll have to give it.'

'I'll talk him through it.'

'Okay. Capcom, let's get Griggs on comm.'

As they waited for Griggs to respond, Todd kept a close eye on the monitor. What he saw worried him. Diana's pulse rate was increasing: 135, 140. Now a brief burst of 160, the spikes almost lost in a flutter of patient movement or electrical interference. What was happening up there?

Capcom said, 'Commander Griggs is not responding.'

'She needs that lidocaine,' said Todd.

'We can't get him on comm.'

Either he can't hear us or he's refusing to answer, thought Todd. They'd been worried about Griggs's emotional health. Had he withdrawn so completely he'd ignore an urgent communication?

Todd's gaze suddenly froze on his console screen. Diana Estes was going in and out of V tach. Her ventricles were contracting so rapidly, they could not pump with any efficiency. They could not maintain her blood pressure.

'She needs that drug *now!*' he snapped.

'Griggs is not responding,' said Capcom.

'Then get the EVA crew inside!'

'*No,*' Flight cut in. 'They're at a delicate point in repairs. We can't interrupt them.'

'She's turning critical.'

'We pull in the EVA crew, that ends all repairs for the next twenty-four hours.' The crew could not pop inside and go right back out again. They needed time to recover, additional time to repeat the decompression cycle. Though Woody Ellis didn't say it aloud, he was probably thinking the same thing as everyone else in the room: Even if they did call the crew inside to assist, it would make little difference to Diana Estes. Her death was inevitable.

To Todd's horror, the EKG tracing was now in sustained V tach. It was not recovering.

'She's going downhill!' he said. 'Get *one* of them inside now! Bring in Watson!'

There was a second's hesitation.

Then Flight said, 'Do it.'

Why isn't Griggs responding?

Frantically Emma pulled herself from handhold to handhold, moving as fast as she could along the main truss. She felt slow and clumsy in the Orlan-M suit, and her hands ached from the effort of flexing against the resistance of bulky gloves. She was already weary from the repair work, and now fresh sweat was soaking into her suit lining, and her muscles quivered from fatigue.

'Griggs, respond. Goddamnit, respond!' she snapped into her comm link.

ISS remained silent.

'What's Diana's status?' she demanded between panted breaths.

Todd's voice came on. 'Still in V tach.'

'Shit.'

'Don't rush, Watson. Don't get careless!'

'She's not going to last. Where the fuck is Griggs?'

She was breathing so hard now she could barely keep up the conversation. She forced herself to concentrate on grabbing the next hand rung, on keeping her tether untangled. Clambering off the truss, she made a lunge for the ladder, but was suddenly snapped to a halt. Her sleeve had caught on a corner of the work platform.

Slow down. You're going to get yourself killed.

Gingerly she unsnagged her sleeve and saw there was no puncture. Heart still hammering, she continued down the ladder and pulled herself into the air lock. Quickly she swung the hatch shut and opened the pressure equalization valve.

'Talk to me, Todd,' she snapped as the air lock began to repressurize. 'What's the rhythm?'

'She's now in coarse V fib. We still can't get Griggs on comm.'

'We're losing her.'

'I know, I know!'

'Okay, I'm up to five psi –'

'Air-lock integrity check. Don't skip it.'

'I don't have time.'

'Watson, *no fucking shortcuts*.'

She paused and took a deep breath. Todd was right. In

the hostile environment of space, one must never take short-cuts. She completed the air-lock integrity check, finished repressurization, and opened the next hatch, leading into the equipment lock. There she swiftly removed her gloves. The Russian Orlan-M suit was easier to doff than the American EMU, but it still took time to swing open the rear life-support system and wriggle out. *I'll never make it in time*, she thought as she furiously kicked her feet free from the lower torso.

'Status, Surgeon!' she barked into her comm assembly.

'She's now in fine fib.'

A terminal rhythm, thought Emma. This was their last chance to save Diana.

Now clad only in her water-cooling garment, she opened the hatch leading into the station. Frantic to reach her patient, she pushed off the wall and dove headfirst through the hatch opening.

Wetness splashed her face, blurring her vision. She missed the handhold and collided with the far wall. For a few seconds she drifted in confusion, blinking away the sting. *What did I get in my eyes?* she thought. *Not eggs. Please, not eggs* . . . Slowly her vision cleared, but even then, she could not comprehend what she was seeing.

Floating all around her in the shadowy node were giant globules. She felt more wetness brush her hand, and she looked down at the blackish stain soaking into her sleeve, at the dark splotches blooming here and there on her water-cooling garment. She held her sleeve up to one of the node lights.

The stain was blood.

In horror she gazed at the giant globules hanging in the shadows. So much of it . . .

Quickly she closed the hatch to prevent the contamination from spreading into the air lock. It was too late to protect the rest of the station; the globules had spread everywhere.

She dove into the hab, opened the CCPK, and donned protective mask and goggles. Maybe the blood was not infectious. Maybe she could still protect herself.

'Watson?' said Cutler.

'Blood . . . there's blood everywhere!'

'Diana's rhythm is agonal – there's not much left to jump-start!'

'I'm on my way!' She pushed out of the node and entered the tunnellike Zarya. The Russian module seemed blindingly bright after the barely lit U.S. end, the globules of blood like gaily colored balloons floating in the air. Some had collided with the walls, splattering Zarya a brilliant red. Popping out the far end of the module, she could not avoid one giant bubble floating directly in her path. Reflexively she closed her eyes as it splattered her goggles, obscuring her view. Drifting blindly, she wiped her sleeve across the goggles to clear away the blood.

And found herself staring straight at Michael Griggs's chalk-white face.

She screamed. In horror she thrashed uselessly at empty air, going nowhere.

'Watson?'

She stared at the large bubble of blood still clinging to the gaping wound on his neck. This was the source of all the blood – a slashed carotid artery. She forced herself to touch the intact side of his neck, to search for a pulse. She could not feel one.

'Diana's EKG is flat line!' said Todd.

Emma's stunned gaze shifted to the hatch leading to the RSM, where Diana was supposed to be isolated. The plastic sheeting was gone; the module was open to the rest of the station.

In dread, she entered the RSM.

Diana was still strapped to the patient restraint board.

Her face had been battered beyond recognition, her teeth smashed to splinters. A balloon of blood was oozing from her mouth.

The squeal of the cardiac monitor at last drew Emma's attention. A flat line traced across the screen. She reached over to turn off the alarm, and her hand froze in midair. Glistening on the power switch was a blue-green gelatinous clump.

Eggs. Diana has already shed eggs. She has already released Chimera into the air.

The monitor alarm seemed to build to an unbearable shriek, yet Emma remained motionless, staring at that cluster of eggs. They seemed to shimmer and recede out of focus. She blinked, and as her vision cleared again, she remembered the moisture hitting her face, stinging her eyes as she had dived through the air-lock hatch. She had not been wearing goggles then. She could still feel the wetness on her cheek, cool and clinging.

She reached up to touch her face, and stared at the eggs, like quivering pearls, on her fingertips.

The squeal of the cardiac alarm had become unbearable. She flipped off the monitor, and the squeal ceased. The silence that followed was just as alarming. She could not hear the hiss of the vent fans. They should be drawing in air, pulling it through the HEPA filters for cleansing. *There's too much blood in the air. It has blocked all the filters.* The rise in the pressure gradient across those filters had tripped the sensors, automatically shutting off the overheated fans.

'Watson, please respond!' said Todd.

'They're dead.' Her voice broke into a sob. 'They're both dead!'

Now Luther's voice broke into the loop. 'I'm coming in.'

'No,' she said. 'No –'

'Just hang on, Emma. I'll be right there.'

309

'Luther, you can't come in! There's blood and eggs every-where. This station is no longer habitable. You have to stay in the air lock.'

'That's not a long-term solution.'

'There *is* no fucking long-term solution!'

'Look, I'm in the crew lock now. I'm closing the outer hatch. Starting repress –'

'The vent fans have all shut off. There's no way to clean this air.'

'I'm up to five psi. Pausing for integrity check.'

'If you come in, you'll be exposing yourself!'

'Going to full repress.'

'Luther, I've already been exposed! I got splashed in the eyes.' She took a deep breath. It came out in a sob. 'You're the only one left. The only one with any chance of surviving.'

There was a long silence. 'Jesus, Emma,' he murmured.

'Okay. Okay, listen to me.' She paused to calm herself. To think logically. 'Luther, I want you to move into the equipment lock. It should still be relatively clean in there, and you can take off your helmet. Then turn off your personal comm assembly.'

'What?'

'*Do it*. I'm heading for Node One. I'll be right on the other side of the hatch, talking to you.'

Now Todd broke in: 'Emma? Emma, do *not* break off air-to-ground loop –'

'Sorry, Surgeon,' she murmured, and turned off her comm assembly.

A moment later, she heard Luther say, over the station's hardline intercom system, 'I'm in the equipment lock.'

They were talking in private now, their conversation no longer monitored by Mission Control.

'There's one option left for you,' said Emma. 'The one

you've been pushing for all along. I can't take it, but you can. You're still clean. You won't bring the disease home.'

'We already agreed on this. No one stays behind.'

'You've got three hours left of uncontaminated air in your EMU. If you keep your helmet on in the CRV and go straight to deorbit, you could make it down in time.'

'You'll be stranded.'

'I'm stranded here anyway!' She took another deep breath, and spoke more calmly. 'Look, we both know this goes against orders. It could be a very bad idea. How they'll respond is anyone's guess – that's the gamble. But, Luther, it's your choice to make.'

'There'll be no way for you to evac.'

'Take me out of the equation. Don't even think of me.' She added, softly, 'I'm already dead.'

'Emma, no –'

'What do *you* want to do? Answer that. Think only about *yourself*.'

She heard him take a deep breath. 'I want to go home.'

So do I, she thought, blinking away tears. *Oh, God, so do I.*

'Put on your helmet,' she said. 'I'll open the hatch.'

311

24

Jack ran up the stairs to Building 30, flashed his badge at Security, and headed straight to Special Vehicle Operations.

Gordon Obie intercepted him just outside the control room. 'Jack, wait. You go in there and raise hell, they'll toss you right out. Take a minute to cool down, or you won't be any help to her.'

'I want my wife home *now*.'

'Everyone wants them home! We're trying the best we can, but the situation has changed. The whole station is now contaminated. The filter system's off. The EVA crew never had a chance to complete the gimbal repairs, so they remain in power down. And now they're not talking to us.'

'What?'

'Emma and Luther have cut off communications. We don't know what's going on up there. That's why they rushed you back – to help us get through to them.'

Jack stared through the open doorway, into the Special Vehicle Operations Room. He saw men and women at their consoles, performing their duties as always. It suddenly enraged him that those flight controllers could remain so calm and efficient. That the deaths of two more astronauts did not seem to alter their cold professionalism. The cool demeanor of everyone in the room only magnified his own grief, his own terror.

He walked into the control room. Two uniformed Air Force officers stood beside Flight Director Woody Ellis, monitoring the comm loops. They were a disturbing reminder that the room was not under NASA's control. As Jack moved along the back row, toward the surgeon's console, several controllers shot him sympathetic looks. He said nothing, but sank into the chair next to Todd Cutler. He was acutely aware that just behind him, in the viewing gallery, other Air Force officers from U.S. Space Command were watching the room.

'You've heard the latest?' said Todd softly.

Jack nodded. There was no longer any EKG tracing on the monitor; Diana was dead. So was Griggs.

'Half the station's still in power down. And now they've got eggs floating in the air.'

And blood as well. Jack could picture what it must be like aboard the station. The lights dimmed. The stench of death. Blood splattering the walls, clogging the HEPA filters. An orbiting house of horrors.

'We need you to talk to her, Jack. Get her to tell us what's happening up there.'

'Why aren't they talking?'

'We don't know. Maybe they're pissed at us. They have a right to be. Maybe they're too traumatized.'

'No, they must have a reason.' Jack looked at the front screen, showing the station's orbital path above the earth. *What are you thinking, Emma?* He slipped on the headset and said, 'Capcom, this is Jack McCallum. I'm ready.'

'Roger, Surgeon. Stand by, and we'll try them again.'

They waited. ISS did not respond.

At the third row of consoles, two of the controllers

suddenly glanced back over their shoulders, at Flight Director Ellis. Jack heard nothing over the comm loop, but he saw the Odin controller, the controller in charge of onboard data networks, rise from his chair and lean forward to whisper across his console to the second-row controllers.

Now the OPS controller, in the third row, took off his headset, stood up, and stretched. He started up the side aisle, walking casually, as though headed for a bathroom break. As he passed by the surgeon's console, he dropped a piece of paper in Todd Cutler's lap and continued out of the room.

Todd unfolded the note and shot Jack a stunned look. 'The station's reconfigured their computers to ASCR mode,' he whispered. 'The crew's already started CRV sep sequence.'

Jack stared back in disbelief. ASCR, or assured safe crew return, was the computer config meant to support crew evacuation. He glanced quickly around the room. None of the controllers was saying a word about this over the loop. All Jack saw were rows of squared shoulders, everyone's gaze focused tightly on their consoles. He glanced sideways at Woody Ellis. Ellis stood absolutely motionless. The body language said it all. *He knows what's going on. And he's not saying a thing, either.*

Jack broke out in a sweat. This was why the crew wasn't talking. They had made their own decision, and they were forging ahead with it. The Air Force would not be in the dark for long. Through their Space Surveillance Network of radar and optical sensors, they could monitor objects as small as a baseball in low earth orbit. As soon as the CRV separated, as soon as it became an independent orbital object, it would come to the attention of Space Command's control center in Cheyenne Mountain Air Station. The million-dollar question was: How would they respond?

I hope to God you know what you're doing, Emma.

After CRV sep, it would take twenty-five minutes for the evac vehicle to bring up guidance and landing targets, another fifteen minutes to set up the deorbit burn. Another hour to land. U.S. Space Command would have them identified and tracked long before the CRV could touch down.

In the second row, the OSO flight controller raised his hand in a casual thumbs-up. With that gesture, he'd silently announced the news: The CRV had separated. For better or worse, the crew was on its way home.

Now the game begins.

The tension in the room coiled tighter. Jack hazarded a glance at the two Air Force officers, but the men seemed oblivious to the situation; one of them kept looking at the clock, as though anxious to be elsewhere.

The minutes ticked past, the room strangely quiet. Jack leaned forward, his heart hammering, sweat soaking his shirt. By now the CRV would be drifting outside the station's envelope. Their landing target would be identified, their guidance system locked onto GPS satellites.

Come on, come on, thought Jack. *Go to deorbit now!*

The sound of a ringing telephone cut the silence. Jack glanced sideways and saw one of the Air Force monitors answer it. Suddenly he went rigid and turned to Woody Ellis. 'What the hell is going on here?'

Ellis said nothing.

The officer quickly typed on Ellis's console keyboard and stared at the screen in disbelief. He grabbed the phone. 'Yes, sir. I'm afraid that's a confirmation. The CRV has separated. No, sir, I don't know how it – Yes, sir, we have been monitoring the loop, but—' The officer was red-faced and sweating as he listened to the tirade spewing from the receiver. When he hung up, he was shaking with rage.

'Turn it around!' he ordered.

Woody Ellis answered with barely disguised contempt. 'It

isn't a *Soyuz* capsule. You can't command it to drive around like a goddamn automobile.'

'Then stop it from landing!'

'We can't. It's a one-way trip home.'

Three more Air Force officers walked swiftly into the room. Jack recognized General Gregorian of U.S. Space Command – the man now in authority over NASA operations.

'What's the status?' Gregorian snapped.

'The CRV is undocked but still in orbit,' the red-faced officer replied.

'How soon before they reach atmosphere?'

'Uh – I don't have that information, sir.'

Gregorian turned to the flight director. 'How soon, Mr Ellis?'

'It depends. There are a number of options.'

'Don't give me a fucking engineering lecture. I want an answer. I want a number.'

'Okay.' Ellis straightened and looked him hard in the eye. 'Anywhere from one to eight hours. It's up to them. They can stay in orbit for four revolutions max. Or they can deorbit now and be on the ground in an hour.'

Gregorian picked up the phone. 'Mr President, I'm afraid there's not much time to decide. They could deorbit any minute now. Yes, sir, I know it's a hard choice. But my recommendation remains the same as Mr Profitt's.'

What recommendation? thought Jack with a surge of panic.

An Air Force officer called out from one of the flight consoles, 'They've started their deorbit burn!'

'We're running out of time, sir,' said Gregorian. 'We need your answer now.' There was a long pause. Then he nodded, with relief. 'You've made the right decision. Thank you.' He hung up and turned to the Air Force officers. 'It's a go.'

'What's a go?' said Ellis. 'What are you people planning to do?'

His questions were ignored. The Air Force officer picked

316

up the phone and calmly issued the order: 'Stand by for EKV launch.'

What the hell is an EKV? thought Jack. He looked at Todd and saw by his blank expression that he didn't know what was being launched, either.

It was Topo, the trajectory controller, who walked over to their console and quietly answered the question. 'Exoatmospheric kill vehicle,' he whispered. 'They're going to intercept.'

'Target must be neutralized before it descends to atmosphere,' said Gregorian.

Jack shot to his feet in panic. *'No!'*

Almost simultaneously, other controllers rose from their chairs in protest. Their shouts almost drowned out Capcom, who had to yell at the top of his voice to be heard.

'I have ISS on comm! ISS is on comm!'

ISS? Then someone is still aboard the station. Someone has been left behind.

Jack cupped his hand over his earpiece and listened to the downlinked voice.

It was Emma. 'Houston, this is Watson on ISS. Mission Specialist Ames is *not* infected. I repeat, he is *not* infected. He is the only crew member returning aboard CRV. I urgently request you allow the vehicle's safe landing.'

'Roger that, ISS,' said Capcom.

'You see? There's no reason to shoot it down,' Ellis said to Gregorian. 'Stop your EKV launch!'

'How do we know Watson's telling the truth?' countered Gregorian.

'She must be telling the truth. Why else would she stay behind? She's just stranded herself up there. The CRV was the only lifeboat she had!'

The impact of those words made Jack go numb. The heated conversation between Ellis and Gregorian suddenly seemed to fade out. Jack was no longer focusing on the fate of the CRV. He could think only of Emma, alone now, and trapped on the station, with no way to evacuate. *She knows she is infected. She has stayed behind to die.*

'CRV has completed deorbit burn. It's descending. Trajectory is on the front screen.'

Tracing across the world map at the front of the room was a small blip representing the CRV and its lone human passenger. They heard him now, on comm.

'This is Mission Specialist Luther Ames. I am approaching entry altitude, all systems nominal.'

The Air Force officer looked at Gregorian. 'We're still standing by for EKV launch.'

'You don't have to do this,' said Woody Ellis. 'He's not sick. We can bring him home!'

'The craft itself is probably contaminated,' said Gregorian.

'You don't know that!'

'I can't take that chance. I can't risk the lives of people on earth.'

'Godddamnit, this is *murder*.'

'He disobeyed orders. He knew what our response would be.' Gregorian nodded to the Air Force officer.

'EKVs have been launched, sir.'

Instantly the room hushed. Woody Ellis, pale and shaken, stared at the front screen, at the multiple trajectory tracings, hurtling toward an intersecting point.

The minutes went by in dead silence. At the front of the room, one of the women controllers began to cry softly.

'Houston, I'm approaching entry interface.' It was a shock to hear Luther's cheery voice suddenly crackle on the comm. 'I'd greatly 'preciate it if you'd have someone meet me on the ground, 'cause I'm gonna need help getting out of this EMU.'

No one responded. No one had the heart to.

'Houston?' said Luther, after a moment of silence. 'Hey, you guys still there?'

At last Capcom managed to reply, in an uneven voice, 'Uh, roger, CRV. We'll have the beer keg waiting for you, Luther ol' buddy. Dancing girls. The whole works . . .'

'Geez, you guys have loosened up since we last spoke. Okay, looks like I'm 'bout ready for LOS. You keep that beer cold, and I –'

There was a loud burst of static. Then the transmission went dead.

The blip on the front screen exploded into a shocking sunburst of fragments, scattering into delicate pixels of dust.

Woody Ellis crumpled into his chair and dropped his head in his hands.

August 19

'Securing air-to-ground loop,' said Capcom. 'Stand by, ISS.'

Talk to me, Jack. Please talk to me, Emma pleaded silently as she floated in the hab's semidarkness. With the circulation fans shut down, the module was so quiet she could hear the whoosh of her own pulse, the movement of air rushing in and out of her lungs.

She was startled when Capcom's voice suddenly said, 'Air-to-ground secure. You may proceed to PFC.'

'Jack?' she said.

'I'm here. I'm right here, sweetheart.'

'He was clean! I told them he was clean –'

'We tried to stop it! The order came straight from the White House. They didn't want to take any chances.'

'It's my fault.' Her exhaustion suddenly gave way to tears. She was alone and scared. And haunted by her catastrophically wrong decision. 'I thought they'd let him come back. I thought it was his best chance of staying alive.'

'Why did you stay behind, Emma?'

'I had to.' She took a deep breath and said, 'I'm infected.'

'You were *exposed*. That doesn't mean you're infected.'

'I just ran my own blood tests, Jack. My amylase level is rising.'

He said nothing.

'I'm now eight hours postexposure. I should have another twenty-four to forty-eight hours before I . . . can no longer function.' Her voice had steadied. She sounded strangely calm now, as though she were talking about a patient's impending death. Not her own. 'That's enough time to get a few things in order. Jettison the bodies. Change out some of the filters, and get the fans working again. It should make cleanup easier for the next crew. If there is a next crew . . .'

Jack still hadn't spoken.

'As for my own remains . . .' Her voice had steadied to numb dispassion, all emotions suppressed. 'When the time comes, I think the best thing I can do, for the good of the station, is to go EVA. Where I can't contaminate anything after I die. After my body . . .' She paused. 'The Orlan is easy enough to get into without assistance. I have Valium and narcotics on hand. Enough to put me under. So I'll be asleep when my air runs out. You know, Jack, it's not such a bad way to go, when you think about it. Floating outside. Looking at the earth, the stars. And just drifting off to sleep . . .'

She heard him then. He was crying.

'Jack,' she said softly. 'I love you. I don't know why things fell apart between us. I know some of it had to be my fault.'

He drew in a shuddering breath. 'Emma, *don't*.'

'It's so stupid that I waited this long to tell you. You probably think I'm only saying it now because I'm going to die. But, Jack, the honest-to-God truth is –'

'You're not going to die.' He said it again, with anger. 'You are not going to die.'

'You've heard Dr Roman's results. Nothing has worked.'

'The hyperbaric chamber has.'

'They can't get a chamber up here in time. And without a lifeboat, I can't get home. Even if they'd let me return.'

'There's got to be a way. Something you can do to reproduce the chamber's effect. It's working on infected mice. It's keeping them alive, so it's doing *something*. They're the only ones who've survived.'

No, she suddenly realized. *Not the only ones.*

Slowly, she turned and stared at the hatchway leading into Node 1.

The mouse, she thought. *Is the mouse still alive?*

'Emma?'

'Stand by. I'm going to check something in the lab.'

She swam through Node 1, into the U.S. lab. The stench of dried blood was just as strong in here, and even in the gloom, she could see the dark splatters on the walls. She floated across to the animal habitat, pulled out the mouse enclosure, and shone a flashlight inside.

The beam captured a pitiful sight. The bloated mouse was in its agonal throes, limbs thrashing out, mouth open, drawing in gulps of air.

You can't be dying, she thought. *You're the survivor, the exception to the rule. The proof that there's still hope for me.*

The mouse twisted, body corkscrewing in agony. A thread of blood curled out from between the hind legs, broke off into swirling droplets. Emma knew what would come next: the final flurry of seizures as the brain dissolved into a soup of digested proteins. She saw a fresh pulse of blood stain the white fur of the hindquarters. And then she saw something else, something pink, protruding between the legs.

It was moving.

The mouse thrashed again.

The pink thing slid all the way out, writhing and hairless.

321

Tethered to its abdomen was a single glistening strand. An umbilical cord.

'Jack,' she whispered. *'Jack!'*

'I'm here.'

'The mouse – the female –'

'What about it?'

'These last three weeks, she's been exposed again and again to Chimera, and she hasn't gotten sick. She's the only one who's survived.'

'She's still alive?'

'Yes. And I think I know why. She was pregnant.'

The mouse began to writhe again. Another pup slid out in a glistening veil of blood and mucus.

'It must have happened that night when Kenichi put her with the males,' she said. 'I haven't been handling her. I never realized . . .'

'Why would pregnancy make a difference? Why should it be protective?'

Emma floated in the gloom, struggling to come up with an answer. The recent EVA and the shock of Luther's death had left her physically drained. She knew that Jack was just as exhausted. Two tired brains, working against the ticking time bomb of her infection.

'Okay. Okay, let's think about pregnancy,' she said. 'It's a complex physiological condition. It's more than just the gestation of a fetus. It's an altered metabolic state.'

'Hormones. Pregnant animals are chemically high on hormones. If we can mimic that state, maybe we can reproduce what's happened in that mouse.'

Hormone therapy. She thought of all the different chemicals circulating in a pregnant woman's body. Estrogen. Progesterone. Prolactin. Human chorionic gonadotropin.

'Birth control pills,' said Jack. 'You could mimic pregnancy with contraceptive hormones.'

322

'We have nothing like that on board. It's not part of the medical kit.'

'Have you checked Diana's personal locker?'

'She wouldn't take contraceptives without my knowledge. I'm the medical officer. I'd know about it.'

'Check it anyway. Do it, Emma.'

She shot out of the lab. In the Russian service module, she quickly pulled open the drawers in Diana's locker. It felt wrong, to be pawing through another woman's private possessions. Even a dead woman's. Among the neatly folded clothes she uncovered a private stash of candy. She hadn't known that Diana loved sweets; there was so much about Diana she would never know. In another drawer she found shampoo and toothpaste and tampons. No birth control pills.

She slammed the drawer shut. 'There's nothing on this station I can use!'

'If we launched the shuttle tomorrow – if we got the hormones up to you –'

'They won't launch! And even if you could send up a whole damn pharmacy, it'd still take three days to get to me!'

In three days, she would most likely be dead.

She clung to the blood-splattered locker, her breaths coming hard and fast, every muscle taut with frustration. With despair.

'Then we have to approach this from another angle,' said Jack. 'Emma, stay with me on this! I need you to help me think.'

She released a sharp breath. 'I'm not going anywhere.'

'*Why* would hormones work? What's the mechanism? We know they're chemical signals – an internal communication system at the cellular level. They work by activating or repressing gene expression. By changing the cell's programming . . .' He was rambling now, letting his stream of consciousness lead him toward a solution. 'In order for a

323

hormone to work, it has to bind to a specific receptor on the target cell. It's like a key, in search of the right lock in which to fit. Maybe if we studied the data from SeaScience – if we could find out what other DNA Dr Koenig grafted onto this organism's genome – we might know how to shut off Chimera's reproduction.'

'What do you know about Dr Koenig? What other research has she worked on? That might be a clue.'

'We have her curriculum vitae. We've seen her published papers on Archaeons. Other than that, she's something of a mystery to us. So is SeaScience. We're still trying to dig up more information.'

That will take precious time, she thought. *I don't have much of it left.*

Her hands ached from gripping Diana's locker. She relaxed her hold and drifted away, as though swept along on a tide of despair. Loose items from Diana's locker floated around her in the air, evidence of Diana's sweet tooth. Chocolate bars. M&M's. A cellophane package of crystallized ginger candy. It was that last item that Emma suddenly focused on. Crystallized ginger.

Crystals.

'Jack,' she said. 'I have an idea.'

Her heart was racing as she swam out of the Russian service module and headed back into the U.S. lab. There she turned on the payload computer. The monitor glowed an eerie amber in the darkened module. She called up the operations data files and clicked on 'ESA.' European Space Agency. Here were all the procedures and reference materials required to operate the ESA payload experiments.

'What are you thinking, Emma?' came Jack's voice over her comm unit.

'Diana was working on protein crystal growth, remember? Pharmaceutical research.'

'Which proteins?' he shot back, and she knew he understood exactly what she was thinking.

'I'm scrolling down the list now. There are dozens . . .'

The protein names raced up the screen in a blur. The cursor halted on the entry she'd been searching for: '*Human chorionic gonadotropin.*'

'Jack,' she said softly. 'I think I've just bought myself some time.'

'What've you got?'

'HCG. Diana was growing the crystals. I'd have to do an IVA to get to it. They're in the ESA module, and that's at vacuum. But if I start depress now, I could get to those crystals in four or five hours.'

'How much HCG is on board?'

'I'm checking.' She opened the experiment file and quickly scanned the mass measurement data.

'Emma?'

'Hold on, hold on! I've got the most recent mass here. I'm looking up normal HCG levels in pregnancy.'

'I can get those for you.'

'No, I've found it. Okay. Okay, if I dilute this crystal mass in normal saline . . . plug in my body weight as forty-five kilograms . . .' She typed in the numbers. She was making wild assumptions here. She didn't know how quickly HCG was metabolized, or what its half-life would be. The answer at last appeared onscreen.

'How many doses?' said Jack.

She closed her eyes. *It's not going to last long enough. It's not going to save me.*

'Emma?'

She released a deep breath. It came out as a sob. 'Three days.'

The Origin

25

It was 1:45 A.M., and Jack's vision was blurred from fatigue, the words on the computer screen fading in and out of focus. 'There must be more,' he said. 'Keep searching.'

Gretchen Liu, seated at the keyboard, glanced up at Jack and Gordon in frustration. She had been sound asleep when they called her to come in, and she'd arrived without her usual camera-ready makeup and contact lenses. They had never seen their normally elegant public affairs officer looking so unglamorous. Or wearing glasses, for that matter – thick horn-rim glasses that magnified her pinched eyes. 'I'm telling you guys, this is all I can find on Lexis-Nexis search. Almost nothing on Helen Koenig. On SeaScience, there's only the usual corporate news releases. And as for the name *Palmer Gabriel*, well, you can see for yourself he doesn't court publicity. In the last five years, the only place his name turns up in the media is on the financial pages of *The Wall Street Journal*. Business articles about SeaScience and its products. There's no biographical data. There's not even a photo of the man.'

Jack slumped back in his chair and rubbed his eyes. The three of them had spent the last two hours in the Public Affairs Office, combing every article about Helen Koenig and

SeaScience they could find on Lexis-Nexis. They had turned up numerous hits for SeaScience, dozens of articles in which its products had been mentioned, from shampoos to pharmaceuticals to fertilizers. But almost nothing had turned up on Koenig or Gabriel.

'Try the name *Koenig* again,' said Jack.

'We've done every possible spelling variation on her name,' said Gretchen. 'There's nothing.'

'Then type in the word *Archaeons*.'

Sighing, Gretchen typed in *Archaeons* and clicked on 'Search.' A numbingly long string of article citations filled the screen.

'Alien Earth Creatures. Scientists Hail Discovery of New Branch of Life.' *(Washington Post)*

'Archaeons to Be Subject of International Conference.' *(Miami Herald)*

'Deep Sea Organisms Offer Clues to Life's Origins.' *(Philadelphia Inquirer)*

'Guys, this is hopeless,' said Gretchen. 'It'll take us all night to read every article on this list. Why don't we just call it a night and get some sleep?'

'Wait!' Gordon said. 'Scroll down to this one.' He pointed to a citation at the bottom of the screen: '"Scientist Dies in Galápagos Diving Accident" *(New York Times)*.'

'The Galápagos,' said Jack. 'That's where Dr Koenig discovered the Archaeon strain. In the Galápagos Rift.'

Gretchen clicked on the article and the text appeared. The story was two years old.

COPYRIGHT: *The New York Times*.

SECTION: International News.

HEADLINE: 'Scientist Dies in Deep Sea Diving Accident.'

BYLINE: Julio Perez, NYT Correspondent.

BODY: An American scientist studying Archaeon marine organisms was killed yesterday when his one-man submersible became wedged in an undersea canyon of the Galápagos Rift. The body of Dr Stephen D. Ahearn was not recovered until this morning, when cables from the research vessel *Gabriella* were able to haul the minisub to the surface.

'We knew he was still alive down there, but there was nothing we could do,' said a fellow scientist aboard *Gabriella*. 'He was trapped at nineteen thousand feet. It took us hours to free his submersible and haul it back to the surface.'

Dr Ahearn was a professor of geology at the University of California, San Diego. He resided in La Jolla, California.

Jack said, 'The ship's name was *Gabriella*.'

He and Gordon looked at each other, both of them struck by the same startling thought: *Gabriella. Palmer Gabriel.*

'I'll bet you this was a SeaScience vessel,' said Jack, 'and Helen Koenig was aboard.'

Gordon's gaze shifted back to the screen. 'Now this is interesting. What do you make of the fact Ahearn was a geologist?'

'So what?' said Gretchen, yawning.

'What was a geologist doing aboard a marine research vessel?'

'Checking out the rocks on the sea floor?'

'Let's do a search on his name.'

Gretchen sighed. 'You guys owe me a night's worth of beauty sleep.' She typed in the name *Stephen D. Ahearn* and clicked on 'Search.'

331

A list appeared, seven articles in all. Six of them were about his undersea death in the Galápagos.

One article was from the year prior to his death:

'UCSD Professor to Present Latest Findings on Tektite Research. Will Be Keynote Speaker at International Geological Conference in Madrid.'
(San Diego Union)

Both men stared at the screen, too stunned for a moment to utter a word.

Then Gordon said softly, 'This is it, Jack. This is what they've been trying to hide from us.'

Jack's hands had gone numb, his throat dry. He focused on a single word, the word that told them everything.

Tektite.

JSC director Ken Blankenship's house was one of the anonymous tract homes in the suburb of Clear Lake, where so many JSC officials lived. It was a large house for a bachelor, and in the glare of the security lights, Jack saw that the front yard was immaculately groomed, every hedge clipped into submission. That yard, so well lit at three A.M., was exactly what one would expect of Blankenship, who was notorious for his perfectionism as well as his almost paranoid obsession with security. *There's probably a surveillance camera trained on us right this moment*, thought Jack as he and Obie waited for Blankenship to answer the front door. It took several rings of the doorbell before they saw lights come on inside. Then Blankenship appeared, a squat little Napoleon dressed in a bathrobe.

'It's three in the morning,' said Blankenship. 'What are you guys doing here?'

'We need to talk,' said Gordon.

'Is there something wrong with my phone? You couldn't have called first?'

'We can't use the phone. Not about this.'

They all stepped into the house. Only after the front door swung shut did Jack say, 'We know what the White House is trying to hide. We know where Chimera comes from.'

Blankenship stared at him, his irritation over a disturbed night's sleep instantly forgotten. Then he looked at Gordon, seeking confirmation of Jack's statement.

'It explains everything,' said Gordon. 'USAMRIID's secrecy. The White House's paranoia. And the fact that this organism behaves unlike anything our doctors have ever encountered.'

'What did you find out?'

Jack answered the question. 'We know Chimera has human, mouse, and amphibian DNA. But USAMRIID won't tell us what other DNA is on the genome. They won't tell us what Chimera really is, or where it comes from.'

'You told me last night the bug was sent up in a SeaScience payload. A culture of Archaeons.'

'That's what we thought. But Archaeons are not dangerous organisms. They're incapable of causing disease in humans – that's why the experiment was accepted by NASA. Something about this particular Archaeon is different. Something SeaScience didn't tell us.'

'What do you mean, different?'

'Where it came from. The Galápagos Rift.'

Blankenship shook his head. 'I don't see the significance.'

'This culture was discovered by scientists aboard the vessel *Gabriella*, a ship belonging to SeaScience. One of those researchers was a Dr Stephen Ahearn, who was flown out to *Gabriella*, apparently as a last-minute consultant. Within a week, he was dead. His minisub became trapped at the bottom of the rift, and he suffocated.'

Blankenship said nothing, but his gaze remained focused on Jack's.

'Dr Ahearn was known for his research on tektites,' said Jack. 'Those are glassy fragments produced whenever a meteor collides with the earth. That was Dr Ahearn's field of expertise. The geology of meteors and asteroids.'

Still Blankenship said nothing. *Why isn't he reacting?* Jack wondered. *Doesn't he understand what this means?*

'SeaScience flew Ahearn to the Galápagos because they needed a geologist's opinion,' said Jack. 'They needed confirmation of what they'd found on the sea floor. An asteroid.'

Blankenship's face had gone rigid. He turned and walked toward the kitchen.

Jack and Gordon followed him. 'That's why the White House is so scared of Chimera!' said Jack. 'They know where it comes from. They know what it is.'

Blankenship picked up the telephone and dialed. A moment later, he said, 'This is JSC director Kenneth Blankenship. I need to speak to Jared Profitt. Yes, I know what time it is. This is an emergency, so if you could connect me to his home . . .' There was a moment's silence. Then he said into the phone, 'They know. No, I did not tell them. They found out on their own.' A pause. 'Jack McCallum and Gordon Obie. Yes, sir, they're standing right here in my kitchen.' He handed the receiver to Jack. 'He wants to speak to you.'

Jack took the phone. 'This is McCallum.'

'How many people know?' was the first thing Jared Profitt asked him.

That question instantly told Jack how sensitive this information was. He said, 'Our medical people know. And a few people in Life Sciences.' That was all he'd say; he knew better than to name names.

'Can you all keep it quiet?' asked Profitt.

'That depends.'

'On what?'

'On whether your people cooperate with us. Share information with us.'

'What do you want, Dr McCallum?'

'Full disclosure. Everything you've learned about Chimera. The autopsy results. The data from your clinical trials.'

'And if we don't share? What happens?'

'My colleagues at NASA start faxing every news agency in the country.'

'Telling them what, exactly?'

'The truth. That this organism is not terrestrial.'

There was a long silence. Jack could hear his own heartbeat thudding in the receiver. *Have we guessed right? Have we really uncovered the truth?*

Profitt said, 'I'll authorize Dr Roman to tell you everything. He'll be expecting you at White Sands.' The phone went dead.

Jack hung up and looked at Blankenship. 'How long have you known?'

Blankenship's silence only fueled Jack's anger. He took a threatening step forward, and Blankenship backed up against the kitchen wall. '*How long have you known?*'

'Only – only a few days. I was sworn to secrecy!'

'Those were *our* people dying up there!'

'I had no choice! This has got everyone terrified! The White House. Defense.' Blankenship took a deep breath and looked Jack straight in the eye. 'You'll understand what I'm talking about. When you get to White Sands.'

August 20

With one end gripped in her teeth, Emma yanked the tourniquet tight, and the veins of her left arm plumped up like blue worms beneath the pale skin. She gave her antecubital vein a quick swipe of alcohol and winced at the prick of the

335

needle. Like a junkie desperate for a fix, she injected the entire contents of the syringe, loosening the tourniquet halfway through. When she was finished, she closed her eyes and allowed herself to drift as she imagined the HCG molecules, like tiny stars of hope, coursing up her veins, swirling into her heart and lungs. Streaming out into arteries and capillaries. She imagined she could already feel its effect, the headache melting away, the hot flames of her fever smothered to a dying glow. *Three doses left*, she thought. *Three more days*.

She imagined herself drifting out of her own body, and she saw herself, as though from a distance, curled up like a mottled fetus in a coffin. A bubble of mucus spilling out of her mouth, breaking into bright squirming threads like maggots.

Abruptly she opened her eyes and realized that she had been sleeping. Dreaming. Her shirt was saturated with sweat. It was a good sign. It meant that her fever had eased off.

She massaged her temples, trying to force out the images from her dream, but she could not; reality and nightmares had merged into one.

She stripped off the sweat-soaked shirt and put on a clean one from Diana's locker. Despite the bad dreams, that brief nap had refreshed her, and she was alert again, ready to search for new solutions. She floated into the U.S. lab and pulled up all the Chimera files on the computer. It was an extraterrestrial organism, Todd Cutler had informed her, and everything NASA now knew about the life-form had been transmitted to her onboard computers. She reviewed the files, hoping to find some new inspiration, some fresh approach that no one else had thought of. Everything she read was dismally familiar.

She opened the genome file. A nucleotide sequence spilled across the monitor in an unending stream of *A*s, *C*s, *T*s, and

Gs. Here was Chimera's genetic code – parts of it, anyway. The parts USAMRIID had chosen to share with NASA. She stared, hypnotized, as the lines of code marched down the screen. This was the essence of the alien life-form now growing inside her. It was the key to the enemy. If only she knew how to use it.

The key.

She suddenly thought of what Jack had said earlier, about hormones. *In order for a hormone to work, it has to bind to a specific receptor on the target cell. It's like a key in search of just the right lock in which to fit.*

Why would a mammalian hormone like HCG suppress the reproduction of an alien life-form? she wondered. Why would an extraterrestrial organism, so foreign to anything on earth, possess properly fitting locks to *our* keys?

On the computer, the nucleotide sequence had finished scrolling to the end. She stared at the blinking cursor and thought of the earth-born species whose DNA had been raided by Chimera. By acquiring those new genes, this alien life-form had become part human. Part mouse. Part amphibian.

She got on the comm with Houston. 'I need to speak to somebody in Life Sciences,' she said.

'Anyone in particular?' asked Capcom.

'An amphibian expert.'

'Stand by, Watson.'

Ten minutes later, a Dr Wang from NASA Life Sciences came on the loop. 'You had a question about amphibians?' he asked.

'Yes, about *Rana pipiens*, the northern leopard frog.'

'What can I tell you about it?'

'What happens if you expose the leopard frog to human hormones?'

'Any hormone in particular?'

'Estrogen, for instance. Or HCG.'

Dr Wang answered without hesitation. 'Amphibians in general are adversely affected by environmental estrogens. It's been studied quite a bit, actually. A number of experts think the worldwide decline in frog populations is due to estrogenlike substances polluting streams and ponds.'

'What estrogenlike substances?'

'Certain pesticides, for instance, can mimic estrogens. They disrupt the frogs' endocrine systems, making it impossible for them to reproduce or thrive.'

'So it doesn't actually kill them.'

'No, it just disrupts reproduction.'

'Are frogs in particular sensitive to this?'

'Oh, yes. Far more than mammals. Plus, frogs have permeable skin, so they're susceptible to toxins in general. That's sort of their, well, Achilles' heel.'

Achilles' heel. She fell silent for a moment, thinking about that.

'Dr Watson?' said Wang. 'You have any other questions?'

'Yes. Is there any disease or toxin that would kill a frog, but not harm a mammal?'

'That's an interesting question. When it comes to toxins, it would depend on the dose. You give a little arsenic to a frog, you'd kill it. But arsenic would kill a man as well, if he's given a larger dose. Then again, there are microbial diseases, certain bacteria and viruses, that only kill frogs. I'm not a physician, so I'm not absolutely certain they're harmless to humans, but –'

'Viruses?' she cut in. 'Which ones?'

'Well, Ranaviruses, for instance.'

'I've never heard of those.'

'Only amphibian experts are familiar with them. They're DNA viruses. Part of the Iridovirus family. We think they're the cause of tadpole edema syndrome. The tadpoles swell up and hemorrhage.'

338

'And that's fatal to them?'

'Very much so.'

'Does this virus kill people as well?'

'I don't know. I don't think anyone does. I do know Ranaviruses have killed off whole populations of frogs around the world.'

The Achilles' heel, she thought. *I've found it.*

By adding the leopard frog's DNA to its own genome, Chimera had become part amphibian. It had also acquired an amphibian's vulnerabilities.

She said, 'Is there any way to obtain live samples of one of these Ranaviruses? To test against Chimera?'

There was a long silence. 'I get it,' said Dr Wang. 'No one's tried that yet. No one's even considered –'

'Can you get the virus?' she cut in.

'Yes. I know two amphibian research labs in California who are working with live Ranaviruses.'

'Then do it. And get hold of Jack McCallum. He needs to know about this.'

'He and Gordon Obie just left for White Sands. I'll reach them there.'

Tumbleweeds skittered across the road, swept along in a stinging cloud of sand. The men drove past the guardhouse, past the electrified fence, and into the barren Army compound. Jack and Gordon stepped out of the vehicle and squinted up at the sky. The sun was a dusky orange, obscured by wind-blown dust. The color of sunset, not high noon. They had managed to catch only a few hours of sleep before they'd taken off from Ellington, and it hurt Jack's eyes just to see the light of day.

'This way, gentlemen,' the driver said.

They followed the soldier into the building.

It was a different reception from the last time Jack had

339

visited. This time the Army escort was polite and respectful. This time Dr Isaac Roman was waiting at the front desk, although he did not look particularly happy about their arrival.

'Only you are allowed to come with me, Dr McCallum,' he said. 'Mr Obie will have to wait here. That was the agreement.'

'I made no such agreement,' said Jack.

'Mr Profitt did, on your behalf. He's the only reason you're being allowed in this building. I haven't a great deal of time, so let's get this over with.' He turned and walked to the elevators.

'Now, there's your standard Army-issue asshole,' said Gordon. 'Go on. I'll wait here.'

Jack followed Roman into the elevator.

'First stop is sub-basement level two,' said Roman, 'where we house our animal trials.' The elevator door opened, and they confronted a wall of glass. It was a viewing window.

Jack approached the window and stared at the laboratory beyond. Inside were a dozen workers wearing biocontamination suits. Cages held spider monkeys and dogs. Right beside the window were glass-enclosed rat cages. Roman pointed to the rats. 'You'll notice each cage is labeled with the date and time they were infected. I can think of no better way to illustrate Chimera's lethal nature.'

In the Day 1 cage, the six rats appeared healthy, vigorously spinning their exercise wheels.

In the cage labeled 'Day 2,' the first signs of illness appeared. Two of the six rats were shivering, their eyes a bright bloodred. The other four were huddled in a lethargic heap.

'The first two days,' said Dr Roman, 'is Chimera's reproductive phase. You understand, this is completely opposite to what we see on earth. Usually a life-form must reach maturity before it begins to reproduce. Chimera reproduces *first*, and then begins to mature. It divides at a rapid rate, producing up to a hundred copies of itself by forty-eight hours. They start out microscopic in size – not visible to the naked eye. Small enough so that you could breathe them in, or absorb them through your mucous membranes, and not even know you've been exposed.'

'So they're infectious at this early stage in their life cycle?'

'They're infectious at *any* stage of their life cycle. They only have to be released into the air. Usually it happens around the time of the victim's death, or when the corpse bursts open several days post mortem. Once Chimera's infected you, once it's multiplied inside your body, each individual copy begins to grow. Begins to develop into . . .' He paused. 'We don't really know what to call them. Egg sacs, I suppose. Because they contain a larval life-form inside them.'

Jack's gaze moved on to the Day 3 enclosure. All the mice were twitching, limbs thrashing as though repeatedly jolted by electric shocks.

'By the third day,' said Roman, 'the larvae are growing rapidly. Displacing the victim's brain matter by sheer mass effect. Wreaking havoc with the host's neurologic functions. And by day four . . .'

They looked at the fourth enclosure. All but one were dead. The corpses had not been removed; they lay stiff-legged, mouths gaping open. There were still three cages to go; the process of decomposition had been allowed to continue.

By day five, the corpses were beginning to bloat.

On day six, the bellies had grown even larger, the skin stretched drum-taut. Viscous fluid seeped from the open eyes and glistened on the nostrils.

And on day seven . . .

Jack halted beside the window, staring into the seventh enclosure. Ruptured corpses littered the bottom like deflated balloons, the skin torn open to reveal a black stew of dissolved organs. And adhering to one rat's face was a gelatinous mass of opaque globes. They were quivering.

'The egg sacs,' said Roman. 'By this stage, the corpse's body cavities are packed with them. They grow at an astonishing rate, feeding on host tissues. Digesting muscles and organs.' He looked at Jack. 'Are you familiar with the life cycle of parasitic wasps?'

Jack shook his head.

'The adult wasp injects its eggs into a living caterpillar. The larvae grow, ingesting their host's hemolymph fluid. All this time, the caterpillar is *alive*. Incubating a foreign lifeform that's eating it from the inside, until the larvae finally burst out of their dying host.' Roman looked at the dead rats. 'These larvae, too, multiply and develop inside a living victim. And that's what finally kills the host. All those larvae, packing into the cranium. Nibbling away at the surface of the gray matter. Damaging capillaries, causing intracranial bleeding. The pressure builds. Vessels in the eyes engorge, burst. The host experiences blinding headaches, confusion. He stumbles around as though drunk. In three or four days, he is dead. And still the life-form continues to feed on the corpse. Raiding its DNA. Using that DNA to speed its own evolution.'

'Into what?'

Roman looked at Jack. 'We don't know the end point. With every generation, Chimera acquires DNA from its host. The Chimera we're working with now is not the same one we started out with. The genome has become more complex. The life-form more advanced.'

More and more human, thought Jack.

'This is the reason for absolute secrecy,' said Roman. 'Any

terrorist, any hostile country, could mine the Galápagos Rift for more of these things. This organism, in the wrong hands . . .' His voice trailed off.

'So nothing about this thing is manmade.'

Roman shook his head. 'It was found by chance in the rift. Brought up to the surface by *Gabriella*. At first Dr Koenig thought she'd discovered a new species of Archaeons. Instead, what she found was this.' He looked at the wriggling mass of eggs. 'A thousand years, they've been trapped in the remains of that asteroid. At a depth of nineteen thousand feet. That's what has kept it in check all this time. The fact it came to rest in the deep sea, and not on land.'

'Now I understand why you tested the hyperbaric chamber.'

'All this time Chimera has existed benignly in the rift. We thought, if we reproduced those pressures, we could make it benign again.'

'And can you?'

Roman shook his head. 'Only temporarily. This life-form has been permanently altered by exposure to microgravity. Somehow, when it was brought to ISS, its reproductive switch was turned on. It's as if it was preprogrammed to be lethal. But it needed the *absence* of gravity to start that program running again.'

'How temporary is hyperbaric treatment?'

'Infected mice stay healthy as long as they're in the chamber. We've kept them alive ten days now. But as soon as we take any of them out, the disease continues its progression.'

'What about Ranavirus?' Only an hour ago, Dr Wang from NASA Life Sciences had briefed Jack by phone. At that very moment, a supply of the amphibian virus was winging its way by Air Force jet to Dr Roman's lab. 'Our scientists believe it could work.'

'Theoretically. But it's too early to launch a rescue shuttle. First we have to *prove* Ranavirus works, or you'd risk the lives of another shuttle crew. We need time to test the virus. Several weeks, at least.'

Emma doesn't have weeks, thought Jack. *She has only three days' worth of HCG.* In silence he gazed down at the cage of rat corpses. At the eggs, glistening in their nest of slime. *If only I could buy more time.*

Time. A thought suddenly occurred to him. The memory of something Roman had just said.

'You said the hyperbaric chamber has kept mice alive for ten days so far.'

'That's correct.'

'But it was only ten days ago that *Discovery* crashed.'

Roman avoided his gaze.

'You planned the chamber tests right from the start. Which means you already knew what you were dealing with. Even before you performed the autopsies.'

Roman turned and started to walk back to the elevator. He gave a gasp of surprise when Jack caught him by the collar and spun him around.

'That wasn't a commercial payload,' said Jack. '*Was it?*'

Roman pushed away and stumbled backward, against the wall.

'Defense used SeaScience as a cover,' said Jack. 'You paid them to send up the experiment for you. To hide the fact that this life-form is of military interest.'

Roman sidled toward the elevator. Toward escape.

Jack grabbed the man's lab coat and tightened his grip on the collar. 'This wasn't bioterrorism. This was your own fucking *mistake!*'

Roman's face had turned purple. 'I can't – can't breathe!'

Jack released him, and Roman slid down the wall, his legs collapsing beneath him. For a moment he didn't speak, but sat slumped on the floor, struggling to catch his breath. When at last he did talk, all he could manage was a whisper.

'We had no way of knowing what it would do. How it would change without gravity . . .'

'But you knew it was alien.'

'Yes.'

'And you knew it was a chimera. That it already had amphibian DNA.'

'No. No, we didn't know that.'

'Don't bullshit me.'

'We don't know how the frog DNA got onto the genome! It must have happened in Dr Koenig's lab. A mistake of some kind. She was the one who found the organism in the rift, the one who finally realized what it was. SeaScience knew we'd be interested. An extraterrestrial organism – of course we were! Defense paid for their KC-135 experiments. We funded the payload space on ISS. It couldn't go up as a military payload. There'd be too many questions asked, too many review committees. NASA would wonder why the Army cared about harmless sea microbes. But no one questions the private sector. So it went up as a commercial payload, with Sea-Science as sponsor. And Dr Koenig as principal investigator.'

'Where is Dr Koenig?'

Slowly Roman rose to his feet. 'She's dead.'

That information took Jack by surprise. 'How?' he asked softly.

'It was an accident.'

'You think I believe that?'

'It's the truth.'

Jack studied the man for a moment and decided Roman was not lying.

'It happened over two weeks ago in Mexico,' said Roman. 'Just after she resigned from SeaScience. The taxi she was riding in was completely destroyed.'

'And USAMRIID's raid on her lab? You weren't there to investigate, were you? You were there to see that all her files were destroyed.'

'We are talking about an alien life-form. An organism more dangerous than we realized. Yes, the experiment was a mistake. A catastrophe. Just imagine what could happen if this information leaked out to the world's terrorists?'

This was why NASA had been kept in the dark. Why the truth could never be revealed.

'And you haven't seen the worst of it yet, Dr McCallum,' said Roman.

'What do you mean?'

'There's one more thing I want to show you.'

They rode the elevator down to the next level, to subbasement three. Deeper into Hades, thought Jack. Once again they stepped out to face a wall of glass, and beyond it, another lab with more space-suited workers.

Roman pressed the intercom button and said, 'Could you bring out the specimen?'

One of the lab workers nodded. She crossed to a walk-in steel vault, spun the massive combination lock, and disappeared inside. When she emerged again, she was wheeling a cart with a steel container on a tray. She rolled it to the viewing window.

Roman nodded.

She unlatched the steel container, lifted out a Plexiglas cylinder, and set it on the tray. The contents bobbed gently in a clear bath of formalin.

'We found this burrowed inside the spinal column of Kenichi Hirai,' said Roman. 'His spine protected it from the force of impact when *Discovery* crashed. When we removed it, it was still alive – but only barely.'

Jack tried to speak, but could not produce a single word. He heard only the hiss of the ventilation fans and the roar of his own pulse as he stared in horror at the contents of the cylinder.

'This is what the larvae grow into,' said Roman. 'This is the next stage.'

He understood, now. The reason for secrecy. What he had seen preserved in formalin, coiled up in that Plexiglas cylinder, had explained everything. Though it had been mangled during extraction, its essential features had been apparent. The glossy amphibian skin. The larval tail. And the fetal curl of the spine – not amphibian, but something far more horrifying, because its genetic origin was recognizable. *Mammalian*, he thought. Maybe even human. It was already beginning to look like its host.

Allowed to infect a different species, it would change its appearance yet again. It could raid the DNA of any organism on earth, assume any shape. Eventually it could evolve to the point where it needed no host at all in which to grow and reproduce. It would be independent and self-sufficient. Perhaps even intelligent.

And Emma was now a living nursery for these things, her body a nourishing cocoon in which they were growing.

Jack shivered as he stood on the tarmac and stared across the barren airstrip. The Army jeep that had brought him and Gordon back to White Sands Air Force Base had receded to barely a glint now, trailing a fantail of dust into the horizon. The sun's white-hot brilliance brought tears to his eyes, and for a moment, the desert shimmered out of focus, as though underwater.

He turned to look at Gordon. 'There's no other way. We have to do it.'

'There are a thousand things that can go wrong.'

'There always are. That's true for every launch, every mission. Why should this one be any different?'

'There'll be no contingencies. No safety backups. I know what we're dealing with, and it's a cowboy operation.'

'Which makes it possible. What's their motto? *Smaller, faster, cheaper.*'

'Okay,' said Gordon, 'let's say you *don't* blow up on the launchpad. Say the Air Force *doesn't* blast you out of the sky. Once you get up there, you're still faced with the biggest gamble of all: whether the Ranavirus will work.'

'From the very beginning, Gordon, there was one thing I couldn't figure out: Why was amphibian DNA on that genome? How did Chimera get frog genes? Roman thinks it was an accident. A mistake that happened in Koenig's lab.' Jack shook his head. 'I don't think it was an accident at all. I think Koenig *put* those genes there. As a fail-safe.'

'I don't understand.'

'Maybe she was thinking ahead, to the possible dangers. To what could happen if this new life-form changed while in microgravity. If Chimera ever got out of control, she wanted a way to kill it. A back door through its defenses. And this is it.'

'A frog virus.'

'It will work, Gordon. It has to work. I'll bet my life on it.'

A whorl of dust spun between them, kicking up sand and stray scraps of paper. Gordon turned and gazed across the tarmac at the T-38 they had flown from Houston. And he sighed. 'I was afraid you'd say that.'

26

August 22

Casper Mulholland was gobbling down his third package of Tums, and his stomach still felt like a bubbling cauldron of acid. In the distance, *Apogee II* glinted like a bullet casing planted point up in the desert sand. She was not a particularly impressive sight, especially to this audience. Most of them had heard the earth-shaking roar of a NASA launch, had been awed by the majesty of the shuttle's giant columns of fire streaking into the sky. *Apogee II* looked nothing like the shuttle. She was more like a child's toy rocket, and Casper could see disappointment in the eyes of the dozen or so visitors as they climbed the newly erected viewing stand and gazed across the bleak desert terrain, toward the launchpad. Everyone wanted *big*. Everyone was in love with size and power. The small, the elegantly simple, did not interest them.

Another van pulled up at the site, and a fresh group of visitors began piling out, hands lifting at once to shield their eyes from the morning sun. He recognized Mark Lucas and Hashemi Rashad, the two businessmen who had visited Apogee over three weeks ago. He saw the same disappointment play across their faces as they squinted toward the launchpad.

349

'This is as close to the pad as we can get?' said Lucas.

'I'm afraid so,' said Casper. 'It's for your own safety. We're dealing with explosive propellants out there.'

'But I thought we were going to get an in-depth look at your launch operations.'

'You'll have full access to our ground-control facility – our equivalent of Houston's Mission Control. As soon as she's off the pad, we'll drive over to the building and show you how we guide her into low earth orbit. That's the real test of our system, Mr Lucas. Any engineering grad can launch a rocket. But getting one safely into orbit, and then guiding her to a flyby of the station, is a far more complicated matter. That's why we moved up this demonstration four days – to hit just the right launch window for ISS. To show you our system is already rendezvous-capable. *Apogee II* is just the kind of bird NASA's looking to buy.'

'You're not actually going to dock, are you?' said Rashad. 'I heard the station is in quarantine.'

'No, we're not going to dock. *Apogee II*'s just a prototype. She can't physically hook up with ISS because she doesn't have an orbital docking system. But we'll fly her close enough to the station to demonstrate we can do it. You know, just the fact we're able to change our launch schedule on short notice is a selling point. When it comes to spaceflight, flexibility is key. Unexpected things always pop up. My partner's recent accident, for example. Even though Mr Obie's laid up in bed with a broken pelvis, you'll notice we didn't cancel the launch. We'll control the entire mission from the ground. Gentlemen, *that's* flexibility.'

'I can understand why you might delay a launch,' said Lucas. 'Say, for bad weather. By why did you have to move it *up* four days? Some of our partners weren't able to make it here in time.'

350

Casper could feel the last Tums tablet bubble away in a fresh spurt of stomach acid. 'It's simple, really.' He paused to take out a handkerchief and wipe the sweat from his forehead. 'It has to do with that launch window I mentioned. The space station's orbit is at an inclination of fifty-one point six degrees. If you look at a tracing of its orbital path on a map, it makes a sine wave varying between fifty-one point six degrees north and fifty-one point six degrees south. Since the earth rotates, the station passes over a different place on the map with each orbit. Also, the earth isn't entirely spherical, which adds another complication. When that orbital trace passes over your launch site, that's the most efficient time to lift off. Adding up all those factors, we came up with various launch options. Then there's the question of daytime versus nighttime launches. Allowable launch angles. The most current weather forecasts . . .'

Their eyes had begun to glaze over. He'd already lost them.

'Anyway,' Casper finished with a profound sense of relief, 'today at seven-ten A.M. turns out to be the best choice. That all makes perfect sense to you, right?'

Lucas seemed to give himself a shake, like a startled dog coming out of a nap. 'Yes. Of course.'

'I'd still like to get closer,' said Mr Rashad on a wistful note. He gazed at the rocket, a snub-nosed blip on the horizon. 'From this far away, she's not much to look at, is she? So small.'

Casper smiled, even as he felt his own stomach digest itself in nervous acid. 'Well, you know what they say, Mr Rashad. It's not the size that matters. It's what you do with it.'

This is the last option, thought Jack as a bead of perspiration slid down his temple and soaked into the lining of his flight helmet. He tried to calm his racing pulse, but his heart was like a frantic animal trying to batter its way out of his chest.

For so many years, this was the moment he had dreamed of: strapped into the flight seat, helmet closed, oxygen flowing. The countdown ticking toward zero. In those dreams, fear had not been part of the equation, only excitement. Anticipation. He had not expected to be terrified.

'You are at T minus five minutes. The time to back out is now.' It was Gordon Obie's voice over the hardline comm. At every step of the way, Gordon had offered Jack chances to change his mind. During the flight from White Sands to Nevada. In the early morning hours, as Jack suited up in the Apogee Engineering hangar. And finally, on the drive across the pitch-black desert to the launchpad. This was Jack's last opportunity.

'We can stop the countdown now,' said Gordon. 'Nix the whole mission.'

'I'm still a go.'

'Then this will be our last voice contact. There can't be any communication from you. No downlink to the ground, no contact with ISS, or everything's blown. The instant we hear your voice, we'll abort the whole mission and bring you back.' *If we still can*, was what he didn't add.

'I roger that.'

There was a silence. 'You don't have to do this. No one expects you to.'

'Let's get on with it. Just light the damn candle, okay?'

Gordon's answering sigh came through loud and clear. 'Okay. You're a go. We're at T minus three minutes and counting.'

'Thank you, Gordie. For everything.'

'Good luck and Godspeed, Jack McCallum.'

The hard link was severed.

And that may be the last voice I'll ever hear, thought Jack. From this point on, the only uplink from Apogee ground control would be command data streaming into the onboard

352

guidance and nav computers. The vehicle was flying itself; Jack was nothing more than the dumb monkey in the pilot's seat.

He closed his eyes and focused on the beating of his own heart. It had slowed. He now felt strangely calm and prepared for the inevitable, whatever that might be. He heard the whirs and clicks of the onboard systems preparing for the leap. He imagined the cloudless sky, its atmosphere dense as water, like a sea of air through which he must surface to reach the cold, clear vacuum of space.

Where Emma was dying.

The crowd in the viewing stand had fallen ominously silent. The countdown clock, displayed on the closed-circuit video feed, slid past the T minus sixty seconds mark and kept ticking. *They're going for the launch window*, thought Casper, and the fresh sweat of panic bloomed on his forehead. In his heart, he had never really believed it would come to this moment. He had expected delays, aborts, even a cancellation. He had lived through so many disappointments, so much bad luck with this damn bird, that dread rose like bile in his throat. He glanced at the faces in the stands and saw that many of them were mouthing the seconds as they ticked by. It started as a whisper, a rhythmic disturbance in the air.

'Twenty-nine. Twenty-eight. Twenty-seven . . .'

The whispers became a chorus of murmurs, growing louder with each passing second.

'Twelve. Eleven. Ten . . .'

Casper's hands were shaking so hard he had to clutch the railing. His pulse throbbed in his fingertips.

'Seven. Six. Five . . .'

He closed his eyes. Oh, God, what had they done?

'Three. Two. One . . .'

The crowd sucked in a simultaneous gasp of wonder. Then

the roar of the boosters spilled over him, and his eyes flew open. He stared at the sky, at the streak of fire lifting toward the heavens. Any second now it would happen. First the blinding flash, then, lagging behind at the speed of sound, the pulse of the explosion battering their eardrums. That's how it had happened with *Apogee I.*

But the fiery streak kept on rising until it was only a pale dot punched in the deep blue sky.

A hand clapped his back, hard. He gave a start and turned to see Mark Lucas beaming at him.

'Way to go, Mulholland! What a gorgeous launch!'

Casper ventured another terrified glance at the sky. Still no explosion.

'But I guess you never had any doubts, did you?' said Lucas.

Casper swallowed. 'None at all.'

The last dose.

Emma squeezed the plunger, slowly emptying the contents of the syringe into her vein. She removed the needle, pressed gauze to the puncture site, and folded her arm to hold it in place while she disposed of the needle. It felt like a sacred ceremony, every action performed with reverence, with the solemn knowledge that this was the last time she would experience each sensation, from the prick of the needle, to the hard lump of gauze pressing into the flesh at the crook of her arm. And how long would this final dose of HCG keep her alive?

She turned and looked at the mouse cage, which she had moved into the Russian service module, where there was more light. The lone female was now curled in a shivering ball, dying. The hormone's effect was not permanent. The babies had died that morning. *By tomorrow*, thought Emma, *I will be the only one alive aboard this station.*

No, not the only one. There would be the life-form inside her. The scores of larvae that would soon awaken from dormancy and begin to feed and grow.

She pressed her hand to her abdomen, like a pregnant woman sensing the fetus inside her. And like a real fetus, the life-form she now harbored would carry bits and pieces of her DNA. In that way, it was her biological offspring, and it possessed the genetic memory of every host it had ever known. Kenichi Hirai. Nicolai Rudenko. Diana Estes. And now, Emma.

She would be the last. There would be no new hosts, no new victims, because there would be no rescuers. The station was now a sepulchre of contagion, as forbidden and untouchable as a leper colony had been to the ancients.

She floated out of the RSM and swam toward the powered-down section of the station. There was barely enough light to guide her through the darkened node. Except for the rhythmic sigh of her own breathing, all was silent on this end. She moved through the same molecules of air that had once swirled in the lungs of people now dead. Even now, she sensed the presence of the five who had passed on, could imagine the echoes of their voices, the last faint pulses of sound fracturing at last into silence. This was the very air through which they had moved, and it was still haunted by their passing.

And soon, she thought, *it will be haunted by mine.*

August 24

Jared Profitt was awakened just after midnight. It took only two rings of the phone to propel him from deep sleep to a state of complete alertness. He reached for the receiver.

The voice on the other end was brusque. 'This is General Gregorian. I've just spoken to our control center in Cheyenne Mountain. That so-called demo launch from Nevada continues to be on a rendezvous path with ISS.'

'Which launch?'

'Apogee Engineering.'

Profitt frowned, trying to remember the name. Every week there were numerous launches from sites around the world. A score of commercial aerospace firms were always testing booster systems or sending satellites into orbit or even blasting off cremated human remains. Space Command was already tracking nine thousand manmade objects in orbit. 'Refresh my memory about this Nevada launch,' he asked.

'Apogee is testing a new reusable launch vehicle. They sent it up at oh-seven-ten yesterday morning. They informed the FAA as required, but didn't let us know until after the fact. This flight is billed as an orbital trial of their new RLV. A launch into low earth orbit, a flyby past ISS, and then reentry. We've been tracking it for a day and a half now, and based on its most recent on-orbit burns, it seems possible they'll approach the station closer than they told us.'

'How close will they get?'

'It depends on their next burn maneuvers.'

'Close enough for an actual rendezvous? A docking?'

'That's not possible with this particular vehicle. We have all the specs on their orbiter. It's just a prototype, with no orbital docking system. The best it can do is a flyby and a wave.'

'A wave?' Profitt suddenly sat up in bed. 'Are you telling me this RLV is manned?'

'No, sir. That was just a figure of speech. Apogee says the vehicle is unmanned. There are animals aboard, including a spider monkey, but no pilot. And we've picked up no voice communication between ground and vehicle.'

A spider monkey, thought Profitt. Its presence aboard the spacecraft meant they could not rule out the possibility of a human pilot. The craft's environmental monitors, the carbon dioxide levels, would not distinguish between animal or

356

human life. He was uneasy about the lack of information. He was even more uneasy about the timing of the launch.

'I'm not certain there's any cause for alarm,' said Gregorian. 'But you did ask to be notified of any orbital approaches.'

'Tell me more about Apogee,' Profitt cut in.

Gregorian gave a dismissive snort. 'A minor player. Twelve-man engineering firm out in Nevada. They haven't had a lot of luck. A year and a half ago, they blew up their first prototype twenty seconds into launch, and all their early investors vanished. I'm sort of surprised they're still hanging in there. Their booster's based on Russian technology. The orbiter's a simple, bare-bones system with a parachute reentry. Payload capacity's only three hundred kilos, plus a pilot.'

'I'll fly out to Nevada at once. We need to get a better handle on this.'

'Sir, we can monitor every move this vehicle makes. Right now, we have no reason to take action. They're just a small firm, trying to impress some new investors. If the orbiter presents any real concern, we can have our ground-based interceptors standing by to bring that bird down.'

General Gregorian was probably right. The fact that some hotshot ground jockeys decided to launch a monkey into space did not constitute a national emergency. He had to move very carefully on this. The death of Luther Ames had unleashed a national uproar of protest. This was not the time to shoot down another spacecraft – one built by a private American firm, no less.

But so much about this Apogee launch disturbed him. The timing. The rendezvous maneuvers. The fact they could neither confirm nor rule out a human presence.

What else could it be but a rescue mission?

He said, 'I'm leaving for Nevada.'

Forty-five minutes later, Profitt was in his car and pulling out of the driveway. The night was clear, the stars like bright pinpricks in blue velvet. There were perhaps one hundred billion galaxies in the universe, and each galaxy contained a hundred billion stars. How many of those stars had planets, and how many planets had life? *Panspermia*, the theory that life exists and is distributed throughout the universe, was no longer merely speculation. The belief that there was life only on this pale blue dot, in this insignificant solar system, now seemed as absurd as the ancients' naive belief that the sun and the stars revolved around the earth. The only strict requirements for life were the presence of carbon-based compounds plus some form of water. Both were in abundance throughout the universe. Which meant that life, however primitive, could be abundant as well, and that interstellar dust might be seeded with bacteria or spores. From such primitive creatures did all other life spring.

And what happened if such life-forms, arriving as bits of cosmic dust, seeded a planet where life already existed?

This was Jared Profitt's nightmare.

Once, he had thought the stars beautiful. Once he had viewed the universe with awe and wonder. Now, when he looked at the night sky, he saw infinite menace. He saw biological Armageddon.

Their conqueror, descending from the heavens.

It was time to die.

Emma's hands were shaking, and the pounding in her head was so severe she had to grit her teeth just to keep herself from crying out. The last morphine shot had barely taken the edge off the pain, and she was so dazed by the narcotic she could barely focus on the computer screen. On the keyboard beneath her fingers. She paused to still the trembling of her hands. Then she began to type.

Personal E-mail to: Jack McCallum

If I could have one wish, it would be to hear your voice again. I don't know where you are, or why I can't speak to you. I only know that this thing inside me is about to claim victory. Even as I write this, I can feel it gaining ground. I can feel my strength retreating. I have fought it as long as I can. But I'm tired now. I'm ready to sleep.

While I can type these words, this is what I most want to say. I love you. I have never stopped loving you. They say that no one who stands poised at the doorway to eternity steps through it with a lie on his lips. They say that deathbed confessions are always to be believed. And this is mine.

Her hands were shaking so badly she could not type any more. She signed off and pressed 'send.'

In the medical kit, she found the supply of Valium. There were two tablets left. She swallowed them both with a gulp of water. The edges of her vision were starting to black out. Her legs felt numb, as though they were not part of her body at all, but the limbs of a stranger.

There was not much time left.

She did not have the strength to don an EVA suit. And what did it matter now where she died? The station was already diseased. Her corpse would be just one more item to clean up.

She made her last passage into the dark side of the station.

The cupola was where she wanted to spend her final waking moments. Floating in darkness, gazing down at the beauty of the earth. From the windows, she could see the blue-gray arc of the Caspian Sea. Clouds swirling over Kazakhstan and snow in the Himalayas. *Down there are billions of people going about their lives*, she thought. *And here am I, a dying speck in the heavens.*

'Emma?' It was Todd Cutler, speaking gently over her comm unit. 'How are you doing?'

'Not . . . feeling so good,' she murmured. 'Pain. Vision's starting to fade. I took the last Valium.'

'You have to hang in there, Emma. Listen to me. Don't give up. Not yet.'

'I've already lost the battle, Todd.'

'No, you haven't! You have to have faith –'

'In miracles?' She gave a soft laugh. 'The real miracle is that I am up here at all. That I'm seeing the earth from a place so few people have ever been . . .' She touched the window of the cupola and felt the warmth of the sun through the glass. 'I only wish I could speak to Jack.'

'We're trying to make that happen.'

'Where is he? Why can't you reach him?'

'He's working like crazy to get you home. You have to believe that.'

She blinked away tears. *I do.*

'Is there anything we can do for you?' said Todd. 'Anyone else you want to speak to?'

'No.' She sighed. 'Only Jack.'

There was a silence.

'I think – I think what I want most now –'

'Yes?' said Todd.

'I'd like to go to sleep. That's all. Just go to sleep.'

He cleared his throat. 'Of course. You get some rest. I'll be right here if you need me.' He closed with a soft, 'Good night, ISS.'

Good night, Houston, she thought. And she took off her headset and let it float away into the gloom.

27

The convoy of black sedans braked to a stop in front of Apogee Engineering, tires churning up a massive cloud of dust. Jared Profitt stepped out of the lead car and gazed up at the building. It looked like an airplane hangar, windowless and bleakly industrial, its rooftop studded with satellite equipment.

He nodded to General Gregorian. 'Secure the building.'

Barely a minute later, Gregorian's men gave the all-secure signal, and Profitt stepped into the building.

Inside, he found a ragtag group of men and women herded into a tense and angry circle. He immediately recognized two of the faces: Director of Flight Crew Operations Gordon Obie and shuttle Flight Director Randy Carpenter. So NASA was here, as he'd suspected, and this featureless building in the middle of the Nevada desert had been turned into a rebel Mission Control.

Unlike the Flight Control Room at NASA, this was clearly a shoestring operation. The floor was bare concrete. Spaghetti tangles of wires and cables were strung everywhere. A grotesquely overweight cat picked its way among a pile of discarded electronic equipment.

361

Profitt walked over to the flight consoles and saw the data streaming in. 'What's the orbiter's status?' he asked.

One of Gregorian's men, a flight controller from U.S. Space Command, said, 'It's already completed its Ti-burn, sir, and it's now moving up the R-bar. It could rendezvous with ISS within forty-five minutes.'

'Halt the approach.'

'No!' said Gordon Obie. He broke away from the group and stepped forward. 'Don't do this. You don't understand –'

'There can be no evacuation of station crew,' said Profitt.

'It's *not* an evacuation!'

'Then what's it doing up there? It's clearly about to rendezvous with ISS.'

'No, it's not. It *can't*. It has no docking system, no way of connecting with the station. There's no chance of cross-contamination.'

'You haven't answered my question, Mr Obie. What is *Apogee II* doing up there?'

Gordon hesitated. 'It's going through a near-approach sequence, that's all. It's a test of *Apogee*'s rendezvous capabilities.'

'Sir,' said the flight controller from Space Command. 'I'm seeing a major anomaly here.'

Profitt's gaze shot back to the console. 'What anomaly?'

'The cabin atmospheric pressure. It's down to eight psi. It should be at fourteen point seven. Either the orbiter has a serious air leak, or they've purposely allowed it to depressurize.'

'How long has it been that low?'

Quickly the flight controller typed on the keyboard, and a graph appeared, a plot of the cabin pressure over time. 'According to their computers, the cabin was maintained at fourteen point seven for the first twelve hours after launch. Then around thirty-six hours ago, it was depressurized to

362

ten point two, where it held steady until an hour ago.' Suddenly his chin jerked up. 'Sir, I know what they're doing! This appears to be a prebreathe protocol.'

'Protocol for what?'

'An EVA. A spacewalk.' He looked at Profitt. 'I think someone's aboard that orbiter.'

Profitt turned to face Gordon Obie. 'Who's aboard? Who did you send up?'

Gordon could see there was no longer any point in holding back the truth. He said, in quiet defeat, 'It's Jack McCallum.'

Emma Watson's husband.

'So it's a rescue mission,' said Profitt. 'How was it supposed to work? He goes EVA, and then what?'

'The SAFER jet pack. The Orlan-M suit he's wearing is equipped with one. He uses it to propel himself from *Apogee II* to the station. Enters via the ISS airlock.'

'And he retrieves his wife and brings her home.'

'No. That wasn't the plan. Look, he understands – we *all* understand – why she can't come home. The reason Jack went up was to deliver the Ranavirus.'

'And if the virus doesn't work?'

'That's the gamble.'

'He's exposing himself to ISS. We'd never let him come home.'

'He wasn't planning to come home! The orbiter was going to return without him.' Gordon paused, his gaze fixed on Profitt's. 'It's a one-way trip, and Jack knows it. He accepted the conditions. It's his wife dying up there! He won't – he can't – let her die alone.'

Stunned, Profitt fell silent. He looked at the flight console, the monitors streaming with data. As the seconds ticked by, he thought of his own wife, Amy, dying in Bethesda Hospital. Remembered his frantic sprint through the Denver airport to catch the next flight home to her, and remembered his despair as he'd arrived breathless at the gate to see the plane pulling away. He thought of the desperation that must be driving McCallum, the anguish of being so heartbreakingly close to his goal, only to see it drift inexorably out of reach. And he thought, *This will bring no harm to anyone here on earth. To anyone but McCallum. He has made his choice, with full knowledge of the consequences. What right do I have to stop him?*

He said, to the Space Command flight controller, 'Return control of the console to Apogee. Let them resume their mission.'

'*Sir?*'

'I said, let the orbiter continue its approach.'

There was a moment of stunned silence. Then the Apogee controllers scrambled back into their seats.

'Mr Obie,' said Profitt, turning to look at Gordon. 'You do understand that we'll be monitoring every move McCallum makes. I am not your enemy. But I'm charged with protecting the greater good, and I'll do what's necessary. If I see any indication you plan to bring either of those people home, I will order *Apogee II* destroyed.'

Gordon Obie nodded. 'It's what I'd expect you to do.'

'Then we both know where we stand.' Profitt took a deep breath and turned to face the row of consoles. 'Now. Go ahead and get that man to his wife.'

Jack hung poised at the edge of eternity.

No amount of EVA training in the WET-F pool could have prepared him for this visceral punch of fear, for the paralysis that now seized him as he stared into the emptiness of space. He had swung open the hatch leading into the open payload bay, and his first view, through the bay's gaping clamshell doors, was of the earth, a dizzying drop below. He could not see ISS; she was floating above him, out of view. To

364

reach her, he would have to swim down past those payload doors and circle around to the opposite side of *Apogee II*. But first, he had to force himself to ignore every instinct that was now screaming at him to retreat back into the air lock.

'Emma,' he said, and the sound of her name was like a murmured prayer. He took a breath and prepared to release his grip on the hatchway, to surrender himself to the heavens.

'*Apogee II*, this is Capcom Houston. *Apogee* – Jack – please respond.'

The transmission over his comm unit caught Jack by surprise. He had not expected any contact from the ground. The fact Houston was openly hailing him by name meant all secrecy had been shattered.

'*Apogee*, we urgently request you respond.'

He remained silent, uncertain if he should confirm his presence in orbit.

'Jack, we have been advised that the White House will not interfere with your mission. Provided you understand one essential fact: This is a one-way trip.' Capcom paused and then said quietly, 'If you board ISS, you can't leave it again. You can't come home.'

'This is *Apogee II*,' Jack finally answered. 'Message received and understood.'

'And you still plan to proceed? Think about it.'

'What the hell do you think I came up here for? The fucking view?'

'Uh, we roger that. But before you proceed, you should be aware of this. We lost contact with ISS about six hours ago.'

'What do you mean, "lost contact"?'

'Emma is no longer responding.'

Six hours, he thought. *What has happened in the last six hours?* The launch had been two days ago. It had taken that long for *Apogee II* to catch up with ISS and complete the rendezvous maneuvers. In all that time, he'd been cut off from all communication, from any knowledge of what was happening aboard the station.

'You may already be too late. You might want to reconsider –'

'What does biotelemetry show?' he cut in. 'What's her rhythm?'

'She's not hooked up. She chose to disconnect her leads.'

'Then you don't know. You can't tell me what's going on.'

'Just before she went silent, she sent you a final E-mail.' Capcom added gently, 'Jack, she was saying good-bye.'

No. At once he released his grip on the hatchway and pushed out of the air lock, diving headfirst into the open payload bay. *No.* He grabbed a handhold and scrambled up over the clamshell door, to the other side of *Apogee II.* Suddenly the space station was *right there,* looming above him, so big and sprawling he was momentarily stunned by the wonder of it. Then, in panic, he thought, *Where is the air lock? I don't see the air lock!* There were so many modules, so many solar arrays, fanned out across an area as large as two football fields. He could not orient himself. He was lost, overwhelmed by the dizzying spread.

Then he spotted the dark-green *Soyuz* capsule jutting out. He was underneath the Russian end of the station. Instantly everything snapped into place. His gaze shot to the American end, and he identified the US hab. At the upper end of the hab was Node 1, which led to the air lock.

He knew where he was going.

Here came the leap of faith. With only his SAFER jet pack to propel him, he would be crossing empty space without tethers, without anything to anchor him. He activated the jet pack, pushed off from *Apogee,* and launched himself toward ISS.

It was his first EVA, and he was clumsy and inexperienced,

unable to judge how quickly he was closing in on his goal. He slammed into the hab hull with such force he almost caromed off, and barely managed to grab onto a handhold.

Hurry. She is dying.

Sick with dread, he clambered up the length of the hab, his breaths coming hard and fast.

'Houston,' he panted. 'I need Surgeon – have him standing by –'

'Roger that.'

'Almost – I'm almost to Node One –'

'Jack, this is Surgeon.' It was Todd Cutler's voice, speaking with quiet urgency. 'You've been out of the loop for two days. You need to know a few things. Emma's last dose of HCG was fifty-five hours ago. Since then, her labs have deteriorated. Amylase and CPK sky-high. Last transmission, she was complaining of headaches and visual loss. That was six hours ago. We don't know her current condition.'

'I'm at the air-lock hatch!'

'Station control software has been switched to EVA mode. You're a go for repress.'

Jack swung open the hatch and pulled himself into the crew lock. As he twisted around to close the external hatch, he caught a glimpse of *Apogee II*. She was already moving away. His only lifeboat was going home without him. He'd passed the point of no return.

He closed and sealed the hatch. 'Pressure-equalization valve open,' he said. 'Beginning repress.'

'I'm trying to prepare you for the worst,' said Todd. 'In case she –'

'Tell me something useful!'

'Okay. Okay, here's the latest from USAMRIID. The Ranavirus does seem to work on their lab animals. But it's only been effective in early cases. If it's given during the first thirty-six hours after infection.'

'What if it's given after that?'

Cutler didn't respond. His silence confirmed the worst.

The crew lock pressure was up to fourteen psi. Jack opened the middle hatch and dove into the equipment lock. Frantically he detached his gloves, then doffed his Orlan-M suit and wriggled out of the cooling garment. From the Orlan's zippered pockets he pulled out various packets containing emergency medications and prefilled syringes of Ranavirus. By now he was shaking with fear, terrified of what he would find inside the station. He swung open the inner hatch.

And confronted his worst nightmare.

She was floating in the gloom of Node 1, like a swimmer adrift in a dark sea. Only this swimmer was drowning. Her limbs jerked in rhythmic spasms. Convulsions wracked her spine, and her head snapped forward and back, her hair lashing like a whip. Death throes.

No, he thought. *I won't let you die. Goddamnit, Emma, you are not going to leave me.*

He grasped her around the waist and began to pull her toward the Russian end of the station. Toward the modules that still had power and light. Her body twitched like a live wire jolted by electric shocks, thrashing in his arms. She was so small, so fragile, yet the strength now coursing through her dying body threatened to overpower his grip on her. Weightlessness was new to him, and he bounced drunkenly off walls and hatchways as he struggled to maneuver them both into the Russian service module.

'Jack, talk to me,' said Todd. 'What's going on?'

'I've moved her into the RSM – getting her onto the restraint board –'

'Have you given the virus?'

'Tying her down first. She's seizing –' He fastened the Velcro straps over her chest and hips, anchoring her torso to the medical restraint board. Her head slammed backward, her eyes rolling up into the orbits. The sclerae were a brilliant and horrifying red. *Give her the virus. Do it now.*

A tourniquet was looped around the restraint-board frame. He whipped it free and tied it around her thrashing arm. It took all his strength to forcibly extend her elbow, to expose the antecubital vein. With his teeth he uncapped the syringe of Ranavirus. Stabbing the needle into her arm, he squeezed the plunger.

'It's in!' he said. 'The whole syringe!'

'What's she doing?'

'She's still seizing!'

'There's IV Dilantin in the med kit.'

'I see it. I'm starting an IV!' The tourniquet floated by, a startling reminder that in weightlessness, what was not tied down would quickly drift out of reach. He snatched it from midair and reached, once again, for Emma's arm.

A moment later he reported, 'Dilantin's going in! IV's running wide open.'

'Any change?'

Jack stared at his wife, silently demanding, *Come on, Emma. Don't die on me.*

Slowly her spine relaxed. Her neck went limp and her head stopped battering the board. Her eyes rolled forward, and he could see her irises now, two dark pools ringed by bloodred sclerae. At his first glimpse of her pupils, a moan rose in his throat.

Her left pupil was fully dilated. Black and lifeless.

He was too late. She was dying.

He cupped her face in his hands, as though by sheer will he could force her to live. But even as he pleaded with her not to leave him, he knew that she would not be saved by mere touch or prayer. Death was an organic process. Biochemical functions, the movement of ions across cell membranes, slowly ceased. The brain waves flattened. The

369

rhythmic contractions of myocardial cells faded to a quiver. Just wishing it so would not make her live.

But she was not dead. Not yet.

'Todd,' he said.

'I'm here.'

'What is the terminal event? What happens to the lab animals?'

'I don't follow –'

'You said Ranavirus works, if given early enough in the infection. Which means it must be killing Chimera. So why doesn't it work when given later?'

'Too much tissue damage has occurred. There's internal bleeding –'

'Bleeding where? What do the autopsies show?'

'Seventy-five percent of the time, in dogs, the fatal hemorrhage is intracranial. Chimera's enzymes damage blood vessels on the surface of the cerebral cortex. The vessels rupture, and the bleeding causes a catastrophic rise in intracranial pressure. It's like a massive head injury, Jack. The brain herniates.'

'What if you stop the bleeding, stop the brain damage? If you get the victims past the acute stage, they might live long enough for Ranavirus to work.'

'Possibly.'

Jack stared down at Emma's dilated left pupil. A terrible memory flashed into his head: Debbie Haning, unconscious on a hospital gurney. He had failed Debbie. He had waited too long to take action, and because of his indecision, he had lost her.

I will not lose you.

He said, 'Todd, she's blown her left pupil. She needs burr holes.'

'What? You're working blind. Without X-ray –'

'It's the only chance she has! I need a drill. Tell me where the work tools are kept!'

370

'Stand by.' Seconds later, Todd came back on comm. 'We're not sure where the Russians stow their kit. But NASA's are in Node One, in the storage rack. Check the labels on the Nomex bags. The contents are specified.'

Jack shot out of the service module, once again colliding with walls and hatchways as he clumsily barreled his way into Node 1. His hands were shaking as he opened the storage rack. He pulled out three Nomex bags before he found the one labeled 'Power drill/bits/adapters.' He grabbed a second bag containing screwdrivers and a hammer, and shot back out of the node. He'd been away from her for only a moment, yet the fear that he would return to find her dead sent him flying through Zarya and back into the service module.

She was still breathing. Still alive.

He anchored the Nomex bags to the table and removed the power tool. It was meant for space station repair and construction, not neurosurgery. Now that he actually held the drill in his hand and considered what he was about to do, panic seized him. He was operating in unsterile conditions, with a tool meant for steel bolts, not flesh and bone. He looked at Emma, lying flaccid on the table, and thought of what lay beneath that cranial vault, thought of her gray matter, where a lifetime of memories and dreams and emotions were stored. Everything that made her uniquely Emma. All of it dying now.

He reached into the medical kit and took scissors and a shaving razor. Grasping a handful of her hair, he began to snip it away, then shaved the stubble, clearing an incision site over her left temporal bone. *Your beautiful hair. I have always loved your hair. I have always loved you.*

The rest of her hair he bound up and tucked out of the way, so it would not contaminate the site. With a strip of adhesive tape, he restrained her head to the board. Moving more quickly now, he prepared his tools. The suction catheter.

371

The scalpel. The gauze. He swished the drill bits in disinfectant, then wiped them off with alcohol.

He pulled on sterile gloves and picked up the scalpel.

His skin was clammy inside the latex gloves as he made his incision. Blood oozed from the scalp, welling into a gently expanding globule. He dabbed it with gauze and sliced deeper, until his blade scraped bone.

To breach the skull is to expose the brain to a hostile universe of microbial invaders. Yet the human body is resilient; it can survive the most brutal of insults. He kept reminding himself of this as he tapped a nick into the temporal bone, as he positioned the tip of the drill bit. The ancient Egyptians and the Incas had successfully performed skull trephinations, opening holes in the cranium with only the crudest of tools and no thought of sterile technique. It could be done.

His hands were steady, his concentration fierce as he drilled into the bone. A few millimeters too deep, and he could hit brain matter. A thousand precious memories would be destroyed in a second. Or a nick of the middle meningeal artery, and he could unleash an unstoppable fountain of blood. He kept pausing to take a breath, to probe the depth of the hole. *Go slow. Go slow.*

Suddenly he felt the last filigree of bone give way, and the drill broke through. Heart slamming in his throat, he gently withdrew the bit.

A bubble of blood immediately began to form, slowly ballooning out from the breach. It was dark red – venous. He gave a sigh of relief. Not arterial. Even now the pressure on Emma's brain was slowly easing, the intracranial bleed escaping through this new opening. He suctioned the bubble, then used gauze to absorb the continuing ooze as he drilled the next hole, and the next, punching a one-inch-diameter ring of perforations in the skull. By the time the last hole was drilled, and the circle was complete, his hands were cramping, his face beaded with sweat. He could not pause to rest; every second counted.

He reached for a screwdriver and ball peen hammer.

Let this work. Let this save her.

Using the screwdriver as a chisel, he gently dug the tip into the skull. Then, teeth gritted, he pried off the circular cap of bone.

Blood billowed out. The larger opening at last allowed it to escape, and it gradually spilled out of the cranium.

So did something else. *Eggs.* A clump of them gushed out and floated, quivering, into the air. He caught them with the suction catheter, trapping them in the vacuum jar. Throughout history, mankind's most dangerous enemies have been the smallest life-forms. Viruses. Bacteria. Parasites. *And now you*, thought Jack, staring into the jar. *But we can defeat you.*

The blood was barely oozing out the cranial hole. With that initial gush, the pressure on her brain had been relieved.

He looked at Emma's left eye. The pupil was still dilated. But when he shone a light into it, he thought – or was he imagining it? – that the edges quivered just the slightest bit, like black water rippling toward the center.

You will *live*, he thought.

He dressed the wound with gauze and started a new IV infusion containing steroids and phenobarbital to temporarily deepen her coma and protect her brain from further damage. He attached EKG leads to her chest. Only after all these tasks had been done did he finally tie a tourniquet around his own arm and inject himself with a dose of Ranavirus. It would either kill them both or save them both. He would know soon enough.

On the EKG monitor, Emma's heart traced a steady sinus rhythm. He took her hand in his, and waited for a sign.

August 27

Gordon Obie walked into Special Vehicle Operations and gazed around the room at the men and women working at their consoles. On the front screen, the space station traced its sinuous path across the global map. At this moment, in the deserts of Algeria, villagers who chanced to glance up at the night sky would marvel at the strange star, brilliant as Venus, soaring across the heavens. A star unique in all the firmament because it was created not by an all-powerful god, nor by any force of nature, but by the fragile hand of man.

And in this room, halfway around the world from that Algerian desert, were the guardians of that star.

Flight Director Woody Ellis turned and greeted Gordon with a sad nod. 'No word. It's been silent up there.'

'How long since the last transmission?'

'Jack signed off five hours ago to get some sleep. It's been almost three days since he got much rest. We're trying not to disturb him.'

Three days, and still no change in Emma's status. Gordon sighed and headed along the back row to the flight surgeon's console. Todd Cutler, unshaven and haggard, was watching Emma's biotelemetry readings on his monitor. And when had Todd last slept? Gordon wondered. Everyone looked exhausted, but no one was ready to admit defeat.

'She's still hanging in there,' Todd said softly. 'We've withdrawn the phenobarb.'

'But she hasn't come out of the coma?'

'No.' Sighing, Todd slumped back and pinched the bridge of his nose. 'I don't know what else to do. I've never dealt with this before. Neurosurgery in space.'

It was a phrase many of them had uttered over the last few weeks. *I've never dealt with this before. This is new. This is something we've never seen.* Yet wasn't that the essence of exploration? That no crisis could be predicted, that every new problem required its own solution. That every triumph was built on sacrifice.

And there *had* been triumphs, even in the midst of all this tragedy. *Apogee II* had landed safely in the Arizona desert, and Casper Mulholland was now negotiating his company's first contract with the Air Force. Jack was still healthy, even three days after being aboard ISS – an indication that Ranavirus was both a cure and a preventive against Chimera. And the very fact that Emma was alive counted as a triumph as well.

Though perhaps only a temporary one.

Gordon felt a profound sense of sadness as he watched her EKG blip across the screen. *How long can the heart go on beating when the brain is gone?* he wondered. *How long can a body survive a coma?* To watch this slow fading away of a once-vibrant woman was more painful than to witness her sudden and catastrophic death.

Suddenly he sat up straight, his gaze frozen on the monitor. 'Todd,' he said. 'What's happening to her?'

'What?'

'There's something wrong with her heart.'

Todd raised his head and stared at the tracing shuddering across the monitor. 'No,' he said, and reached for the comm switch. 'That's not her heart.'

The high whine of the monitor alarm sliced through Jack's twilight sleep, and he awakened with a start. Years of medical training, of countless nights spent in on-call rooms, had taught him to surface fully alert from the deepest sleep, and the instant he opened his eyes he knew where he was. He knew something was wrong.

He turned toward the sound of the alarm and was briefly disoriented by his upside-down view. Emma appeared to be suspended facedown from the ceiling. One of her three EKG

375

leads floated loose, like a strand of sea grass drifting under-water. He turned a hundred eighty degrees, and everything righted itself.

He reattached her EKG lead. His own heart was racing as he watched the monitor, afraid of what he would see. To his relief, a normal rhythm blipped across the screen.

And then – something else. A shuddering of the line. *Movement.*

He looked down at Emma. And saw that her eyes were open.

'ISS is not responding,' said Capcom.

'Keep trying. We need him on comm now!' snapped Todd.

Gordon stared at the biotelemetry readings, not under-standing any of it, and fearing the worst. The EKG skittered up and down, then suddenly went flat. *No,* he thought. *We've lost her!*

'It's just a disconnect,' said Todd. 'The lead's fallen off. She may be seizing.'

'Still no response from ISS,' said Capcom.

'What the hell is going on up there?'

'Look!' said Gordon.

Both men froze as a blip appeared on the screen. It was followed by another and another.

'Surgeon, I have ISS,' Capcom announced. 'Requesting immediate consultation.'

Todd shot forward in his chair. 'Ground Control, close the loop. Go ahead, Jack.'

It was a private conversation; no one but Todd could hear what Jack was saying. In the sudden hush, everyone in the room turned to look at the surgeon's console. Even Gordon, seated right beside him, could not read Todd's expression. Todd was hunched forward, both hands cupping his headset, as though to shut out any distractions.

Then he said, 'Hold on, Jack. There are a lot of folks down here waiting to hear this. Let's tell them the news.' Todd turned to Flight Director Ellis and gave him a triumphant thumbs-up. 'Watson's awake! She's talking!'

What happened next would remain forever etched in Gordon Obie's memory. He heard voices swell, cresting into noisy cheers. He felt Todd slap him on the back, hard. Liz Gianni gave a rebel whoop. And Woody Ellis fell into his chair with a look of disbelief and joy.

But what Gordon would remember most of all was his own reaction. He looked around the room and suddenly found his throat was aching and his eyes were blurred. In all his years at NASA, no one had ever seen Gordon Obie cry. They were damn well not going to see it now.

They were still cheering as he rose from his chair and walked, unnoticed, out of the room.

Five Months Later
Panama City, Florida

The squeal of hinges and the clank of metal echoed in the vast Navy hangar as the door to the hyperbaric chamber at last swung open. Jared Profitt watched as the two Navy physicians stepped out first, both of them taking in deep breaths as they emerged. They had spent over a month confined to that claustrophobic space, and they seemed a little dazed by their sudden transition into freedom. They turned to assist the last two occupants out of the chamber.

Emma Watson and Jack McCallum stepped out. They both focused on Jared Profitt, crossing toward them.

'Welcome back to the world, Dr Watson,' he said, and held out his hand in greeting.

She hesitated, then shook it. She looked far thinner than her photographs. More fragile. Four months quarantined in space, followed by five weeks in the hyperbaric chamber, had taken its toll. She had lost muscle mass, and her eyes seemed huge and darkly luminous in that pale face. The hair growing back on her shaved scalp was silver, a startling contrast against the rest of her brown mane.

Profitt looked at the two Navy doctors. 'Could you leave us alone, please?' He waited until their footsteps faded away.

Then he asked Emma, 'Are you feeling well?'

'Well enough,' she said. 'They tell me I'm free of disease.'

'None that can be detected,' he corrected her. This was an important distinction. Though they had demonstrated that Ranavirus did indeed eradicate Chimera in lab animals, they could not be certain of Emma's long-term prognosis. The best they could say was that there was no evidence of Chimera in her body. From the moment she'd landed aboard *Endeavour*, she'd been subjected to repeated blood tests, X rays, and biopsies. Though all were negative, USAMRIID had insisted she remain in the hyperbaric chamber while the tests continued. Two weeks ago, the chamber pressure had been dropped to a normal one atmosphere. She had remained healthy.

Even now, she was not entirely free. For the rest of her life she would be a subject of study.

He looked at Jack and saw hostility in the man's eyes. Jack had said nothing, but his arm circled Emma's waist in a protective gesture that said clearly, *You are not taking her from me.*

'Dr McCallum, I hope you understand that every decision I made was for a good reason.'

'I understand your reasons. It doesn't mean I agree with your decisions.'

'Then at least we share that much – an understanding.' He did not offer his hand; he sensed that McCallum would refuse to shake it. So he said simply, 'There are a number of

378

people waiting outside to see you. I won't keep you from your friends any longer.' He turned to leave.

'Wait,' said Jack. 'What happens now?'

'You're free to leave. As long as you both return for periodic testing.'

'No, I mean what happens to the people responsible? The ones who sent up Chimera?'

'They are no longer making decisions.'

'And that's it?' Jack's voice rose in anger. 'No punishment, no consequences?'

'It will be handled in the usual manner. The way it's done at any government agency, including NASA. A discreet shuffle to the sidelines. And then a quiet retirement. There can't be any investigation, any disclosure whatsoever. Chimera is too dangerous to reveal to the rest of the world.'

'But people have died.'

'Marburg virus will be blamed. Accidentally introduced to ISS by an infected monkey. Luther Ames' death will be attributed to a mechanical malfunction of the CRV.'

'*Someone* should be held accountable.'

'For what, a bad decision?' Profitt shook his head. He turned and looked at the closed hangar door, where a slit of sunlight shone through. 'There's no crime to punish here. These are people who simply made mistakes. People who didn't understand the nature of what they were dealing with. I know it's frustrating for you. I understand your need to blame someone. But there are no real villains in this piece, Dr McCallum. There are only . . . heroes.' He turned and looked directly at Jack.

The two men regarded each other for a moment. Profitt saw no warmth, no trust in Jack's gaze. But he did see respect.

'Your friends are waiting for you,' said Profitt.

Jack nodded. He and Emma crossed to the hangar door. As they stepped out, a burst of sunlight shone in, and Jared

379

Profitt, squinting against the brightness, saw Jack and Emma only in silhouette, his arm around her shoulder, her profile turned to his. To the sound of cheering voices, they walked out and vanished into the blinding light of midday.

The Sea

28

A shooting star arced across the heavens and shattered into bright bits of glitter. Emma took in a sharp breath in awe, inhaling the smell of the wind over Galveston Bay. Everything about being home again seemed new and strange to her. This unbroken panorama of sky. The rocking of the sailboat's deck beneath her back. The sound of water slapping *Sanneke*'s hull. She had been so long deprived of simple, earthbound experiences that just the sensation of the breeze on her face was something to be treasured. During the last months of quarantine on the station, she had stared down at the earth, homesick for the smell of grass, the taste of salt air, the warmth of the soil under her bare feet. She had thought, *When I am home again, if I am ever home again, I will never leave it.*

Now here she was, savoring the sights and smells of earth. Yet she could not help turning her wistful gaze toward the stars.

'Do you ever wish you could go back?' Jack asked the question so softly his words were almost lost in the wind. He lay beside her on *Sanneke*'s deck, his hand clasping hers, his gaze also fixed on the night sky. 'Do you ever think, "If they gave me one more chance to go up there, I'd take it"?'

'Every day,' she murmured. 'Isn't it strange? When we were up there, all we talked about was coming home. And now we're home, and we can't stop thinking about going back up.' She brushed her fingers across her scalp, where the shorter hair was growing back as a startling streak of silver. She could still feel the knotty ridge of scar tissue where Jack's scalpel had cut through skin and galea. It was a permanent reminder of what she had survived on the station. An enduring record of horror, carved in her flesh. Yet, when she looked at the sky, she felt the old yearning for the heavens.

'I think I'll always be hoping for another chance,' she said. 'The way sailors always want to go back to sea. No matter how terrible their last voyage. Or how fervently they kiss the ground when they reach land. In time, they miss the sea, and they always want to return.'

But she would never return to space. She was like a sailor trapped on land, with the sea all around her, tantalizing yet forbidden. It was forever out of her reach because of Chimera.

Although the doctors at JSC and USAMRIID could no longer detect any evidence of infection in her body, they could not be certain Chimera had been eradicated. It could be merely dormant, a benign tenant of her body. No one at NASA dared predict what would happen should she return to space.

So she would never return. She was an astronaut ghost now, still a member of the corps, but without hope of any flight assignment. It was up to others to pursue the dream. Already, a new team was aboard the station, completing the repairs and biological cleanup that she and Jack had begun. Next month, the last replacement parts for the damaged main truss and solar arrays would be launched aboard *Columbia*. ISS would not die. Too many lives had been lost to make an orbiting station a reality; to abandon it now would be to render that sacrifice meaningless.

Another shooting star streaked overhead, tumbled like a dying cinder, and winked out. They both waited, hoping, for another. Other people who saw falling stars might think them omens, or angels winging from heaven, or consider them occasions to make a wish. Emma saw them for what they were: bits of cosmic debris, wayward travelers from the cold, dark reaches of space. That they were nothing more than rocks and ice did not make them any less wondrous.

As she tilted her head back and scanned the heavens, *Sanneke* rose upon a swell, and she had the disorienting impression that the stars were rushing toward her, that she was hurtling through space and time. She closed her eyes. And without warning, her heart began to pound with inexplicable dread. She felt the icy kiss of sweat on her face.

Jack touched her trembling hand. 'What's wrong? Are you cold?'

'No. No, not cold . . .' She swallowed hard. 'I suddenly thought of something terrible.'

'What?'

'If USAMRIID's right – if Chimera came to earth on an asteroid – then that's proof other life is out there.'

'Yes. It would prove it.'

'What if it's intelligent life?'

'Chimera's too small, too primitive. It's not intelligent.'

'But whoever sent it here may be,' she whispered.

Jack went very still beside her. 'A colonizer,' he said softly.

'Like seeds cast on the wind. Wherever Chimera landed, on any planet, in any solar system, it would infect the native species. Incorporate their DNA into its own genome. It wouldn't need millions of years of evolution to adapt to its new home. It could acquire all the genetic tools for survival from the species already living there.'

And once established, once it became the dominant species on its new planet, what then? What was its next step? She didn't know. The answer, she thought, must lie in the parts of Chimera's genome they could not yet identify. The sequences of DNA whose function remained a mystery.

A fresh meteor streaked the sky, a reminder that the heavens are ever-changing and turbulent. That the earth is only one lonely traveler through the vastness of space.

'We'll have to be ready,' she said. 'Before the next Chimera arrives.'

Jack sat up and looked at his watch. 'It's getting cold,' he said. 'Let's go home. Gordon will go ballistic if we miss that press conference tomorrow.'

'I've never seen him lose his temper.'

'You don't know him the way I do.' Jack began to haul on the halyard, and the main sail rose, flapping in the wind. 'He's halfway in love with you, you know.'

'Gordie?' She laughed. 'I can't imagine.'

'And you know what I can't imagine?' he said softly, pulling her close beside him in the cockpit. 'That any man wouldn't be.'

The wind suddenly gusted, filling the sail, and *Sanneke* surged ahead, slicing through the waters of Galveston Bay.

'Ready about,' said Jack. And he steered them through the wind, turning the bow west. Guided not by the stars, but by the lights of shore.

The lights of home.

Glossary

NASA has been dubbed the 'National Acronym-Slinging Agency' and with good reason. Conversations between NASA employees are often so peppered with acronyms the uninitiated may believe they are hearing a foreign language. Here are definitions for some of the acronyms and abbreviations used in *Gravity*:

AFB: Air Force Base.

ALSP: Advanced Life Support Pack; the onboard medical kit that provides advanced cardiac life support.

APU: Auxiliary Power Unit.

ASCR: Assured Safe Crew Return; a space-station-control software mode that supports emergency separation and departure of evacuation vehicles.

ATO: Abort to Orbit; an abort mode that allows the vehicle to achieve a temporary orbit prior to returning to earth.

Capcom: Capsule Communicator.

CCPK: Crew Contaminant Protection Kit.

CCTV: Closed-Circuit Television.

CRT: Cathode-Ray Tube.

CRV: Crew Return Vehicle; the space station's lifeboat.

C/W: Caution and Warning.

DAP: Digital Autopilot.

ECLSS: Environmental Control and Life Support System.

ECS: Environmental Control System.

EKG: Electrocardiogram.

EKV: Exoatmospheric Kill Vehicle; missile designed to destroy objects before they enter earth's atmosphere.

EMU: Extravehicular Mobility Unit; a spacewalking suit (American); see also Orlan-M.

EPS: Electrical Power System.

ESA: European Space Agency.

EVA: Extravehicular Activity; a spacewalk.

FAA: Federal Aviation Agency.

Falcon: Flight controller in charge of monitoring ISS power systems and solar arrays.

FCR: Flight Control Room.

FDO: Flight Dynamics Officer.

FGB: (Russian initials) Functional Cargo Block; one of the space station modules; also called *Zarya*.

Flight: Flight Director.

GC: Ground Control.

GDO: Guidance Officer.

GNC: Guidance, Navigation, and Control.

GOES: Geostationary Operational Environmental Satellite; a weather satellite.

GPC: General Purpose Computer.

Hab: (American) Habitation Module.

HCG: Human Chorionic Gonadotropin; a hormone of pregnancy.

HEPA filter: High-Efficiency Particulate Air filter.

ISS: International Space Station.

IVA: Intravehicular Activity; a spacewalk inside a decompressed vehicle or module.

JPL: Jet Propulsion Laboratory.

JSC: Johnson Space Center (Houston).

KSC: Kennedy Space Center (Cape Canaveral, Florida).

Ku-band: Ku-band communication subsystem.

LCC: Launch Control Center.

LEO: Low Earth Orbit; orbit within a few hundred miles of earth.

LES: Launch and Entry Suit; the bright orange suit astronauts wear during liftoff and for return to earth. It is a one-piece partial pressure suit which provides a thermal barrier as well as anti-g protection.

LOS: Loss of Signal.

MCC: Mission Control Center.

ME: Main Engines.

MECO: Main Engine Cutoff.

MMACS: Maintenance, Mechanical Arm, and Crew Systems engineer.

MMT: Mission Management Team.

MMU: Mass Memory Unit.

MOD: Mission Operations Director.

MSFC: Marshall Space Flight Center.

NASA: National Aeronautics and Space Administration.

NASDA: The Japanese space agency.

NOAA: National Oceanic and Atmospheric Administration.

NORAD: North American Air Defense Command.

NSTS: National Space Transportation System.

Odin: Flight controller for ISS onboard data networks and computers.

ODS: Orbital Docking System.

OMS: Orbital Maneuvering System.

Orlan-M: A spacewalking suit (Russian).

ORU: Orbital Replacement Unit.

Oso: Flight controller for ISS Mechanical/Maintenance/Latches.

PAO: Public Affairs Officer.

PFC: Private Family Conference.

PI: Principal Investigator; the earth-based scientist in charge of an on-orbit experiment.

PMC: Private Medical Conference.

POCC: Payload Operations Control Center.

Psi: Pounds per square inch.

PVM: Photovoltaic Module.

RCS: Reaction Control System; one of the shuttle engine systems used on orbit to maneuver the spacecraft.

RLV: Reusable Launch Vehicle.

RPOP: Rendezvous and Proximity Operations Program (software).

RSM: Russian Service Module.

RTLS: Return to Launch Site; a launch-abort mode that requires the shuttle to fly downrange to dissipate fuel, then turn around for a landing at or near the launch site.

SAFER: Simplified Aid for EVA Rescue; a jet pack that allows a spacewalking astronaut to pilot himself to safety in the event he becomes untethered.

Sim: Short for flight simulation.

SRB: Solid Rocket Boosters.

STS: Shuttle Transportation System.

Surgeon: The call sign for the mission flight surgeon.

SVOR: Special Vehicle Operations Room; the flight control room for the International Space Station.

TACAN: Tactical Air Navigation.

TAEM: Terminal Area Energy Management.

TAL: Transatlantic Landing; an abort mode in which the shuttle lands on the other side of the Atlantic Ocean.

TDRS: Tracking and Data Relay Satellite.

Topo: Flight controller for ISS trajectory control.

TVIS: Treadmill with Vibration Isolation System.

UHF: Ultrahigh Frequency.

United Space Alliance (USA): A private contractor chartered

to maintain and conduct certain aspects of NASA's operations.

USAMRIID: United States Army Medical Research Institute of Infectious Diseases.

U.S. Space Command: Part of the Unified Command of the Department of Defense, USSPACECOM monitors manmade objects orbiting earth and supports military as well as civilian operations involving space.

WET-F: Weightless Environment Training Facility.

KillerReads.com

The one-stop shop for the best in crime and thriller fiction

Be the first to get your hands on the **latest releases, exclusive interviews** and **sneak previews** from your favourite authors.

Browse the site and sign up to the newsletter for our pick of the **hottest** articles as well as a chance to **win** our monthly competition!

Writing so good it's criminal

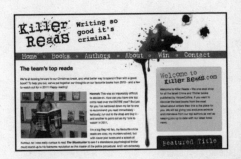